A MATTER OF TRUST

Belfast girl Liz O'Hara is devastated to discover that her fiancé, Danny, has been unfaithful and a teenage girl is pregnant by him. To make matters worse, after the shotgun wedding the couple intend living in Danny's parents' house across the street from Liz's home. Danny is far from happy at being forced into a loveless marriage and pursues Liz relentlessly. To escape his passionate advances Liz agrees to marry David, her boss, although she still loves Danny – but can she make her marriage work? Or will she succumb to the charms of her former fiancé?

A MATTER OF TRUST

A MATTER OF TRUST

by

Mary A. Larkin

Magna Large Print Books
Long Preston, North Yorkshire,
BD23 4ND, England.

British Library Cataloguing in Publication Data.

Larkin, Mary A.
    A matter of trust.

    A catalogue record of this book is
    available from the British Library

    ISBN   0-7505-1691-7

First published in Great Britain in 2000 by
Judy Piatkus (Publishers) Ltd.

Published in Large Print 2001 by arrangement with
Judy Piatkus (Publishers) Ltd.

Magna Large Print is an imprint of Library Magna Books Ltd.

Printed and bound in Great Britain by
T.J. (International) Ltd., Cornwall, PL28 8RW

To my sisters Margaret and Sue,
and their husbands Joe and Billy

Acknowledgements

I would like to express my sincere gratitude to Billy and Sue McDowell, for all their encouragement and help which was always readily available throughout my writing career.

Author's Note

The geographical areas portrayed in *A Matter Of Trust* actually exist and historic events referred to in the course of the story are, to the best of my knowledge, authentic. However, I would like to emphasise that the story is fictional; all characters are fictitious and any resemblance to real persons, living or dead, is purely coincidental.

Chapter One

David Atkinson felt tired and weary. Removing his spectacles, he rubbed the bridge of his nose gently between finger and thumb to ease the pressure. It had been a long day; stock taking always involved a lot of time and extra paper-work. Of course as owner of the clothing factory he could afford to delegate the work, but what had he to go home to except for an empty house? Well, time to call it a day and return to that showpiece he called home. He swung round in the big leather maroon-coloured swivel chair, one of the few luxuries he allowed himself at the factory, and rose slowly to his feet, stretching his six-foot frame to relieve the tension in his muscles. Only then did he realize a light still burned in the small adjoining office. Good heavens, Liz O'Hara must be still working away. A glance at the desk clock showed it was half-past six. She should have been gone an hour ago.

In the doorway that connected the offices he stood silently watching his assistant. The lamp on the desk highlighted her dark chestnut hair. Cut short and shaped close to her head, it revealed small shell-like ears and a long graceful neck. She was a fine-looking girl, with a wide sensuous mouth and eyes of bright hazel with dark rings circling the irises which twinkled and sparkled at the slightest provocation. She had worked here since leaving college four years ago. He'd often wondered why a girl of her ability chose to work in a factory, even if it was in the office, when she must have other more lucrative avenues open to her.

She gave a little start when he moved forward, and he apologized. 'I'm sorry. I thought you were aware of me.'

She smiled ruefully. 'No, I was lost in a world of my own.'

'Do you know what time it is, Liz?'

A glance at her watch brought a cry of dismay from her lips. 'Good heavens! Is it really that time already? I hadn't realized it was so late.'

'Well, come on now. Time to go home.'

He lifted her coat from the hanger behind the door and held it while she put the ledger away in the safe and locked it.

'Thank you, Mr Atkinson.' She smiled broadly, revealing even white teeth as she slipped her arms into the coat he held ready for her.

Warm colour washed her face as his gaze intensified, studying her as if seeing her for the first time. She hoped he wouldn't notice the blush. Imagine colouring because 'Old Atkie', as he was affectionately labelled by the girls, was eyeing her. Not that he was all that old. His pale blonde hair and fair complexion was aging well. He would pass for a man in his early thirties although she imagined he was older. Still, she could be forgiven for blushing; her boss rarely seemed to notice anyone. He was a very reserved man.

Fully aware of her embarrassment, he smiled

14

and to ease the tension that was suddenly there between them, chided her, 'What will your young man think of me for keeping you back so late, eh? He'll think me a slave driver, that's what he'll think! And I wouldn't blame him. Let's get a move on before he comes looking for you.'

They walked the length of the sewing room, passing the now silent rows of machines, and descended the steep flight of stairs to the dispatch department on the ground floor. At the foot of the stairs he turned to her. 'I'll give you a lift home, if you like?'

'Oh, no. That won't be necessary,' she cried. Imagine what the neighbours would think if she arrived home in her boss's big shining Jaguar. And him a widower, too. There would be all kinds of rumours flying about. 'I'm not going directly home,' she lied, 'I'm going to call in and see Danny.' After all, Mr Atkinson wasn't aware that she and Danny lived in the same street.

'Well, I'll take you there then.' When she would have objected, he said, 'No more protests. It's the least I can do when you were working so late. Although, mind you, I do appreciate it.'

Liz watched him set the alarm and lock up, then followed him across the empty yard to the car. 'I'm getting married,' she confided, as she climbed into the passenger seat beside him. Then silently berated herself. What on earth had made her mention that? Probably because it had been on her mind all day. He certainly would not be interested in her private affairs.

'When are you getting married, Liz?' he asked. 'I hope I'm not going to lose you. You're one of

15

my most valuable assets, you know.'

She felt a warm glow at the compliment but warned herself not to gabble too much. He was just making polite conversation. He wouldn't really be interested in her life story. 'No chance of that,' she retorted. 'At least not for a while. We haven't set the date yet.' She lapsed into silence. Sinking back against the soft leather upholstery, she let her mind mull over past events. Would Danny mind bringing the wedding forward? Hardly. She was the one who had insisted on waiting until they had enough money saved for the deposit on a house and some cash over to furnish it. Now she conceded it wasn't fair to keep him waiting. Men had needs. But the very idea of starting married life under the same roof as her mother didn't appeal in the slightest. Though it might be better than trying to keep Danny at arm's length. The strain was beginning to show in their relationship. They were already snapping at each other over the slightest thing.

The car travelled smoothly up Grosvenor Road and until they neared the Springfield Road junction she remained locked in her own thoughts. With a sideways glance, her employer asked quietly. 'Is anything worrying you?'

She turned a startled look on him. 'No. What made you ask that?'

'The frown that's furrowed your brow this past few minutes!' The words were accompanied with a slight laugh.

'Oh.' She touched her forehead and laughed with him. 'No, I've no real worries that I can think of, thanks be to goodness. Just drop me

16

here, will you, Mr Atkinson,' she said as the car stopped at the traffic lights. 'It's no distance. And thanks a lot. Oh ... by the way, are we working tomorrow morning?'

'I'll certainly be in, and I'd be very glad of your help if you could make it.'

A wide smile brightened her face. 'Yes, please. I need the overtime. And good night.'

'Good night, Liz.'

She watched the long sleek car turn right down the Falls Road towards the town centre, before making her way across the busy crossroads and heading towards Dunlewey Street where both she and Danny lived. His family had moved up from the Pound Loney just a year ago. They had bought one of the kitchen houses on the left-hand side of the street. She lived in one of the big parlour houses above St Vincent's School on the opposite side. Mr Atkinson had gone out of his way to give her a lift. He had a big bungalow over on Somerton Road, or so she had heard. It had been very kind of him, she thought.

Striding up Dunlewey Street, she decided to call in and see Danny, and smiled to herself. He would be surprised to see her. He was coming over for her at eight o'clock to go to the pictures. Aware that she would never be ready by then and that her mother would not be too pleased if she had to entertain Danny for any length of time, she thought it only prudent to call in and warn him to come over at half past instead. They would still be in time for the main feature film in the Broadway picture house. She never for one moment doubted he would be anything but glad

17

to see her: They were very much in love after all.

She stepped up into the small hall of the terraced house and raised her hand to knock on the inner door before entering the living room. Raised voices brought her to a standstill, hand hovering uncertainly in mid-air.

Jane McGowan's voice, full of consternation, reached her ears. 'Does Liz know yet? Have you told her?'

'No, Ma. I only learned about it myself last night, remember. Just like you! I haven't seen Liz yet. We're going to the pictures tonight. I'll have to tell her then.'

Jane lamented, 'This will kill her! How could you be so stupid? Why, Bridget Kelly's only a child. No wonder her father came over here breathing fire. How far on is she?'

A short silence, then: 'She can't be more than six weeks.'

'How can they be so sure she's pregnant then? Maybe she's trying it on, eh, son?'

'No, Ma. She's not like that. You heard her da. She's been sick every morning.'

'But is it yours, son?'

'Why, of course it is!' Although he tried to sound certain, even in her hurt and dismay Liz heard the thread of doubt in Danny's words.

A combination of anger, fear and pain brought tears to her eyes. Like a blind woman she groped her way out of the hall, all the while praying she would escape unobserved. Instinctively, like a wounded animal, she headed for home. At the door, though, she faltered. She couldn't face her mother. The state she was in, she would probably

18

blurt everything out and would get no sympathy there. She needed time to think; time to still the terrible thoughts racing wildly through her mind. Time to compose herself before facing her mother. Abruptly she turned tail and hurried back down the street and across the Falls Road, towards the Dunville Park. Here she would have comparative privacy, in which to face up to this terrible betrayal.

Soon, sitting on a frost-covered bench, she was hugging herself for warmth. How could Danny have done this to her? She dreaded going home and having to face her mother. Kath O'Hara had never liked Danny McGowan. From the first day he'd arrived in Dunlewey Street, she had not been able to find a good word to say about him or his family. For this very reason Liz had not wanted to start her married life under her mother's roof. Kath had never thought Danny good enough. That was a laugh! Not good enough for an illegitimate daughter? Sometimes her mother had ideas above her station. She should have been glad that a handsome young man like Danny was willing to take her daughter on. But no, she would be better pleased to hear about Bridget Kelly and unable to hide her satisfaction that Liz's marriage would not now be taking place.

Liz knew Bridget Kelly. Not to speak to, but by sight. Was aware that she worked in one of the department stores in town. A small pretty girl with a mass of curly dark hair, she must be only about seventeen. And from what Liz had just heard, Danny had got her into trouble. Six weeks

19

into trouble. Which meant it must have been when she and Danny ... about the time she had convinced him they must wait until they were married. A bitter laugh escaped her. Obviously he couldn't wait. Still, how could he do that to her? And with a young girl like Bridget?

Had Danny been any different these past six weeks? Surely there must have been some telltale sign he was carrying on with Bridget, some hidden excitement. Some sign of guilt. No, she hadn't noticed anything different. But then, she admitted to herself, she had been very preoccupied. Taking all the overtime she could get to boost their savings. Fool! She'd been an idiot to leave him alone in the evenings. Men were easily tempted. But did she really want a husband who was so easily led astray? And then realized in despair that, easily led or not, she wanted Danny McGowan. She loved him. And it was too late for them now.

Dragging her mind back from the past, she took a couple of deep breaths and willed her emotions under control. She couldn't sit here all night; she had to go home.

A quick glance at her watch showed it was seven o'clock. There was no way she could face Danny tonight and be confronted in person by this awful news. She needed time to think; to decide what to do. Becoming aware that she was under scrutiny from the foot patrol soldiers who paced the pavements, alert and ready for action, she quickly rose to her feet and headed for home. She must get a message to Danny somehow.

Kath O'Hara came from the living room into the hall when she heard her daughter's key in the lock. 'Where on earth have you been?' she cried plaintively. 'I was so worried. I thought you had been knocked down or something.'

'Mam, I'm a big girl now,' Liz retorted, unable to hide her resentment. 'There's no need for you to worry about me. I'm quite capable of looking after myself. As it happens, I worked back to help Mr Atkinson with the books. Anyway, I can be as late as I like,' she added peevishly.

'Not when your dinner is spoiling, you can't,' Kath retaliated. However, when Liz moved further into the hall and light from the living room fell on her daughter's face, Kath's attitude immediately changed. She came towards her in concern. 'What's wrong, love? You look awful.'

'I don't feel very well,' Liz admitted truthfully. 'Perhaps I'm sickening for something.' Like a broken heart, she thought distractedly. Dear God, how would she ever get through this ordeal?

'Come and sit by the fire, love. I'll make you a hot drink.' Helping Liz off with her coat, her mother hustled her into the living room to a chair by the fire and turned to leave the room.

To her surprise, Liz caught at her sleeve. 'Mam, I'm supposed to be going to the Broadway with Danny tonight. Will you run across and explain that I'm full of the cold? Warn him not to come over and catch my germs. Tell him I'll see him over the weekend, just as soon as I feel better.'

'Of course I will, love. You're obviously in no fit state to go out tonight.'

To say that Danny was relieved when Kath O'Hara knocked on the door and coolly delivered her message would be putting it mildly. He had been reprieved, albeit for a short time only. How would he ever get the courage to confess to Liz how stupid he had been? Since the minute he had set eyes on her a year ago almost to the day, he had loved Liz O'Hara. Had hounded her until she consented to date him. In no time they became inseparable. Now he couldn't imagine life without her. She was everything he admired in a woman: attractive, intelligent, and to his great joy she professed to love him. Now he had blown it. For the sake of a few minutes' lust with Bridget Kelly, he had ruined his chance of happiness. How could he have been so daft? His only excuse was it had all been so new to him, Bridget so small and willing in his arms. He had been unable to control himself and to his shame had even gone back for more.

But then, he had never dreamed anything like this would happen. Had assuaged his guilt with the thought that Liz need never know he had strayed. Even as he had betrayed her, at the back of his mind he had planned somehow or other to make it up to her. No chance of that now! Soon the whole district would know. He dreaded telling Liz how foolish he had been. It would break her heart. She would be so hurt. Was there any way out of this awful predicament?

His mother saw the expression on his face when he returned to the living room, and cried, 'What's up now?'

'That was Mrs O'Hara. Liz isn't feeling too well. I won't be seeing her tonight after all.'

'Well, you should make a point of going over to see her. Tell her about Bridget. Get it over with,' his mother remonstrated. 'It's not fair to leave her in the dark like this.'

He shied away from the idea. 'No. She's probably in bed, and can you see her mother allowing me up the stairs? I'll tell her tomorrow or Sunday, if she's feeling any better.'

'Coward! You're nothing but a big coward.'

His head bowed low in shame, Danny silently agreed with her. They were both still stunned. He had been in a daze all day, going about his duties in a trance, trying to come to terms with the shock he had received last night. Jane had answered a loud summons to the door to find a young girl standing in the hall and a tall heavyset man glowering on the pavement outside.

'Can I help you?' she asked, looking from one to the other in bewilderment.

'It's your son we want to see,' the man informed her in a far from friendly manner.

'Which son? I've three, you know.'

'No, I didn't.' He glared at the girl. 'What's his name?'

'Danny,' she whispered through pale, trembling lips.

Sensing trouble and not wanting the whole street to hear about it, Jane quickly moved aside. 'I think you'd both better come in.' With a motion of her head she beckoned them into the living room.

Danny rose from his seat by the fire, his face

23

lengthening in dismay as he recognized the girl. Running to him, she gripped his arm and gazed imploringly up into his face. 'Danny, I'm sorry. Truly sorry. I didn't want to come. Me da wouldn't listen to me...'

'I should think not!' There was a look of utter contempt on the man's face as his eyes fixed on Danny. 'My daughter has been sick every morning, so she has. You know what I'm talking about, don't you? I take it you intend to marry her?'

'What on earth do you mean?' cried Jane. 'He's already engaged to someone else.'

'He should have remembered that before he took advantage of my girl, and believe me ... this child's going to have a father or I'll know the reason why!' The man's voice and attitude were threatening, causing Jane to take an involuntary step backwards in alarm. 'Are you going to do the honourable thing and marry her?' he thundered, moving menacingly in Danny's direction.

Stunned, he stood silent, Adam's apple jerking up and down as he sought for control of his voice. His mother watched in growing alarm as his mouth opened and closed like a grounded fish's, words eluding him. Danny couldn't believe he had made Bridget pregnant, but obviously he had. Why had he never considered the possibility? Slowly, he nodded his head in assent. What choice did he have, after all?

'Good! The sooner the better then. Tomorrow night we'll all go down and see the priest.'

'No!' Danny quickly intervened. 'Please wait until Saturday morning. I must tell my fiancée first.'

24

Thinking that the girl was well rid of him, Barney Kelly agreed. 'You do that. Saturday morning then.' He turned away before the urge to smash his fist into Danny's handsome face became too much. This young bastard had ruined his daughter's life. Barney's wife was devastated; she had hoped that Bridget, their youngest, whom they had encouraged to obtain work in the Bank Buildings, though it was for pittance the first year, would one day marry someone worthwhile. She was now in a position where she could work her way up and make a good career for herself. But Barney very much doubted if her employers would want her attending to customers when she started to show.

Still, he admitted, it could have been worse. At least Danny was a Catholic and, according to Bridget, had a good job in Mackie's foundry. Yes, it could have been much worse. Even so, there were tears in his eyes as he led his daughter from the house. His youngest was only just turned seventeen, and now she was to become a mother herself. Her whole life was in ruins, for heaven's sake.

When the door had closed behind them, Jane rounded on her son in a fury. 'How could you, you stupid idiot? This will be the talk of the neighbourhood now.' She had always prided herself that her sons were the pick of the bunch. Three strapping lads the girls would be glad to get their hooks into. But not like this! She had been so proud that, in spite of her mother's obvious disapproval, Liz had consented to marry Danny. No matter if she was illegitimate, Liz

25

O'Hara had class! There was a regal quality about her. Jane had often wondered just who her father was. On her arrival in Dunlewey Street, she had discreetly questioned the neighbours, but Kath O'Hara had covered her tracks well. No one had been able to find out who had fathered Liz. Now Jane was beside herself with rage. 'Wait till your da hears about this. He'll hit the roof, so he will. He's very fond of Liz. We all are. I'll have to tell him and the boys as soon as they come in.'

'Why? It's none of their bloody business, so it's not. Just keep your mouth shut. They'll know soon enough.'

'They'll be better hearing it from us than on the grapevine, son.'

'I'll have to tell Liz first.'

'I suppose you're right.' Jane's sigh was from the heart. 'You owe her that much at least. The poor, poor girl. She really cares for you – this'll break her heart. But the family will have to be told, you know. That big Barney Kelly fellow won't keep quiet for long. And, you mark my words, the wedding will have to be soon. He'll want a ring on his daughter's finger before she starts to show. And I can't say I blame him.'

'Who'll want a ring on whose finger?' Peter McGowan entered the house on a blast of cold air, quickly closing the door behind him to retain the heat. Jane had reared her sons well where economy was concerned. He waited patiently for an answer, eyebrows raised as he looked from one to the other.

An inch or two smaller than Danny, at nineteen Peter still had some growing and filling out to do.

26

Jane returned his glance then looked appealingly at Danny. 'Perhaps you'd better...'

'You just can't wait, Ma. Sure you can't,' Danny bellowed, glad of the excuse to let off steam. 'Well, go ahead and tell him – I don't care. Broadcast it in the *Irish News*, if you like!' With these words he grabbed his coat off the rack at the foot of the stairs and left the house.

When the door had finally settled back on its hinges, Peter turned a questioning look on his mother. 'What's the matter with him?'

Jane sighed dramatically. 'He's just gone and got a young girl into trouble, so he has, and now there's to be a shotgun wedding. *That's* what's the matter with him.'

Bewilderment clouded Peter's face. 'But he's engaged to marry Liz O'Hara.'

'I know that. You know that. But it seems Danny forgot it long enough to get a wee girl pregnant.'

'Who's the girl?'

'A child. That's all she is, a child. Her name's Bridget Kelly.'

Peter looked flabbergasted. 'Wee Bridget? The dirty bastard! Why, she really is only a child.'

Jane gaped at him in surprise. 'You know her?'

'I went to school with her brother. She's much younger than me.'

'Well, she was old enough to let him. Remember, it takes two.'

'The sly, dirty bastard! That's what he is. He should have known better.'

'Here ... less of that vulgar talk in this house.'

'I don't understand. What about Liz? I thought

27

our Danny idolized her?'

'He does, son, let there be no doubt about that. Believe me, he's heartbroken. He must have had plenty of encouragement from Bridget Kelly or he wouldn't have strayed. Nevertheless, he'll have to do the decent thing.'

'Bloody selfish fool, that's what he is! He doesn't know when he's well off.'

As he continued on his journey down the Falls, David Atkinson was surprised at the number of army jeeps and Saracen armoured personnel carriers, manned by armed soldiers, that stood on street corners or travelled in slow convoy along the roads. Since the arrival of the British army in Northern Ireland in '69, the media often reported outbreaks of armed confrontation between the soldiers and local civilians, some ending in carnage and death, but this was as close as David ever got to it. It was quiet where he lived, with only the odd army patrol seen now and again. He had no reason to travel the Falls or Shankill Roads usually and tonight's detour brought home to him how awful it must be to live in areas such as these where young men were constantly stopped and searched. No wonder they were bitter and ready to join paramilitary organisations to fight for their beliefs.

Once the town centre was left behind and he was heading towards Fort William Park and to Somerton Road where he lived, he was surprised to find himself dwelling on thoughts of Liz O'Hara. He had been aware that she was attractive but had never really given her a second thought. She was just there to keep the books in order and protect him from unwanted salesmen. No one got through the outer office if he didn't want to see them. She also dealt with inquiries and complaints from customers and workforce alike. His 'Girl Friday', she helped to keep the factory running on an even keel. When had he last given her a rise? Too long ago, if he wasn't mistaken. He would have to look into that and put things right. Once married, would she leave work? He sincerely hoped not. How could he ever replace her?

He considered his other female employees, only to discard them one by one. Some of them were beauties and cheeky with it, but no one showed any sign of being brainy as well. One in particular was dark and passionate-looking, and had way-laid him one evening and had the audacity to offer to model some of the lingerie they manu-factured, just for him. A weaker man might have been tempted to see those luscious curves encased in artificial silk but since his wife's death four years earlier David had never sought any female company. Victoria had been everything to him. Her sudden death from a brain tumour had knocked the bottom out of his world. Their friends had rallied round but he could no longer bear to be in their company without his wife by his side. Gradually, he had broken away from the clique. Hard work had been his only salvation.

He admitted there were times when he was desperately lonely. How he wished they'd had a child, but it was not to be. He was utterly alone in the world now. An only child himself and orphaned at an early age, he had determined to make something of himself. He had excelled in the management course he had taken and had then been employed by Victoria's father for a trial period. In no time David was running the factory, taking most of the burden off her father's shoulders. Dedication and hard work had paid dividends and in due course a partnership was offered and gratefully accepted.

A year younger than he, Victoria was also an only child and the apple of her father's eye. They had been attracted to each other from the start, and to David's great relief no objections were raised when he asked for her hand in marriage. Even without children, the next fourteen years had been happy. Then disaster had struck and within a week he was a widower. Utterly bereft, he had buried himself in running the factory. Her parents, both elderly and heartbroken, had followed her within the year. At the age of thirty-seven, he found himself the sole owner of a very profitable concern with no one to share its proceeds.

In his haste to escape his mother's sharp tongue, Danny had grabbed the first jacket to hand instead of his overcoat. Now he hunched his shoulders against the biting wind as he quickly walked the length of the Falls Road to his favourite pub. He intended getting drunk. He knew it wouldn't solve anything, but for a while at least he would escape from his problems.

Clasping a pint of Guinness in his fist, he looked neither to right nor left as he headed to a secluded corner of the pub, hoping to avoid company. It was not to be.

'What about ye, Danny? Has Liz let you off the hook tonight?'

It was a well-known fact that Liz didn't like him frequenting the pubs. She'd put a stop to that early in their relationship. It was only right. After all, they were saving to get married and his mates understood, even if they did frequently rib him about it.

Now one of the lads he used to drink with joined him, grinning from ear to ear. 'Don't tell me the wedding's off?' he joked with a wink and a nod.

'You're probably right, Oliver,' Danny gloomily agreed with him.

'Ah, you've had a tiff.' Already the worse for drink, Oliver nodded sagely. 'It will blow over. Remember, the course of true love never runs smooth,' he jested, giving his mate a dig in the ribs.

This caused Danny's glass to spill liquid over his fingers. 'Give over, for heaven's sake, Oliver,' he growled. 'Watch what you're doing.'

'You're in a right mood, old mate. Never mind, it will soon blow over,' Oliver repeated consolingly.

'You're probably right,' Danny once more agreed with him. 'Just leave me alone.' He didn't want to be tempted to cry on anyone's shoulder, least of all Oliver's. He would only regret it later. When the truth came out he would be the laughing stock of the area, there was no doubt about that. Losing a girl like Liz O'Hara because of a kid like Bridget? The gossips would have a field day.

'Well now, you'd better be careful, big fellow. A lot of men would be only too willing to fill your shoes beside Liz O'Hara. She's a fine-looking girl, you know.'

Sadly, Danny knew that this was all too true. Liz would have no trouble getting herself a new man. No trouble at all.

After a sleepless night, Saturday morning saw a heavy-eyed Liz up and about before seven o'clock. She wanted to be away from the house before her mother got up. She also wanted to avoid the chance of bumping into any of the Mc-Gowans who were all early risers. In spite of her endeavours Peter McGowan caught up with her and fell into step beside her as she hurried down the street.

'You're out early this morning, considering it's Saturday,' he greeted her.

'We're stock taking today. The earlier I get in, the sooner I get home again.'

She gave him a tight smile. Did he know all about Danny and Bridget? Well, if he did, he wasn't likely to say anything to her as she was still supposed to be in the dark about it.

He studied her in concern. 'You don't look very well, Liz.'

'No, I don't feel too good, but I promised my boss I'd come in this morning. He depends on me to take some of the work off his shoulders.'

Peter bit hard on his lip when he thought of the bad news lying in store for her. He would gladly kick his brother the length of the street if he could save her the pain, so enraged was he at the terrible hurt Danny would inflict on her. His brother deserved a good hiding. They had reached the corner when to Liz's relief Peter waved his hand and bade her goodbye, heading down the Falls Road. She proceeded to the top of Grosvenor Road to catch a bus.

Early though she was, she saw that Mr Atkinson had beaten her to it. The big shining Jaguar was already in the factory yard.

One glance at her dark-ringed eyes in a face the colour of putty and he cried, 'Don't you dare take that coat off. Why, you shouldn't be out! You look like death warmed up. What you need is a hot toddy and then to bed with a hot water bottle. Come on, I'll run you back home.'

To his dismay great tears welled up in Liz's eyes and ran down her ashen cheeks. 'Please don't send me home, Mr Atkinson. I can't bear to face everybody,' she wailed.

'In the name of goodness, what on earth has happened that's so awful? Nothing is worth getting into a state like this over. Nothing!' Putting an arm around her shoulders, he led her to a chair and pushed her gently down on to it. A spotless white handkerchief was thrust into her hand and her boss tactfully withdrew into his own office, leaving her sobbing away.

Liz was distraught; what must he think of her, blubbering like a child? Had he gone to phone a taxi? Where would she go? She couldn't bear the thought of returning home again, not right away.

'Here, drink this.' A glass was thrust into her hand.

At the smell of whiskey, she tried to push it away. 'I don't drink.'

'This will help settle you down. Drink it.'

She gulped at the golden liquid and spluttered as the whiskey slid down her throat, warming her all the way down to her stomach. 'I'm sorry for making such a fool of myself,' she muttered.

'Obviously something has upset you badly. Tell me about it. I might be able to help.'

'No one can help me.' She sounded so forlorn, David found he wanted to gather her close and comfort her.

Resisting the urge, he said, 'You never know. Come on, tell me about it. A trouble shared and all that.'

'Danny has found himself another girl.'

'You mean, he's called the wedding off?'

'Not yet. I'm not supposed to know. He's going to break the news to me today. I can't face him, not at the moment, that's why I don't want to go home for a while.'

David was bewildered and showed it. 'If he hasn't said anything, then how do you know?'

She told him the whole sordid story. How she had overheard Danny admit he had got a young girl in trouble and would now have to marry her.

'Do you love him?'

Liz looked scornful at this stupid question. 'Of course I love him. I wouldn't have agreed to marry him otherwise. I love him with all my heart. There will never be anyone else for me. I don't know what I'm going to do now. My

34

mother won't be able to hide her joy. She never liked Danny. Thought he wasn't good enough for me.'

'Perhaps she's right,' David said gently. 'Sometimes others can see faults that those in love are blind to.'

'You don't understand – I'm illegitimate. All my life the finger has been pointed at me. I was the only one in the street with no dad and suffered miserably because of it. My mother won't even tell me who my father is. I don't know if he's alive or dead. All she would ever say was, "You've got good blood in you, girl. One day you may be glad of it." I can tell you, that was cold comfort when I was crying my eyes out because I was being called a bastard! The way I see it, she should have been glad someone like Danny was willing to have me.'

It was David's turn to gape now. 'You're talking nonsense,' he admonished her. 'You're a person in your own right. It wasn't your fault your mother fell by the wayside.'

She smiled sadly at him, amused by the quaint expression. 'You live in a different world from us, so you do, Mr Atkinson. It doesn't work like that where I come from. *I'm* the one who is the bastard. *I'm* the one who is looked down on. To be truthful, Mam didn't get off lightly. Every time there was a dispute of any kind, it was thrown in her face how she couldn't get a man of her own. So obviously my father was already married.'

He had the sense to realize she spoke the truth. When a girl of his class was unfortunate enough to get into trouble, she was whisked away to a distant relative and in due course the baby was adopted. Had not he and Victoria tried to adopt one such child? But in vain. The young mother had fought her parents tooth and nail and had succeeded in keeping it. Although disappointed that the child was to be denied them, he had admired her greatly for her courage.

Slowly, Liz rose to her feet. 'I'm sorry for taking up so much of your valuable time like this, Mr Atkinson, when I know how busy you are. I have to face Danny sometime, so it may as well be today. But I'll never forget your kindness.'

She headed for the door but with a gesture of his hand he stopped her. 'Let's both take the day off, Liz. Come for a drive with me.' He was as surprised at the suggestion as she was.

Hope rose in her breast. Oh, if only she could get away for a while. 'But ... what about the stock taking?' she queried.

'Well, I trust you'll be willing to work late next week to get it squared up, so let's give it a miss for today, eh, Liz?'

'You're too kind, Mr Atkinson.'

He saw tears threaten to fall anew and hastened towards her, ushering her out of the door in front of him. 'No more crying. We're going to have a wonderful day, you'll see.'

Liz tried to keep her eyes open but after her sleepless night the warmth and comfort of the car proved too much and soon she was lulled to sleep. David watched her head nod and bit on his lip, already regretting his impulsive offer. She was just a girl, young enough to be his daughter. How would he pass the day with her? Where could he take her? In the tearful condition she was in there was only one place they'd be away from prying eyes. With a sigh, he headed the car in the direction of Somerton Road.

'Liz, wake up.'

A gentle shake of her shoulder brought her back from a pleasant dream. One glance at her boss's face and reality returned like a cold blast of wind.

He helped her from the car and she glanced around her apprehensively. 'Where are we?'

'This is my home, Liz. I thought perhaps you'd like to freshen up before we move on?'

Awed, she took in the big detached bungalow and surrounding gardens. Never in her life had she seen such grandeur. Slowly she followed him to the big double oak doors and waited while he unlocked them. Inside she was even more flabbergasted. The hall was immense with a marble floor and great domed ceiling. Four doors led off it, one to each side and two facing the entrance.

Opening the one to the left-hand side, David said, 'You will find the bathroom at the end of the corridor on the left.' He nodded towards the door on the far side of the hall. 'That's the lounge. I'll be in there if you need me.' With these words he gave her a gentle push on her way.

Liz stood in the beautiful gold and black bathroom and gaped. So this was how the other half lived? Luxury indeed. The bath was a sunken corner type with steps leading down into it; the sort she saw advertised in glossy magazines. All the fittings were gold, and it looked like the real McCoy. A mirror ran the full length of one wall. The sight of her face in the mirror sent all other thoughts from her mind. No wonder Old Atkie had brought her here to freshen up. She looked awful. He must have been ashamed to be seen with her, and she didn't blame him. Her swollen eyes were almost slits and encased in a smudged mess of mascara. Her nose was shiny and her lipstick non-existent; her hair spiky and tangled.

By splashing her eyes alternately with hot and cold water, she managed to reduce most of the swelling. Next she repaired the damage to her make-up and combed her hair until it clung smoothly to her head. Still not quite satisfied with the results of her labours, she grimaced at her reflection. She had done her best. Replacing all her bits and pieces in her handbag, she squared her shoulders and went to join her employer.

David quickly crossed the floor of the lounge to the drinks cabinet and poured himself a stiff whiskey. What on earth had possessed him? Liz O'Hara was young enough to be his daughter he reminded himself again. They had nothing whatsoever in common. Where could they go? What did twenty-two year olds do these days for entertainment? He had no idea. It was so long since he had entertained a young girl, he didn't know where to start.

They couldn't just drive around all day. What would they find to talk about? And they must eat. But where?

Moving to the window he gazed out across manicured lawns to the boundary of his garden where large conifers screened his house from neighbours' eyes. He wished with all his heart Victoria was here. She would know what to do. But then, if his wife were here, Liz certainly wouldn't be.

The door swung silently inward and Liz had time to observe her boss before he became aware of her. His profile was towards her and she noted the worried frown on his brow. He was probably regretting his offer of a day out. She must let the poor man off the hook as soon as possible.

'Mr Atkinson?'

He swung round to face her and was amazed at the change in her. Gone was the distraught tearful girl and in her place stood a composed young lady. 'Ah, Liz ... I was just wondering how we would spend the day. I'll need your advice on where we should go to eat and so forth.' He smiled wryly. 'You see, I'm out of practice with this sort of thing.'

'It is all right Mr Atkinson. I've decided to face the music and get it over with. If you would phone for a taxi, please, I'll be on my way.'

'I'll do no such thing!' he exclaimed. 'It's a long time since I've had a day out and I'm looking forward to it. Surely you're not going to do me out of my treat, eh, Liz?' The words came across sincerely because he had discovered he really did want to spend the day with this attractive young woman. It was time to stop mourning and get on with his life. He was suddenly confident Victoria

39

would have wanted that.

Her eyes held his for a long moment and at last she nodded, satisfied at what she saw there. 'If you're sure?'

'I'm sure.'

It was a wonderful crisp autumn day. A huge ball of sun hung in the sky, highlighting the yellow, red and bronze foliage of the trees along the way. They drove for miles out into the countryside and eventually David pulled into the car park of a quaint village pub.

'If my memory serves me right the food here is delicious. Of course, I'm going back five years or more. Shall we give it a try?'

Eyes aglow, Liz nodded her approval. The low one-storey thatched building with leaded windows and ivy-covered walls enchanted her. Nor did the inside of the pub disappoint her. It gave off an air of opulence, with thick carpets beneath their feet and well-polished wooden furniture. They passed through the lounge and into the bar. Here the floor was formed of random-patterned stone and a turf fire burned brightly in a massive iron grate, blackened by years of service. On the stonework over the fire hung a conglomeration of brightly polished brasses. This was the first time she had set eyes on a turf fire and she thought it was the perfect final touch to their surroundings.

Seeing her obvious pleasure, David suggested they should have a drink by the fire while they studied the menu. Flushed with excitement, Liz removed her coat. This was immediately whisked out of sight by a waiter and, once settled in a great armchair close to the fire, a menu was placed in her hands.

'What would you like to drink, Liz?'

'A fruit juice, please.'

Recalling that he had already had one whiskey, David followed her example.

Liz blinked in astonishment at the prices. She and Danny ate out now and again, but not like this. Frantically, she searched for the lowest priced dish.

As if reading her thoughts, David leaned towards her and in a conspiratorial whisper said, 'Have anything you like, Liz.'

With a quick glance at a nearby waiter, she returned his whisper, 'You're sure?'

He nodded and without further ado she ordered a prawn cocktail followed by roast lamb with all the trimmings.

Drinks finished, they were ushered to a table by a window with a breathtaking view over a small lake. It glittered like silver in the pale midday sun and a pair of proud-necked swans swam lazily on its surface while ducks waddled about on the banks. David had been right, the food was indeed delicious. She cleared her plate and sat back with a contented sigh.

His eyes twinkled across the table at her. 'I'm glad you haven't lost your appetite,' he teased.

Bewilderment clouded her face as she realized Danny was very much at the back of her mind at the moment. How could she be so fickle? But then, all this was new to her. She would be back in Dunlewey Street and the real world all too soon. 'I haven't given Danny a single thought for the last couple of hours,' she admitted, and shook her head in confusion. 'I can't believe it,' she confessed. 'I'm having a wonderful time. I didn't realize some people had it so good.'

Touched by her honesty, he said gently, 'Perhaps you don't love him as much as you think?'

'Oh, but I do! He's so handsome and kind...'

'Handsome is as handsome does, my late wife often said.'

'I noticed her photograph on the sideboard. She was very beautiful. You must miss her,' she said softly.

'She was, and I do. No one can ever take her place,' he agreed.

Silence fell for a while and then, with an abrupt movement, David dispelled it by inquiring if she would like dessert. Liz declined. With a smile, he signalled the waiter and asked for the bill.

Back in the car, he turned to her. 'Where now? Have you any suggestions?'

'I have a confession to make. I've never been to the Giant's Causeway. Unless my geography's all wrong, I have a feeling we're quite close to it at the moment, so...?'

'Your wish is my command. If my reckoning is correct we're just about fifteen minutes or so away, but will you be warm enough in that coat?'

She threw her head back and laughed aloud. It was a wonderful musical sound and he was enchanted. She had turned out to be a wonderful companion and he was enjoying himself immensely.

'Let me tell you something, Mr Atkinson. This

coat is just one month old and is the height of fashion at the moment. Whether or not it's warm doesn't enter into it. I dress for style, not comfort.' Her hand caressed the soft wool. 'My mother insisted on buying it for my birthday. She said once I was married to Danny McGowan and the kids came along, I'd have to scrimp and save, but at least I'd have a decent coat if I got the chance to go out. And, to be truthful, it's quite warm. I usually only wear it on special occasions, but today I needed something to buoy me up.' She laughed once more and his expression softened. 'And as it has turned out, it is a special occasion. Indeed, the most special I've ever had.'

'It suits you. That colour brings out the yellow in your eyes.'

She threw him a startled look and he warned himself to go carefully or he would spoil the day. She must never know he was attracted to her. They had to continue working together and another man already held her heart.

David parked close to the Giant's Causeway and assisted Liz from the car. A cold wind was blowing in from the sea and Liz pulled her collar close around her throat as she walked down the path to the causeway itself.

Her eyes took in the wild stark beauty of the famous rocks for the first time. She was aware from local history lessons at school that this splendid phenomenon was formed many, many years ago when molten rock spilled out from the earth's core. As it cooled it split into numerous closely fitting pillars, mostly with five or six sides.

Irish folklore had it that this natural phenomenon was the beginning of a road built by a giant named Finn MacCool, one that stretched from Ireland to Staffa, one of the Western Islands of Scotland. At its narrowest point the pillars rose as high as twenty feet. At one point these pillars were curiously shaped into what was known as the giant's chair.

Liz walked timidly along the wet rocks that shone like dark marble and David followed close behind. This was all old hat to him. He had lost count of the times he had clambered over these rocks. Once he was earning enough to own a car, this was one of his favourite haunts. Now he followed Liz, trying to see it anew through her eyes. Turning back to him, she cried, 'I never guessed it would be this beautiful. The pictures I've seen don't do it justice. It's wonderful! Thank you for bringing me here. You miss out on so much when you don't own a car.'

'What does Danny work at?'

'He's a foreman fitter in Mackie's Foundry.'

'That sounds like a well-paid job. Why hasn't he a car?'

'Oh, his mother rules the roost in their house. He and Peter, and I suspect their father too, hand over their wage packets every Friday night and get pocket money in return. Granted, Peter isn't out of his time yet. He works for a plumbing firm. Joseph – he's the youngest – goes to St Malachy's College. He's very clever, won a scholarship, and Jane will see he goes on to university.' A grimace twisted her face. 'No matter who else goes to the wall! To be fair, he's

44

a nice lad and the apple of his mother's eye. She's very wise where money is concerned. Danny says she was able to pay cash for their house across from us when it came on the market last year.'

No wonder, David thought, if she was getting three wage packets handed to her every week! He heard Liz out in silence, sensing her resentment that Danny still handed over his wages. Now he asked, 'How old is Danny?'

'The same age as me – twenty-two.'

David pursed his lips but held his counsel. He wasn't about to tell her her business but thought perhaps Danny wasn't man enough for her if he let his mother rule him like that.

Liz's arms stretched wide as she embraced the scene before her. 'I'll never forget this,' she said softly. 'Thank you.'

On the journey back to Belfast she thanked him once again. 'I'll always remember this day. Especially seeing the Giant's Causeway for the very first time.'

David shot a sideways glance at her. 'It's not over yet, I trust.'

'It's five o'clock, Mr Atkinson. My mother will be frantic with worry.'

'I was hoping to spend the evening with you, too. Can we not call up and let your mother know you're safe, then go on somewhere else?'

Liz turned to him in amazement. He kept his eyes on the road ahead and she examined his profile. He had an aristocratic, almost imperious face which she had to admit was quite attractive; not as handsome as Danny's of course, but he was much older. The fair hair starting to recede at the temples and the thick golden brows made him look quite stern. The thought of Danny brought a sinking feeling to her stomach. Soon she must face him. Maybe tonight. But what if she took Old Atkie at his word and arrived in Dunlewey Street in the Jaguar? If Danny happened to see her, what would he do then?

David waited patiently, amazed to discover how very much he wanted to spend more time with her. At last he glanced over at her. 'Well, you've certainly given it some thought, so what's your decision?'

'If we're going out for the evening, I'd need to change.'

Unable to believe his luck, he grinned in delight. 'You mean it?'

'Yes, I'd love to spend the evening with you. Will you drop me off at the corner and pick me up again about seven?'

'Where would you like to go then?'

She dithered and he suggested, 'What about the Opera House? There's a play on this week. It gets great reviews.'

'That would be wonderful. I've never been to a live stage show before,' she admitted.

'I'll see if I can get some tickets.' They had arrived back at Dunlewey Street and at the corner he drew in close to the kerb. He made to get out to open the door for her. Quickly Liz forestalled him by hurriedly stepping out.

'Will you pick me up here, please?'

'No, I'll come to the door for you. What number do you live in?'

She didn't think this a good idea and demurred. 'Here will be fine.'

'I will come to your home,' he insisted, quietly but firmly.

Reluctantly, she told him.

'Until seven o'clock then.'

She watched the car out of sight and then walked quickly up the street, keeping her eyes averted. She sincerely hoped Danny would not see her and come over. She did not want to spoil the wonder of this day. Time enough to face up to her worries tomorrow.

'Where have you been?' her mother greeted her. 'Danny McGowan has been over here three times today, so he has! I don't think he believed me when I said you were working.'

'What did he want?'

'He wouldn't leave a message. Said he must see you himself.'

'Huh! Well, he was quite right not to believe you, Mam. I haven't been working,' Liz confessed. 'I have had the most wonderful day out with my boss,' she gaily informed her mother. 'Furthermore, I'm going to the Opera House with him tonight. He's picking me up at seven. What do you think of that?'

Slowly Kath sank down on a chair, gaping slightly. 'Have you and Danny had a tiff?' she queried.

'No, I wouldn't call it a tiff exactly. Look, Mam, I haven't time to explain now. I must have a bath and choose something decent to wear. I promise I'll tell you all about it tomorrow. All right, love?'

'I suppose it will have to be,' Kath answered

huffily. 'Will I make you something to eat?'

'No, Mam. I had a delicious lunch in a lovely country pub today, and I imagine Mr Atkinson will invite me to dine with him after the show.'

Halfway up the stairs, Liz dropped her final bombshell. Turning, she looked down at her mother. 'Oh, by the way, he's coming here to collect me. If I'm not quite ready, will you let him in, Mam?' She laughed outright at her mother's comical expression. 'Don't worry, I think you'll like him.'

Stunned, Kath sat for some time, trying to figure out what it was all about. First Danny McGowan popping back and forth, looking the picture of misery. She had questioned him but he'd been evasive, telling her nothing was wrong. Had they really fallen out? Oh, she hoped so. She really hoped so. It would be the answer to her prayers. Danny was not good enough by half for Kath O'Hara's daughter whereas a well set up man like her boss... Ah well, all would be revealed in due course. Meanwhile, she must be patient and tidy the place up before Liz's boss arrived. She would show him into the parlour. After all, she always kept it prepared for visitors, although they were few and far between. Rising to her feet she started to fuss around a room that was already spotlessly clean. Straightening curtains that already hung perfectly and plumping up cushions that needed no attention.

Shortly before seven, Kath took up her stance behind the net curtains at the parlour window. She wanted to have a look at this man with whom her daughter had spent the day, before he was aware of her. This was so unexpected. For the last year, since the McGowans had come to live opposite them, to Kath's great annoyance Liz had had eyes for no one but Danny. The girl had been besotted with him. Now he was running around looking miserable and Liz was dating her boss! Kath couldn't make head nor tail of it. First Danny popping back and forth looking quite perturbed, but telling her nothing. Then Liz arriving home and announcing she had spent the day with her boss and intended spending the evening with him as well. Was she trying to make Danny jealous? Was that why he looked so unhappy? It didn't sound like Liz to be unkind. All kinds of ideas plagued Kath but no satisfactory answers were forthcoming.

She straightened to attention, eyes widening in surprise when the big gleaming car drew up to the kerb in front of the house and David Atkinson climbed out. He was not at all what Kath had expected. She had always imagined Liz's boss to be elderly. The man who was approaching their door was quite young; about the same age as herself. Instinctively her hand went to her hair and smoothed pale blonde locks back from her brow. Pausing in front of the hall mirror, she examined her reflection, biting her lips to give them colour and smoothing her skirt over slim hips. Then, with an amused smile at the antics of herself, she went to answer his knock.

'Come in, please.' She stood to one side for him to enter, very much aware that the nets on the McGowans' window were twitching.

Offering her hand, she said, 'You must be Mr Atkinson. I'm Kath, Liz's mother.'

David could see who Liz got her looks from. Except for the colour of the hair she was the picture of her mother. He was a bit embarrassed to find this woman so young and attractive. Why did one always assume that mothers must look maternal?

'I'm very pleased to make your acquaintance, Kath. My name is David.'

She led the way into the parlour and nodded towards an easy chair. 'Liz isn't quite ready. Can I offer you a cup of tea or something while you're waiting, David?'

Before he could answer, Liz entered the room. 'No need, Mam. I'm here.'

He rose slowly to his feet, his eyes sweeping her from head to toe. How come, during years of working with her, he had never realized just how lovely she was? But then, she didn't come to work in fitted suits that showed off her slim figure and long slender legs, and make-up that made her eyes dark and mysterious-looking.

He smiled in appreciation and said sincerely, 'You look wonderful, Liz.'

Colour stained her cheeks. 'Did you manage to get tickets for the show?' she asked huskily.

'I did indeed. And the play starts at half-seven, so shall we make tracks?'

'Yes. Mam, I might be home late so don't wait up for me.'

'I'll see she comes to no harm,' David promised Kath.

She stood at the door and waved them off

proudly, aware that the neighbours were all furtively watching her daughter climb into the Jaguar. She was proud, but also uneasy. What was Liz playing at? David Atkinson was old enough to be her father. But who was she to point the finger? He was in fact about the same age Liz's father had been when he'd seduced Kath, an eighteen-year-old virgin then. Unbidden memories crowded her mind, of hot summer evenings spent in the park or in other out-of-the-way places where no one would recognize them. By the time she found out he was married, it was too late; she was too much in love to care. It had all been wonderful until she had discovered she was pregnant. He, of course, wouldn't hear tell of leaving his wife.

When she could hide it no longer and her parents realized that she was pregnant, they had hit the roof. Demanded to know his name. Kath had refused to tell them. He was a family friend. The shock of learning that a man they looked up to and admired had betrayed their trust would have proved too much, and they were suffering enough already. There was also the chance they might not believe her and he would never willingly acknowledge that he was the father. She had been afraid to take the chance of disclosing his name.

He had not abandoned her completely. In return for her silence he had bought her this house. He had never openly acknowledged that Liz was his, but funding for her secondary schooling had been made readily available. Kath wondered sometimes if he would have liked to acknowledge her, especially after the death of his wife the year before. His two sons had followed in his footsteps and were teaching, apparently. Would he have liked to have had a daughter? She still saw him about town occasionally, but thank God the flame had diminished over the years. Time is a great healer and there was nothing now. Was Liz going to land herself in the same predicament? Kath hoped not; it was a lonely existence bringing up a child on your own. Could this man David be carrying on with her daughter? At his age he must surely be married. She told herself she'd better have a heart to heart chat with Liz before things got out of hand.

Danny also watched the Jaguar out of sight, his face a tight mask of anger. His mother had beckoned him to the window and he had been just in time to see a tall, distinguished-looking man hand Liz into a Jag, of all cars! And a new one at that. She looked ravishing, all aglow. All silk-clad, slender legs and shining chestnut hair. He had never seen her look so lovely and knew the deep amber colour of the suit she wore would darken her eyes to a tawny colour. He guessed the man was her boss. Old Atkie, she affection-ately called him.

Since learning of Bridget's condition he had been sick with worry. Dreading breaking the news to Liz. And here she was ... swanning about with her boss! Had she been two-timing him all along? All the overtime she had put in lately ... was it a cover up for something else? Was she playing around with a man old enough to be her father? Not Liz! Surely not Liz? He would bank on her integrity. Still, he had just seen her with his own eyes and she had looked very much at home with her boss. He would make a point of calling on her tomorrow and finding out just what she was playing at.

Jane watched all the different expressions flit across her son's face. Bewilderment, doubt, jealousy, and lastly rage. He was absolutely seething. Wasn't that just like a man? After several futile attempts to see Liz, he and Bridget, accompanied by Barney Kelly, had been down to see the priest that very morning and in three weeks time they would be man and wife. It was almost laughable, the idea of him being angry that Liz had the gumption to go out with another man, and him practically married himself.

'Well, it looks like Liz won't be exactly heartbroken about your news,' his mother taunted him.

'What do you mean?'

'It looks to me like she also has other fish to fry. She must have been seeing him as well as you. And considering the way *you* turned out, good luck to her.'

'Are you daft? That old man must be well over forty, Ma. Liz has more sense than to take on a sugar daddy. It must be that big car that's the attraction. She always lamented the fact that I hadn't a car.'

'He didn't look all that old to me. In fact, I thought him quite handsome.'

The look he threw her was full of venom. 'Well, you would think that, wouldn't you? You're about the same age!'

Jane hid a smile. She was glad Danny was annoyed. He wasn't exactly in her good books at the moment. He and Bridget would be living here for a while until they got rooms elsewhere. Then there was the added expense of the wedding. Danny had admitted he had very little savings, had even had the audacity to blame her, saying he couldn't save much out of the pocket money she gave him. Jane didn't fancy sharing her home with another woman. It also meant another mouth to feed and she didn't for one moment delude herself that she would continue to receive most of Danny's wages every week. Not once the knot was tied. Bridget might be young but her mother would be prompting her as to what to expect. And all this because Danny couldn't control himself. Bloody fool!

Now she said curtly, 'Here's Bridget. You'd better open the door to her. And, for goodness' sake, go for a walk or something. That wee girl and I don't talk the same language. Liz may have gotten herself a sugar daddy, but you ... you've robbed the cradle!'

Danny had also found that he and Bridget were on different wavelengths. But then, they had other things to do to pass the time. Wasn't that why he was in this predicament?

They arrived at the Opera House with only minutes to spare and had just taken their seats when the curtain was raised. It was a murder drama and for the next hour and a half Liz sat on the edge of her seat, thoroughly engrossed.

When the curtain descended at the inter-mission, David turned to her. 'Well, what do you think of it so far?'

'Wonderful! Absolutely wonderful. You just get lost in the plot. Don't want to miss a word or an action. The cast are all great.'

He smiled at her enthusiasm and rose to his feet. 'Let's go to the bar and get a drink or a coffee.'

Anxiety clouded her features. 'Will we have time?'

He laughed gently. 'Don't worry, I promise to get you back before the curtain rises again.'

The bar was crowded and to David's dismay old friends came over to greet him and be introduced to his friend. He should have realized that some of the old clique would be here. It had been a favourite haunt of his and Victoria's. Not that he was ashamed to be seen with Liz. On the contrary, he was proud to see the admiring looks cast in her direction. However, it would start rumours circulating and there would be no truth in them. No truth whatsoever, worse luck.

Liz took it all in her stride. Determined not to let him down, she was gracious and ladylike and he was proud of her. When they were once again seated and the curtain about to rise, she whis-pered confidentially, 'I'm afraid you've started tongues wagging.'

He gave a little laugh. 'I was just thinking the same thing myself. Still, it's about time I started getting out and about again. This has broken the ice for me.'

To her surprise, it saddened her to think of him

55

taking up with someone new. Anyone he took an interest in should be very proud. One woman in particular had seemed perturbed to see him out with Liz. He had introduced her as Irene Brennan, and she had stressed that he must call her *soon*. Liz had noticed a warmth in David's manner when he had assured her that he would indeed telephone her, and soon. Would this dark attractive woman prove to be the new interest in his life?

After the show, while they ate supper at a small select restaurant in the town centre, they discussed the play.

'I never dreamt that she was the murderess, did you? I was so sure it was the doctor.'

'I have to admit, I did. I saw the play some years ago and remembered the outcome, but I enjoyed seeing it again. And I'm glad you enjoyed it, too. I could see it was a new experience for you. We must go to see another one.' He saw her startled glance and hastily added, 'Only if you're free, of course.'

They found that they had a lot of mutual interests and spent a long time talking over coffee. Afterwards David invited her to accompany him to a club he used to frequent. Here they met up again with the crowd from the Opera House and were waved over to join them. David consulted Liz first, asking if she minded and explaining it would be churlish to refuse. She assured him that she didn't mind in the slightest.

She found herself seated between two strangers and David was somehow propelled to a chair that had mysteriously appeared beside Irene Brennan.

'David is a dark horse. Imagine keeping you hidden away.'

Liz turned to the man on her right, a slight frown on her brow. 'I beg your pardon?'

She had not meant to put him in his place but she saw that he was embarrassed. 'I mean, if I had a girlfriend as young and attractive as you, I'd be showing her off to everyone.'

'Oh, would you really?'

'Don't listen to my husband, dear. He always tries to impress people and usually ends up putting his big feet in it.'

Liz turned to the blonde woman at her left-hand side. 'No offence taken, Mrs ... ? You'll have to forgive me, I can never remember names first time round.'

'I'm Joan and he's John. Have you known David long?'

'A few years.' Liz looked across the table at David and caught his eye. He smiled encouragingly at her and mouthed the words, 'Are you OK?' She nodded and smiled. Irene Brennan followed his gaze and Liz was dismayed to see the dislike reflected in her eyes. She wondered whether David would want them to know that he was out with one of his employees. That would be sure to raise a few eyebrows.

Time passed slowly for her as she tried to stave off impertinent questions from the inquisitive John and Joan without giving offence. In reality barely half an hour had elapsed before David rose to his feet and made his excuses. 'You'll all have to pardon me but I must get this young girl home,' he explained, and his eyes twinkled as he observed them trying to stem their curiosity. 'Good night all.'

Outside Liz was dismayed to smell whiskey on his breath in the cold night air. How much had he had to drink? They crossed to the car and she wondered whether or not it would be tactful to suggest they phone for a taxi. The words stuck in her throat and she silently got into the car. The short journey home was spent in silence. It was very late when the car drew up to her front door and she was not surprised to find the house in darkness.

'Would you like to come in for a cup of coffee or tea?' she asked tentatively, and was relieved when he declined.

'No, thank you, but I'll see you safely indoors.'

Liz rummaged through her handbag and at last produced the key. Taking it from her, he opened the door and motioned her inside.

In the doorway she turned. 'Thank you once again for a wonderful day.'

'It was my pleasure, Liz.' The words that had hovered on his lips all evening at last took shape. 'Have you had any contact with Danny yet?'

'No. Mam says he was over here three times today but he wouldn't tell her why he was so anxious to see me. She's in for a big shock!' Liz gave an exaggerated sigh. 'Tomorrow's the evil day. Danny will probably come over to break the bad news, and I've promised Mam to explain everything to her.' With a grimace she confessed, 'I have to admit I'm not looking forward to it.'

She motioned across the road. 'Danny lives in that house with the green door. He'll probably have to bring Bridget there to live. At least for a while. As far as I'm concerned that's the biggest snag, having to watch them together. If they were moving away it would be easier to bear. But I can't see any alternative, so I can't. He has no spare cash.'

By the light of the street lamp David could see which door she meant. He heard her out while staring fixedly at it. 'Perhaps they will live with her parents?' he suggested.

'I can't see it. She lives in Leeson Street and I think there's quite a big family of them.'

'How will you be able to bear seeing them come and go together?'

'I won't. I'll go round the bend if I have to. I'll have to look for rooms somewhere else, out of this area.' For a moment her voice trembled but she quickly regained control. 'Mam is going to be very annoyed. She never did like him in the first place. She'll probably run over there and claw his eyes out if she gets half a chance.'

'It's not fair your life here will be disrupted, through no fault of your own?'

'Well, at least I've had the most wonderful day of my life. I dread to think how I would have managed if you had insisted that I go back home this morning. I feel a different person now, I really do. You've given me the strength to conquer all before me tomorrow. I hope!'

'It's very kind of you to say that.' He took her hand between his. 'Good night, Liz. Thank you for pleasing an old man.'

'You're not old!' she exclaimed. 'And you're wonderful company.' Impulsively, she reached up and kissed him on the cheek. It proved too much for David. Without further thought he reached for her and held her close, his mouth covering hers. For a moment she stood rigid. This was the whiskey acting, she told herself, giving him Dutch courage. He would never have dared kiss her otherwise. He would regret this tomorrow. Then, relaxing in his arms, she returned the kiss. It was the least she could do, and even with the taste of whiskey on his lips it was pleasant.

They strained together for some moments but as his passion rose and she started to push him away, he released her at once. 'I'm sorry, my dear,' he apologized. 'It has been so long since I held a woman in my arms. And don't you go blaming the whiskey.' So he had been aware of her unease. 'I'm far from drunk. I had one small drink and it gave me the courage I needed to kiss you. Please don't hold it against me. See you Monday.'

Before she could utter a word, he was outside and pulling the door closed behind him. She stood breathless, her heart racing, until the sound of the car zooming off receded into the night. She sent a prayer heavenward that he would get home safely. If he continued at that speed he would be stopped by the army. Her lips still tingled from his kiss and she covered them with her fingers. It had been pleasant, very pleasant. So you didn't have to be in love to enjoy a man's attentions? That was good to know. Perhaps one day she would get over Danny and meet someone else. But there was sadness in her heart as she slowly climbed the stairs. That day seemed very remote indeed.

Liz was still in bed when early next morning her mother answered a knock on the door.

From the foot of the stairs she called, 'Liz! Liz, are you awake? Mr Atkinson is here.'

Kath was annoyed; if her daughter had made arrangements to see her boss so early, she should at least have had the decency to be up and dressed for him coming. Showing David into the parlour, she excused herself and, closing the door on him, quickly climbed the stairs.

Pushing open the bedroom door, she glared at her daughter. Liz forestalled her. 'Before you blow your top, Mam ... I didn't know he was coming. Talk to him, please? Give me a chance to freshen up and brush my hair. I'll be as quick as I can.'

'Oh, all right, but hurry up.'

Five minutes later, still in her old worn dressing gown but with face scrubbed clean and hair tidily brushed, Liz faced her boss across the parlour. He looked alert and fresh with no sign that he had retired late and was now here at this unearthly hour. Her mother had discreetly left them alone. There was a puzzled look in Liz's eyes as she waited for him to speak.

David returned her look and quailed inside. Without make-up, she looked about seventeen. He had obviously come here on a fool's mission. He debated within himself whether he should make some excuse and leave. The idea that had come to him during a sleepless night had seemed the answer to all their problems. Here, in the cold light of day, with Liz waiting for him to explain his presence, it struck him as ludicrous.

He began in a rush, 'Liz, I'm sorry for arriving out of the blue like this but I must talk to you.' She continued to look at him wide-eyed and he said, 'Look, please sit down. This isn't easy for me.'

Crossing the room she sat down on the small settee, bewildered. What was he doing here so early in the morning? And a Sunday morning at that!

'Liz, I've spent a sleepless night worrying about you. It's wrong that you should have to move because that idiot across the street was stupid enough to let you down.'

She gave a slight laugh. 'It's nice of you to worry about me, but it's hardly your concern. It's my problem. I'll solve it myself, in my own way.'

'The thing is... I think I have a solution for you.'

She remained quiet and aloof. She was still having difficulty coming to terms with him being here.

Throwing caution to the wind he blurted out, 'Liz, will you marry me?'

She gaped at him in amazement. Had he gone mad?

'Don't look like that,' he entreated. 'Think about it. You would save face if we were to announce that we intended getting married. I have friends in the right places – we could get a special licence and be married right away. You need never see Danny and Bridget come and go.'

In his excitement he was on his knees beside her. Gripping her hand tightly, he explained, 'I came this early so that when you see Danny boy today you'll be able to hold up your head and laugh in his face.'

'Hold on, Mr Atkinson. This is ridiculous! You hardly know me and I certainly know very little about you.'

He interrupted her. 'I trust my instincts that you are a good person. I know I enjoy your company very much indeed, and I think you enjoy mine. I think we could make a go of it, Liz.'

At her wit's end, she pulled her hand free and rose to her feet. 'It wouldn't be right. We'd be marrying for all the wrong reasons. I don't love you, I love Danny.'

'I know that. I know you love him. But you like me, don't you?'

'Yes, but not enough to ... to ... you know.' She shrugged and looked away in embarrassment.

'If you're thinking of the physical side of it... I can wait. I'd never rush you. And you don't exactly find me repulsive, do you?'

'No!'

'There you are then. There's hope for us.'

'You don't understand. You don't know the ins and outs of it.' She shook her head as if to clear it. 'It just wouldn't be right.'

'Liz, I'll take whatever you offer. No strings attached. If you find you can't bear me near you, I'll accede to your wishes. Just grace my home and be my companion, and we'll take it from there. We could make a go of it, I know we could. I'll do everything in my power to make you happy.'

She stood shaking her head in rejection. He didn't realize what he was saying.

When at last he left the house, after begging her to give his proposal serious consideration, Liz sank down on the settee and stared straight ahead, her mind in a whirl. She couldn't possibly marry him. For a start he was too old. Still, she had never thought of his age when in his company. That was because she had considered him a father figure, wasn't it? No! She was deluding herself there. She had never once thought of him as a father figure.

She remembered the feel of his arms around her the night before; the pressure of his lips on hers. It had been pleasant, she couldn't deny that. Very pleasant. Not in the least fatherly, and she had enjoyed it. But a kiss was just a kiss; different from the other thing. Besides she loved Danny. It would be wrong to marry anyone else. And there were other things to consider, things she would be ashamed to admit to.

Her mother had stayed out of the way while David was there. Now she tentatively pushed the door open and thrust her head round it to look at her daughter. 'What was that all about?'

'Come in, Mam. Prepare yourself for a shock. A couple in fact. Mr Atkinson has just asked me to marry him.' She smiled grimly as she watched her mother grope for a chair and sit down.

'He never did!'

'Oh, but he did, Mam.' Mirth bubbled over at the comical expression on her mother's face, but the laughter was tinged with hysteria.

Kath recognized it and, going to her daughter, sat beside her and clasped her hands tightly. 'Get a grip on yourself, love. Is he not already married?'

'He's a widower.'

'Oh, I see. What did you say to him?'

'I said it wouldn't be right to marry him when I was in love with someone else. Mam, I promised to tell you the truth today. The long and short of it is, I won't be marrying Danny after all. That's why Mr Atkinson asked me to marry him. He feels sorry for me, so he does.'

'Oh, be sensible, Liz. Men don't propose marriage out of pity. But tell me ... what changed your mind about Danny?'

'He's got another girl into trouble. He has to marry her.'

Fury brought Kath bounding to her feet and she was actually spitting little specks of froth when she spluttered: 'Danny McGowan was two-timing you? The bastard! The dirty rotten bastard. I warned you not to trust him. I told you he wasn't good enough for you, but you wouldn't listen.'

Liz flapped her hand in Kath's direction. 'Ah, Mam, give over. It happens all the time. I'll get over it. But I'm sure they'll have to live with his mother for a time, and I can't stay here. Watching them come and go together... I couldn't stand that.'

'And just what do you suggest doing, eh? Leaving home to make it easier for him? Are you daft, girl?'

'Mam, I don't want any fuss.'

Kath's mind was still struggling with all this information. 'I don't understand. When did Danny tell you this?'

65

'He hasn't told me yet. I'm not supposed to know.' She went on to explain how she had overheard him and his mother talking on Friday night. 'I broke down at work yesterday morning and that's why Mr Atkinson treated me to a day out. He's a very kind man.'

'He's much older than you, Liz.'

'I know that.'

'I can understand the attraction of an older man, though.'

'Yes, I'm sure you can,' Liz said wryly. 'But I'm not attracted to him.' Remembering her response to his kiss, her voice faltered. 'At least, I don't think I am.'

'You would want for nothing if you did marry him.'

'You're right there. I didn't realize how wealthy he was until I saw his home. It's absolutely beautiful.'

'Well then, give him a chance to woo you. Thumb your nose at that big galoot across the street!'

'You surprise me, Mam. You must surely guess that David's a Protestant?'

'Given time, he might turn.'

'No, Mam, I'm afraid he wants to get a special licence so we can be married right away. That means a register office. Think of the scandal. Me getting married in a register office. I'd be away, Mam. You'd get the brunt of it all.'

She watched her mother turn this over in her mind. To her amazement Kath retorted. 'I still think you should go for it. Never worry about me, I can look after myself. You could do a lot

66

worse for yourself, you know.'

Two hours later, Liz faced Danny in the living room. Her mother never showed him into the parlour. She didn't think he was worthy of it; even less so now.

Usually the minute they were alone they were in each other's arms, craving the closeness. Now, an awkward silence hung between them. After a long pause, during which Liz stood motionless and Danny fidgeted restlessly, he spoke. 'I was surprised to see you swanning off in your boss's car yesterday. I thought you were supposed to be ill. At least, I take it that was Old Atkie?'

'You're quite right. It was Mr Atkinson,' she said stiffly. She didn't like the way Danny stressed the 'Old'.

'What happened to the bad cold you were suffering from on Friday night? It was bad enough to stop you going out with me, but obviously not with him.'

'I made a remarkable recovery, and when Mr Atkinson asked me to go for a ride out into the country with him, I agreed. We had a wonderful time. He even took me to see the Giant's Causeway. Something you never did.'

Danny had the grace to look ashamed. He had known how much she wanted to visit the great phenomenon. Lord knows, the times she had hinted they should have a day out especially to visit it were countless. With a bit of effort he could have taken her, but he wasn't interested in viewing the Giant's Causeway so hadn't bothered.

'Mam says that you were looking for me yesterday?'

Danny's lips twisted in a sneer. She was trying to change the subject; trying to get away from the fact that she had been out with her boss. 'Where else did you go, eh? You were home very late. I saw you kissing him,' he said accusingly.

Liz gazed at him in wonder. He was actually jealous. And considering the news he had come to impart to her, he had a cheek. Keeping a tight rein on her temper, she answered him truthfully. 'We went to the Opera House and then to supper afterwards.' Her head went back and she eyed Danny suspiciously. 'You must have been up late. Were you spying on me?'

'I had every right to spy, as you put it. We're engaged to be married, in case you've forgotten. How long has this been going on, Liz? And, more important still, how far has it gone? All this overtime you've put in lately while you left me twiddling my thumbs...'

Thinking that he hadn't twiddled his thumbs for long, she interrupted him. 'That's enough, Danny. I spent one day with Mr Atkinson and enjoyed it very much. What you saw was just a good night kiss, and I won't hear a bad word said against him.' Again she came back to the matter in hand. 'Mam said you wanted to tell me something?' she persisted.

'Yes, as a matter of fact...' Before she could move he came close and his arms circled her waist; his eyes pleaded with her. 'Ah, Liz, Liz, I love you so much. I've been such a fool.' His lips met hers and she struggled against the emotion he had always aroused in her, right from the very beginning. She struggled in vain. The longing and need in her were too great to be kept at bay. They were swept away on a great wave of passion, stronger than ever before. At last self-loathing came to her rescue. How could she let him maul her like this after what he had done? Had she no pride?

She broke away from him and he looked at her in bewilderment. You would think that she already knew. She avoided his eye, wishing he would get it over with. At last he burst out, 'Liz, you'll never guess how stupid I've been!'

'Try me,' she said tersely.

'I'm so sorry. I didn't mean for it to happen...' Shamefaced, he turned aside. 'I've been stupid enough to get a girl into trouble. I have to marry her.'

'I know.'

Startled, he spun round to face her again. 'You know?' he gasped.

'Yes, I heard you and your mother bawling at each other on Friday night. I called over to tell you I'd be late for the pictures. I couldn't help but hear what you were talking about.'

Horror spread over his face. For her to have heard like that! It must have been awful for her. 'Ah, Liz, I'm so sorry. I wouldn't deliberately hurt you, you know that, don't you? I care too much.'

'Really? What were you doing out with Bridget Kelly then?'

He made to hold her again but she deftly eluded him. 'Liz, it was your fault, you know,' he growled.

Her voice rose shrilly. 'My fault? How do you make that out?'

'You gave me a taste for it, remember? Then your morals, or more likely the priest in confession, came to the fore and you said once was enough and we must wait until we were married. And marriage was in the far, far distant future, remember? I know it's no real excuse but when it was handed to me on a plate, I couldn't resist.' He shrugged as if it was the most natural thing in the world to betray your loved one.

'And why do you think I insisted we wait, eh? Because I didn't want to become pregnant. I wanted to be married decently. But you couldn't wait, Danny, sure you couldn't,' she jeered. 'You had to take away a young girl's innocence.'

'Innocence? Huh! You have to be joking. She knew more about it than I did. You know I was a novice. I thought perhaps that was another reason why you backed down. You didn't seem to enjoy it. I thought if I learnt a thing or two you might...' His voice trailed off and he tried to catch Liz's eye. 'If I hadn't done the right thing and promised to marry her, would you still have had me?'

'You know I wouldn't.'

'I thought not. Is that why you went out with Old Atkie then? Because you already knew? You're not really carrying on with him, are you, Liz?'

'Don't judge me by your own standards, Danny McGowan. I went out with Mr Atkinson because I wanted to. And since it matters so much to you, no, I'm not carrying on with him, as you put it.

He is a gentleman.' Danny had the grace to look ashamed and she asked, 'How soon will you be married?'

'In three weeks. Her da wants a ring on her finger before she starts to show.'

A great ache was where her heart should be and tears smarted in her eyes. 'Where will you live?'

'We'll have to live with me ma for a while. You must have guessed that, Liz.'

'I did. But I'd hoped you might find somewhere else. Surely you can see how hard it will be for me? Afraid of bumping into you every time I go out.'

The words were heartfelt and Danny's heart ached as he reached for her again. She pulled roughly away and he said humbly, 'I'm so sorry, Liz. I know it will be awkward for all concerned, but it can't be helped.'

Suddenly the unfairness of it all was too much for her to bear and she lashed out at him. 'Oh, but it can. Mr Atkinson has asked me to marry him. If we get married at once, I'll not even be here to see you leave for the church. What do you think of *that*, Danny McGowan?'

His face fell and then anger came to the fore. 'I think you'd be a mug. That's what I think, Liz O'Hara. He's an old man, for God's sake!'

'He's a rich man and I have great respect for him. He's a wonderful companion and I enjoy his company immensely. I think *he* might just prove to be a wonderful lover as well.' She knew this was beneath the belt after Danny's confession that maybe he had failed her. Didn't he realize that guilt and shame had made it seem so wrong

71

that time? Had taken all the joy out of it. It hadn't been his fault.

In two strides he was on her. Gripping her by the arms, he shook her roughly. 'Don't taunt me, Liz. And don't even joke about marrying him. You're just saying this to punish me. You'll live to regret it. You don't love him. You love me, I know you do!'

Her head rose. 'Don't you love Bridget?'

'Of course I don't! But there's the child to consider.'

'I admire your principles, Danny, but it works both ways. If you can marry without love ... why can't I, eh? Am I supposed to go through life alone just because you lusted after a young girl?'

'Don't do it, Liz. Please don't make my burden even harder.'

'*Your* burden? Hah! That's a gag. That's all you ever think of, isn't it? Yourself! Oh, get out of my sight, Danny McGowan. I don't know what I ever saw in you in the first place.'

With one last baleful look she turned away. He gazed at her rigid back for a few seconds, then with a muffled oath, spun on his heel and left the room. The slam of the outer door brought Kath from the kitchen.

Liz was standing dry-eyed and her mother said, 'I'm glad to see he didn't reduce you to tears. That fellow's not worth one single tear drop.'

At this Liz's mouth trembled and she wailed as tears started to fall, 'I know that, but how will I live without him? Eh, Mam? How will I get through this?'

'That's easy. Marry David Atkinson.'

'But I don't love him.'

'Liz, I've been standing out there thinking about it. Everybody has their own idea of what love is like. Take me, for instance. I thought that no one had ever felt as strongly as I did for your father. I was willing to give up everything just to be with him. He was forty years old and I was eighteen. But what did it get me? Shame, misery, loneliness. The only good thing to come out of it was you. I love you dearly and want to see you happy. Don't let what you feel for Danny blind you to other facets of love. Trust me, love, you could do a lot worse than marry David Atkinson.'

'Ah, Mam. No matter what he has done, I love Danny with all my heart.'

Going to her, Kath took her in her arms and rocked her gently. She wished she could banish the tears as easily as she had when Liz was small. 'It will pass, love. It will pass.' Would it? she derided herself. How long had it taken before the pain of her own love affair had eased? Many, many years. But then, she had not given another man the chance to get to know her, to soften the blow. David Atkinson was the answer to any girl's prayers.

Giving Liz a light shake, she once more urged her, 'Go for it, love. If it doesn't work out for you, I'll still be here. I love you and I'll always be here for you. Just you remember that.'

Chapter Two

Still in a turmoil, Liz climbed the stairs to her office the following morning with a heavy heart. Sunday had been spent going from one extreme to the other; from hopeful anticipation that somehow things could be put right to absolute despair. Egged on by her mother, she had actually pictured herself living on Somerton Road, happily married to Mr Atkinson. Imagine! She couldn't even think of him as David, but she could picture herself living with him in his beautiful bungalow. Just him and her. She could never bring herself to picture them together in the bedroom, though. No, her mind shied away from that thought.

Now and then a word or gesture brought memories that tormented her. Never again to be in Danny's arms and feel her heart thudding in rhythm with his. To be denied the joy of planning a future together and having his children broke her heart. It wasn't fair. She had done nothing to deserve this. Why must she be the one to suffer? He didn't love Bridget Kelly. Everybody was going to be miserable, except maybe Bridget who would have Danny and his child to fill her life. But Liz and Danny at least could have happiness together. A word from her and she knew he would pack his bags and they could run away together.

Now she was being daft. Run away to where? Leave another child with the stigma of being born a bastard? Never. Liz had enough experience of that and would not wish it on her worst enemy. She would never willingly condemn an innocent child to that fate. But the very fact she'd been tempted, even momentarily, put paid to everything else. Under the circumstances, how could she even contemplate marrying David Atkinson?

Pale-faced and dull-eyed, she was aware she looked far from her best this morning. Maybe seeing her like this would put Mr Atkinson off. She dreaded facing him. Would have loved to have called in sick, but she knew he would not be fooled by lame excuses. Besides, there was the stock taking to be done. Hadn't she promised to work late and help him with it? If only he hadn't proposed. What on earth had possessed him? If he was beginning to feel that way inclined, Irene Brennan would be a far better match for him. She was at least in the same age group and very attractive. It was also obvious she fancied him, so why hadn't he picked her?

What would his attitude be towards Liz when she turned him down? Perhaps it was pity that had triggered off this silly idea in the first instance and now he was regretting it. Oh, wouldn't it be great if he was hoping to be let off the hook? It would make things so much easier all round. She sent a prayer heavenward that this would be so. However, it brought a different worry to the fore. Would they still be able to work together after all that had passed between them

76

in such a short space of time? To have to look for another job on top of everything else would be the final straw. Liz didn't know which way to turn; what to do for the best. She was quite literally at her wits' end.

There was no easy way out. It was all right her mother egging her on to marry David, but how could she lie beside him, night after night? Danny would always be there between them. She stifled a hysterical laugh as she pictured three in a bed. God, what was she thinking of?

Her heart in her mouth, she tentatively pushed open the office door, to find at least some of her worries were in vain. David looked up from the papers he was working on and greeted her in his usual pleasant manner, as if the weekend had been a figment of her imagination. Her mind balked at this thought. Was it possible? Had she dreamed it all up? A closer look showed the concern in his eyes and she knew it was no dream.

Once Liz had removed and hung up her coat, it was business as usual. Soon she was caught up in her duties and spent most of the morning out on the shop floor in the company of the two overseers, seeing to the distribution of different batches of work to the girls. Petticoats to some and french knickers to others. Usually they could be trusted to get on with it, but this was a special order from a new client and she wanted to make sure that the girls knew just what quality of work was expected of them. Except for the two young trainees, who would not be on this particular order, they were all experienced cutters and stitchers and it wasn't often a mistake was made.

However, it was a new design and if handled successfully, could lead to further lucrative orders. The material was pure silk and therefore very expensive; any mistakes would be severely frowned on. Liz made the machinists aware of this, and after some good-natured banter left them to get on with it. The rest of the morning was spent with the cutters, examiners and dispatch room workers.

The mid-day break was from twelve-thirty until one-thirty. If the weather was dull, wet or severely cold like today, most of the stitchers remained in the spacious warm cloakroom where there was a radio to listen to, tea-making facilities and a small gas ring where soup could be heated. Liz usually fetched a cup of tea to her office and read a book while eating sandwiches she brought in with her each day. That some of the staff thought this a bit standoffish she never realized, or she would have been very hurt. She was just not one for idle gossip, and preferred to get engrossed in a good book or magazine.

At half-twelve on the dot David entered her office. 'I hope you don't mind, but I have booked a table for lunch for us.'

'Oh, but I can't...'

'Why not, Liz?'

'If we go out to lunch together it will start the girls' tongues wagging. You know what they're like!'

'Does that mean you're saying no to my proposal of marriage?'

'Of course I am, Mr Atkinson. You must surely see it wouldn't work? You're letting pity blind you to reality.'

He smiled grimly. 'I've heard it called many a thing, but never pity. No, what I feel for you, Liz, is definitely not pity. Come to lunch with me, please,' he insisted.

She opened her mouth to refuse but he cried, 'Surely I've at least the right to know how Danny conducted himself over the weekend?'

For some moments she sat pondering, head bent, then nodded. He had every right to know. She had given him that right when she had blubbered, here in this very office, in his presence on Saturday morning and then accepted his invitation to spend the day with him. He reached for her coat and held it while she slipped her arms into the sleeves. Lifting her handbag, she preceded him from the office, eyes downcast. As she had already foreseen, heads came around the cloakroom door as they passed and eyes followed their progress down the length of the stitching room. Excited chatter burst forth and followed them down the stairs. The girls were agog with excitement. And who could blame them? After all, it was unheard of for Old Atkie to take Liz O'Hara to lunch. And where else could they be going at this hour of the day?

She could imagine the turn the conversation would take. Age difference was sure to be mentioned; the fact that he was old enough to be her father would cause raised brows. And they all knew she was engaged to Danny McGowan; some had even met him with her and had enviously declared him a handsome devil. They would wonder what on earth she was playing at.

'See what I mean,' she muttered, grumpily.

David smiled grimly. He also hated the idea of being gossiped about, especially by his own workforce, but this had become a crusade with him. He was determined to do all in his power to persuade Liz to marry him. He was sure he could make her happy. The more she resisted him, the more he admired her and determined to win her over.

The restaurant he had chosen was close to the factory and after a short walk in the crisp air, they entered the embracing warmth of its interior. Being the lunch hour it was packed. They were escorted to a table in a corner and David asked for the wine list. He ordered, and then while they waited, leant across the table and said quietly, 'Now tell me, what did Danny have to say?'

She smiled slightly as she recalled Danny's reaction. 'You'll never believe me but he was very angry because I spent the day with you. He implied we had been "carrying on", as he put it, while we were supposed to be working overtime.'

'Trying to shift the blame. What did you say to that?'

'I told him I'd spent just the one day with you, but I doubt if he believed me. He ranted on about me being a prude. He said he was a virile young man and since I wasn't willing, I shouldn't blame him for taking what was handed to him on a plate. I'm afraid there was a lot of anger and cross words and in the heat of it all, I couldn't resist telling him that you had asked me to marry you.'

With a slight tut of annoyance at the interruption, David drew back and examined the label on the bottle offered by the waiter. He nodded permission for it to be poured. He handed Liz the menu but she refused it, saying she wasn't hungry. His lips tightened and he ordered for both of them.

When they were alone again, he asked, 'What had Danny to say about that?'

'He was outraged. Said I loved him, and I'd live to regret it. And he's right, you know, Mr Atkinson. I do still love him, in spite of everything he's done.'

He appreciated that she was being honest with him and did not refute this. The food arrived and he said, 'Now eat up. Remember, you're working late tonight and I don't want you passing out on me.'

Having eaten very little the day before, Liz looked at the food, smelt its appetising aroma, and regained her lost appetite. When she had cleared her plate and drunk two glasses of wine she smiled across the table at him.

'I enjoyed that, thank you.'

'Do you feel any better?'

'Yes, I do actually.'

He was glad the wine had brought colour to her cheeks and put a sparkle in her eyes. Her ashen face and dark-ringed eyes had dismayed him. Indeed, it had taken all his self-control not to take her in his arms and commiserate with her this morning. Now he wanted to tell her that he thought she looked wonderful but settled for, 'Nothing ever looks half as bad on a full stomach.'

'I wish you wouldn't be so kind, Mr Atkinson. It makes it so awkward for me.'

'Liz, do you think you could call me David?'

Wide-eyed, she cried, 'No! What would the girls think?'

'To hell with the girls. I beg your pardon. Ah, Liz, how can I get through to you how much I want you to marry me? Look at it this way. You're in a position where you need to get away from Dunlewey Street. I am offering you that outlet.'

'I only need rooms, not a commitment for life, Mr...' She saw his mouth open in protest and hastily said, 'David.'

A slight smile showed his approval. 'That's better. If the worst comes to the worst, we can always get divorced, you know. And I'd see to it you were settled for life. You can't lose, Liz. No matter what.'

'That's no way to enter into marriage. I wish things were different. I wish I had more time to think. I can't imagine what you see in me. What about Irene Brennan? She's beautiful! And she's upper-crust and would be a much better match for you.'

'Liz, if I had been attracted to Irene, I would have done something about it long ago. She was Victoria's best friend and that's how we'll remain, just good friends. Take my word for it.'

Remembering the way Irene had looked at him she found this hard to believe, but apparently it was all one-sided. 'Give me a couple of days to think it over. All right?'

Relieved, he nodded his agreement. There was hope yet.

During the next couple of days Liz blew hot and cold. They worked late stock taking and David insisted on seeing her home each evening, staying for a coffee and chat with her and her mother. He soon discovered he had an ally in Kath. The more she saw of him, the more she liked him and the more pressure was put on Liz to marry him.

The turning point came on Wednesday. David had dropped her off as usual but declined to come in, saying he had some business to attend to. Kath, who worked in the chemist's shop facing Dunville Park had also been late home, the shop being open for prescriptions that particular night. They decided that instead of cooking they would have fish and chips for tea and Liz nipped down to the chip shop at the corner of Spinner Street to buy some. With the fish suppers wrapped in newspaper against the cold and clasped close to her breast, she hurried across the Falls Road. Head bent against the sharp wind, she quite literally bumped into Danny, a laughing Bridget hanging on his arm. He caught hold of her arm to steady her and they all stopped in confusion. Bridget fell quiet as Danny and Liz couldn't help staring at each other. Waves of naked longing flowed like electricity between them. After what seemed like ages but in reality was seconds, Liz dragged her eyes from his and with an abrupt nod, angrily disengaged her arm and continued up the street.

Danny stood stock still looking after her, forgetful of the girl by his side. Heart thudding against his rib cage, fingers tingling from their contact with Liz's arm, a great ache filled his chest. What on earth had he done? He and Liz were meant for each other. No one else could ever take her place!

Tentatively, Bridget tugged at his sleeve. 'Danny, it is going to be all right, isn't it?'

He looked down into her big worried brown eyes and tried to force a smile. 'Of course it is. Aren't we going to become parents?' The false brightness of his voice made it sound like a prison sentence and fear entered Bridget's heart. He must not change his mind. The sooner they were married the better.

Tears blinding her, Liz reached the sanctuary of her own home. How could she bear to watch them? See that young girl grow bigger with Danny's child? Inside the house, her mother was hovering anxiously. 'You saw them then.' It was a statement, not a question. Liz's misery was plain to be seen. 'I saw them go down the street and hoped you wouldn't bump into them.'

'Mam, do you think I could be a good wife to David, feeling the way I do about Danny? Is it at all possible?'

Kath was quick to seize the opportunity to fight on David's behalf. 'It is, love. You would make him a wonderful wife, I know you would. You would give it your best shot and no one could ask for more.'

'Ah, Mam, it's awful. I can't bear to see them together. Still, it doesn't seem fair to offer David second best.'

'He knows the score, Liz. He won't expect any

miracles. You won't regret it, love. David Atkinson is a good man.'

Liz smiled through her tears. 'I hope you still think it's a good idea when the priest comes banging on the door. He's sure to hear about it if we get married in a register office, and all hell will break loose then. The clergy will be up in arms about it, you know that.'

'They won't know until you're married. So don't you worry about the priest. I'll deal with him when the time comes.'

In the small hall that led into Bridget's home, Danny took her in his arms and kissed her good night. Her parents had yet to forgive him for disgracing their daughter and he avoided any contact with them. 'Danny, are you sure you want to marry me?' Tears hung on Bridget's long thick lashes and, stifling the bitterness that engulfed him, he brushed them gently away. It was all his fault. At his age he should have known better. He had done the dirty deed; now he must play the part.

'Of course I do. Do you think I would let a child of mine be branded a bastard?'

It wasn't what she wanted to hear. She was aware that he was being evasive. Nevertheless she pretended to believe him and once more offered him her lips.

He brushed them briefly with his and gave her a gentle push towards the door. 'Good night. Get away in out of the cold or your da will be after my skin. I'll see you tomorrow night.'

Reluctantly, she entered the house and, heavy

of heart, he made his way up Leeson Street on to the Falls Road. He remembered little of the film they had seen earlier on. Sitting in the darkness of the picture house beside the girl he was going to marry, his mind had been full of Liz and all that could have been. He couldn't bear the thought of losing her. There must be something he could do. But what?

In the act of opening his own front door, he came to a sudden decision. Swinging round, he crossed the street and knocked on the O'Haras' door. It was quite late but he knew they had not retired for the night, a light still burned downstairs.

The door was opened by Kath. She glowered at him and he apologized. 'I'm sorry for disturbing you this late, Mrs O'Hara, but I would like to speak with Liz, please?'

'She's in bed and I'm sure she's fast asleep by now,' Kath lied hoping Liz wouldn't follow her into the hall and prove her a liar. She hoped in vain.

'It's all right, Mam. I'll speak to him.'

Reluctantly, Kath moved aside and Danny passed her, his eyes never leaving Liz's pale face. He could see she had been crying recently. Was it because of him?

'You go on up to bed, Mam.'

'Are you sure, Liz?'

'Yes, Mam. I won't be too long behind you.'

Leading the way into the living room, Liz turned to face Danny. She could see the lines of strain on his face, the dark shadows under his eyes that spoke of sleepless nights. She was glad he was suffering too.

'What brings you here at this time of night, Danny?'

'Liz, we have to talk.'

'What about?'

'Us! The future. I realized tonight that it would be wrong to marry Bridget feeling as I do about you.'

A great ball of joy rose in her breast; her prayers had been answered. He must have found a way out. It was going to be all right after all. She willingly entered his arms. His fingers threaded through her hair and they kissed hungrily. Forgetful of everything but his nearness, Liz returned his passionate caresses. Only when he eased her on to the settee and started to undo her blouse did sanity return.

What was different? She must find out. 'What has happened, Danny? Will Bridget not marry you after all?' she asked. She knew at once by the look on his face that nothing had changed! Maybe he didn't want to marry Bridget, but there was still the child to consider. Pushing him angrily away, Liz cried, 'What about the baby?'

'I'll provide for it. My name can go on the birth certificate. I'll do all I can for Bridget, but I can't marry her. Surely you can see that, Liz? It just wouldn't work!'

'Don't be silly. If you don't marry her the child will still be a bastard.'

'I can't, Liz. I can't live without you. Please don't ask me to.'

Sadness engulfed her. It was so easy to be wise after the event. 'There is no other way, Danny.

87

But I'll make it easier for you,' she added. 'I'm marrying David Atkinson as soon as it can be arranged.'

He jumped to his feet and pulled her roughly to hers. 'I won't let you. Do you hear me? How can you even think of it after that display of passion? You love me. We're meant for each other. And you know it!'

'It's a pity you didn't remember that when Bridget offered it to you on a plate. What a lame excuse! If you really loved me it wouldn't have mattered who offered it to you, you would have been man enough to say no. Good night, Danny. You're wasting my time. There's nothing more to be said. You're history now as far as I'm concerned. That's the way it has to be.'

'Don't you play the holy act on me, Liz O'Hara! You wouldn't be rushing into marriage with Old Atkie unless you and him were closer than you let on. Don't take me for a fool.'

'I can't help your warped view of things. I would never have known that David was attracted to me if you hadn't let me down. But you did.'

A harsh laugh interrupted her. 'Ah, so it's *David* now!'

'Yes, *David!* I've discovered what a wonderful person he is, and I do intend to marry him. So don't you do anything foolish where Bridget is concerned, because I won't change my mind. You've made your bed, now lie on it.'

He moved towards her again but with a disdainful flick of the wrist Liz dismissed him and turned her back on him. He was never to know that as he skulked from the room, tears coursed down her cheeks.

Striding up the street, Peter McGowan watched his brother turn tail at the door and cross over to Liz's home. What was he up to now? No good, that was for sure. The house was silent; everyone else had retired for the night. Making himself a cup of tea, Peter sat down to await his brother's return. He had not long to wait; Liz must have chucked him out on his ear, he thought with satisfaction.

Raising his cup, he gestured towards the kitchen. 'There's enough left in the pot for another one.'

'Oh, thanks.'

Tea poured, Danny took the chair opposite Peter's and sat hunched forward, gazing into the dying embers of the fire.

He looked so down that for a moment Peter actually felt sorry for him. Only for a brief moment. Danny had brought all this trouble on himself. There was no one else to blame. 'Did I see you go into the O'Haras' house a while ago?'

Danny's head jerked and a scowl twisted his mouth. 'What if you did?'

'I just wondered what business you had over there now?'

'Oh, you did, did you? And what gives you the right to poke your nose into my affairs?'

'Do you not think you should let Liz get on with her own life? You'll be married in a couple of weeks' time. Concentrate on that and leave the poor girl alone.'

89

'Will I?'

'You're talking in riddles, man. Will you what?'

'Will I be getting married?'

'You had better! Or you won't just have Barney Kelly and his three sons to answer to ... you'll have me as well.'

'Well, now, isn't Bridget the lucky one to have so many champions in her corner? If I didn't know better, I'd think you fancied her yourself. Now *that* would be an answer to everybody's problems. You would get what you wanted. The baby would have the family name. What would it matter which brother was its father? And I would be able to follow my heart's desire.'

Peter was on his feet instantly. With clenched fists he towered over Danny. 'No, strange as it may seem, I'm not interested in infants. Because that's all Bridget is, you know. A child. But she is a lovely wee girl and I won't see you make a fool of her. Have you no pride at all, man?'

'Hah! Everybody seems to think that I'm the big bad wolf. But let me tell you something, Peter McGowan. It takes two and she was willing – more than willing. In fact, in hindsight, I'd go so far as to say she seduced me.'

Peter's jaw dropped in shock. 'How low can you go? Blaming it on her. You should have had more sense at your age. Just do the right thing by her, do you hear me?'

Slowly Danny rose to his feet and faced his brother. 'If Liz would still have me, I'd face you, Barney Kelly and his three sons any day of the week. But unfortunately, she's going to marry her boss. What do you think of that? What does that

90

suggest to you, eh? That *she's* not as lily white as she's painted either. Who knows? Maybe I'm doing her an injustice. But since she does intend to marry her boss, I may as well give my child a name. Just don't you think for one minute I'm scared of any of you, 'cause I'm not.' On this note he turned on his heel and left the room.

Peter stared after him. Well, well, so Liz was marrying her boss? He found that hard to take in. She'd been daft about Danny and you don't just change your mind overnight. Then comprehension dawned. She was running away from him! Tying herself to an older man. That's what she was doing. God, but his brother had a lot to answer for.

David was quiet and pensive on Thursday morning. Liz watched him covertly over her typewriter, waiting for a convenient time to tell him of her decision to marry him. Now that she had made up her mind she wanted to commit herself before she faltered. Mid-morning he informed her he was meeting a client for lunch and would probably be back late. Liz nodded her understanding but inwardly questions were bombarding her. What client? She usually made notes in her desk diary of all his appointments.

Because he was lying, dark ugly colour stained David's pale skin as he avoided her eye. She looked at him in amazement. What on earth was the matter? At half-past twelve, perplexed, she watched from the window as he crossed the yard and opened the car door. He looked up and raised his hand in farewell. Embarrassed at being

91

caught spying on him, she quickly drew back without acknowledging his gesture. Was he having second thoughts but too embarrassed to admit it?

Easing the car out of the yard, David was feeling far from happy. He was meeting Irene Brennan for lunch. What had possessed him? Two nights ago he had found a message on his answering machine at home, asking him to ring her at eight last night. That was why he'd had to miss out on the pleasure of having coffee with Liz and her mother. Irene had been delighted he had answered her call, subtly reminding him of all the others he had not returned and making him feel ashamed. But he had known she wanted to further their friendship and had not intended giving her any encouragement. Her husband had died six years ago and even before Victoria's death, he had been dismayed to realize she was sending out vibes in his direction, behind his wife's back.

Still, she had sounded so unhappy on the phone the night before, he had felt compelled to accept her invitation to lunch. Now he was on his way to Fortwilliam Golf Club where she was a member, to have lunch and a chat with her. Why hadn't he told Liz where he was going? She would have understood. Indeed, she would probably have been delighted to hear that he was meeting Irene. For that very reason he hadn't told her! He didn't want to give her any excuse to continue putting him off.

Irene was already in the car park waiting for him. She locked the door of her small Austin

Mini and came to meet him with her hand extended. Her smile was warm and implied an intimacy between them that didn't exist. Apprehensively, David clasped the small cool hand and avoiding the pursed lips, brushed his lips lightly against her cheek. He followed her to the door of the clubhouse, already regretting the impulsive gesture that had resulted in his being here. Opening the door with her member's key, she entered the hallway and motioned him inside.

They climbed the wide staircase to the restaurant in silence. He and Victoria had often frequented the golf club and he was glad to note that the lounge was empty. Irene had booked a table and he was relieved that a *tête-à-tête* in one of the lounge's secluded alcoves could be avoided. At least they would not have to sit and mull over old times in one of those intimate enclosures while they waited. A waiter came towards them and Irene addressed him by his Christian name. They were led straight into the dining room.

'I warned them that you were on your lunch break and would be in a hurry to get back, so the service should be quick,' she explained. Once their order was taken, she leant across the table towards him. 'I hope you didn't mind my asking you to lunch today, David?'

'Not at all, Irene. It was the least I could do. You sounded so upset on the phone last night and if I can be of any assistance whatsoever, I will be only too happy.'

'You promised you would keep in touch, David,' she reminded him plaintively, while playfully tapping with long sensitive fingers on his hand where it rested on the table.

Resisting the impulse to snatch his hand away, he said quietly, 'Yes, I did, but you know how it is. Time goes on, and to be truthful at the beginning I couldn't bring myself to meet any of the old clique, so I buried myself in my work.'

'I had hoped you would have at least kept in touch with *me*, David. After all, I was Victoria's best friend.'

'That's the very reason I didn't. You brought the loss of her too close to me.'

Irene was unwilling to let go of her grievance. 'I left messages on your answer machine?'

'I know but it was too soon. I was still grieving.'

'So you have at last come to terms with her death, then?'

'Yes,' he agreed sadly. 'Of course I'll never forget her, but it has been four years now and time is a great healer. Victoria would want me to make a new life for myself.'

'That's what I thought when I saw you at the Opera House on Saturday night.'

'It was nice seeing you all again.'

'That was a lovely young girl you were with, David.'

'Yes, she's very nice.'

'Have you known her long?'

'Yes, quite a few years.'

'Oh.' Irene sounded nonplussed and suddenly became intense. 'You know I care for you, don't you, David?'

'You have always been a good friend, Irene,' he said evasively, dismay in his heart. What had he let himself in for?

'We could become closer. I care deeply for you.' Her dark blue eyes were trying to draw him in and he squirmed uncomfortably.

To his great relief a waitress arrived with their soup and he was able to lean back, away from Irene's relentless patting fingers and compelling gaze. The next hour passed slowly. The conversation was stilted and he carefully picked his words to avoid saying anything that might lead her to think he cared, even slightly.

It was with relief that he said farewell to her outside the club. He had managed to ward off a definite meeting in the future by promising to ring her when he was free. He knew she was disappointed and felt a bit of a cad, but he had never given her any indication that he was interested in her. Never!

Liz lifted her head and looked him full in the face when he passed through her office fifteen minutes past the lunch hour.

'Any calls?' David asked, avoiding her gaze; his voice sounding strange even to his own ears. Why did he feel and sound so guilty?

She shook her head and the intensity of her gaze made him aware she knew that something was wrong.

She followed him into his office and, closing the door, stood with her back to it. 'Have you changed your mind about me, David?' she blurted out. 'Don't be afraid to say if you have. I'll understand.'

He stared at her in amazement. 'No! What on

earth makes you think that?'

Her eyes scanned his face, noting the high colour in his cheeks. 'You're acting very strangely today.'

'I'm sorry, Liz, but something cropped up. Something I can't talk about at the moment. Perhaps later. Were you wanting to ask me something?'

She hesitated. Perhaps she should wait for the right moment? No, there would never be a right moment. She had better get it over with. If she was going to marry him, the sooner the better for all concerned. She licked dry lips and forced the words out of her mouth. 'If you still want me, I will be happy to become your wife, David.'

He could not contain himself. To her amazement he threw back his head and let out a great yelp of pure delight. Then, taking her by the arm, he led her through her office and out on to the shop floor. Calling for attention, he said, 'I know there has been a lot of gossip about Liz and me lately and I want to put an end to it once and for all.' He paused dramatically, one hand grasping Liz's and the other held up to command their attention though it was not really necessary. The girls were all agog. With a wide grin he announced, 'I would like you all to know that Liz has just done me the honour of agreeing to become my wife.'

Stunned silence greeted his words and startled glances were exchanged. Then bedlam broke out as they all left their machines and vied with each other to offer their congratulations.

Liz was acutely embarrassed. They would all

think she had dumped Danny in favour of David. They would be sure to think it was David's money she was after. Well, did she want them to know it was the other way about? That Danny had dumped her for a young girl? They would probably find out the truth in due course. Two of them came from around Leeson Street, so would probably hear it on the grapevine. And did it really matter what they thought?

To her surprise, David continued. 'And, as I don't believe in beating about the bush, just in case she changes her mind, we shall be married as quickly as possible. Thank you for your good wishes, but now I'm afraid it's back to work. I would like that order out before the deadline.' They started to drift back to their machines and he added a word of warning. 'I don't want a rush job, mind you. If you do well on it, there'll be a bonus for each of you.' He was feeling in a benevolent mood.

In the privacy of his office, David took Liz in his arms. She stiffened and threw him an apologetic look. 'It's all right, Liz. I promised I wouldn't rush you, and I won't.' He kissed her gently on the cheek. She gazed up into kind grey eyes fringed with long golden lashes and inwardly wept for Danny's dark good looks. 'You have made me very happy, Liz, and I'll do all in my power to make you happy in return. I shall see about a special licence and we will marry as soon as possible.'

Seeing his great happiness, doubts began to gnaw at her. 'David ... I hope you don't live to regret this.'

'If I do, I'll have no one to blame but myself. Lord knows, you've tried hard enough to put me off.'

Big haunted eyes gazed up at him. Slowly, he lowered his head, giving her every chance to draw away. She tilted her head back slightly and waited for his lips. The kiss was deep, tender and satisfying. To his great delight she pressed closer.

It was pure coincidence that both marriages took place on the same day. In St Peter's Pro-cathedral Church, Danny and Bridget were married during eleven o'clock Mass. Her mother had insisted she marry in white and a long dress and veil was purchased for the occasion. Gazing at her reflection in the full-length mirror that morning, Bridget had squirmed with embarrassment. There was as yet no sign of a bump, just a slight thickening of the waist. The dress really was very pretty, with a modest neckline and long sleeves. She looked sweet and pure, but those not already in the know must surely guess the reason for the quick wedding. Even the priest had been unable to hide his disapproval. She felt a right hypocrite dressed in virginal white.

Her only sister Marie, who was already married, was matron of honour. She wore a pale blue dress and her four-year-old daughter was flower girl. Thankfully the rain had stopped. Bridget had always found St Peter's church cold, and now as she stood in the front porch she shivered in the chilly air. There was sadness in her heart as she gazed around the group waiting for instructions from the photographer. Danny,

Peter who was best man, her father who was giving her away, her three brothers and Joe, her new father-in-law, all looked handsome in lounge suits. Even shy young Joseph was dressed to kill, in a new sports jacket and dark grey flannel trousers. Her mother and Jane also wore new suits and festive hats. They were all smiling and hearty but this didn't lessen her sadness. It was such false gaiety, like some half-baked soap opera unfolding before her eyes.

Her mother had cried oceans of tears before leaving the house and her face was puffy, her eyes swollen. She looked far from being the happy mother of the bride. She had expected so much of her beautiful daughter and could not hide her disappointment. In her eyes, Danny had spoilt everything. Bridget's father was grim-faced. He hadn't smiled since he had learnt of her pregnancy. How she wished she could turn the clock back. See her father smiling and relaxed, her mother happy again. But then there would be no Danny beside her and she needed him above all others.

Jane McGowan dabbed furtively at her tears. They were certainly not tears of joy. It should have been tall, elegant Liz O'Hara up there beside her son, she inwardly lamented. How proud she would have been to welcome Liz as a daughter-in-law. As it was she was not in the least looking forward to having Bridget and Danny living with her. And for how long? Would they still be there when the baby arrived? The prospect of nappies and baby clothes cluttering up her home did not appeal to her. She'd had her fair share of that, thank you very much!

Her husband had convinced her they must do the decent thing and let the newly weds have their lovely big bedroom. The bedrooms in their house in Pound Loney had been small and cramped. Her spacious new room was her pride and joy. Jane had put her heart and soul into decorating it. A beautiful rose-patterned fitted carpet that your feet sank into, the best of bed linen, and furniture that gave her great pleasure to polish. Now she was to be denied it all. Joe had argued it would be uncomfortable for Bridget in the smaller bedroom, what with her expecting a baby. But what about Jane? Hadn't she a right to be pampered in her twilight years? Still, there was nothing else for it. Peter and Joseph had agreed to doubling up in the other large room so she had agreed, with great reluctance, to let the newly weds have their precious room and had prepared what was little more than a box room for her and Joe. She did it with bad grace. A man of few words, Joe McGowan didn't often voice an opinion and when he did, his wife nearly always submitted to his wishes, but that didn't mean she had to pretend to like it.

She gazed at the wedding group, sorrow in her heart. She had hoped to hold on to her sons for some years yet. Danny had said it would be years before he and Liz could afford to get married because Liz wanted the best of everything, which had pleased Jane. His money coming in for another year or so would have helped her to save enough money to put Joseph through university, and have some security for her old age. Some would call her selfish but she looked on it as just reward for rearing her sons through hard times.

Instead there was this awful rushed affair. Her first-born son married and it had to be a shotgun wedding. Nothing whatsoever to brag about. And all that money laid out on new suits for them. Joe had insisted that the best and only the best would do for the occasion. They were not to let Danny down even under these trying circumstances. She had demurred, asking him where he thought the money was coming from. He had fixed a stern eye on her and assured her he was confident she would come up trumps, considering all the money she raked in each Friday night. Imagine Joe, who rarely criticized anyone, saying that to her! It was all Danny's fault and Jane would never forgive him for letting her down like this.

Barney Kelly didn't realize just how grim he looked. He was doing everything in his power to make this a memorable day for his daughter. He had hired a hall in Bread Street, within walking distance of St Peter's to cut out the necessity of hiring cars. With so little time it was the best he could manage. He might have managed to scrape up enough money for a proper reception but the hotels were booked for months in advance, with the exception of those posh places which were well beyond his pocket.

The female members of the family had rallied round, aunts and cousins and even neighbours lending a helping hand. The buffet that was laid on proved to be very appetizing, but a long stretch from what he would really have liked for his youngest daughter, the apple of his eye. He had also persuaded a popular local group, The Starlights, to provide entertainment for a small payment well below their usual fee, as a special favour to him. For Bridget's sake he wanted things to go well and tried to be friendly towards Danny. He had made the typical father-in-law speech, jokingly warning Danny what would befall him if he failed to live up to his daughter's expectations. How was he to know that it actually came out more like a threat?

He'd succeeded in being amicable enough, as he thought; making small talk and dancing with all the ladies, until the bride and groom had changed into suitable clothes for travelling and were preparing to leave for their honeymoon – a few days in Dublin. Before they left Barney took Danny by the elbow and led him to a secluded corner. 'If I ever see so much as a tear on my daughter's face, I'll break your bloody neck! And that's a promise,' he growled menacingly.

Danny looked up into the face of the big man who could give him four inches and two stone; the man who had scowled and frowned at him since that fateful day they'd first met. The man who couldn't say a civil word to him but was happy enough to push his pregnant daughter into marriage with him. Did they think he'd wanted this rushed affair? Liz and he had aspired to higher things. Oh, yes, indeed they had. *Their* wedding would have been something! Hurt pride gave him Dutch courage. 'She's my wife now, and what you think or say doesn't

102

enter in to it any more.'

Rage blurred Barney's vision but his aim was nevertheless true. 'Oh, no?' he growled, and a fist like a shovel smashed into Danny's face and lifted him right off his feet.

'Dad!' Bridget's piercing cry brought Barney back to his senses. The mist slowly evaporated from before his eyes and he bent to assist his new son-in-law to his feet. Knocking the hand away, Danny was nevertheless glad to accept help from Peter.

'I expect you deserved that,' he couldn't resist muttering in his brother's ear.

'Oh, frig off, the lot of you. And thanks for all your good wishes on this day that's supposed to be the happiest of my life,' Danny muttered, tenderly fingering his rapidly swelling lip. He glared around until his eye lit on Bridget, now being comforted by her mother. 'Come on. Let's get out of here.' Gripping her by the arm, he led her out of the front door and into her brother's car. A hushed, dismayed crowd watched them out of sight.

It was Barney who broke the awkward silence. Running a hand wearily over his face, he avoided his wife's tearful, accusing look and cried, 'Come on, let's not waste any more time. There's still plenty of drink and grub to get through so let's get on with it. I feel like a good drink after that exhibition.'

David and Liz were married at half-past two in the afternoon. He had gone to a lot of trouble and expense and the register office, usually bare and bleak, was festooned with great bouquets of flowers. Kath, and Dick Kennedy, a friend of David's, were witnesses. A hired photographer was there to take photographs, and unknown to Liz, David had arranged for copies to be sent to the two main newspapers, the *Belfast Telegraph* and the *Irish News.* That way friends on both sides should become aware that they were married.

Liz had broken into her savings and splashed out on her wedding outfit which was exquisite. Bought from one of the smarter boutiques in town, it was of the purest silk: a cream, full-skirted dress with a close-fitting bodice that showed off her figure to perfection, topped by a loose matching full-length coat. A large pink picture hat framed a cameo face, lending colour to the skin and shadowing Liz's high cheek bones. She looked radiant. Her eyes were dark and haunted with emotion. Afraid she might break down and cry, David clasped her hand tightly and smiled reassuringly at her throughout the short ceremony.

Liz had difficulty pushing pictures from her mind of herself walking up the aisle of St Peter's in a long white dress and floating veil, and Danny waiting at the altar to claim her. Tears brimmed in her eyes but she must not let David down. To her relief the service was over all too soon and he kissed her on the cheek. He sensed that she was all keyed up and didn't want to push his luck by claiming her lips. She was his wife now and that was all that mattered. He was content to wait.

After a slap-up meal in one of the posh restaurants in the city centre, they prepared to take their leave. Dick was running them to Aldergrove Airport to catch the plane. Before leaving, David took Kath to one side.

'Thank you. I owe you a lot. I will do all in my power to make her happy. And dare I say, you look wonderful in that suit?'

She smiled with pleasure at the compliment. She knew that she did look her best in the dark blue suit and white hat. 'I know you will, David. She's a very lucky girl.'

'You will look after that other matter for me?' he asked quietly. She nodded. 'Thank you. See you soon.' He gathered her up in a bear hug and kissed her cheek.

While the men put the suitcases in the boot of the car, Liz faced her mother. 'Well, Mam, the deed is done. For better or worse, as they say. I just hope I don't live to regret it.'

'Don't you dare have any regrets concerning Danny McGowan! I didn't tell you sooner but he was married too this morning. I saw all the McGowans, dressed to kill, getting into a taxi while you were having your bath.'

Stifling the swift pain these words caused her, Liz said, 'I hope he'll be happy, Mam. He can be so hot-headed at times.'

Inwardly cursing Danny for the way he had spoilt things for her daughter, Kath urged her, 'Just you forget all about him, love. He's not your problem any more. That is a real man you're married to.'

A taxi had been ordered to take Kath home. David pushed some money at the driver and told him to look after her. The delighted man respect-fully touched his forelock and promised to see her safely into her own house.

To her great surprise, Liz enjoyed the flight; another first for her. She had been apprehensive, thinking she would be nervous, but she loved the new experience of floating above the clouds and gazed in awe at the frothy whiteness below them. Their destination was unknown to her, but David promised her that she would love where they were going. In this restful atmosphere, all the tension eased from her body and eventually she dozed off.

David watched his sleeping wife and marvelled at the way fate had made her his. He had a lot to thank Danny McGowan for. If he had not been so stupid, David might never have discovered how wonderful a woman Liz really was. His eye ran over her bosom as it rose and fell beneath the fine silk material. He felt his cheeks redden at the thoughts that started going through his head, and derided himself. Was she not his wife? Didn't he have the right to picture her naked? Tonight, hopefully, she would be his, wholly and com-pletely. He couldn't wait to possess her, but he would follow her lead.

As if aware of his intense gaze, Liz moved restlessly in her sleep. When she opened her eyes he was reading the daily paper and seemed un-aware of her. She covertly eyed his hands with their long sensitive fingers and manicured nails. She shivered slightly when she imagined them on her body. Would she be able to bear him touching her? She gave all her attention to the view until their meal was served. By then she was in control of her emotions. David had said that he would be prepared to wait. But why should he? It wasn't as if she was recovering from an illness or something. No, there would be no waiting. She would do her duty.

The white sands and blue green waters of the Bahamas were like paradise to her. She had dozed off again and David had awakened her as they approached Nassau. He wanted to see her reaction to his choice of venue for their honeymoon. He was not disappointed. She was thrilled.

Their days were spent swimming and sunbathing on white sandy beaches; their evenings exploring the island and afterwards relaxing in one of the beautiful lounges that were located back and front of the hotel, each looking out on to breath-taking scenery. Here they sipped Bacardi-based cocktails and enjoyed the Calypso music provided by the resident steel band.

The nights proved to be no great problem. Liz found in David a considerate and tender lover. Their future looked promising indeed. If at times she looked on the pale golden body of her husband and longed for Danny's swarthy form, his intense passion, David never knew. The only blot on an otherwise contented horizon was her inability to block Danny completely from her mind. David guessed this but showed no sign of resentment. Liz was his wife and it was up to him to make her love him and forget the past.

Tears blinding her, Bridget sat in the back of her brother's old banger and begged God to let things work out right for them. Danny sat hunched at his side of the car, the picture of misery. The swelling around his mouth was more pronounced now and he dabbed at it with his handkerchief, scowling down at the bloody evidence of his encounter with his father-in-law.

They arrived at Victoria Street station with little time to spare and, gripping their suitcase, Patrick Kelly raced towards the platform, leaving them trailing in his wake. He hated seeing his sister in such a state. What on earth had possessed his da? Hitting Danny like that, after warning them all to be on their best behaviour for Bridget's sake. It was an awful thing to have done. It would be the talk of the district. Danny must feel a right fool. It was to his credit he had not retaliated. But then, perhaps he'd realized that that would be another mistake on his part. It was a well-known fact his father had been a fairly good amateur boxer in his younger days and could still handle himself with the best.

Throwing open the door of an empty carriage, Patrick threw the case onto the seat and waited for them to catch up. His heart was wrung with pity at the sight of his sister's despair. Imagine, her wedding day and she was the picture of misery. He scowled at Danny; the idiot should be trying to cheer her up instead of striding along as if he was on his own.

Putting a comforting arm across his sister's shoulders, he whispered, 'Sis, you know me da will regret that episode back there until his dying

108

day, don't you? I don't know what possessed him.'

The pain and hurt pride held in check for so long suddenly erupted and Bridget lashed out at him. 'And so he should! I'll never forgive him. Don't expect to see me back in Leeson Street when we come home. And you can tell him that.'

'Ah, sis, you don't mean it?'

'Just see if I don't,' she told him through tight lips.

Rocking her gently, he said, 'Don't do anything rash. You might need me ma and da one day. Don't cut yourself off from them. All right, love?'

She knew he spoke the truth and nodded mutely. 'Thanks, Patrick. Thanks for all your help.'

Turning to Danny, he held out his hand. 'All the best, mate. Try to make her happy, eh?' he said brightly.

Danny roused himself from his self-pitying thoughts to assure Patrick, 'She'll want for nothing. I'll see to that!'

'Just so long as she's happy. We can't ask for more.'

They were lucky enough to have a carriage to themselves. As the train pulled out of the station, taking his hand in hers, Bridget pleaded, 'Danny, please don't look so miserable.'

'Your da shouldn't have done that, you know, Bridget. I feel a right fool for letting him get away with it.'

'Yes, I know that, but please don't take it out on me. It's not my fault. I'm cold... Please hold me, Danny.'

Suddenly all else faded away as he became aware of his wife's distress. 'Ah, don't look like that, love. I'm sorry. It's just your da smacking me like that in front of everybody was the last straw.' Putting his arm around her, he drew her close. 'We'll show them, love. We'll show them all. We will be the best parents in the world. Our child will want for nothing.'

She smiled contentedly as, snuggling her head on his shoulder, she agreed with him. She only hoped he remembered these words later, when things got tougher still; as she was sure they would.

The Atkinsons arrived back from the Bahamas to cold winds and snow. Dick Kennedy was waiting for them in the arrival lounge at Aldergrove Airport.

Running his eye over their tanned figures, he greeted them enviously. 'You lucky people! We have had nothing but snow while you were away, and look at you. It's not fair.'

Dick had been divorced some years ago. Now a thought struck David. 'Your turn will come, Dick. Irene Brennan's a very lonely woman. Why don't you ask her out?'

'She's a fine woman, I admit that. I also admit I find her very attractive. I didn't stand a chance while you remained single, but now – who knows? Since lunching with you a couple of weeks ago, I think she had high hopes. Then she saw your wedding photo in the paper. Mind you, it was a bit of a shock for her. She seemed inconsolable.' He smiled slightly as if at some pleasant memory. 'However, I'm doing my best to comfort her.'

David sensed rather than saw Liz's look of surprise and coloured deeply under his pale golden tan. She noted the blush and was amused. For all his years, there were times when he acted like a young boy. When they reached the bungalow, Dick refused to come in for refreshments, saying with a twinkle in his eye that he had more important things to do with his spare time. They stood at the door to wave him off.

Unlocking the door, David turned to her. 'Now, my dear, I intend carrying you over the threshold.'

She laughed delightedly. 'I'm no light weight, mind, you could easily get a hernia!'

He swept her up in his arms as if she was as light as a feather and carried her into the hall. Setting her down gently, with a brief kiss, he left and went out to retrieve their suitcases.

Liz stood in the hall and eyed the great domed ceiling and dark oak doors. This was her new home. She felt unworthy of such splendour. Felt she was here under false pretences; an intruder. She recalled the day she had told David she would marry him. He had been out to lunch with a client that day although she'd had no record of it in her diary. He had seemed flustered when he returned. Could that client have been Irene? Could that maybe have been the start of a romance between them? Had Liz spoken out at the wrong time? Remembering David's great pleasure at the time, Liz doubted it. He had been overjoyed when she had at last agreed to marry him. But what if she had refused? Would he and Irene be companions by now?

Quietly approaching her from behind, David put his arms around her. 'Not having regrets, I hope?' he whispered in her ear.

'I'm just wondering if maybe you are?'

Her voice was low and he wasn't sure he'd heard her properly. Twisting her around to face him, he asked, 'What did you say?'

'I was wondering if you had any regrets? I didn't know that you were seeing Irene or I'd have kept my big mouth shut.'

'I had lunch with her once, and only once. It was the day you at last said that you'd marry me, remember?'

'I thought as much. Some client, eh? I couldn't understand why you were acting so guilty at the time.'

'The reason I didn't mention my date with her was because I knew you would think there was a chance she and I might come together.'

'And was there?'

'Never! Not once I fell in love with you. Do you know when that was?'

She shook her head and he continued. 'The very day you stood on the Giant's Causeway. Finn MacCool must have put a spell on me, and thank God all my conniving worked because here you are, my wife, Mrs Atkinson. And I'm so proud of you.'

'Ah, David, I don't deserve you, but I will try to be a good wife. I really will.'

Taking her by the hand, he led her towards the main bedroom and thrust open the door. It was all newly decorated. Together they admired the decor, the pastel blues and greys showed off the splendour of the dark furniture. 'I left a key with your mother and she saw to all this. I must admit, she's excelled herself. I don't want you thinking you're replacing my wife. I loved her dearly, but what I feel for you is unique. No one ever felt like this before.'

Liz remembered her mother saying those self-same words about her father, and was afraid. 'I hope you won't live to regret our marriage, David. I'll do all in my power to make you happy but...'

'You already have, my dear,' he assured her.

With a long look around, she sighed. 'It really is beautiful, but then Mother has always had such good taste.' Then, with a knowing smile, she took him by the hand. Kicking the door closed, with a deep chuckle he let himself be led towards the big inviting double bed.

Bridget came back from Dublin with stars in her eyes. After the bad start to their honeymoon Danny had concentrated on making his wife happy. The weather had been dry, and although cold and frosty with an occasional flurry of snow, it didn't deter them from touring the sights of the beautiful city. The first morning they walked along O'Connell Street (reputed to be one of the widest streets in the world), over O'Connell Bridge towards St Stephen's Green where they spent an hour just sitting on a bench watching the world go by until the chilliness sent them in search of warmth. This was found in a cafe in

Grafton Street where they had lunch, laughing and giggling at absurd little things, just like honeymooners should.

Retracing their steps, they passed Trinity College. 'That's where the *Books of Kells* is kept,' Danny informed Bridget, drawing to a standstill in front of the great buildings. 'In there in the library. Did you know it's known as "the most beautiful book in the world"? he asked with a knowing air.

'I've heard about it, of course, but what exactly is the *Book of Kells?*'

'It's a hand-written manuscript of the four gospels. You know what they are, don't you?'

'Of course I do! Everybody knows that.'

'Well, every page is decorated with designs of gold and glowing colours, so they look illumin-ated. That's why it's called the most beautiful book in the world.'

Bridget was looking at him in awe. 'You're so well educated, Danny.'

A mite embarrassed at all this admiration, he said, 'I must confess I read all about it in a book I borrowed from the library. It fired my imagin-ation.'

'Do you think we could get in there and have a look at it?'

'I don't know, love. As you can see, it's closed at the moment. I'll make inquiries and if so we can see it the next time we come to Dublin. Perhaps at Easter, eh?'

'That would be wonderful, Danny.'

Wanting to impress her still further, he asked, 'Do you know him that wrote *Gulliver's Travels* –

Jonathan Swift?' She nodded and he continued. 'Well, his body is entombed in St Patrick's Cathedral, over that way somewhere.' He gestured vaguely and she dutifully nodded.

'Perhaps we could go to Mass there tomorrow and have a look at it?' she volunteered.

These words brought a burst of laughter from him. 'Don't be silly,' he chided. 'It's a Protestant cathedral.'

Bewildered, she retorted, 'I thought you said St Patrick's. That's a Catholic name, isn't it?'

'That may well be, but it certainly isn't a Catholic church.'

'You seem to know a lot about the history of Dublin.' Her admiration was genuine but she had difficulty in hiding a smile when she saw his chest swell with pride.

'Well, I do like reading about Irish history,' he admitted, getting into his stride. 'Remember that statue we passed at the end of O'Connell Street? That was a monument to Daniel O'Connell, one of the old Irish statesmen. Hence the name of the street. He was also called The Liberator. At the other end of the street is a statue of Charles Stewart Parnell. You surely must have heard of him? He caused a scandal in his time, having an affair with a married woman.'

Bridget was beginning to flag. She was once again chilled to the bone and didn't find history all that enthralling, as Danny appeared to. They crossed the River Liffey again and to her delight he at last headed towards the big department stores which were already decorated for the Christmas season. As they went from one shop to another, he grew bored. Like most men, he found shopping a drag, especially as they couldn't afford to buy anything; the price tags on the goods took his breath away. However, Bridget was content just to browse, exclaiming in delight when something she liked caught her eye. Danny trailed beside her, managing to hide his ennui.

Bridget had never been happier. As she pressed close to him and exclaimed over the beauty of everything, she silently vowed she would do all in her power to make Danny happy. He had come into her life at just the right time. She had craved popularity but had gone the wrong way to win it. To her great dismay, although only two boys had received favours from her, she had earned herself a tarnished reputation. She had been delighted when dark, handsome Danny McGowan, in spite of being engaged to Liz O'Hara, had wanted her. What if he hadn't fallen for her? What if she had become pregnant by one of the other boys? Why, her dad would have throttled her, favourite daughter or not. No, she was indebted to Danny, more than he knew or she would ever be likely to confess to.

She remembered the night she had first met him. She had been queuing up to have her books checked out at the library when a voice behind her had exclaimed, 'Surely you're not Patrick Kelly's wee sister?'

Gazing up into his dark handsome face, she had been overcome with shyness. Cheeks pink with embarrassment, she had admitted she was indeed Bridget Kelly. She recognized him as one of the handsome McGowan boys who had recently come to live in Dunlewey Street.

'My, but you have grown! If I hadn't seen your name on the library ticket I'd never have recognized you.'

His books were checked out while they were talking, and tucking them under his arm he fell into step beside her and they left the library together.

Seeing traces of recent tears, he asked solicitously, 'Why so sad, Bridget?'

The tears had been the result of Noel Gibson's rejecting her. She had been so sure he loved her. Were all men liars? Were they all only after one thing? Not that Noel was a man! Not by a long shot. The same age as herself, he was really only a boy. Girls matured so much more quickly than boys and she had been foolish to give into his boyish lust. Danny was eyeing her questioningly, waiting for a reply. Quickly she fabricated a lie, saying that a friend had promised to accompany her to a dance that night in a hall near the town centre, but had let her down.

The dance hall she mentioned had a bad name and Danny's brows had drawn together in disapproval. 'What are you doing, going to a dive like that?'

She had thought it very daring to go to the weekly dance there. Now, not wanting him to think badly of her, she once again lied. 'I don't usually go there but I would have been safe enough with Noel Gibson, only he let me down. And I promised to deliver a book to a friend. She'll be so disappointed.'

He had eyed her closely and she'd gazed

117

steadily back, wondering if he guessed that she was telling fibs. Imagine delivering a book to a friend in a dance hall. But it was the only excuse that sprang to mind on the spur of the moment. She felt guilt must be written all over her face. At last Danny seemed satisfied. 'Is it important she receives the book tonight?'

'Well, I know she was looking forward to reading it over the weekend.'

He smiled slightly, remembering how, when he was seventeen, everything had to be done yesterday. 'Tell you what, let's leave the rest at home and then I'll walk down with you to give your friend the book.'

'Really? Would you really do that for me?'

'Why not? I've nothing better to do. My fiancée is working late tonight. I'll meet you back here in ten minutes, all right? By the way ... is Noel your steady boyfriend? I don't want to be treading on anyone's toes.'

'No, I've only been out with him a few times. Are you sure you don't mind walking me down there?'

Danny smiled at her enthusiasm and shook his head. Just wait until Liz heard that he had been a knight in shining armour and had come to the rescue of a maiden in distress. She would be tickled pink.

On their arrival back in Belfast the snow that blanketed the North dampened Bridget's spirits somewhat. Was the honeymoon really over? She dreaded returning to her mother-in-law's house. What kind of reception would she receive from

Jane? She appeared to be a right old battle axe, though Danny said her bark was worse than her bite.

It was early-afternoon when they arrived in Dunlewey Street. Jane was alone in the house, the others still at work or college. The house was warm and appetizing aromas wafted in from the kitchen. Jane's greeting was friendly enough.

When Bridget had removed her coat and boots she was led to a chair by the fire. 'Sit down here, dear. You look absolutely frozen. I'll make a pot of tea. That will soon thaw you out.'

Sipping from the big mug of tea and biting hungrily into a freshly baked soda farl, oozing butter, Bridget congratulated her mother-in-law on the tempting aromas. 'Whatever is cooking sure smells delicious and this soda is scrumptious.'

'The soda farls are just off the griddle. I bake every Tuesday. And that's a pork casserole you smell,' Jane proudly informed her. 'No doubt you'll create delicious dishes yourself now you're married. Shall we take it in turns to cook the meals or would you like to cook separately for you and Danny?' she asked coyly.

'I don't know. I'm not a very good cook. I'm afraid my mam does all the cooking in our house.' Bridget threw a scared look at Danny for support. She had confessed to him that she couldn't cook and he had assured her it didn't matter as his mother would look after that. Danny was sorting through the mail that had come while they were away and was unaware of her entreating gaze.

'Oh, dear.' Jane looked at her wide-eyed, as if amazed at this confession. 'Then perhaps you had better learn by cooking for yourself and Danny. Joe and the boys love their food!'

Bridget felt like weeping. How would she be able to cook alongside an experienced woman like Jane? How she wished they were living with her mother, then she wouldn't have to worry about cooking at all.

Bridget continued to work in the Bank Buildings and as the Christmas period gathered momentum, was rushed off her feet. Though tired and despondent, each evening she put on a brave smile as she faced her in-laws. Mr McGowan was kindness itself, always asking after her welfare, and the two lads were friendly enough, but Jane remained distant and aloof. She had made it abundantly clear she was not going to wait on the newly weds hand and foot. Disappointed at the loss of Danny's money, she was determined to make them pull their weight, one way or another.

After one disastrous attempt at Sunday dinner, to her great relief Bridget was not invited to do any further cooking, but since Jane didn't believe that a man should demean himself with housework, after dinner each evening it was Bridget who was constantly on the go in the kitchen. Between dinner and bedtime she washed dishes, surfaces and floors. Tuesday and Thursday she was also expected to do the family ironing as Jane laundered all the clothes. Her final chore each night before she could retire was to prepare their sandwiches for the following day. This was all carried out under the eagle eye of her mother-in-law as she sat knitting by the fire and tut-tutting at everything and nothing.

To crown it all Danny still expected her to be full of beans in bed. The idea that the rest of the family could hear them embarrassed her; besides, she was so very tired. Her lack of enthusiasm annoyed him and, in a fit of pique, one Friday night he arranged to go out with his mates. This visit to the pub soon became a weekly habit. On these occasions she visited her parents and put on a brave front, succeeding in convincing them that all was wonderful with married life in the McGowans' home.

Shortly before Christmas misery engulfed her like a heavy mantle she was unable to shrug off. Unable to contain herself any longer, Bridget turned to her husband for understanding. She just had to get out. It was a Sunday and a bright crisp day. She suggested to Danny that they take a walk up to the Falls Park to get rid of the cobwebs. He cried off, confessing that he had a headache and was feeling quite ill. The night before he had gone out with his mates again and she guessed it was a hangover he suffered from. He never once suggested that they have a night out together. Was he ashamed to be seen with her?

This idea depressed her still further. He was wasting so much money on booze when they were supposed to be saving for a deposit on a house. At this rate they would never be able to afford a home of their own. Was Saturday night out with his mates about to become another habit? Bad habits were so easily started and so hard to break.

Really in the doldrums now, without a further word to her husband she slipped quietly out of the house. She felt as if she was being slowly strangled and needed to get away from this cloying atmosphere for a while; away from her mother-in-law's ill-concealed disapproval and ever-watchful eye. Last-minute Christmas shopping had resulted in Bridget's being rushed off her feet at work the day before. Her pregnancy was beginning to show. Just a slight bump, but the waistband on all her work skirts were now too tight for comfort. What with that and swollen ankles, she had been sore and miserable all day. Combined with putting on a cheerful appearance for the sake of the customers, she felt a complete wreck by closing time. The comfort and tenderness she craved from her husband had been sadly lacking, and after some muttered words of censure, Danny had taken the huff and resorted to going out with his mates. So much for all his promises and good intentions!

Outside on the pavement, she dithered. It would be no fun going to the park alone. She decided to visit her mother on the off chance of finding her alone. Maybe she would be able to pluck up the courage to ask for advice. Luck was with her; the house was silent when she tapped on the inner door and entered the living room.

'Hello ... oo. Anybody home?'

Her mother came down the stairs tidying her hair. 'This is a surprise. I didn't expect to see you today.'

Remembering belatedly, that her mother always took a nap after dinner, which was early on a Sunday afternoon, Bridget cried, 'Ah, Mam … have I disturbed you? Were you having a wee nap?'

'Never worry. Your dad will be here soon. I was just about to get up when I heard you arrive,' she lied.

'Where is everybody else?'

'Your dad is over in the Royal Hospital, visiting a workmate. As for the lads, God knows where they are. They never confide in me where they're going. Probably playing cards in one of their mates' homes, or up to some other mischief, no doubt.'

Even in her misery, Bridget had to smile at her mother's words. 'They think you know nothing of their gambling habits, Mam.'

'There is very little escapes me, as you well know. If they want to be foolish with their money, that's their look out. Just so long as they don't try to borrow any money from me or turn my home into a gambling den. You look tired, love. Are you all right?'

'I'm exhausted. I've never felt so tired in my life before. I was run off my feet at work yesterday.'

'The fatigue will soon pass, love,' her mother consoled her. 'That's just your body adjusting to carrying a baby. But don't just stand there. Take off your coat, love, and sit down. I'll make us something hot to drink.'

Removing the spark guard, Martha Kelly poked the coals into life and added some coal from the brass shuttle at the side of the hearth, before retiring to the kitchen to make the drinks. Soon they were sitting each side of the brightly burning fire in silence, drinking hot chocolate. Martha guessed from her daughter's demeanour that all was not well with her and waited patiently for the confidences she was sure would come. The silence stretched and Martha cast a furtive glance across at her daughter. To her dismay great tears were rolling down Bridget's cheeks and dripping unheeded off her jaw on to her chest. This display of grief was made all the worse for the silence in which it was conducted.

Deeply concerned, Martha set her cup on the hearth and went to clasp her daughter close. Bridget tried desperately to check the flood of tears but they gushed from a well of pain in which her whole being was engulfed and there was no stopping them.

'There, there, this will never do,' Martha urged. 'You'll make yourself ill.' Still the tears fell and, distracted, she cried. 'Think of the baby! What in the name of God brought all this on?' She rocked her daughter gently in her arms and surrounded by all this love and tenderness, Bridget let loose and quite literally howled, great sobs tearing at her body. 'I can't stand it any longer,' she kept repeating, over and over. Under her mother's gentle persuasion she sobbed out her tale of woe.

Martha was silent throughout the lamentation, her concern mounting as she listened to her daughter's grievances. At last the flow of tears ebbed and, blowing her nose, Bridget grimaced, shamefaced. 'Sorry, Mam, but I needed to get that of my chest.'

'Why on earth did you pretend everything was hunkydory when it wasn't? You had us all fooled, you know. Your dad was just saying the other day how surprised he was you'd settled in so quickly with the McGowans.'

'I know, but I kept hoping Danny would give in to pressure and help me look for a place of our own to live. We would be all right if we were on our own. I'm sure we could get rooms at a reasonable rent and still be able to save, but he won't hear tell of it. In my heart I don't really blame him, Mam. You know what a lousy cook I am and Jane is forever dishing up wonderful appetizing dinners. No wonder Danny doesn't want to leave. He gets lifted and laid over there.'

'Few of us could cook before we were married. Learning is all part of married life. I bet Jane McGowan was no different from the rest of us once. Seems to me she's creating unnecessary mischief for you.'

At the sound of footsteps approaching the house and entering the hall, Bridget gripped frantically at her mother's arm. 'It's Dad! Mam, don't tell him. Sure you won't? Promise?'

Martha was saved from giving her word by her husband's appearance.

Barney sensed something was amiss but decided not to say anything but play it by ear. Squeezing his daughter's shoulder, he asked kindly, 'And how are you today, love?'

Blowing noisily into a handkerchief, Bridget kept her head bowed. 'I think I've caught a cold. I've been sneezing all day and my eyes are all watery.'

'You should be in bed then. I'll give you a wee drop of whiskey home with you for a hot toddy. God, but it's dark today. Will I put on the light, Martha?' Barney stretched his arm towards the light switch but drew back, startled, when both his wife and daughter quickly cried, 'No!' in unison.

'Dad, could we leave the light off for a while, please? I've a headache,' Bridget said.

'Oh ... will I make you a wee drop of punch now?'

'No, I'd better be making tracks. I just popped out for a breath of fresh air, to see if it would clear my head,' she lied.

Her father peered at her in the dim light. 'You look a wee bit peaky to me, love. Are you taking your iron tablets?'

Bridget was shrugging into her coat again, avoiding looking directly at her father. She must escape before he saw the state of her face. 'Yes, Dad. I take them religiously, morning and night. I'll have to go now. See you soon.'

Still he delayed her and she hovered restlessly while he poured some whiskey into a small bottle, all the while avoiding his gaze. At last, clutching the bottle in her gloved hand, she again wished him farewell and, giving him a brief kiss on the cheek, turned with relief towards the door.

Her mother accompanied her. 'What are you going to do?' she asked, her voice fraught with worry.

'What can I do? Grin and bear it, I suppose. I feel much better now I've had a chance to grouse. Thanks for listening to me. It does make

126

a big difference, so it does.' Bridget squeezed her eyes tight shut and then opened them again. 'My eyes feel awful. I think I'll go down the street and walk up Grosvenor Road, give my face a chance to cool down, or there'll be all sorts of inter-rogations when I get home. I'll see you soon, Mam.' She reached across and kissed Martha on the cheek.

'I wish I could be of some help to you, love.'

'You know what they say, Mam. You make your bed and you must lie on it.'

'But you do love Danny, don't you, Bridget? I mean, you did want to marry him, didn't you?'

The way she was feeling at the moment, a truthful answer to this would be, 'I don't know'. Danny was so handsome and the fact he apparently loved her had thrilled her to bits. She had longed to be loved and wanted and had been carried along on the crest of a wave of happiness. Now she said, 'Of course I do. Don't look so worried, Mam. I'll be all right.' She patted her mother's arm consolingly and headed down the street.

Martha slowly returned indoors with a frown puckering her brow. Barney had drawn the blinds and switched on the light. Now he looked at her in concern. 'Is anything wrong?'

'No.'

'Come off it, Martha. I can see you're worried about something. Is he hitting her?'

'Don't be silly.'

'I'm not stupid, I know she didn't want me to see her face. Has that bastard marked her?'

Exasperated, she turned on him. 'Barney Kelly,

you are always ready to jump to conclusions. No, he isn't hitting her. She didn't want you to see her face because she's been crying. She's unhappy living with that Jane McGowan woman.'

'Oh, I see. And what is *he* going to do about it, eh?'

'Bridget wants to get rooms somewhere away from his mother, but she says Danny won't hear tell of it.'

'Well, then, until such time as he sees sense, tell her to come home here.'

'Don't be silly! Where would she sleep? We couldn't expect the lads to go back to how it was before. Her in the small room and the three of them sharing the other one. It wouldn't be fair on them, Barney.'

'She can bed down with you and I'll sleep on the settee. Okay?'

'It wouldn't work, Barney. You're not a young man any more. You need a decent night's sleep to face going to that shipyard every day.'

He knew she was right. It was far from a pleasure to go to work each morning. Tension hung over the Yard and he had to watch his tongue. Still, he insisted, 'If we bring her home, perhaps Danny will be shamed into finding somewhere else to live. She can at least spend Christmas with us, can't she?'

'But what if he doesn't, Barney? What will we do then? Mmm?'

'We will cross that bridge when we come to it. I'll go and fetch her.'

'What?' Martha quite literally squealed. He had taken the breath from her. She gulped, and cried,

128

'Now? No! Leave it for another couple of days, Barney. She won't thank you for interfering.'

'I'm not looking for thanks. And the sooner that big galoot realizes she's not chained to him the better.' His voice heavy with emotion, Barney muttered, 'Sometimes I'm sorry we forced her to marry him.' Without further ado, he lifted his coat and left the house.

Martha stood gnawing at her lower lip and gazing blankly at the door. Had they forced Bridget? Didn't she love Danny? She sighed. That was beginning to look very doubtful. But then, why had she let him touch her in the first place?

And now what on earth had *she* done? She should have kept her big mouth shut. Bridget would never forgive her for betraying her confidences. Barney was anything but subtle. God knows what he might say or do. A thought struck her, bringing her to her feet in dismay. Bridget was taking a walk first. Would Barney get there before her? Feverishly she sent a prayer heavenward, begging God not to let her husband lose control of his temper and resort to fisticuffs.

Barney crossed over to Dunlewey Street, sorting out in his head what he would say. He knew he would have to be very careful. For Bridget's sake he must not give offence. He would just say that his wife thought the girl looked a bit peaky and would she not come and stay with them over Christmas? He would be polite. At all costs, he warned himself, he must not lose his temper with that big galoot of a husband of Bridget's.

He knocked on the door, a polite greeting hovering on his lips should it be opened by anyone other than Bridget. As he waited he became aware of a big Jaguar on the opposite side of the street. That would belong to Liz O'Hara's husband. He had heard all the gossip from Martha. The car was a beauty. And rumour had it the guy also owned his own business. His eyes met those of the man behind the wheel and Barney nodded in acknowledgement. The man returned his nod with a wave of his hand. He was distinguished-looking. Looked like his Bridget had done Liz O'Hara a good turn by taking Danny McGowan off her hands.

It was Peter who answered his knock. 'Hello, Mr Kelly.' He had difficulty hiding his surprise. This was the first time any of the Kellys had come to the house since that initial meeting.

'Hello, Peter. Could I have a word with Bridget, please?'

'I'm afraid she isn't here at the moment, but do come in and wait.'

Taking his cap off, Barney stuffed it into his overcoat pocket and, wiping his feet carefully on the mat, entered the living room. He nodded politely to Jane who was coming from the kitchen, drying her hands on her apron. 'Hello, there.' For the moment her name eluded him. 'Nasty weather we're having at the moment, isn't it?'

Jane, who detested being addressed as 'there', was grim-faced, but determined to be polite and friendly at all costs. 'Hello, Barney, take a seat. Bridget and Danny both disappeared some time ago. I don't know where they can be. Can I offer you a drink? Tea, coffee, a beer? We have some booze in for Christmas.'

'No. It's very kind of you to offer, but if Bridget doesn't come soon I'll go on home. Martha will have something ready for me.'

He chose an upright chair near the door and sat down, looking very intimidating. Soon Peter and he were exchanging polite conversation about the weather and football. Relieved that her son was entertaining him, Jane excused herself and returned to the kitchen.

Bridget was more frightened than surprised when, approaching the house, she recognized her father's deep voice. What on earth had brought him here? she wondered. Would he cause trouble? Pushing open the door, she nervously entered the living-room. One glance informed her Danny was not there. She must get rid of her dad before Danny put in an appearance.

'Hello, Dad, what are you doing here?'

Barney rose to his feet and said gently, 'Your mother thought you looked a bit peaky when you were over earlier on. She was wondering if you might like to spend Christmas with us?'

Bridget's jaw dropped. She was dumbstruck! Had her dad lost his marbles or something? What on earth would Jane think?

No one had heard Danny quietly enter the house. His voice came across the silence, soft and insinuating. 'Well now, Bridget. What do you think of that proposition?'

She spun round in surprise. 'Danny, I didn't

131

hear you come in.'

He moved closer to her and placed an arm possessively around her shoulders. She smelt the drink on his breath and her heart quailed. Where had he got it on a Sunday afternoon? His eyes still on Barney Kelly's face, Danny repeated, 'What do you think of that suggestion, Bridget? Would you like to spend Christmas with your parents, instead of here with me?'

Before she could open her mouth, her father spoke. A hand wagged in her direction. His voice was mild. 'Look at her, Danny,' he said in a placating tone. 'Do you not think she looks a bit off colour?'

'Surely I have no need to remind you she's expecting our baby?'

'Martha had five children and when she looked off colour like that, I made sure she got plenty of rest.'

'Are you suggesting Bridget doesn't get any rest here?' These words came from Jane who stood at the kitchen door, hands on her hips. They earned her a scowl from Danny.

'No, I'm not. But since you mention it, does she?'

Agitated, Bridget cried in a shrill voice, 'Dad, I get plenty of rest. I'm all right, I tell you. And I wouldn't dream of spending Christmas anywhere but with Danny.'

With difficulty Barney controlled his temper. He was aware that in spite of his good intentions he had handled it all wrong. Here in the harsh glare of the electric light his daughter looked awful with swollen eyes and haggard face. She looked positively ill. He longed to hustle her out of here, over to the comforting arms of her mother, but if she chose to stay what could he do about it? 'So be it then.' He took Bridget's small hand in his. It was cold and he squeezed it tightly. 'If you should change your mind, love, remember, I'm just over across the Falls Road.'

He nodded at Jane, relieved her name came to mind now. 'Thank you for your hospitality, Jane. Good night, Peter.' And he turned to leave the house.

He was on the pavement when Danny followed him out. Voice loud and belligerent, he yelled, 'Let me tell you something, Barney Kelly, you are not welcome here! Don't you ever come to my home again and expect Bridget just to go off with you. For better or for worse, she's my wife and will do as I say.'

Barney's bushy eyebrows drew together. '*Your* home? Why, if you were half a man, my daughter would have a home of her own by now. She wouldn't be sitting in a corner of your mother's house while you're out drinking all your wages. And tell me this: when was the last time you took her out, eh?'

'Why, you cheeky bastard!' Danny lunged at the big man but Barney was ready for him.

Gripping Danny's fist he looked over his shoulder to where Bridget stood in the hall, a hand to her mouth. 'I'm sorry, love. I didn't mean for it to end like this.'

With a powerful thrust he pushed Danny away and strode off down the street. With a howl of rage Danny made to go after him, but Peter

133

caught hold of him. 'Come in, man. You're making a spectacle of yourself.'

Only then did Danny realize he had an audience. He glared across the street and saw Liz standing there. She looked beautiful in a camel-hair coat with a large fur collar and matching Cossack-style fur hat. His face filled with yearning. She could have been his. His eyes pleaded with her before he allowed Peter to push him indoors.

Honeymoon over, Christmas seemed to come in a rush for the Atkinsons. The order for the silk underwear had been finished in plenty of time and the client, delighted at the finished product, promised more orders in the new year. Thus a hefty Christmas bonus was promised to all the staff. Mindful of the beautiful china dinner service the staff had collected money for and given to them for a wedding present, Liz suggested to David they should throw a party for the girls. He willingly agreed and the day after they broke up for the Christmas holiday, a Saturday, the dispatch room was cleared, a catering firm was brought in and a delicious buffet laid on. The workers all turned out in their glad rags and David confessed to Liz he'd had some difficulty recognizing half of them.

There was plenty of wine and beer flowing and a good time was had by all. The staff were also delighted at the size of the bonus in their Christmas pay packets and many became quite tipsy on the free booze. David was concerned, and for those who didn't intend taking the town by storm to spend their bonuses, laid on taxis to see them safely home.

Afterwards Liz and he did some late shopping while the foreman supervised the clearing of the dispatch room and locked the windows and doors. David later returned to set the alarm.

Liz had dispensed with the services of the small restaurant that had daily cooked and delivered David's dinner when he lived alone. Each evening they spent time together in the big kitchen and while Liz prepared delicious meals and David assisted her, they discussed work, argued about current affairs and had a good laugh together. They were content with their lot.

This evening as he chopped vegetables and she prepared the roast, he remarked, 'I really am very lucky, you know.'

'What do you mean?'

'I have a beautiful, sexy wife who can also cook. Not many men are so blessed. How come you're such a good cook, Liz?'

'Mam has always had to work so I have been preparing the evening meal since I was no age.'

'Liz, I think we should train someone to take over your job at the factory. Would you not like to be a full-time wife and housekeeper?'

Her working was a bone of contention between them. He did not like the idea that his wife worked when she could afford to stay at home. With a sigh she reminded him, 'I'd be bored stiff, David. Time enough when I become pregnant to think along those lines. Anyway, you know I love working in the office. I can keep an eye on you there and make sure you don't flirt with any of the girls.'

He came up behind her and buried his face in her hair. 'Liz, what if we don't have children? Would you be very disappointed?'

She twisted around in his arms and gazed into his face. 'Do you not like children, David? Is that what you're saying? Would you not like a family? Someone to pass the business on to?'

'Oh, I'd love a family, but...'

'No buts about it. Just give me five minutes to finish here and while this is cooking, we'll have an hour or so to maybe make a start on a family.'

She pulled his head down and kissed him on the lips. He gazed at her and thanked God for having let her be his. 'Don't be long.'

A great tenderness swelled in Liz's breast as she pictured what was to come. Surely this was love she felt for David? A different kind of love but a deep abiding emotion nevertheless. She would never do anything that might hurt this wonderful man who had given her so much.

They had persuaded Kath to leave her own home and spend some time with them over the Christmas break. On Sunday afternoon they arrived in Dunlewey Street to fetch her. David waited in the car while Liz knocked on the door to alert her mother of their arrival. The door opened and Kath grabbed her arm and, pulling her inside, quickly closed the door 'What on earth...'

'Come in here,' Kath ordered. Bemused, Liz followed her mother into the parlour where she took up a stance behind the nets, beckoning her daughter to join her. 'Barney Kelly has just gone in to the McGowans. I was watching for the car and saw him.' She turned excitedly to Liz. 'Look, there's Bridget now.'

Liz's lips tightened in contempt. She could scarcely believe her ears. This wasn't like her mother. Usually she respected other people's privacy. 'Mam, why shouldn't Mr Kelly visit his daughter? I don't know what all the excitement is about.'

'Well, I've never seen any of them visit before.'

'Mam! How can you stand there spying on your neighbours? It's none of your business what they do. Come away from that window at once,' Liz pleaded.

'It's just the McGowans,' Kath retorted, as if that excused her bad behaviour. 'Look! Look, there's Danny coming up the street now,' she cried excitedly.

Liz returned to the hall and lifted the small suitcase sitting ready. 'Come on, Mam. Put on your coat and lock up. David is outside.' She opened the front door and stood waiting, leaving a disgruntled Kath no option but to shrug into her coat and follow.

To Liz's dismay, but Kath's great delight, the McGowans' door swung open and Barney Kelly came out. It was obvious from his expression he was very angry. His lips were a small tight knot and his bushy black eyebrows, puckered together, made him ferocious-looking. Two steps were as far as he got before Danny appeared in the doorway. It was obvious he too was angry. He also appeared to be the worse for drink.

Liz wanted to get away before Danny saw her

witnessing this awful spectacle, but her mother stood stock still between her and the car door.

Angry words were exchanged and Liz thought for one awful moment they were going to exchange blows. To her relief Peter grabbed his brother. Whatever he whispered in Danny's ear caused him to turn and look across the street at her. Their eyes locked and she found herself unable to turn away, the love and yearning in his were so unbearable. Her heart went out to him in his misery. He looked so unhappy. Surely he deserved some happiness – had he not done his duty and married Bridget?

From the seclusion of his car, David had witnessed all the comings and goings across the street at the McGowans' home. He had even guessed the identity of the big man. Now he turned round in his seat. He needed to see his wife's face. See if the yearning on Danny's was reflected there. If it was, he was not to witness it. He could only see up as far as his wife's shoulder.

Walking around her mother, Liz opened the car door and almost pushed her inside. Then, quickly entering the car, she said tersely, 'Let's go.'

Aware of her daughter's deep displeasure, Kath excused her actions. 'I was watching for the car when all that bother started. I don't stand at the window all day, you know.'

Liz remained silent and David, with a perplexed glance at his wife, said gently, 'It was only natural for you to be interested, Kath. I must admit I was enthralled, and I only know one of those taking part.'

Liz stirred herself from her inner thoughts and

138

said, 'It was rude to stand there gawking.'

'It was natural, Liz,' he gently contradicted her.

'Let's forget all about it, shall we? After all, it's no concern of ours,' she said testily.

'Thank God for that,' he said feelingly. He was dismayed at the effect the scene had on his wife. She looked gutted. She must still care deeply for Danny. Well, she hadn't made any promises. He had said he was willing to take what she had to offer. She had appeared to give her all and he had dared to hope that perhaps she was falling in love with him. It seemed he was wrong. What more could he do? Was he fighting a lost cause?

The journey home was conducted in an uneasy silence.

Chapter Three

As the day progressed, David silently cursed Danny McGowan. On the run up to the Christmas break they had been borne along on a wave of euphoria. For the first time since the death of Victoria, he had been eagerly looking forward to the holiday. The house was weighed down with decorations and a huge Christmas tree swamped the hall. Liz had even persuaded him to thread coloured light bulbs through the trees near the house. A happiness he savoured had enveloped them and all was well with his world.

Then Danny had appeared on the scene, spoiling everything. Now Liz was depressed and a damper had been cast on their preparations. A few attempts on his part to lighten the atmosphere proved fruitless, and unable to bear the glum detachment of his wife, he decided to go for a drive. He hovered about for some minutes on the edge of her vision, hoping against hope she would notice him and speak; put an end to the tension, but in vain. She was lost in a world of her own. Recent events had put a discontented droop to her usually laughing lips and blinded her to his need. At last, unable to bear it any longer, he strode across the hall and out, closing the great oak door none too gently. Liz, immersed in worried thoughts about Danny's welfare, didn't even notice him go.

Kath, however, from a window in the lounge, watched David leave the house, a dejected figure with bowed head and slumped shoulders. A great surge of anger built up inside her against her thoughtless daughter. This good man didn't deserve the cold shoulder treatment. What she would give to be in a position to pander to someone like him! She was beginning to feel Liz's absence from the house. Sometimes ... not often, but now and again, she pondered on how things would be if she could meet someone like David. All her life had been devoted to rearing Liz. No man had ever penetrated her defences. It was different now that Liz had flown the nest; Kath was lonely living on her own without her daughter to cater for and fuss over.

Now that she had her alone, Kath decided to have a quiet word in her daughter's ear. She cornered Liz in the kitchen. 'Do you know something, my girl? You're a fool! You're making a big mistake worrying about Danny McGowan. He isn't worth it. Do you think if the positions were reversed, he would worry about you? Huh! No chance.'

Liz rounded on her and snapped angrily, 'Mam, keep your nose out of it! It's none of your business whatsoever. Besides, how can I help worrying? Did you not see how miserable he looked? It broke my heart just to see his despair, so it did. He appears to be at the end of his tether. I'm worried because I know how hot-headed he can be. He's very likely to get into some sort of trouble. I wouldn't wish that on any-one, least of all Danny.'

'He's not your concern any more, Liz. God knows, when you were engaged to him you had to look out for his interests. However, he chose Bridget Kelly to be his wife and hurt you deeply in the process. Don't you forget that, Liz. Let her look after him. Meanwhile, there's a man who is very much your concern who has just left this house, in case you didn't notice, every bit as miserable as Danny McGowan. Probably Danny deserved all he got, but David certainly doesn't. It's not fair the way you're acting towards him.'

Liz gaped at her mother in disbelief. 'David, gone? Where?'

'See what I mean? You didn't even miss him. And how should I know where he's gone? He didn't confide in me. Is it any wonder he's gone out? You're walking about with a face a mile long. In fact, you're positively sullen. No wonder he's puzzled and upset. Surely you can't still love Danny?'

'Did you ever grow out of loving my father? Honestly, now, Mam, did you? Isn't that why you're still single? You above all should understand how I feel. I can't help it. I made no secret of the fact I still love him and David was willing to take a chance. But I will never deliberately hurt David, that's for sure. I respect him too much.'

Kath bit on her lip. It had taken her a long time to forget the man who had seduced her. Who had made her the happiest woman in Belfast for one short year. It had been a long time before the pain dimmed. Still, there was no need to let Liz know that. 'How long it took me to get over your father is neither here nor there, my girl. I had no one to turn to. You have David. Show him you care! Don't spoil your first Christmas together over the likes of Danny McGowan.'

Liz saw the wisdom of her words and grimaced slightly. 'You're right as usual, Mam. I'll try to make things right. When he comes back, make yourself scarce.'

David left Somerton Road and headed the car along Downview Avenue towards the Antrim Road. He intended visiting Bellevue Zoo. Since Victoria's death he had, when lonely, often visited the zoo. It had a soothing effect on him to watch the big animals pacing about; see the ripple of powerful muscles beneath thick shining coats. The puma in particular fascinated him. Beautiful and disdainful of her surroundings, she restlessly padded to and fro. The beasts were out of their natural habitat, but still managed to look proud and in control of their situations.

He hadn't been to the zoo since persuading Liz to marry him. He had been too happy. Now he felt the need to be at one with nature for a time. Parking the car he made his way to the entrance gate and paid his fee. Then he dandered over to the animal enclosures. First he visited the chattering monkeys, standing for some time watching their antics. However they only received half his attention, his mind being elsewhere. Would Liz miss him out of the house? In fact, would she even notice he had gone?

He moved on, mildly surprised to find the zoo so empty on a Sunday. Perhaps this was due to

144

Christmas being so near. Besides it was a bleak, bitterly cold day, with a biting wind blowing up from the lough and scudding heavy clouds haphazardly across a slate grey sky. Soon it must surely rain. That could account for the lack of sightseers. The more sensible ones were probably sitting in the warmth of their own cosy homes. Some of the animals were even curled up in their lairs, sheltered from the cold.

The puma was last on his list. Pulling up the collar of his Crombie coat, he sank his ears into its warmth as he approached her cage. His disappointment was acute when he saw her enclosure was empty. Then, as if sensing his presence, a head was thrust from the entrance to the lair; he was obviously found wanting as she gave him the once over and slowly withdrew her great black head. Still he patiently waited, and at last she reappeared and emerged from her lair and started stomping about. He was glad she had defied the cold and was now prowling about, her breath crystallizing on the cold air. He was pleased he and the beautiful black beast with the bright amber eyes were alone for the moment.

Standing as close to the cage as the protection barrier would allow, he watched the animal pace to and fro. Thrilled at the sight of the powerful muscles rippling beneath the thick shining coat; saw the head rise and the nostrils widen as they caught his scent. With a disdainful toss of her head she decided to ignore him. He stood and admired that feline quality of being imperious and untouchable although behind bars. He again waited patiently watching every move she made,

145

and in the end was rewarded. With a switch of her tail and long graceful strides she at last approached the railings and eyed him back. He was tempted to reach out and stroke the dark shining fur but thought better of it. She probably didn't feel as at home with him as he did with her.

Her glowing tawny eyes reminded him so much of Liz's, the ache in his chest deepened. He couldn't understand his wife. Was she, like the puma, out of her natural habitat? Sometimes, like today, in her withdrawn state, she reminded him of the puma: disdainful and aloof. Did she too feel caged? Did she wish that she was free of their marriage? In his heart he didn't really think so. Most times she seemed content with her lot and he had dared to hope that she was learning to love him. Then one glimpse of her old flame and she had become some stranger he couldn't reach. He supposed the circumstances were unusual, and had to admit that Danny had indeed looked wretched. However, David did not intend to let it spoil their first Christmas together. He would have it out with Liz. Between them surely they could put things in their true perspective. But had he the right to harass her after promising there would be no strings attached? What if she threw that in his face? Come what may, he had to give it a try.

He must attempt to reach his wife and reason with her. Leaning closer to the cage for a last look of farewell, he drew hastily back when the puma bared her teeth and growled low in her throat. One great heavy paw reached through the rails, its long sharp claws extended, almost reaching the safety barrier.

'There, girl, it's all right,' David assured her. Then feeling a real idiot he left the enclosure, glad that no one had witnessed him consoling the great beast.

His mind made up. It would be awkward with Kath there, but he must have a word with his wife in private. Must begin as he intended to go on. Danny McGowan must not be allowed to become an insurmountable barrier between husband and wife.

The house was quiet when he returned an hour or so later. His wife's voice hailed him from the lounge. 'I'm in here, David.'

She lay stretched out on the settee, a book on her lap. Drawing her knees up to make room for him caused the split in her pencil skirt to slide up one silk-clad thigh. She looked tempting and very approachable. Determined not to be too easily won over, he appeared not to notice the silent invitation and took a chair close by. 'Where's Kath?'

'Mam has gone to have a nap. I put dinner on hold when you disappeared so mysteriously without a word of farewell,' Liz gently chided.

He closed his eyes and tapped the side of his head with a clenched fist. 'I completely forgot about dinner,' he confessed. 'I was preoccupied. I'm sorry,' he apologized.

She held out her hand to him. 'No harm done.' She'd had time to think and wanted to make amends. 'I'm the one who should apologize. I'm sorry if I upset you, David. I really didn't mean to.'

Resistance crumbled as he gripped her hand and gazed into amber eyes, so like the puma's. Sinking slowly to his knees beside the settee, he clung tightly to her hand. 'You still care for him, don't you, Liz?' he probed softly.

She heard the tremor in his voice and sought to allay his fear. Cupping her hands tenderly around his face, she held his gaze. 'David, when we married I didn't pretend I was over Danny, remember? And, I hate to remind you, you did say you would be content with what I had to offer. And we are getting along all right, aren't we?'

'Yes! I know ... I know. It's just that ... it's hard to bear. It's heartbreaking for me, to say the least. After today, I'll dread you visiting your mother in case you run into him again. I never imagined I would be unable to control my jealousy.'

Her hand covered his mouth. 'You have no need to fear, David. After all, nothing has changed. He's married to Bridget and I'm your wife. I'll never deliberately hurt you. If ever I find that I can't go on as we are, you will be the first to know. Meanwhile, I care deeply for you and I'm very content to be here with you.' She gently touched his lips with hers. His arms circled her and he savagely crushed her lips, passion making him rough.

Kath's bedroom was on the far side of the bungalow from theirs, and relieved there was to be no confrontation, he whispered against her lips. 'Come to our room, Liz. Show me you really care.'

Willingly, she rose to her feet and entered his arms. They barely made it to the bedroom.

Things were far from quiet in the McGowans' house in the wake of Barney Kelly's visit. Having witnessed the love and yearning in the look he had bestowed on Liz O'Hara, Bridget gaped at her husband in horror. She felt sure everyone else must also have noticed it; must realize, like her, where his heart really lay. And could she blame him? Liz had been dressed to kill and had looked absolutely stunning. Whereas she was a complete mess. But that was Danny's fault. If he was even trying to please her, she wouldn't be crying her eyes out and looking a sorry sight. Before she could come to terms with this turn of events, to her dismay Danny laid all the blame for the recent fracas firmly at her door.

'What brought your da over here today, eh, Bridget? Have you been whingeing to your parents you're not happy here?'

'No, Danny! No. You've got it all wrong. I just confided in my mam that I would like us to have a place of our own. That's all I said. Honest.'

'Huh! Why? Is my family not good enough for you?'

Bridget's face crumpled at the unfairness of it all. How could she answer this accusation in front of Jane and Peter, without looking ungrateful?

Peter came to her rescue. 'Look, do you two not think you should have this out in private? Dad and Joseph will be here shortly and it's not right we should all have to be involved in your quarrel.

149

Especially Joseph. The antics of you will put him off marriage completely.'

Mortified colour blazed in Bridget's cheeks and, turning on her heel, she climbed the stairs in a rush. She'd had enough of this. They had no privacy whatsoever here in this house. The house in Leeson Street, that had always seemed so overcrowded when she had lived there, had never looked so homely. The invitation to spend Christmas there so tempting.

Danny glared at his brother. 'Can you not mind your own business, just for once?' he snarled through bared teeth.

'You're making it everybody's business, so you are. Bridget's right, man! You should get a place of your own. It isn't natural, being cooped up here with all of us. That wee girl must feel like she's in a prison. And another thing ... you're drinking far too much. Huh, even now you stink of the stuff.'

'Oh, like you never have a drink?'

'Oh, yes, I'd be the first to admit to being partial to a pint or two. But nowhere near as much as you do. And I'm not married. And I'm not supposed to be saving for a house.'

'Well, the way Ma fleeces you every week, you couldn't afford to get drunk. That's what did the damage to my life. I'm not used to having money in my pocket. It's great to be able to go out and not count the pennies. When you come out of your time next year, make sure you get a fair whack of your wages. Don't let her get her greedy claws on it all.'

Jane visibly bristled. 'Don't you dare go

blaming me for your filthy drinking habits, Danny McGowan! I was only trying to teach you to be careful with money. That's what I was trying to do. You have to admit you didn't get drunk very often before you got married.' Her voice was shrill with offence and she faced him, arms akimbo.

'Oh, so that was the reason?' His voice was derisive. 'You were teaching me to be prudent where my money was concerned? Then no doubt you have a wee nest egg tucked away somewhere for me. Is that right, Ma? Am I in for a big surprise?'

'It was spent on your wedding! That's where it went. So don't you try blaming me for your own stupidity.'

'Why wouldn't I blame you, Ma? Eh? If you had been fair, I'd have been able to save more money this past few years, I'd have had a bit behind me when I met Liz and we would probably have been married long ago and then all this wouldn't have happened.' He shook his head in disbelief. 'I can't believe I was such a mug where money was concerned. Handing it over to you, every week.'

'Hah! That's a gag if ever I heard one. Don't you dare try to put the blame on me. The only reason you and Liz parted company was because you couldn't keep your trousers buttoned.' She gave sway to Peter's words. 'And your brother's right. Don't wash your dirty linen in public, please. There's a time and place for everything.'

'Oh, give over, for heaven's sake. The pair of you sicken me, you're such know-alls.'

Danny glared from one to the other of them, then with a muttered oath dejectedly followed his wife upstairs. Here he was amazed to find Bridget packing a holdall. 'And just what the hell do you think you're doing?' he cried in consternation.

She gave him a tight-lipped glare and retorted, 'Surely it's obvious! See.' She removed some more clothes from a drawer, held them aloft and neatly placed them in the holdall. 'This is how it's done. I'm packing. I've decided to take my parents up on their offer. If I stay here after all this bother, it will be like a bomb ticking away, ready to go off any minute. To tell you the truth, I'll be glad to spend Christmas with Mam and Dad. Even if it will be a bit cramped.'

Danny thrust his face close to hers and growled. 'Don't you act smart with me, madam. You leave this house over my dead body. Do you hear me?'

She grimaced in distaste and turned aside as whiskey fumes filled her nostrils. 'I smell you've started celebrating Christmas already. That would be enough to send anyone packing. The thought of you lying about the house nursing a hangover all Christmas would try the patience of a saint. I'll be glad not to witness it.'

At a loss as to how to deal with the situation, he attempted to put his arms around her but she shrugged them roughly away. 'Don't you love me any more, Bridget?'

She stared him full in the face and he couldn't believe the doubt he saw in her eyes. 'I don't know. I honestly don't,' she whispered. 'What difference does it make anyhow? I saw the way you looked at Liz O'Hara and I'm sure everybody else did as well. It's obvious you still love her. Why did you marry me, Danny? At the beginning you couldn't get enough of me and I was daft enough to think you loved me. Now I feel a right eejit.'

She sounded so bewildered he gaped at her in wonder. Why did she think he'd married her? She surely couldn't be gullible enough to think he had fallen in love with her? Love had never ever been mentioned between them. Certainly not that first night he had been stupid enough to dance with her on the crowded floor at the jig down in that dive. Her small frame had pressed close to his body and his desire had been roused. They had taken the back streets home and she had not demurred when he had drawn her into the shadows of Raglin Street School. There in the dark she had been so eager to please, but it had been all lust and passion; high-pitched emotions. He had been tempted and succumbed to the weakness of the flesh. She had been so warm and willing, it had been balm to his hurt pride so soon after Liz's rejection of him. Forgetful of her age, he had taken her that first night.

It had been wonderful. He admitted it had been much more exciting than his fumbled attempt with Liz. Bridget had been unstinting in her passionate response to his advances. There, in the shadows of the school, uncaring that someone might pass, she had given her all. Wanting more of this forbidden fruit, he had made arrangements to see her again. And yet again. Six weeks

153

of stolen bliss. But all the time Liz was the only girl he loved.

Then that awful rude awakening. Never once had it crossed his mind Bridget might conceive a child. How could he have been so stupid? If she hadn't conceived, there was no way in the wide world he would have married her. Liz was the only woman for him and ever would be.

He had however, big-headed fool that he was, believed Bridget had fallen in love with him. Why else had she allowed him to make love to her in the first place? Had he been a mug? Could she possibly be promiscuous? Would any man have satisfied her? A bit late to think of all that now. He was truly bewildered. Seeking reassurance in her eyes, he had seen only doubt reflected in their dark troubled depths. She couldn't do this to him. He wouldn't let her! Had he not given up all his hopes and dreams to marry her?

For some moments she watched conflicting emotions flit across his face, wondering what lay behind them. Then, with a sigh, she snapped shut the holdall and heaved it off the bed. Men would always be a mystery to her; there was no pleasing them. He gripped her arm and tried to wrestle the bag from her grasp but she hung grimly on. 'I'm going, Danny. If you have any feelings at all for me ... cut out the drinking and find some-where else for us to live. And maybe then we'll be able to make a go of it.' With these words she brushed roughly past him and descended the stairs.

At the foot of the stairs she dropped the bag and sought her mother-in-law out in the kitchen.

'None of this is your fault, Jane. In the circumstances it was good of you to take me in and I thank you for it. Goodbye.'

Jane was saddened by the wretched look on her daughter-in-law's face, but she had no one to blame but herself. She should not have conned Danny into a shotgun wedding. She followed her into the living-room. 'You'll be back, love. This will all blow over.'

Bridget shook her head and as she shrugged into her coat and wound a scarf around her neck, glanced at Peter. 'Goodbye, Peter.'

He smiled wryly at her. 'You will at least visit us, I trust?'

A slight smile touched her lips and was gone before it came to fullness. 'That depends on Danny and his drinking habits.'

He reached for the holdall. 'I'll walk you home with that bag, Bridget. It looks heavy.'

Danny had followed her downstairs and now swung round on his brother with a snarl.

'You will do no such thing. Since I can't persuade her otherwise, I'll walk her home.' He shook his head. He couldn't believe he had just said that. Walk her home? Home was *here* with him.

Donning his overcoat, he grabbed the bag and preceded his wife from the house; rage evident in every gesture. Peter winked at Bridget, and giving her the thumbs up sign, whispered, 'Stick to your guns. Don't let him walk all over you.'

Jane hovered about, feeling that she should hug the girl or something, but she was no hypocrite; already the thought of returning to her own comfortable bedroom was uppermost in her mind. She made do with, 'Take care now, Bridget.'

Glad that it was a bitter cold day, the biting wind keeping people indoors, Danny trudged along the deserted street. His spirits were low. This would be the latest tit-bit of scandal locally. Something to be mulled over during the Christmas break. Word would soon get round. They would be saying Danny McGowan couldn't hold on to a woman. First Liz, now a slip of a girl like Bridget walking out on him. He was making a muck of his life. Would be the laughing stock of the district. Shame would keep him from showing his face in public after this.

At the top of Leeson Street he drew her into the shadowed doorway of a shop away from the interested gaze of the soldiers on duty. He dropped the bag at his feet. 'I'll not come any further, Bridget. No good getting your da all worked up again.' He gazed at her and she swayed towards him; willing him to hold her; to make her feel wanted. He pretended not to notice. At the moment she was repugnant to him. Her hair was a tangled mess, her face ravaged after her recent breakdown. Liz's fine pale face beneath that fur hat was uppermost in his mind. But he had to say something. Bridget was his wife. He had to provide for her. 'If I find somewhere for us to live, will you come back to me?' he asked tentatively.

Her eyes lit up and she cried, 'Of course I will. We'll be all right if we're on our own, Danny. I'll learn to cook, and you must learn to go easy on the booze.'

Remembering the ruined Sunday dinner, he smiled ruefully. 'Are you trying to put me off?' he jested. Now his arms did reach for her, drawing her close. 'I'll find somewhere for us to live. Will you come over to see me on Christmas Day?'

She gave a happy laugh. 'I'll have to, won't I? My presents are still under the tree, remember.'

'I'll see you then. If you want me beforehand, just come on over. Right?'

'Right!'

A brief kiss, and then the comfort of his arms was removed and without another word he was gone. Dejected and alone, Bridget stared after him until he reached the corner of Dunlewey Street, willing him to turn and wave. Without a backward glance he turned the corner and was out of sight. She stifled a sob. What did the future hold for her and her child? One thing she was grateful for: Liz O'Hara was safely married.

She was glad her father was not present when she hauled the heavy bag into the living room. Danny would have sunk even lower in his eyes, if that were possible, for allowing her to carry such a weight in her condition.

Her mother rose slowly from her chair by the fire, her eyes questioning.

'Do you still want me home, Mam?'

Clasping her close, Martha cried, 'Of course we do.' Pushing her back, she searched Bridget's eyes. 'Was there any unpleasantness, love?'

'Not really, Mam, but I can't go back there. Can I stay here until Danny finds us somewhere else?'

'You can stay as long as you like, love. I only

wish we hadn't pushed you into marriage with the likes of Danny McGowan.'

She waited tensely for her daughter to avow her undying love for Danny. Her heart sank when Bridget replied, 'It's too late now for regrets, Mam. I'll just have to make the best of it.'

They made some inquiries and were told some addresses where rooms were available to rent. They trudged around back streets to have a look at these but Bridget always shook her head firmly and refused to consider any of them. She had no intention of living in cramped conditions and sharing a kitchen and toilet with strangers.

There was no need for it. She was happy enough staying with her parents until such time as decent accommodation was found. She had insisted on sleeping on the big comfortable settee so there was no guilt about putting her father out of his bed. He had purchased a secondhand screen down in Smithfield Market and in the mornings and at night she was shielded from her brothers' eyes as they returned late after a night out or left the house early for work.

On her days off, she and her mother shopped for the coming confinement. Bridget's health appeared to have settled down and her pregnancy continued smoothly. Although she spent a lot on maternity clothes, she was pleasantly surprised by how much she still managed to save from her wages and wondered if Danny was doing likewise. She refused to follow her mother's advice and ask him for weekly maintenance. Hopefully he too was saving like mad so that they could soon be together.

Martha was uneasy about her daughter. It wasn't natural the way the two of them adapted to living apart. Neither of them seemed unduly worried about the situation. 'It isn't natural, so it isn't,' she confided in her husband.

'I know what you mean, love. But what can we do about it? You know what would happen if I tried to talk some sense into that husband of hers. It would probably finish up with me having another bash at him. He has that effect on me.'

Two months slowly passed and nowhere suitable was found. Bridget was beginning to despair. Danny of course refused to visit her at home and she felt uncomfortable in his house when Jane was there, which was usually the case. Therefore, they had few precious moments to themselves. Barney was quick to criticize Danny's feeble attempts at finding suitable accommodation for them and this caused further tension between him and his daughter. It was he who eventually heard tell of a flat going on the Antrim Road. A young lad who worked in the Yard with him had rented it for some time but was getting married at Easter and now buying a house. Hearing that Barney was asking after rooms, he told him about it and assured him it was in a quiet district and the rooms were spacious and clean.

When Bridget showed Danny the piece of paper with the address scribbled on it, he scowled. 'The Antrim Road? That will be well beyond our pockets, so it will.'

'We can at least look at it, so we can. Billy

McCormack who lives there at the minute says we can call over tonight to view it. He is doing us a favour, you know. The owners will have no difficulty re-letting it.'

He still dithered, and she pleaded, 'Please, Danny. It will only cost us our bus fares to go and look at it. We're not committed to anything. In fact we can even call into a pub and have a drink before we come home. It will be like a night out for me.'

Saddened, she considered that a night out, he reluctantly agreed and made arrangements to meet her at the corner of the street at half-past six.

Bridget fell in love with the big roomy flat. It would be let unfurnished and she pictured how it would look when she could fill it with her own things. A great big terraced house with bay windows, it was divided into three flats. The one Billy McCormack leased was on the ground floor. He led them into the living room and, saying he would pop out to the shop, left them alone to look it over in privacy. Bridget was wide-eyed with delight as she surveyed the spacious living room, with the gas fire built into the wall. It wouldn't take much to furnish it. A three-piece suite and a small table would be enough to be getting on with. The bay window was wide and high but her mother had a sewing machine and would run up some curtains for her.

The kitchen was fair-sized with built-in cupboards, a stainless steel sink with draining board, and a small stove. The floor was covered with red and black linoleum. They had received plenty of crockery and utensils for wedding presents so nothing at all would be required for the kitchen; except food, of course. The bathroom contained the basic essentials and some shelves. Nothing elaborate but clean and sufficient for their needs. She would soon have it looking lovely. A small box room sent her into raptures as she enthused over how it could be converted into a nursery.

Aware that Danny was not sharing her enthusiasm, she cried, 'We must take this!'

Appalled at the rent, he tried in vain to put her off. 'Ah, come on now, Bridget. At this rent we'll never be able to save for a house,' he reasoned. 'We won't even be able to buy any furniture.'

However his wife was not to be deterred. 'Danny McGowan, either we take this flat or we're finished. You might not object to us living like strangers the way we do, but I sure do. I'm sick to the teeth of having nowhere to call my own. Depending on my parents' unending charity. If it wasn't for this ugly big bump, I'd be inclined to think I wasn't married at all.'

'Those rooms we saw in Lincoln Street at the weekend weren't too bad,' he argued. 'And, they're less than half this rent.'

'Weren't too bad? You've got to be joking. There's no comparison. Besides I won't share a kitchen and outside loo. I want somewhere decent for my baby to be born. Somewhere with a bathroom and plenty of hot water. We have all that here. Why, it's an answer to my prayers!'

The more she thought about it, the more

appealing the flat appeared. Here, for instance, Danny would be far removed from his mates. That in itself would be a blessing. Whilst she had been staying with her parents, he'd had far too much time on his hands. God knows what he'd been up to.

'Look,' she pleaded, 'I'll work as long as I can. Then there will be my maternity money coming in for a while. As soon as the baby is old enough, I'll go back to work. Dad says that you must earn good money...' Her voice trailed off. Danny's head reared back and he glared at her. She knew immediately she had said the wrong thing.

He pounced on her words. 'Oh, he did, did he? So he's got me all sorted out, has he?'

'Yes, he did!' she cried indignantly. 'It's ridiculous that I don't even know how much you earn.'

'Why? So that you can tell your da, and he can decide how I spend it? No, Bridget. You will never know how much I earn. My wages will never be discussed in Leeson Street. And another thing. I've had enough of handing in my pay packet and getting pocket money to last me a lifetime. I'll look after the money in our house.'

Tears stung her eyes. How could you reason with someone like this? She turned away, furtively dabbing at her eyes.

'For heaven's sake, turn off the waterworks. Billy McCormack will be back any minute and I don't want you blubbering all over the place. It will be too embarrassing. We just can't afford this place and that's that. God knows how much bond money they'll be looking for, Bridget. And think of the bus fares to and from work. I'm sorry, love, but there's no way we can afford this flat, and that's final.'

Tears forgotten, her eyes narrowed suspiciously and she snapped at him. 'Surely you have enough saved by now to take care of the bond?'

His unwillingness to meet her eye caused her deep concern. What had he been spending all his money on? The sooner she got him under her eye the better. She decided not to mention her savings. 'We'll find the money somehow. Even if we have to borrow it from my da.'

Once more his head came back and he eyed her angrily. 'You can put that idea out of your head right now! There's no way that we will ever borrow from your da. I'll get the money somehow.'

She breathed a sigh of relief. The magic word 'da' had worked wonders. Danny had as good as committed himself.

Bridget didn't inquire where the bond money came from, and didn't really care. Suffice to say it was found somehow and paid over to the landlord. They moved into the flat two weeks later. Jane and Martha between them supplied chests of drawers, a wardrobe and two small tables. Bridget had enough money saved to buy a bed and they went into debt to buy a three-piece suite on the 'never never'. These things, along with their wedding presents, meant that they had quite a comfortable home.

The flat was already tastefully decorated and only the box room needed immediate attention. Peter offered his services and Bridget was glad

163

when Danny accepted the offer. She did not want to cut him off entirely from his family.

They quickly settled into a routine, and if Danny was not as happy as she, Bridget closed her eyes to the fact and pretended all was well. She was in her glory. Each evening she hurried home from work and prepared a meal for him. While living with her mother she had finally learnt a lot about cooking and was quite pleased with her efforts. However, no words of praise were forthcoming from her husband. He usually ate his dinner in silence and then became engrossed in the daily paper. Only in bed did he pay her attention, and then without tenderness or any words of love. She began to feel used, and made all sorts of excuses to avoid his attentions. He became increasingly remote.

Every Tuesday and Thursday evening Peter came to help with decorating the small room. He arrived straight from work and always found something complimentary to say about the dinner Bridget had prepared for them. She began to make special meals those evenings, trying out new recipes given to her by the married women at work. She found herself looking forward to his visits.

The small room soon took shape under Peter's capable hands. After the first evening when he offered a few desultory words of advice, Danny left his wife and brother to get on with it. They worked together in perfect harmony and Bridget found herself fantasizing that Peter was her husband, the father of her child. Oh, if only it were true!

Horrified, she put such thoughts from her mind and concentrated on the decorating. She was delighted with the results of her brother-in-law's labour. An alcove was converted into a cupboard with a sunken top to hold a baby bath. Above it there were shelves to hold all the baby's toiletries and underneath there was space where a plastic pail for soiled nappies and a small linen bin could be stored out of sight. Close to these he had built a shelf for changing and dressing the baby. This lifted up and clipped to the wall out of the way when not in use.

Bridget sighed with pleasure when she surveyed his handiwork. 'I'll pick the paper at the weekend, Peter. Then all that will be needed is the cot and a rug, and eventually a carpet. Thank you for all your help. I don't know how we would have managed without you.'

His smile was wry. 'That sounds like a dismissal, Bridget. Do you not trust me to hang the wallpaper and do a bit of painting?'

'Of course I do!' she cried, alarmed that she might have offended him. 'It's just ... well ... I think that Danny should pull his weight a bit. Don't you agree?'

He laughed softly. 'Point taken. But I'd still like to help out, Bridget. I have to admit I enjoy coming here. I love working with wood. I was always top of the woodwork class at school. Why I became a plumber I'll never know. I suppose it was the only apprenticeship open to me at the time. There are a few things I could still do to make this place look better. For instance, a mantelpiece would set off that grate in the living room and a few shelves in the alcove would hold all your knick-knacks.'

Her eyes went round with wonder. 'Oh, Peter, you make it sound so easy.' Her face clouded over, 'Danny's the one who should be making this into a home.'

'Don't you worry about him. Once all the joinery work is finished, I'll make sure he helps out. Besides,' Peter nodded towards the floor, 'I want to sand down and varnish those floorboards. It will save you the expense of carpet and will finish the room off.'

'Oh, Peter, that would be just wonderful.' She moved closer and placed a hand on his arm. 'You're very good to me. I honestly don't know how I would have managed without you.'

He heard tears in her voice and placed a comforting hand over hers. 'What are brothers-in-law for if not to help?' he asked with a smile. He could never figure out who moved first, but suddenly Bridget was in his arms. Small and tearful, she pressed close against him; her bump barely noticeable against his body. His heart went out to her. His brother was a fool, didn't know when he was well off. Imagine coming home to this every night. Big brown eyes brimming with tears gazed up at him and her trembling lips looked very inviting. The desire to kiss her became overwhelming and Peter's arms tightened around her. His mind boggled at the thoughts that were crowding it. Good God, this was his brother's wife he was lusting after! The same young girl he had accused Danny of taking advantage of. In his present aroused state, he

166

now realized just how easily his brother might have been tempted.

Very much aware that Danny could come into the room at any moment, he gently put her from him. Danny would never believe he was just comforting her. And he would be right too! There was more than comfort on his mind. If Bridget knew the course his thoughts were taking she wouldn't want him back in this flat, that was for sure. As for Danny ... if he got any hint at all, he was so volatile he would erupt. Murder would be done. 'You would have managed fine, Bridget,' Peter assured her. 'I'm only too glad to have been of some help.'

He saw her struggle for control and wished he could really comfort her, but didn't dare touch her again. His heart was racing and he thought he read an invitation in her eyes. That must be his imagination playing tricks on him. Wasn't she married to Danny? To his surprise she moved closer still and whispered, 'I'm so lonely, Peter. Could you not just hold me for a moment, please?'

Suddenly he realized her back was against the door, cutting off his retreat. How had that come about? He'd been between her and the door a minute ago. The heat in the small room was suddenly overpowering and he broke out in a sweat.

Not wanting to give offence, he said gently, 'Bridget, I think it's time that I was going.'

'Well, surely I can at least give you a big thank you kiss, Peter? Mmm?' Her arms crept slowly around his neck and he stood as if mesmerized.

167

She stood on tiptoe and pulled his head down towards her. He lost all will to ward her off. Her lips were soft, moist and slightly parted. The kiss intensified and they pressed closer still. The feel of her against him was electric, sending reason out of the window. Before he lost control completely he managed to push her away.

'Look, I'll really have to be going now, Bridget,' he muttered, shame making him abrupt.

Tears threatened again, and she whispered, 'I'm sorry. I didn't mean to offend you. It was just a kiss. I wouldn't offend you for the world.'

'Offend? Oh, no, I'm not offended. Far from it.'

'Then you will come as usual on Thursday night?'

'Yes, yes, I'll be here.'

Glad that he still intended to help out, Bridget gave him a wobbly smile. 'Thanks, Peter. Thanks for everything.' She turned to open the door. 'I'll make you a cup of tea before you go.'

'That won't be necessary, Bridget.'

Preceding her along the hall, he pushed open the living-room door, staying in its shadows as he spoke to Danny. He felt as guilty as if he had just committed adultery with his brother's wife; felt that if Danny saw his face he would be able to guess what had been in his mind. 'I'm away now, Danny. I'll see you on Thursday.'

Danny rose slowly to his feet and peered over at him. 'Hey, what's the big rush tonight? I've a couple of beers in the fridge. Sit down and have a yarn before you go.'

'I want to catch the next bus. I'm out early tomorrow morning. A job out of town, you know.'

Danny shrugged. 'Suit yourself. See you on Thursday then.'

On the bus journey home, Peter went over the scene in his mind. Had he unwittingly taken Bridget in his arms, or had she engineered it? He gave his head a slight shake at the absurdity of the thought. In the name of God, why would she? It must have been all his fault. He must have been sending out all kinds of signals. He eyed his reflection in the bus window. He was nowhere near as handsome as Danny. So why would Bridget try it on with him eh? Still, he had thought her willing. He remembered Danny saying she had seduced him. Was it possible? One thing was for sure. From now on he would have to tread carefully. He must not give Bridget any reason to suppose that he fancied her. He sighed at this idea. Even the memory of her body close to his and the eagerness of her kiss aroused him and brought an embarrassed flush to his face. What on earth was he going to do? There was only one thing he could do. Make some excuse and stay away from that flat.

The months passed all too quickly for Liz and David. Orders were coming in fast and furious and David was talking about expansion. No sooner said than done. He put in an offer well below the market value for the derelict building adjoining the factory. It had been empty a long, long time and to his great delight, without any quibbling, his offer was accepted. Contractors were immediately brought in to commence renovations.

Dismayed at the cost of all this work, Liz questioned him. 'Are you sure you're doing the right thing? I mean, you will be careful not to overstretch your resources, won't you, David? Last year and this so many factories have closed down, it frightens me to contemplate what you intend doing.'

'I admit, Liz, the government grant isn't enough and I've borrowed heavily from the bank, but I'm confident I'll be able to repay the loan quickly. Now is the time to act. All these clothing factories closing down have left a gap in the market. The Ulidia and Magee's retailers are bound to be looking for alternative sources.'

'But those were makers of men's and boys' clothes.'

'I know that, love. But just think of all those experienced stitchers on the dole. Besides, there's nothing to say we can't start making men's clothes. When the Mayfair stitching company closed down in the sixties, Victoria's father was making handkerchiefs. He saw his chance to expand and that's how he got started in ladies' underwear.'

Open-mouthed, she gaped at him. 'You can't be serious about menswear?'

Drawing her into his arms, David ruffled her hair. 'Why not? But that's all in the future. Don't you be worrying your pretty little head about anything. It will be all right. You just leave everything in my capable hands.'

'I can't help worrying. I admit we're receiving lots of new orders, but it could be a flash in the pan. But I suppose you're right about there being

170

a market for menswear. Still, nothing is sure in this country. This time next year we could be scratching around for work.'

'We've been very lucky, Liz, but you have to take chances in business. Never venture, never gain. You have to speculate to accumulate and I've a gut feeling I'm doing the right thing. But I haven't remortgaged the house or anything like that.'

The worry uppermost in her mind came to the fore. 'What if I become pregnant?'

He pushed her back so he could see her face. 'Are you trying to tell me something, Liz?' he asked roguishly, but she perceived a slight frown on his brow.

Did he not want children? Afraid to put him to the test, she said, 'No, I'm not. But if I were to become pregnant, you would have to employ someone to take my place. And that would be more expenditure. And, I must admit, I am starting to feel a bit broody.' She eyed him closely when she said this but he seemed unconcerned. 'Actually, I thought I would be pregnant by now.'

'There's no hurry, is there?' He sounded a bit anxious. 'Twenty-three is no age at all.'

'It's you I'm thinking of, David. Would you not like to be a father while you're still young enough to enjoy your children? See them grow up?'

'Why, of course I would.'

'Actually I've been thinking of having a word with the doctor.'

'It's only been a few short months, Liz,' he reasoned. 'I think he'll tell you to wait a while.'

She sighed. 'You're probably right, David.

Meanwhile we can put our heads together about this extension you are so determined to build. Who knows what next year will bring?'

April had been a terrible month; dark and dreary with continuous downpours. Then May dawned bright and sunny, showing great promise, giving a lift to the spirits. It was the first Saturday in May. It was also the first Saturday off work the Atkinsons had had in a long time. Liz suggested they breakfast in the conservatory at the back of the bungalow, saying they deserved to have a lazy morning. The sun streamed in through the fine slats of the venetian blinds, teasing chestnut highlights in her hair and making her skin appear transparent. She hummed softly as she set place mats on the wickerwork table. To David she looked beautiful. The yellow housecoat deepened the colour of her eyes and gave a luminous glow to her fine-textured skin. He noticed the venetian blind cast bars of shadows against the bright yellow. Did she feel caged in? Save for a few days in Donegal at Easter, they had socialized very little since their marriage.

The extension to their premises required a lot of attention. He was forever chasing builders about this and that; trying to tie them down to a definite completion date. He was also busy seeking out new orders, and finding out all he could about the manufacture of menswear, leaving the running of the factory completely in Liz's hands. She had seemed to thrive on the extra responsibility. Now he became aware that he was neglecting his wife. She was a young woman. He should be taking her out more often; showing her off, not weighing her down with work. He remembered a phone call from Dick Kennedy the day before. He had tickets for a presentation dance at the club and had asked if David and Liz would care to accompany him and Irene and some of the old crowd to it next Saturday night. David had turned the offer down. Had he been wrong to do so without consulting his wife first? Perhaps Liz would like to go? He hesitated. He didn't particularly want to return to the haunts of his former life. However, he would at least give her the chance to refuse.

'Liz, are you bored?'

She turned a look of baffled surprise on him. 'Bored? No, how could I be? I have a full schedule. Why, I hardly have time to bless myself these days.' A perplexed frown furrowed her smooth brow. 'What made you ask such a silly question?'

'That's what I mean. We've been so pre-occupied with the factory, I've neglected to take you out anywhere.'

'Sure now, didn't we get away for four days at Easter?'

'Yes, but that was such a short break and the weather was lousy.'

She laughed outright at this. 'Unfortunately even you can't control the weather, David. The Shandon Hotel was wonderful and I enjoyed myself. Besides, if I wasn't married to you, I very much doubt I would have had even a single day at Portrush.'

'Have you ever been to Fortwilliam Golf Club?'

Her grin was wide as she confessed, 'No, I'm afraid I've never moved in such circles.'

'Would you care to go next Saturday night? There's a cabaret on.'

She remained silent, waiting for him to continue. He explained, 'I was speaking to Dick Kennedy on the phone yesterday and he asked me if we would care to join him and some friends. I think he's showing off a bit. He has won the something or other trophy for golf. There'll be a presentation and afterwards a cabaret and dance.'

Her back was to him as she poured juice and he could not see her reaction to his request. 'We could go early and have dinner beforehand?' he suggested.

Slowly she turned to face him. 'Do you want to go, David?'

'It would be a night out. Break the monotony.'

She laughed lightly. 'Monotony? Are you bored then?'

He was on his feet instantly. 'Never! It's you I'm thinking of.'

'Will all the old clique be there?'

'Yes,' he confessed. 'I imagine they will be.'

Liz looked at him and for the first time noticed fine lines of strain around his eyes and mouth. She realized he needed a break more than she did.

'All right. Let's go.'

'Liz...' His voice was hesitant now. 'I'm not just asking you to go because of Dick. I mean, his offering me the tickets just brought home to me

174

how little socializing we do. You are a young woman and I should be taking you out and about more often.'

'So it's not a longing to see all your old friends that brought this on?' she teased him.

Taking her in his arms, he gazed earnestly at her. 'No, Liz. I have all I need here with you. Please believe that. If you don't want to go, that's fine by me.'

Her fingers traced the lines around his sensitive mouth. 'I'm only teasing you, silly. I do want to go.' A brief kiss accompanied her words. 'Besides, it will be a chance to show off one of those beautiful dresses you insisted I buy.'

'Don't ever even joke about it, Liz. Always remember, you're all I need.'

A phone had been installed in the flat in the event Bridget might need assistance when alone. Grateful that he didn't have to face her, on Wednesday evening Peter rang to make his excuses. He explained a rush job meant he would be working overtime and would be unable to come to the flat the following night.

'Oh, I'm sorry to hear that, Peter.' Her voice sounded troubled. 'What about next Tuesday?'

'Yes, maybe I won't be so busy next week.'

'I'm sorry if I offended you. Thanks for calling.'

Peter stood looking at the phone for some seconds, then slowly replaced it in its cradle. He hadn't expected her to cut him off like that. What had he expected? Did he want her to grovel? He felt a right cad. Bridget had obviously not been fooled. But surely she realized he had no choice

175

in the matter? He couldn't afford to take chances; perhaps cause a scandal. Sexually attracted to his sister-in-law he might be, but he knew in his heart it wasn't love. There was something so sensual about Bridget, he had to admit he desired her. And if she was willing, as he thought she was, given the chance anything might happen. And that had to be avoided at all costs.

Even if it was love, he reasoned, what difference did it make? He wouldn't be able to do anything about it. She was married to his brother, for heaven's sake! What did she want of him? Just friendship? If that was the case he would be only too willing to oblige. But suppose she wanted more? Would he be able to resist her? A loud knock on the door of the telephone kiosk brought him to his senses.

'Sorry, mate,' he apologized as he exited the booth. 'I was in a world of my own there.'

The young man waiting to get on the phone grinned. 'So I noticed. I hope I didn't waken you from happy dreams?'

'Far from it. I'm glad you interrupted.'

Still lost in troubled thoughts Peter turned up Dunlewey Street with his head bent, and bumped into Kath O'Hara. 'I'm sorry, Mrs O'Hara,' he apologized. 'I wasn't looking where I was going.'

'It's all right, Peter. I do that many a time myself.'

He would have passed on but she stopped and he hesitated to see what she wanted.

'I couldn't help noticing Danny and his wife

176

don't live with your mother any longer. Have they found a place of their own now?'

Nosy old bat, he thought, then scolded himself. It was only because she was Liz's mother he was thinking like that. The woman was probably genuinely interested. Ashamed of himself he volunteered, 'Yes, they have a flat on the Antrim Road.'

Her brows rose. 'The Antrim Road?'

She sounded so surprised, he elaborated. 'Yes, and a lovely big spacious flat it is too.' He added a few lies. 'Our Danny has it looking like a palace, so he has.'

'I'm very glad to hear that, Peter. Give him my regards the next time you see him. And how is his wife keeping? She must be quite near her time.'

A puzzled frown gathered on Peter's brow. 'I don't think she's that near her time, but I'll give them your regards. Good day, Mrs O'Hara.'

As he continued on up the street a smile brightened his face at the memory of her expression at the idea that Danny was turning out a right fellow. The smile soon faded. It was a pity it wasn't true. All Danny was good for was letting Bridget wait on him hand and foot. Poor wee girl. What kind of a marriage was that? These thoughts made him even more depressed.

During next few days Peter found himself worrying about Bridget. On Saturday while in town, he called into the Bank Buildings to see if he could catch a glimpse of her. Just to assure himself she was all right, of course. He watched from a distance as she served customers and

177

came away relieved. Her maternity skirt and top covered her pregnancy and very few people would have guessed her condition. Except for her pallor, she looked fine. His worry appeased, he left the store and finished his shopping with an easy mind. He had a date tonight. He had asked Margaret Rooney to go to the pictures with him. Perhaps she would take his mind off Bridget.

The outing with Margaret was not a success. He had not paid her enough attention and therefore was not surprised when she gently but firmly turned down his offer of another date. He smiled wryly as he bade her farewell; he must be slipping. That was the first time he had been refused a second date.

Contrary to all his good intentions, the following Tuesday night found Peter at the door of the flat. It was some moments before it opened slightly and Bridget peered out.

'Oh, hello, Peter. I didn't expect you.' Her voice was expressionless.

She made no effort to invite him in and he shuffled his feet in embarrassment as he tried to find something to say. 'I would have phoned if I'd been working late,' he at last volunteered.

She seemed to come out of a trance and, moving to one side, with a nod of her head motioned him in. He followed her along the hall and into the kitchen, noting as he did so that the living room was empty.

She turned, brows raised, and said, 'I was just about to make myself a cup of tea. Would you like one?'

'Yes, please.'

There was no welcoming aroma and he realized he would get no dinner tonight. 'Where's Danny?'

'I wish I knew. We had a huge row last night and he walked out. He hasn't been back since. I take it he didn't go to your mother's then?'

'Not last night. But of course he could be there now. I came here straight from work, remember?'

Bridget poured the tea and sat facing him across the kitchen table. 'I'm sorry, Peter, I'm afraid there's no dinner ready. I've been too upset to cook. Anyway, I didn't think you would come.'

She was deathly pale with purple shadows under her eyes. He watched as she raised the cup absent-mindedly to her lips; her hand shook so badly that the tea dripped down over her fingers. She appeared not to notice.

'Bridget, have you been in to work today?'

'Of course I haven't. How could I go in looking like this? I called in sick. Thank God, I only have one more week to go. I stop work at Easter until after the birth.'

'Have you at least eaten today?'

She shrugged negatively. 'I got enough to do me.'

'Look, Bridget, make fresh tea and butter some bread. I'll go and get some fish and chips.'

Her eyes filled with tears. 'Oh, Peter, what am I going to do? What if Danny doesn't come back?'

'Now you're talking nonsense. Of course he'll come back. You're his wife, for heaven's sake.'

'You don't understand – he'll never forgive me.

179

Some awful things were said.'

Peter rose to his feet; he didn't want to hear any confidences she might later regret. 'They usually are in the heat of the moment,' he agreed, and headed for the door. 'Meanwhile we must eat. Get that tea ready. I won't be long.'

As he queued up at the fish and chip shop, he was full of misgivings. He wished now he had stayed away. Danny would probably arrive home full of apologies and he would be in the way of a reconciliation. But until Danny did arrive, he would stay.

On his return to the flat he discovered Bridget still sitting at the table, hands clasped in front of her, staring blankly at the door. There was no light under the teapot. Obviously she had not moved while he was away. He managed to hide his exasperation and, lighting the oven, popped the still wrapped fish suppers into its depths together with two plates to heat. Then, rinsing the teapot, filled it with water and put it on the stove to boil. When the bread was sliced and buttered he added tea to the pot and left it to brew for a minute or two. Then he put the fish suppers on the plates and poured the tea.

Placing a plate in front of her, he admonished, 'Now, Bridget, I expect you to eat that. Don't be wasting my time.'

She rose from the table. 'I'll just wash my hands. I won't be a minute.'

It was obvious when she returned that she had brushed her hair. It was a soft cloud around her pale face and tumbled down over her shoulders. She had also powdered her nose. He gave her an approving look. 'That's better. Now eat up,' he ordered.

She pushed the food about the plate, taking a nibble now and again. At last she pushed the plate to one side. 'I'm sorry, Peter, but it's sticking in my throat.'

'You really should try to eat, Bridget. You'll need all your strength for the birth.'

'It just won't go down.'

'Well, if you can't, you can't, I suppose, and that's that.' He peered intently into her face. 'You look tired. Go and stretch out on the settee and I'll wash these dishes.'

She wouldn't hear tell of lying down and insisted on washing them. He dried in silence, wishing he was anywhere else but here. A glance at the clock showed him it was just eight o'clock. As if sensing his reluctance to hang around, she said, 'You don't have to stay, Peter. I'm sure you have more important things to do than sit with me. I'll be all right, you know.'

He stifled the temptation to take her at her word and asked, 'Did you get the paint and paper at the weekend?'

A slight nod confirmed this. 'Then let's make a start, eh? It'll take your mind off your problems.'

Reluctantly she rose to her feet and he followed her out of the room. The wallpaper was lemon with a fine silver stripe and he could see matching material he guessed was for curtains. He also noticed the window, door and skirting board were freshly painted.

'Somebody's been busy.'

'Danny did some painting at the weekend, under duress.'

'That's good to hear.' He opened out a roll of paper. 'My, this is pretty. It'll make the room seem bigger.'

Her demeanour brightened slightly. 'That's what thought. That's why I chose plain paper. This room's too small for a pattern. Look...' She reached up to a shelf for a narrow roll of paper. 'I thought this border would look nice along the top of the wall.'

Peter took the roll from her and opened it out, to display bright yellow ducks. 'This is lovely. Very nice indeed. What does Danny think of it?'

A grimace twisted her mouth. 'Him! He doesn't pay attention to anything. He barely glanced at it.'

Anger built up inside Peter at the apparent indifference of his brother. As far as he could see Danny wasn't making any effort at all. And Bridget was so easily pleased. He could picture her joy when she showed her husband these precious things for the nursery. How hurt she must have been at Danny's offhand manner. However, he was aware resentment was eating away at Bridget and did not want to say anything that might add fuel to it, so he swallowed the bitter comments against his brother that were hovering on his lips. It was none of his business, after all. Let them sort it out between themselves.

Lifting the packet of cold water paste, he headed for the kitchen. 'I'll get this ready. It has to sit for a while to thicken.'

She stood by his side as he stirred the powder

into a pail of water, staring abjectly into the thickening adhesive. So despondent; so different from the last time he was here. He longed to take her in his arms and give solace. He didn't dare. Take her in his arms in an empty flat? That would really be asking for trouble.

Whilst the paste thickened they worked side by side in silence, stripping the old wallpaper off the walls. The room being so small it took no time at all, and soon one wall was covered with the new paper. He saw her dubiously eye the bubbles that had appeared here and there.

'Those bubbles will disappear when it dries out,' he assured her. 'It's going to look great. You won't be able to appreciate how nice it is until it's all completed.'

It was almost half-past eleven. The last bus into town was due in fifteen minutes. Peter came to a decision. Since he couldn't risk spending the night in the flat with her, he must take her with him. 'Look, I'm not leaving you here alone. Grab a nightdress and toothbrush and I'll take you up to your mam's.'

He saw hope rise in her eyes and guessed she had dreaded spending another night alone. Still she dithered. 'What if Danny comes home?'

'It will give him something to worry about. Though he won't find it hard to guess where you are. Go on, hurry up or we'll miss the last bus.'

Without another word she headed for the bedroom and soon returned with a small bag containing essentials. They left the flat on the quarter hour and caught the bus by the skin of their teeth.

It was, as usual, packed. Peter was glad there was no privacy to talk about her affairs. They sat thigh to thigh on the narrow seat and he was very much aware of the warmth of her body against his. The sensual thoughts this evoked brought him out in a sweat.

Bridget seemed locked in her own world and totally unaware of him. So much for him thinking she fancied him! He had been a stupid fool. An elderly couple got on at the next stop and he was glad to relinquish his seat to the woman. Perhaps now he would cool down.

Peter hung from the strap and gazed down on Bridget's bent head. The artificial light from the bulbs deepened the dark mass of her curls and he saw how her hands were clasped around her stomach as if already holding the baby. She was lovely and would make a grand wee wife. Danny had so much going for him. Why on earth didn't he put the past behind him, forget about Liz O'Hara and make the most of what he had? He could do a hell of a lot worse.

Peter was awakened from his musing by their arrival at Castle Junction. There was no need to rush. They had a few minutes to catch the last bus up the Falls Road. At the corner of Leeson Street Bridget insisted he should leave her. He watched from his stand to make sure her parents were still awake and she was admitted to the house. With a final wave of her hand Bridget entered the house and the door was closed. Peter crossed over to Dunlewey Street, his heart heavy in his chest. Right now he would love to break his brother's neck, the bastard.

184

To his amazement, Danny was sitting by the fireside at home, a mug of tea in his hand, a wide, foolish grin on his face. Coming from the kitchen, Jane gave Peter a warning look and raised her eyes to the ceiling. 'Danny's staying the night. He'll sleep on the sofa.'

Peter ignored his mother's warning look. If his da wakened, too bad! He glared at his brother. 'What about Bridget? Will she not be worried?'

'Bridget's all right.'

'How do you know that? You haven't been home since last night.'

'Hah!' Danny nodded his head sagely. 'You obviously have. Has she been crying on your broad shoulder?' His words were slurred and Peter threw him a look of contempt.

'You're drunk!' he cried in disgust. 'But then, what's new? Just for the record, she didn't say one word against you.'

'No, you're wrong, Peter. I'm not drunk. I'm just happy.' The mug waved in the air, spilling its contents all over the place. 'And you don't know how long it is since I felt this way.'

'You disgust me. I've just left your wife over in her mam's. She's worried stiff about you, so she is. More fool her!'

Anger brought Danny to his feet. He tripped and relinquished his hold on the mug, reaching for the mantelpiece to steady himself. The mug crashed to the tiled hearth and broke into small pieces, bringing words of anguished rebuff from Jane. Trust Danny to use one of her best mugs.

'You brought Bridget up to her da's?' he growled.

185

'I couldn't leave her alone in the flat, could I? What if the baby decided to come early?'

'She would have been all right. That's why we went to the expense of installing a phone, for heaven's sake. So the midwife could be reached in a hurry. And I asked Ian Geddis in the flat above to keep an eye on her. She would have come to no harm.'

'You're the one should be looking after her. Not some stranger.'

'I'm teaching her a lesson, that's what I'm doing. She thinks she can dictate who comes and goes in the flat ... and she can't!' One hand thumped his breast to emphasize his point. 'It's my home as well as hers and it's damned boring sitting there night after night, listening to Bridget ramble on about wallpaper and baby clothes. That's all she talks about – the baby. So if I want to invite Ian down to keep us company on an evening, I will. So there!' The burst of energy died with his temper, and as his knees buckled Danny sank back down on the chair and passed out.

Jane gazed down at him, a look of pity on her face. 'He didn't go in to work. He must have been drinking all day to get into this state. Probably worrying about Bridget. Did she say what happened?'

'Worrying about Bridget, my foot! He thinks of nobody but himself. And not a word did she say. She's at the end of her tether, though. Worried in case he doesn't come back to her. If she but knew it, it'd be the best thing that could possibly happen. She'd be much better off without him.'

186

'That's an awful thing to say, Peter McGowan. They're married and have to make a go of it.'

'You don't understand, Ma. She's in a terrible state. It can't be good for the baby. She's trying to make a go of it but he's not bothered one way or the other. Danny doesn't deserve her. I'd better go across before it gets any later and set her mind at rest. I only hope they're still up.'

'Huh! I'd let her stew for a while, if I was you. Then maybe she'll appreciate our Danny. She got him to move out to the Antrim Road, far away from all his friends, and by the sound of it, she still isn't satisfied.'

The look of contempt Peter bestowed on her made her draw back as if from a blow. 'You would think that, Ma. Our Danny's you all over again. You just can't see any wrong in him.'

The door closed behind him with a click that was more eloquent than any slam would have been. Jane gazed at it for some moments, resentment burning within her breast. Then, with a sigh of regret, she started to clear up the broken mug. She would never have believed that Peter would speak to her like that. Bridget Kelly had a lot to answer for. That was two sons she had turned against Jane. Even her husband was less affable since that girl came on the scene. What had she ever done to deserve their censure? The hearth washed, Jane stood and gazed down on the senseless form of her eldest son. Should she attempt to move him or wait until Peter returned?

A sound caused her to turn round, startled. Her husband stood in the doorway. 'They wakened you, then?'

'I think they probably wakened the whole street, the racket they kicked up. Only the likes of our Joseph could sleep through it.'

She smiled slightly at his exaggeration. 'Leave him be,' her husband admonished. 'If Peter doesn't move him to the settee, he can lie there until the morning. He doesn't deserve any pampering after the way he's treated you. You should have shown him the door when he arrived. His first visit since he moved, and he comes in this state?'

'Where else could he go, Joe, if not to his parents?'

'Come on to bed, love. We will always be here for them. But I tell you now, none of them will walk over us.'

His words warmed her heart and she allowed him to usher her up the stairs before him.

Fortwilliam Golf Club being just round the corner from Somerton Road, David and Liz decided to walk there on Saturday night. It was a beautiful evening and they dandered along, arm in arm. They could see the castle towering through the trees and above it the Cave Hill was capped with a shimmering purple mist. All around them birds twittered in the trees and bushes as they fed their young.

'It's lovely up here, David. So peaceful. You wouldn't dream there was so much trouble and unrest in the town. I consider myself very lucky to be married to you.'

Lucky? He longed to ask her if she thought that perhaps she would be happier married to Danny

McGowan, but was afraid to rock the boat. Why court trouble?

'It's a pity we can't persuade your mother to sell up and buy a house nearby. I'd be happier if she was away from the Falls Road.'

'I know. It's not as if she has any really close friends she can't bear to leave. I don't understand her. Of course there is her wee job and after all ... the Falls is her home. These past few years things have settled down a bit. People are even venturing into the city centre again.'

'She can't earn that much. I'd be willing to reimburse her. And whether or not things are quieter, I'd still like her to be closer to us.'

Liz affectionately rubbed her head against his arm. 'You really are a good man. But, although we were far from rich, Mam always seemed to have something in reserve, I think my father settled some money on her.'

David gazed down at her. 'Are you not at all curious to know who he is?'

Liz shrugged indifferently, but he detected a sadness in her voice when she spoke. 'If he never wanted to acknowledge me, why would I seek him out?'

They turned in at the gates of the golf club and walked up the short drive to the car park. As they crossed to the club itself, Liz gazed at the building and nodded her approval.

'It is very nice.'

'You can't really see it from this angle. The front looks out over Belfast Lough.'

'From this high up the view must be breath-taking.'

'It is, and not just the lough. From the back windows you can see the Cave Hill. I think you'll enjoy yourself tonight.'

They were early, wanting to enjoy a meal in peace before the company they were joining arrived. There was an obstacle. They needed to be signed in. Luckily, an acquaintance of David's saw their plight and did the needful. Once upstairs the waiter showed them to a corner table set for two but as they took their seats Dick Kennedy bounded across the room to them.

'Why on earth didn't you tell me you were coming up for dinner first, David? You could have sat with us. Hello, Liz, how are you? Come on over. I'm sure we can squeeze in two more chairs at our table.'

A glance at Liz's face showed David this idea did not appeal to her. 'No, Dick,' he said cheerfully. 'We prefer to dine alone. Remember, we're practically newly weds. We'll join you later, if we may?'

'I understand. Whatever you like, David. See you later, Liz.'

When he was out of earshot, she breathed an audible sigh of relief. David grinned across the table at her. 'I take it you're pleased we won't be joining them until later.'

Her answer was heartfelt. 'Very.'

'So am I,' he assured her. 'Now let's see what's on the menu.'

They discussed the different courses and ordered the meal. To David's dismay, he saw Irene Brennan leave her own table and approach theirs. Without asking permission, she drew up a

190

spare chair and sat down.

'Don't worry, I'm not about to interrupt your meal. I'll go as soon as the starters arrive. I just want to welcome Liz to Fortwilliam. What do you think of it, Liz?'

'I'm very impressed by what I've seen so far.'

'It's a wonderful club. I'm sure David's already told you of all the marvellous times we had here when Victoria was alive.' She smiled sweetly but Liz noticed that there was no warmth in her eyes. Surely she didn't still harbour feelings for him? From what she had heard, all the indications were that Irene and Dick Kennedy would marry.

'He has indeed told me all about your exploits,' Liz cooed sweetly in return.

She could see Irene was surprised. Her eyes narrowed in a calculating way, but she was not to be thwarted. 'Has he told you about the night we all returned to his house and...'

'That will be enough, Irene.' David's voice held a warning and there was a steely glint in his eye. 'Here come our starters. We'll join you later,' he added dismissively.

Slowly, Irene rose to her feet. David may have cowed her for the moment, but there was nevertheless a triumphant look in her eye. She was aware she had touched a sore spot and obviously ruffled his feathers. This gave her great pleasure; she had not forgiven him for neglecting to return her advances. And then he had the cheek to go and marry this young girl! 'You're quite right, David,' she said softly. 'The less said about our past lives the better. See you both later.'

Liz watched her cross the floor and there was a

twinkle in her eye. 'What was that all about, David? What on earth did you get up to?' she teased.

To her amazement he blushed bright red. 'Hey, I don't really want to know,' she said soothingly. 'Everyone has secrets they wouldn't want broadcast.'

The blush slowly left his face but his eyes remained downcast as the waiter placed dishes in front of them. Once he had gone, however, David leant forward and said earnestly, 'It's not what you're thinking, Liz. I can only remember one incident that she could possibly be referring to and it wasn't anything unsavoury or unlawful. Embarrassing, yes. But only because my manly pride was hurt.'

'David, I don't want to know about your past exploits. I myself have done things I would be embarrassed to tell you about. Let's forget Irene and enjoy our meal. This pâté looks delicious.'

'Liz, you are a wonderful, warm, understanding person and one day I'll reveal all my secrets to you. But not yet. It's not the right time.'

'David, I don't want to know all your secrets. Please forget about it.' She felt a bit agitated. Didn't want David unburdening himself. He might expect confidences in return and there was no way she wanted to tell him of her failed attempt at lovemaking with Danny McGowan. She was too ashamed even to think about it.

'You're right, Liz. Irene is just mischief making.'

'All the more reason to ignore her. Come on, forget her and enjoy your meal.'

When they retired to the lounge they were waved over to one of the alcoves. There were two empty places: one beside Irene, and another over by the big panoramic window. To Liz's dismay Irene patted the empty chair beside her, right at the top of the steps leading down to the small dance floor, indicating that Liz should join her.

David apparently didn't see the gesture. Cupping his hands around his wife's elbow, he headed for the empty space at the window. 'You just have to see the lights on the lough, Liz.'

People obligingly moved round the long padded seat until there was enough room for two. With a grateful smile, David waited until Liz was seated then joined her, all the while ignoring the look of chagrin on Irene's face.

He went to the bar to get drinks and Liz gazed out over Belfast Lough. The reflection of the lights on the opposite shoreline swayed with the motion of the tide, and slicing through these jewels, a ferry bedecked with coloured lights headed out towards the North Sea. Lost in the beauty of it, she came back to reality with a start of surprise when a voice spoke close to her ear.

'It's beautiful, isn't it?' the big burly man seated next to her inquired.

'Very beautiful,' she agreed softly, feeling the words were inadequate, but what else could one say?

'Are you all right there, dear? I'm not crushing you, am I?'

'Oh, no, I'm fine. It was kind of you to make room for us.' She gazed into his face and apologized. 'I'm sorry, I'm afraid I don't know many people here and my husband has neglected to introduce us. I'm Liz Atkinson.' She offered him her hand and he clasped it in a great paw.

'I'm Neville Barnes.' His hand tightened around hers and his eyes scanned her face intently. 'Excuse me, but have we met before?'

Liz returned his gaze. His face was broad, with flat cheekbones, bushy grey eyebrows and a large nose. Thin sensitive lips softened its overall harshness. It was not a face one would easily forget. She shook her head. 'No, I don't think so.'

Realizing he was still holding her hand, he abruptly let go and apologized. 'I'm sorry. There's something very familiar about you. Perhaps you've served me in a bank or shop?' He continued to scan her face, a puzzled look in his eyes.

'I've never worked anywhere since I left college except in my husband's factory.' Liz was intrigued; she was certain she had never met this man before, but he seemed convinced that he knew her.

'Never mind, dear. It will come to me eventually. As for your husband not introducing us ... well, he and I have never met.'

David arrived back with the drinks and Liz introduced the two men, smiling slightly at her husband's bemused expression. However, there was no time for explanations as the club captain called for order and the presentation speeches commenced.

After the presentations were made the cabaret

194

started and the patrons were invited to dance. David was very proud of his wife. He knew all the men were eyeing her, and no wonder. The pale grey chiffon dress she wore moulded itself to her fine figure and floated from the thigh to just above her slender ankles. Silver sandals encased her long narrow feet. She was, in his opinion, the best-looking woman there. They danced most dances together, but as David regretfully pointed out, he did have some duty dances to perform. Liz willingly shooed him off, saying she must pay a visit to the loo anyway.

On her arrival back in the lounge she was surprised when Neville asked her to dance with him. She learnt that he was a retired school teacher and had for a while dabbled a bit in politics. He was now retired and a widower. He had only lately joined the club. Since his wife's death, Dick Kennedy, his nephew, invited him when anything good was on.

David passed them on the floor, dancing with Irene. They were deep in conversation and Liz saw that her husband was talking earnestly, a frown on his brow. She saw Irene throw back her head and actually read her lips quite clearly. 'All right. If it's so important to you, I won't say a word to Liz.'

What was David so worried about? Lost in thought, Liz suddenly became aware that Neville was eyeing her covertly. 'Ah! At last the penny has dropped. I know why you are so familiar-looking.'

'You do?'

'You remind me of a girl I once knew. A very

lovely girl. I should have realized straight away. You're her double.'

Taking this as a compliment, Liz said, 'Thank you.' And as the waltz came to an end thanked him once more as he led her from the dance floor.

The night proved most enjoyable. David gently refused an invitation for him and Liz to join Irene and Dick for a nightcap at her home. When at last they waved them off in a taxi, he turned to his wife with a sigh of relief. 'For a minute there I thought she would invite herself down with us for a drink.'

'So did I. I've been standing here with my fingers tightly crossed,' Liz confessed. 'If she had it would have been churlish to refuse.'

'I know. We must thank God for small mercies.' Drawing her arm through his, David led her out of the club grounds. It was a beautiful calm night. A star-studded sky touched the lough and the beauty of it kept Liz speechless.

'A penny for them?' David asked softly.

She turned a startled glance up at him. 'I was admiring the way the stars seem to disappear into the lough. I still haven't got used to the beauty of it.'

'Yes, the pity of it is, once you get used to it, you take it for granted and cease to notice the beauty so close at hand. Liz, did you enjoy yourself tonight?'

'Yes, I did. Very much.'

'Perhaps we can make a habit of it then. When there's a cabaret on?'

'That sounds lovely.' She hesitated, not wanting

to put him on the spot. 'Do you think maybe we could invite Mam along now and again? She would love it.'

'As often as you like, Liz. You know I'm very fond of Kath.'

Danny braced his shoulders before climbing the steps that led to the door of the flat. Would Bridget be here? During his midday break he had asked a mate, the proud owner of a car, to run him down to the Bank Buildings, only to find that Bridget was on her lunch hour and no one knew just where she was. He had left a note for her, begging her forgiveness and saying he hoped to see her tonight at the flat, even if it was only to air their grievances. Even in writing he couldn't profess to love her. At a loss how to sign off, he wrote, 'Yours forever'.

It had been a long tiring day. His head still throbbed from his night of boozing and his limbs felt leaden. He had been in two minds whether or not to go in to work this morning. Lucky for him that he had. His boss had given him a warning, his second, that if he didn't pull up his socks he faced losing his job. With two verbal warnings against him, the next would be written and then out. Only his track record of good time-keeping up until his marriage had saved him so far. There were hundreds on the dole who would willingly step into his shoes. Imagine letting a woman reduce him to this level. Especially since that same woman was currently swanning about, dressed to kill, in a big Jag. She seemed to have forgotten he existed. Well, he had at last come to his senses. He would show her how little he cared.

This was the reason he needed Bridget back. He had to get himself on an even keel. Become a good family man. To his dismay his hand shook when he placed the key in the lock. Nerves? Or was he more dependent on the drink than he knew? Oh, God, he had been such a fool. Lamenting after what he couldn't have and making his wife miserable. If he couldn't persuade her to return to him what would he do? And she would be right to refuse. Hadn't he treated her like dirt? He wouldn't want to stay in this flat on his own. Neither did he fancy the idea of living in Dunlewey Street again. That was if his ma would even let him back. Everybody would be pitying him and there was no way he could put up with that.

After he had passed out the night before, Peter had gone down to let Bridget know that he was all right. He had relayed a message back to Danny before leaving for work this morning. She was glad that he was all right but had no intention of going back to the flat. Her parents were backing her to the hilt, and she would remain with them until after the birth. Then she would decide what to do. Peter had called him all kinds of a fool, saying a lot of men would be glad to take on a lovely girl like her, baby and all. In his heart Danny agreed with him. He must win Bridget back and make a determined effort to save his marriage.

In the hall a tantalizing aroma assailed his nostrils, making his mouth water. A sigh of relief issued softly from his lips; Bridget was here. Danny had eaten little the past two days and now realized just how hungry he was. He squared his shoulders, preparing to eat humble pie as well.

He walked slowly towards the kitchen, hoping she would come out and meet him halfway. She didn't, and that in itself was an ominous sign. Bridget didn't usually hold a grudge. She must really be mad at him and determined to get her pound of flesh. Well, he was prepared to do anything to win her back. In the kitchen doorway he came to an abrupt halt and gaped at the figure at the stove, turning something over in the pan.

'What the hell are you doing here?' he thundered.

The young man turning to face him was tall with pale blonde hair and slightly built. How come Danny hadn't noticed before how effeminate Ian Geddis was? No wonder Bridget had said all those awful things...

Ian's voice was mild when he replied, 'Since your wife didn't see fit to come home to cook you a meal, I thought I'd rustle up something tasty. I didn't think you'd mind. I thought we were friends?'

Knowing full well he had encouraged this young man to make himself at home in the flat – had even, to spite Bridget's outrage, given him a key – Danny was at a loss for words. But not for long. If he had given this lad the wrong impression, which his wife had accused him of doing, he must put matters right. He had been dumbfounded when Bridget had hinted maybe he also was that way inclined; that it was perhaps why he now showed so little affection towards her. How could she think anything like that about him?

'This is very thoughtful of you, Ian, but it's totally unnecessary. My wife will be returning soon, and I'm afraid...' He hesitated, not knowing how to let Ian down lightly. 'In her present condition she has taken a dislike to you.' He shrugged and stretched his arms wide in apology.

'Well, we can't expect everybody to love us, eh, Danny?' Ian's shoulders rose and fell philosophically. 'Still, there's enough food here for two and it would be a shame to let it go to waste. Since it looks like Bridget isn't coming right away, can I join you? After all, what she doesn't know she can't grieve over. Isn't that right, Danny? We all have our little secrets.'

He waited expectantly, a smile playing around his full-lipped mouth. Danny found himself nodding in agreement. He could only hope Bridget would not arrive until Ian went back upstairs to his own flat.

Hungry though he was, he found the food stuck in his throat. Was his guilty conscience making him imagine there were hidden innuendos in Ian's words? Desperately he tried to remember the events of two nights ago when he'd walked out of the flat in a huff and, ascending the stairs, spent the night in the flat above. Ian had had some home-brew; strong stuff. They had drunk a lot, and in a maudlin mood Danny had told his friend how he came to marry Bridget though he still loved Liz. He distinctly remembered Ian's reply. 'All women are treacherous. Many a man doesn't even like women but finds himself trapped into a loveless marriage by one.'

He had seemed so understanding, sitting there close beside Danny on the settee, giving his thigh a comforting pat now and again. The next morning he had found himself naked in bed in the spare room.

He had thought nothing of it at the time, but now he was terrified. Could anything have happened? Surely there would be some indication? He glanced across the table at his companion and found amused pale blue eyes watching him.

'I'm glad we're friends, Danny,' Ian said softly, his voice a caress. 'I realize you're committed to your wife, but as I say, what she doesn't know won't hurt her. Eh, Danny?'

Slowly, Danny rose to his feet. He must put a stop to this once and for all. Hands pressed firmly on the table, he leant across and ground out through clenched teeth, 'If you're insinuating what I think you are...'

'Insinuating, Danny? Man, but you've a short memory. But never fear, your secret is safe with me.'

These words brought terror to Danny's heart. He hoped his face did not betray how horrified he felt. 'Get out of my flat! And don't ever come back. Do you hear me?'

Eyes still glittering with suppressed laughter, Ian lifted his empty plate. 'I'm finished anyway. I'm sorry you didn't enjoy yours. Perhaps next time?'

'There won't be a next time. I want nothing

201

more to do with you. Just leave that plate there and get out.'

A slight shrug of the shoulders showed Ian's indifference and placing the plate back on the table lifted a hand in salute before heading for the door.

'And – you can leave the key on the hall table on your way out.'

'I'll do that, Danny. But you don't really mean all this. I know you're upset at the moment, but when you've had time to think it over, you know where to find me again.'

Danny didn't like the way he emphasized *again*. What on earth had happened between them?

As he climbed the stairs to his own flat, Ian grinned in triumph. The look on Danny Mc-Gowan's face had been so comical, he'd found it hard to hide his mirth. Serve him right! It was disgraceful the way he was treating that young wife of his. Maybe now he would show her the respect she deserved. Although he knew Bridget viewed him with suspicion, Ian was nevertheless fond of the young girl caught in a loveless marriage. If putting the fear of God into Danny helped to better their marriage, he was content. He couldn't help the way he was, but if Danny only knew it, he wasn't Ian's cup of tea at all. He laughed gently as he let himself into the flat. He would let Danny stew for a while, and then, if he seemed unduly worried, confess he had conned him.

202

Chapter Four

Bridget looked down on the crumpled features of her newborn son and her heart swelled with pride. She'd produced this beautiful wee creature. Her, Bridget McGowan! The wonder of it filled her with awe. It hadn't been easy. Far from it! But worth all the pain and suffering. After many long hours in labour, fearful for the life of the child, the midwife had decided enough was enough and had summoned the doctor. He arrived soon after and agreed with the midwife that Bridget was too exhausted to push the baby into the world without some assistance. An ambulance was quickly on the scene and she was whisked away. At the hospital it was thought the time for forceps was long past and she had been sedated. Her son was delivered by caesarean section.

This was her first sight of him. Washed and wrapped warmly in a blanket, he nuzzled about, seeking her breast. The young nurse who had brought him to her said, 'He's hungry. Let's try him at the nipple.' Directing his mouth to the breast, she teased him until the tiny rosebud mouth at last got the message and clamped itself on to the nipple. The small crumpled face grimaced at first then instinct took over and he sucked happily. 'There now ... isn't he a grand wee lad? He knows his way about already. I'll leave you to get on with it. If he still seems hungry when he's finished there, put him to the other side. I'll be back soon to see how you're getting on.'

With a bright smile the nurse bustled away. Bridget hugged her son close as he suckled contentedly. His head was bald except for a slight fuzz of tawny hair. She knew from experience, having been in close contact with her sister's children, that he would probably lose this hair and become dark like her husband and herself.

Anxiously she watched the door of the ward, waiting to see Danny's first reaction to this wonderful gift God had given them. He was the first visitor through the door and she smiled happily at him as he approached the bed. 'Isn't he lovely?'

'Yes, he's beautiful. I saw him earlier. Just after he was born.' He touched his son's head gently. 'I must admit, he looks much better now he's been washed.'

'Have you given any more thought as to what we'll name him, Danny?'

His grin was wide as he mocked her. 'I suppose one of those many names you've been reeling off every night in bed for the last few weeks. The big question is, which one?'

Her face was one big beam. Since her return to the flat, Danny had been a model husband. Her every wish was carefully considered and, if possible, carried out. He had even managed the promised weekend in Dublin at Easter. Now she said, diffidently, 'I still favour Martin. What do you think? Martin Daniel?'

His hand gently touched hers. 'That's fine by me.' He would agree to anything she said to make up for the hell he'd put her through in the past few months.

'Ah, Danny, I do love you.'

'You weren't so sure of that a couple of months ago when you left me high and dry,' he reminded her.

'I know. I know that. But you were such a pig, I just had to get away from you.'

Laughter filled his eyes and his words as he accused her, 'What if I had been that way inclined, as you so quaintly put it, and turned to Ian for comfort. Eh? What would you have done then?'

Neither of them had noticed a figure approach the bed. 'Who's taking my name in vain?' Ian quipped as he laid a big bunch of flowers beside Bridget.

'Thank you, Ian. They're lovely, so they are. You shouldn't spoil me the way you do.'

'Don't let any of my close friends hear you say that, Bridget McGowan. Me, spoiling a woman? Why, I'd never hear the end of it.'

She laughed outright at these words. It was great that they could talk about him without giving offence. Ian had become a close friend. Still, it was a shame he was that way inclined; in her opinion he'd make some girl a wonderful husband. She had discreetly slipped the child from her breast and quickly covered herself up on his arrival. Luckily, the baby seemed sated and did not kick up a racket at being deprived of his food. Now she gestured towards her precious

205

bundle. 'Here, hold him, Danny. Let Ian have a proper look at him.'

Gingerly, Danny lifted his son from his wife's arms and Ian moved around the bed to peer closely at him. 'He's a handsome wee devil, so he is. He must take after you, Bridget. I can't see anything of his da in him,' he teased.

Bridget looked in gratitude at this young man who had become so much a part of their lives. 'Thank you, Ian. Thanks for all your help.'

'I second that, Ian,' Danny volunteered. 'You've been a true friend.'

Aware that he had helped them over a sticky patch in their marriage, Ian shrugged off their gratitude. 'It's nice to have friends who take you at face value,' he said, 'The pleasure's all mine. Who would have thought that we'd become so close, eh?'

Remembering the night he had ordered him out of the flat, Danny agreed dryly. 'Who indeed?'

Giving him a roguish grin, Ian teased, 'Of course, you and I might have become even closer, Danny, if I'd played my cards right, eh?'

'Don't even joke about it, mate. You had me in a right old state for a while,' Danny laughed. A glance down the ward and his voice changed, becoming lifeless. 'Here's your ma and da, Bridget. There's only two allowed at the bed at a time so Ian and I will wait outside in the corridor for a while.'

He nodded politely at Barney and Martha. Then, thrusting the baby into his mother-in-law's arms, left the bedside followed by Ian. Bridget

206

gazed after them and her spirits sank a little. The nursing staff weren't all that strict. He could have delayed a few minutes to see the proud look on the faces of her parents at this first view of their new grandchild. How much easier life would be if only her dad and husband could be friends, but it looked very unlikely. Perhaps the baby would prove a stepping stone to better relationships, she hoped fervently.

Martha gazed at the baby for long seconds then exclaimed, 'He must take after Danny's side of the family. He doesn't resemble any of ours when they were young.' Her eyes anxiously scanned her daughter's face and she asked gently, 'How are you, love?'

'I'm fine, Mam. Really I am!' At her father's sceptical look she stressed, 'Danny has been very good to me.' Her eyes beseeched him to believe her.

'Hmm! Let's hope he continues that way. You'll be depending on him a lot, stuck out there on the Antrim Road with a baby to look after.'

Martha looked at her husband reproachfully. Why couldn't he keep his big mouth shut? Let well enough alone. 'She looks great, so she does, considering she's just delivered this wee fellow. And by caesarean section too. You must be sore, love. Have you decided what to call him yet?'

'Martin.'

'That's a very nice name. Will you be able to manage all right when you leave here, love? You'll have to be very careful, you know. Your stitches will take a while healing. If only you weren't so far away from us, we could help you over the next couple of weeks until you get your strength back...'

'It's OK, Mam. I'll manage.'

'No matter what your ma says to the contrary, Bridget, I think you look worn out,' Barney said. 'You'd be wise to come to us for a few weeks, wouldn't she, Martha, until she's on her feet again?' he suggested.

'I don't think that would be a good idea, so I don't, Dad. Danny has arranged to take a week of his holidays. I should be well on the mend by the time he goes back to work.'

'Well, I think...'

His wife interrupted him. 'Let it be, Barney. They must do as they see fit. Here's Jane and Joe,' she added warningly as Danny's parents and Peter came into the ward.

Jane looked on her first grandchild and back at Bridget, a wide grin on her face. 'You've done well, love, I have to admit that. He's a bonny baby.'

Joe and Peter agreed with her, and Jane haltingly asked if she could hold the baby for a wee minute.

'You can indeed.' Martha carefully handed over the precious bundle. 'As a matter of fact, we're just going. Have you any dirty clothes I can wash for you, Bridget?' she asked.

'Yes, Mam.' She gestured towards the bedside locker. 'There's some in there in a carrier bag that need washing. Thanks, Mam. It will save Danny having to take them home.'

Martha removed the bag of washing. 'I'll be back tonight with the rest of the clan, Bridget.

Meanwhile they all send their best regards.' She smiled as her eyes passed over the rest of them. And I'm sure I'll see you lot soon. There'll be a christening to look forward to now.'

Barney raised his hand in farewell. ''Bye, everybody.'

They trooped from the ward and Peter moved closer to the bed and presented Bridget with the big bunch of flowers he had been clutching to his breast. To her consternation, his eyes openly admired her, slowly moving over her face and lingering where cleavage showed at the top of her nightdress. Although he visited the flat regularly, it was a long time since they had been alone together. Unable to trust her feelings towards him, she had made sure of that. She'd had no reason to complain at his attitude towards her. He had been the helpful brother-in-law, no more, no less. So the odd moments when she felt low and could have been vulnerable to his attraction had passed without incident.

Now this apparent renewal of interest made her wary. His parents were fully occupied with their new grandchild and it was as if she and he were alone together. She remembered the great pull there had been between them not so long ago, when she had actually wished that Peter was her husband and the father of her unborn child. She knew that with very little effort at the time, in her unhappiness, she could easily have succumbed to the strong emotional attraction between them. Thanks be to God nothing had come of it. It was all over and done with. How could she have been so stupid? She was happy now with Danny, and nothing and no one must be allowed to spoil things between them. Her son would be her main concern from now on. To divert Peter's attention she thanked him for the flowers and asked, 'Where's Joseph?'

He smiled slightly and replied, 'He's outside with Danny, waiting his turn to come in. I couldn't wait any longer to see you and your son, Bridget, so I decided to risk the wrath of the nursing staff. You're looking very pretty, if I may say so. Motherhood obviously agrees with you.' He leant closer and whispered for her ears only, 'Remember, I'm here if you ever need me.'

Colour tinged her cheeks and she tried to form words to put him off once and for all without giving offence, but none would come.

He put her out of her misery. 'I'm only teasing, Bridget. It's obvious you're very happy, and I for one am glad to see it.'

Outside in the corridor Barney stopped in front of his son-in-law and diffidently offered his hand. Danny could be a contrary devil at the best of times and he wasn't sure how his overture would be received but he'd decided for the sake of his daughter and grandson to try and put an end to their enmity. None of his uncertainty appeared on his face as he greeted him. 'Congratulations, Danny. That's a fine son you have in there. Do you think maybe you and I could bury the hatchet once and for all?'

Martha's mouth gaped slightly as she took in the scene before her. Barney Kelly offering a truce to Danny McGowan? If she hadn't seen it

210

with her own eyes, she wouldn't have believed it. Silently she prayed that Danny would receive the olive branch. Taken aback, he just sat there gazing up at the big man before him, waiting for the catch line. Then slowly he rose and reaching out, grasped the proffered hand.

'That's fine by me, Mr Kelly.' He smiled wryly. 'We might never become friends, but I don't see why we can't at least agree to differ.' He gestured towards Ian. 'This is one of our neighbours, Ian Geddis. He lives in the flat above us and has been very good to Bridget and me. Ian, this is Bridget's father and mother.'

Martha moved closer and exclaimed with a wide smile, 'I've heard all about you.'

'Oh, have you? I hope it's not all bad.' Ian's voice was cool. When people greeted him with apparent prior knowledge of him, he always thought the worst. Most times he was right and found himself open to innuendos or snide remarks.

'Yes, our Bridget thinks the world of you and I'm very pleased to make your acquaintance.'

At these words he relaxed. 'And I'm happy to meet any family of Bridget's. She's a fine person.'

Barney eyed him speculatively. He knew a queer when he saw one, but did not hold it against them. In his opinion, there but for the grace of God... He offered his hand. 'Pleased to meet you, son,' he said cordially.

Danny successfully hid his surprise. He would have thought Barney Kelly heartily averse to shaking hands with a homosexual. Just went to

211

show how wrong you could be. Tentatively, he offered, 'Feel free to visit your grandson at the flat, any time you feel like it.'

'Oh, that would be wonderful, Danny.' Martha felt tears of relief sting her eyes. 'Bridget will need plenty of help in the coming months. When you go back to work, I'll pop over as often as I can.'

'We'll be glad of any help we can get.'

'Great! That's great. See you soon, son.'

It was a month before Liz and David got around to going back to the golf club. Pressure at work had slackened off as new stitchers settled into a routine and proved that they were capable of the high-class work required of them. Soon the renovated building would be ready to house more workers and interviews would start again, but meanwhile, David and Liz could relax. He was in his glory. They were making money hand over fist.

Another presentation of golf trophies was taking place on Saturday evening and a well-known group was booked to supply the entertainment. Dick Kennedy phoned and asked them along as his guests. When David mentioned that Liz would like to invite her mother along, Dick assured him he would be happy to renew her acquaintance.

Having received a very definite no to her invitation but determined that her mother should reconsider and accompany them, Liz, now the proud owner of a Morris Minor, called on her to persuade her. Kath seemed a bit down in spirits, and to her daughter's surprise, still flatly refused to go.

'Mam, it will cheer you up no end to get out and about a bit. You're a young woman. I thought you would be delighted to come along with us?'

'Me go to a golf club? You've got to be joking, Liz. I'd stick out like a sore thumb, so I would.'

'Why would you, Mam? They're just ordinary people like you and me and David.'

'Let's face it, Liz, David's upper-class – and as for you, well, I always told you, you've good blood in you and it shows. You would be at home anywhere. But me, I'm just a middle-aged stick-in-the-mud. I'd feel all out of place there.'

Knowing how her mother hated to upset David, Liz stressed, 'David will be very disappointed if you don't come.'

'Ah, Liz, don't make it awkward for me. I'd rather not go, love. My dancing days are over. Besides, who would dance with me?'

'For a start, David.'

'Liz, there's no way I'm going to act as gooseberry, so just forget it.'

'For heaven's sake, Mam, he and I are married! There's no question of you playing gooseberry.' Kath opened her mouth to protest, but with a raised hand Liz stopped her. Afraid to put her mother off by saying that in her opinion she would not lack for partners, she continued, 'If you're worried about dancing, well, you won't be the only one not doing it, you know. You won't have to. Nobody will force you on to the floor. We can have a meal and then just sit in the lounge. We can enjoy listening to the group and watch

213

the dancers. OK?'

Her mother still looked undecided but when she said fretfully, 'What will I wear?' Liz knew she had won her over.

Breathing a sigh of relief, she said, 'Your birthday is coming up soon so I'll treat you to a new dress. Now no more excuses. Tomorrow I will take a couple of hours off work and we'll go shopping.' She was glad her mother had agreed to go with them. She was becoming a regular hermit stuck in the house, her only outing being to and from work. She was too young to retire from the outside world. Who knows? Perhaps she might even become attracted to one of the bachelors or widowers who frequented Fortwilliam Golf Club.

Saturday came all too soon for Kath. David had been very complimentary about her appearance when he picked her up at home. Liz had seconded it all when they arrived back at the bungalow. Still, Kath found she was somewhat nervous when some twenty minutes later she climbed the stairway to the restaurant in Fortwilliam. It was a beautiful place, she had to admit. It was even grander than she'd expected and she only hoped she wouldn't let David down. She felt well out of her depth in these surroundings.

She got through the delicious meal without using the wrong piece of cutlery or dropping gravy down the front of the new dress Liz had insisted on buying her. It was the loveliest Kath had ever possessed. And so it should be! Her daughter had paid a small fortune for it. In soft blues and mauves, it brought out the delicate fairness of Kath's skin and new hair do, and the fitted top and billowing skirt showed off the slimness of her. She felt elegant and pretty wearing it. But was she just mutton dressed as lamb? She had always been conservative when purchasing clothes. There was no way she would have bought this dress if Liz had not been with her and insisted she looked lovely in it. Anyhow, she couldn't have afforded it.

After dinner they retired to the lounge, and with a couple of brandies inside her Kath relaxed and resolved to enjoy herself. She had always loved dancing but, concentrating on rearing her daughter, had had to forgo that pleasure.

However, Liz's father had been a keen ballroom dancer and during their affair had encouraged her to take lessons from a professional. Since he was footing the bill she was only too willing to please him. Thus, when David took her to the floor for a slow foxtrot she was delighted to find that her steps were as sure as ever.

He swung her expertly in and out of the other dancers and she followed him faultlessly. Glancing down at her, he was full of praise. 'Why on earth were you so nervous? You're a marvellous dancer.'

She blushed slightly at his words. 'It's been a long time. I thought I might have forgotten how.'

'After this exhibition, I bet you'll be bombarded with requests for a dance.'

Startled, she cried out, 'Oh, no. I couldn't possibly dance with strangers.'

'Whatever you wish, Kath. But it would be foolish to sit it out because I can tell you're enjoying it, and you'd soon get to know your partners. I hope you don't think me impertinent ... but would you not like to meet someone you could be happy with?'

'Oh, I'm too old now for all that nonsense, David.'

'I don't agree with you there. You're far from too old. You and I are of an age, remember, and I don't consider myself old. If I can be happy with Liz, why not you with someone else?'

'I made a stupid mistake a long time ago and it's too late even to think I might meet another man. All my life has been devoted to caring for Liz. I've forgotten how to make small talk with a man. It would be a waste of time trying to interest someone in an old fogey like me.'

'Now you're being foolish, Kath. If you're asked for a dance, at least don't refuse. If you don't like them they'll soon get the message and leave you alone. Promise me you won't turn down a request offhand?'

To please him she agreed to give it a go. After all, no one else was likely to ask her to dance, surely? She was wrong. When the music started up again, Dick Kennedy approached her. 'May I have the pleasure of this waltz, Kath?'

About to refuse him, she caught David's nod of approval and, remembering her promise to give it a go, allowed Dick to lead her on to the dance floor.

Dick looked down on thick pale blonde hair that was swept back off a face that was as yet

216

barely lined, and wondered why he hadn't followed up his first meeting with this attractive woman. Of course, at the time, glad that David was out of the picture, he'd been hell-bent on pursuing Irene. As a matter of fact, he was still pursuing her. Everybody was expecting their engagement to be announced, but Irene kept putting off naming the day.

Embarrassed at his scrutiny, Kath missed a step, and tutted. Annoyed at herself for letting him embarrass her, she apologized tersely.

'My fault,' Dick said gallantly.

'Too right it is! Why are you staring at me like that? Anyone would think we were meeting for the first time.'

A twinkle lit his eyes. 'I'm sorry. I didn't realize I was staring. It's just that I'd forgotten how lovely you are.'

'Oh, come off it, Dick! Don't talk such rubbish. You don't have to make small talk, you know. Let's just enjoy the music and dance, eh?'

He laughed aloud. 'You're a girl after my own heart, Kath. I like someone who calls a spade a spade. Nevertheless, I just have to say it – you are very attractive, you know.'

She could tell that he was sincere and colour flooded her cheeks. 'Give over. Please? You're embarrassing me.'

He smiled and drew her closer. The dance continued in silence. Very much aware of his body brushing hers as he guided her around the floor, she wondered about him. She had heard all about Dick and Irene from Liz. But as far as she could make out, it seemed a very one-sided affair. For instance, tonight Irene appeared bored. Was she always like this, sitting with a pained expression on her face? True, she was lovely to look at, and rich into the bargain. If that was all Dick was after perhaps she was worth grovelling to.

To Kath's great consternation when they returned to the company, in answer to her smile, Irene gave her a frosty look and ignored Dick altogether. With a smile of thanks to Kath, he took the chair next to Irene and, putting his lips close to her ear, whispered, 'What's the matter? You're sitting there with a face like a Lurgan spade.'

'Nothing. What would be the matter?'

Abashed, he slumped down in his chair. He was finding it increasingly difficult to please her these days. Did he want to go through life like this?

An interval was called and the musical group put aside their instruments and retired to the bar as the presentation was about to take place. During the speeches Dick had difficulty keeping his eyes off Kath. She was very young-looking to be the mother of Liz.

Under cover of the table, a hand was placed on his thigh and fingers dug viciously into the flesh. He turned to find Irene glaring at him. 'Will you kindly remember I'm your partner here tonight?' she hissed.

Annoyed, he retorted, 'Perhaps you'd remember that and dance with me now and again.'

Her nostrils flared in disdain. 'We shall leave straight after the presentation.'

This got him angry. 'I'm sorry, Irene, but if you

218

leave, you go alone. I happen to be enjoying myself. I shall, of course, call a taxi for you.'

Her mouth gaped slightly as she took in his words. How dare he? He was actually putting this stranger in front of her.

'I've had enough. I'm going now.' She was so incensed she forgot the speeches were under way and stormed across the lounge in the middle of the captain's address. Embarrassed apologies dripping from his lips, Dick followed.

'I beg your pardon, Captain. Please forgive us. Irene is feeling unwell.'

He caught up with her at the top of the stairs and, gripping her by the elbow, brought her to a standstill. Aware that they were attracting the attention of those standing near the bar, he urged her down the stairs. At the bottom, in the privacy of the deserted hall, they faced each other. Angrily she pulled herself free from his grasp and glared at him.

It was Dick who spoke first. 'What on earth has got into you, Irene?'

'You actually don't know?'

'No. I'm quite mystified, if you must know.'

'You made a spectacle of yourself on the dance floor with that common little woman, and you wonder why I'm so upset?'

His brows drew together angrily. 'Kath O'Hara is far from common. She's a lady and a terrific dancer, if you must know.'

'If that's how you feel, go back to her. Go on. I can look after myself.'

'I'll walk you home.'

He sounded resigned, and this angered her

further. 'No, thank you. I'd much rather go by taxi.'

He shrugged slightly. 'If that's what you want.' Going to the pay phone under the stairs, he rang for a cab. When he rejoined Irene, she had retrieved her coat and was waiting by the door, looking quite miserable.

Never before had he seen her look so vulnerable and it touched his heart. 'I'm coming with you.'

'There isn't any need. I don't want to take you away from your friends.'

'I want to, Irene. I really do.'

His reward was a wobbly smile and he detected tears glistening in her eyes. 'Ah, Irene. You know it's only you I care for.'

'I'm very glad to hear that, Dick. Very glad indeed.'

The taxi arrived and as he followed her outside his heart soared. Had a bit of jealousy done the trick and made her realize she cared? Was tonight the night?

The speeches dragged on for a long time and Kath had difficulty hiding her boredom. Whispering her excuses, she made her way around the edge of the hall and headed for the ladies' powder room.

As she left the lounge a hand on her arm brought her to a standstill. Surprised, she raised her eyes to the hand's owner. The breath caught in her throat and she almost collapsed.

'What on earth are you doing here?' asked the voice that had once thrilled her to the bone.

Kath gazed into a face from the past. One that used to make her go weak at the knees, and had difficulty finding her tongue. 'The same reason as you, I would imagine,' she at last managed to say dryly, and pulling her arm free proceeded to the cloakroom. It was empty and she stood for some moments drawing deep breaths into her lungs, gazing in the mirror at a face devoid of colour. This would be the last time she would visit Fortwilliam Golf Club, that was for sure. Neville Barnes had ruined her life. He must not find out that Liz was his daughter. Under no circumstances must Liz find out he was her father.

Neville Barnes stood at the landing window and stared blindly through its reflections at the Cave Hill. He was having difficulty believing the evidence of his own eyes. Kath O'Hara here? It was a long time since he had last set eyes on her. They moved in different circles. By God, she hardly looked a day older. He examined his own reflection in the window. Even the blurred image he found wanting. About two stone heavier, jowls drooping, heavily lined. It was a wonder she had recognized him. He certainly had changed.

But then, he was much older than Kath. She had been a slip of a girl when they first met and he was in his forties. She had been like a breath of spring, bubbling over with life and vitality. He had been contented in his marriage, had never strayed before, but the attraction between them had been electric and in spite of being quite happily married he had been unable to resist the

221

magic of her. He'd pursued her relentlessly, over-coming her scruples when she discovered he already had a wife and family. For months they had been gloriously happy. It had been a long hot summer and whenever he could get away, they had lain on sandy beaches on Donegal's coastline and dined in out-of-the-way pubs. He had even managed the odd weekend in classy hotels.

He remembered the shock he'd received when she confessed she was pregnant. She'd been so happy; sure he would leave his wife and family and live with her. But how could he? Give up his job as headmaster of a prestigious boys' school? He couldn't have stayed on in the job if he had left his wife. She was on the board of governors, would have hounded him out. And there was the boys to think about. They were doing their exams. It would have ruined everyone's lives.

He remembered the hurt and pain etched on Kath's face when he'd at last convinced her it just wasn't on. He admitted to being all the low names she called him but was adamant that his family must come first. She'd refused to have an abortion, prepared to give up all they had to-gether sooner than kill an innocent baby. He'd tried to persuade her that as yet it wasn't a person but she'd insisted from the moment of conception a soul was there and she would not murder it. That had been the end of their affair. She had refused to see him ever again.

Over the years, as far as money was concerned, he'd done his best for her and his daughter. The only condition he'd laid down was that no one must ever know he was the father of the child.

Thinking it was for the best, he had refused ever to meet his young daughter. When money was needed for her education it was all handled by his solicitor. He now realized that had been a mistake. He should have kept in touch. For a moment he wondered how his daughter looked now. She'd be twenty-three.

Suddenly, like a bolt from the blue, he knew why Kath was here. She was with that young girl he had found so familiar. In due course he'd realized she resembled his old flame but not once had it crossed his mind she might be his own daughter.

To her great dismay, when she left the cloakroom Kath saw Neville standing gazing out at the Cave Hill. Obviously he was waiting for her. She looked around her in blind panic. There was a door to her right. Where did it lead? The restaurant? She didn't know. Only one route seemed open to her. There was no way she could elude him. He was lost in thought and she endeavoured to slip past unnoticed, but he became aware of her and stepped back into her path.

'Kath, let me talk to you. Please? Can I get you a drink?'

'I'm with company, Neville. I would prefer they didn't know we were once acquainted.'

'While I've been waiting for you I've had time to think. I wondered why Liz Atkinson looked so familiar to me, and now I know. You're here with her. She's my daughter, isn't she?'

Kath's face paled in outrage. 'You've a cheek, so you have. She's *my* daughter,' she whispered furiously. 'All these years you've never once asked her name or how she was getting on. Now you have the cheek to call her yours! She has no idea who her father is and as far as I'm concerned she never will.' Scorn dripped from her lips as she derided him. 'Why, you're not worth knowing, so you're not!'

Neville's brows drew together and he growled, 'None of this changes the fact that she's my daughter. And whether you like it or not, she has the right to know I'm her father.'

Kath felt gutted. How dare he, after all these years? She drew a deep breath. At all costs she must keep her cool. 'Look, Neville, because you deserted me when I most needed you, Liz has never shown any desire to find out about you. If she had, I wouldn't have tried to stop her, but she didn't. She's happy as she is. Let her be. I've never asked a lot from you, but now I beg you not to tell her who you are.'

Her eyes beseeched him but he was loath to give in. 'Let me get you a drink and we can at least talk about it,' he reasoned.

'And how am I going to explain having a drink with a stranger, eh?' The speeches were obviously over as people were heading for the bar and toilets. They were attracting curious glances. 'I'm trusting you to do the decent thing, Neville.' With these words Kath brushed past him and went to join her daughter and son-in-law.

She was ill at ease the rest of the evening, but to her relief Neville left her alone. Then, just before one o'clock, he joined them.

He was obviously on friendly terms with Liz

224

and David. Imagine Liz drinking and laughing and talking with him, never dreaming he was her father. 'Where have you been all night, Neville?' David greeted him cordially.

'I came in late and stayed in the games room.' He gazed at Kath. 'This must surely be Liz's mother? Liz is the picture of her.'

'Yes, this is Kath O'Hara. Kath, meet Neville Barnes.'

Reluctantly, she took the big hand thrust in her direction. It trembled within his grasp and she tried to release it.

Smiling at her nervousness, Neville bowed low over her hand and held her eye. 'I think they're about to play the last dance. Would you do me the honour?'

With ill grace, she snatched her hand away and rose abruptly to her feet. Aware of the startled gaze of her daughter, she preceded him on to the floor. Once out of earshot, she hissed, 'How dare you? I told you I didn't want them to find out I know you.'

'And they won't, if you stop acting so stupid.'

'I may have been stupid when I was young and gullible. Stupid enough then to think you loved me? But I'm not that young foolish girl any-more.'

'No, I realize that. You have grown into a very attractive woman. There's no reason why we can't be friends, Kath. If you come here with them on a regular basis we can at least have a few dances. It won't do any harm and I promise not to reveal any secrets to Liz.'

'That's blackmail, so it is. I won't come back

here ever again.'

'I usually have a dance with Liz, you know, and we've become quite friendly. How will I be able to control my tongue, if you're not here to keep an eye on me?'

'I hate you! But that's nothing new. I've hated you for a long time, Neville Barnes.'

He gazed down into her flushed angry face and felt a stirring of the old passion. They'd been everything to each other for a while. If he could win her over there was no reason they couldn't at least be friends, perhaps even learn to care again. Amazed at the direction of his thoughts he gripped her closer. Her body stiffened and she glared up at him. With a wry smile he loosened his hold on her. The touch of her body against his brought back memories of their fiery lovemaking. A shiver of pleasure trembled through him at the thought. It was a long time since he'd felt like this. It would be pleasant indeed to spend some time with her. Who knew were it might lead?

'Has no one told you that hate is akin to love, Kath? And ... did you know my wife died eighteen months ago?' His voice was like a caress and she drew back in horror.

'Not my hate!' she whispered vehemently. 'And why should I be in the least bit interested whether your wife is alive or dead?' As the music drew to a close she quickly escaped his arms and made her way back to the table. She wished she'd never heard of Fortwilliam Golf Club. Meeting him again was upsetting her no end.

Neville followed her back to the table. 'Thank you very much, Kath. I enjoyed that. Perhaps you'll do me the honour again, the next time you're here?'

She smiled falsely at him and made no response. She had no desire to come back. But could she trust him not to carry out his threat if she didn't?

Unperturbed, he sat down and when last orders were called, accepted David's offer of a drink.

Sensing her mother was disturbed, Liz moved closer to her and whispered, 'What's wrong, Mam? He didn't chance his arm, did he?'

Kath gazed at her in surprise. 'I'd break it if he did,' she exclaimed scornfully.

Liz laughed at these words. Good old Mam! 'Then why are you in such a state?'

'What state am I in? There's nothing wrong with me.'

Liz didn't believe her, but couldn't think why she was so annoyed. When Kath stayed overnight at the bungalow, Liz accompanied her to the Little Flower Oratory to Mass on a morning. Although she didn't mention it to David, she missed attending church and was glad to accompany her mother. She decided to wait until the following day and as they returned from Mass question her further.

When the lights were dimmed and the steward started to circle the room, diplomatically asking guests to drink up and leave the premises, Neville disappeared towards the games room. Relieved, Kath shrugged into her coat and casually drifted towards the door, eager to be shot of him.

David's voice stopped her. 'Hold on a moment, Kath. It's raining and Neville is sharing our taxi.

He lives a few streets from us.'

She turned aside, tears threatening to snap her tightly strung composure. Was there no end to this night?

The taxi arrived and David climbed in beside the driver, leaving the two women to share the back seat with Neville. He handed Liz into the car first and then Kath. Squeezing in beside her, he exclaimed, 'Maybe this isn't such a good idea, girls. I'm squashing you.' He slipped his arm along the back of the seat as if to afford more room but eased his body closer still against Kath's. 'There ... that's better.'

'Don't worry about it. We can suffer a bit of discomfort for a few minutes, Neville,' Liz laughingly assured him, from her safe seat against the other door.

He smiled in the dimness of the cab, remembering other back seats shared with Kath. Peering closely into her averted face, he wondered if she was also remembering?

'Fancy coming in for a coffee, Neville?'

David's voice floating from the front seat made Kath start with dismay. About to decline, Neville felt her reaction to the idea and changed his mind. 'That would be lovely, David, if it's not too late?' He had pursued Kath O'Hara once and won her. Why not again? He intended to cultivate his daughter's friendship and Kath would have to get used to him being around.

'We always have a nightcap,' David assured him. 'You're very welcome to join us.'

His plans soon came awry. In the hall Kath pleaded fatigue and begged to be excused. Liz watched in bewilderment as, avoiding Neville's eye, her mother bade them good night and retired to her room.

Kath sat fully clothed on her bed and listened to the deep drone of Neville's voice. It brought unwanted memories flooding back to torture her. There was a time when that voice had blinded her to any sense of responsibility. She had ignored the fact that he had a wife and children. She had lain in his arms and listened to all his endearments, and thought nothing mattered as long as they were together. All that had changed when she fell pregnant. Then she had been ashamed at her own wantonness. He had just been using her for his own lustful ends.

Now she tried to recapture some of the emotion of long ago but there was nothing there. It didn't seem possible but it was true. Perhaps if he had sought her out when his wife had died they might have salvaged something of the past, but to have the audacity to think he could just waltz back into her life like this ... words to describe his cheek failed her. Probably now he knew how well Liz had turned out and what a lovely person she was, he thought he could have the best of both worlds. Any man would be proud to call her his daughter. But how would Liz react to the knowledge that he was her father?

She felt tears wet on her cheeks and buried her head in her hands. Oh, God, don't let him tell Liz. Struck by another thought, she rocked in anguish. Liz obviously liked him, had she the right to keep them apart?

229

A sleepless night left her heavy-eyed and listless, and she prepared for church with hands that trembled. Liz always accompanied her to the Oratory and would no doubt question her about her behaviour last night. She'd better get her thoughts in order and not let anything incriminating slip out. A tap on the door and Liz entered with her early-morning cup of tea. David would have breakfast prepared for them when they returned.

The Little Flower Oratory was no distance away and Liz decided not to badger her mother until after Mass. She was intrigued and intended getting to the bottom of this.

Kath was grateful for this respite. During Mass she prayed for guidance and convinced herself Liz must never learn the truth.

Leaving the small church, Liz slipped her arm through her mother's and said, 'Now, Mam, tell me why you have taken such an instant dislike to Neville Barnes? And don't beat about the bush. I want the truth.'

Kath pondered a moment. 'Well, to be truthful, it's not that I don't like him. You know, I suppose I should be ashamed to admit at my age to feeling attracted to men ... not just him, mind! But that other man who danced with me, and Dick Kennedy, all had a strange effect on me. I think I'd be as well giving dancing a miss in future.'

'Don't be silly, Mam. I know Dick is spoken for, but Jimmy Smith and Neville are both widowers and Neville is obviously attracted to you. I could see he was disappointed when you

230

went straight to bed last night.'

'Well, I'm too set in my ways now so there'll be no more dancing for me.'

'We'll just have to see about that, Mam. You're too young and have missed out on too much in the past. I'm determined you'll accompany us next time we go to Fortwilliam.'

Kath smiled and patted her arm. 'You're a good daughter, Liz. And who knows? Maybe I will go back,' she said, determined in her mind it would never happen.

Bridget was restless. She should have been happy. Danny was besotted with his baby son. Each night he rushed home from work to bathe young Martin. The child was growing in leaps and bounds and was a joy to behold with his tawny hair and hazel eyes. Danny and her father. had passed the stage where they tiptoed warily round each other like adversaries, looking for their opponent's weakness, and occasionally even shared a joke. They vied with one another for Martin's attention and outwardly everything was great.

Danny was pulling his weight and every spare penny was being salted away towards a deposit on a house of their own. They had even viewed a couple up the Falls Road at Iveagh. That was where Bridget had always wanted to live, and to her delight, Danny agreed with her. Everything was going so well she didn't want to risk upsetting the applecart with her misgivings. And why on earth should she? It was really none of her business.

Her worry stemmed from the fact that Joseph was coming regularly to the flat during his lunch hour. The flat was too handy to St Malachy's College, that was the drawback, and he was a constant visitor. That in itself was nothing to worry about as he was good company, if a mite shy. But when Ian was on the late shift at work, and was there during the day, Joseph spent a lot of time with him.

Perhaps she was doing the lad an injustice, perhaps it was an innocent relationship. Some-how or other she thought not. Sometimes she felt she should mention the fact to Danny. Remove the responsibility from her own shoulders, as it were. After all, Joseph was not yet eighteen and she felt responsible for his welfare while he was in her flat. Then she derided herself. Did she really think something might be going on? That Joseph might be falling under Ian's spell? If he had been an ordinary normal fellow would she have given Joseph's visits a second thought? No of course not! She would have supposed they were playing records and talking about girls. Was it all just in her mind? Hadn't she once been daft enough to think Danny was interested in Ian? Danny would be offended that she thought so little of his brother. If she was wrong, she would lose Ian's friendship which she valued and Joseph's respect. She would also bear the brunt of her husband's wrath again.

Besides, she didn't want to rock the boat just when everything was going so well between them. After all, it really wasn't any concern of hers and Joseph was a very intelligent lad, she reminded herself again. These things happened. She wouldn't have been pleased if anyone had told her parents of her episodes with boys before she got married. But that had been natural. Boy and girl curious about each other. Getting carried away in the heat of the moment. This was different. Joseph wasn't having a kiss and a tickle with some young lass. That would be normal and although Jane would object to his wasting time chasing after girls when he should be studying, it would be laughed over as a passing phase of adolescence.

Sometimes she was so worried she tried to tell Danny her suspicions, but for some reason the words always died on her tongue. What if she was imagining things? Perhaps she was the only one to think Joseph a bit effeminate? She could be chastised and laughed at for suggesting he might prefer Ian Geddis's company to girls'. Surely men could be just good friends? And surely Ian thought more of them than to risk losing their friendship by seducing Joseph? But what if he couldn't help himself? Her tortured thoughts rambled on and on. What if he really fancied Joseph? Oh, dear God, life was complicated enough without worrying about her young brother-in-law.

Even as she worried and fretted, as if she had conjured him up from mind, with a tap on the door Joseph entered the flat.

'Hello, Bridget. Just called in to see if I could be of any help to you?'

She quickly considered what shift Ian was on and her lips tightened. The two to ten. He'd be in his flat at the moment. Well, she'd keep Joseph so busy he wouldn't get time to go upstairs.

'I'm very glad to see you, Joseph. I do need to pop out to the shops for a while. Would you be kind enough to take care of Martin for me?'

Dismay briefly etched his face but he suppressed it and with a smile readily agreed to babysit.

'He's sleeping, so rummage around in the kitchen and make yourself a bite to eat. I won't be long.'

She was pleased to get some shopping done and wondered why she hadn't thought of this sooner. It meant she didn't have to take Martin out later on; she would be able to get her ironing done. In future she would call Joseph's bluff and make full use of him.

Half an hour later she happily let herself into the flat, glad her problem was solved. The quietness warned her it was empty. Unwilling to believe Joseph would take Martin upstairs with him, she looked in each room to confirm they were vacant. Enraged she rushed out to the hall. One foot on the bottom step, she paused in dismay. On the landing at the door of Ian's flat, completely unaware of her, stood the man and the boy. One tall, handsome and assured; the other young and gauche, arms and legs stretching out of his school uniform. Martin's carry-cot was at their feet.

Joseph was obviously besotted. His face was flushed with happiness. Even as she watched he leant closer as if to kiss Ian. With a resigned expression Ian drew back and indicated he should pick up the carry-cot and go. Bridget felt revulsion run through her. It wasn't right, two men acting like that. Joseph was completely unaware of her but Ian caught the look of disgust on her face as he turned to enter the flat and made as if to detain her. Quickly she withdrew, not wanting to face them. She was in the kitchen heating a bottle for Martin when Joseph entered.

'I didn't hear you come back, Bridget. Have you been here long?'

'Long enough,' she muttered ominously.

'I don't understand?'

'Where were you?'

Her tone of voice brought a blush to his cheeks. 'I popped up to see Ian. I didn't think you'd mind. I didn't leave Martin! I took him with me,' he cried defensively.

She swung round to face him. 'Joseph, you're being a very foolish boy, aren't you?'

The blush deepened. 'I don't know what you mean?'

'You know very well what I mean.'

'Ian's a good friend to me.'

'Come off it! You know it goes further than that. I saw you just now at the top of the stairs. I wouldn't have believed it if I hadn't seen it with my own eyes.'

All the rosy colour drained from his face, leaving him deathly pale. 'You won't tell anyone, sure you won't, Bridget?' he whimpered.

'Not if you swear you won't see him again?'

His reply was heartfelt. 'I'd rather die, so I would! Ah, Bridget, Ian's the only person to accept me for what I am. For the first time in my life, I'm happy. But if it gets out, think what it will do to Mam and Dad. They'll be devastated. They might even throw me out of the house. You know how the older generation feel about these things.'

'What if he's just using you, eh, Joseph? Have you thought of that? You're young and impressionable. He could be leading you astray. I can't stand by and be a party to that. What brought it on in the first place?'

He shrugged. 'Nobody's perfect, you know. I am what I am, Bridget. If it wasn't Ian it would be someone else. And I don't expect to be the love of his life. He can have anyone he wants. You don't realize it but there's plenty like me about.'

'If it wasn't for the likes of him there wouldn't be!' She turned aside in despair. 'Ah, Joseph. What am I going to do?'

'Turn a blind eye. Please? Just pretend you never saw us together.'

'I don't know. I don't know what to do for the best. I'll have to have a word with Danny about this and you know what will happen then. He'll kill Ian, so he will.'

At the mention of his brother, suddenly Joseph's temper flared. 'How's about minding your own business, eh, Bridget? Remember, I was in the same class as Noel Gibson. I heard the rumours about you and him, and never said a word to our Danny!'

Seeing the amazement on her face, he cried, 'Have you ever taken a good look at Martin? Eh, have you?'

The enormity of what he was suggesting took

236

the breath from her and she sagged against the sink.

'Don't look like that, Bridget. Your secret's safe with me. I'd never dream of saying a word. Just you do the same thing for me and hold your tongue and everything will be hunky-dory, OK?'

He was heading for the door when she came to her senses. 'I can't believe you're saying these awful things, Joseph. There's no truth in them. None whatsoever.'

He turned to argue but, seeing she was devastated, apologized instead. 'If you say so, Bridget. I'm only telling you the rumours that were going round at the time.'

'Joseph, I won't say anything about you and Ian.' He looked visibly relieved. She hastened to add, 'Not because of your threats, mind, because there's absolutely no truth in what you say, but because I hope you will come to your senses and no one need ever know. But don't use me as an excuse to visit him. Do you hear me? I won't allow it. Do you understand?'

He nodded. 'I'll have to run now or I'll be late for classes. And thanks, Bridget.'

When the door closed on him, she stood rooted to the spot and went over in her mind his insinuations. Had there been rumours? Cries of hunger made her automatically test the baby's bottle against her wrist. With steps that dragged she entered the living room and lifted Martin from his carry-cot. He sucked contentedly on his bottle and for the first time she got no joy from admiring her beautiful son.

She examined him closely. Not once had it

crossed her mind he might not be Danny's son. Not even when his hair remained a light treacle brown and his eyes hazel. She was aware he didn't resemble any of her family or Danny's. But hadn't Jane been quick to point out he favoured *her* mother's side of the family? Couldn't he just be a throwback? If there had been rumours, obviously they hadn't penetrated the family circle. They must have died down long ago, but what if Danny ever heard tell of them? The very thought of his anger made her quail with fright.

It was safe enough out here on the Antrim Road where they never saw any of their old neighbours, but what about their intention to buy a house up on Iveagh Estate? Good God, that's where Noel Gibson lived. They could end up living next door to him. Avidly she examined her son. Did he resemble Noel? She couldn't see it. Was there any chance he was Noel's son?

She might have known things were too good to be true. Tears rolled slowly down her face. Joseph had effectively sealed her lips. As far as he was concerned, she must button her lip. She had no choice in the matter now.

Neville Barnes felt self-conscious as he walked down Dunlewey Street. He had left his car around the corner in O'Neil Street. Now he was asking himself why? There was no need for secrecy. After all, he was a free man and Kath a single woman. He could visit whoever he liked. Would she turn him away from her door. Surely she wouldn't be so heartless?

She looked anything but pleased to see him when she answered his knock. A scowl crossed her face and her greeting was abrupt. 'What do you want?' she asked, making no attempt to let him in.

'Can I come in for a moment?'

'I'd rather you didn't. We have nothing in common any more.'

'You're forgetting Liz.'

'No, I'm not.' Seeing Jane McGowan emerge from her front door and start to cross the street, Kath tutted in frustration. 'Oh, come inside, if you must.'

Passing her, he entered the hall and waited. With a wave of acknowledgement to Jane, Kath closed the door and motioned him along the hall and into the living room. Neville seemed huge in the small room and she found his presence overpowering. He waved a hand around. 'You've made this very nice.'

'It took twenty-three years and a lot of hard work to do it. It's not easy raising a child on your own, you know.'

'I did my best, in the circumstances.'

'Your best wasn't good enough, I'm afraid. Still, it wasn't all your fault. I had earned myself a bad name and wasn't allowed to forget it. No, believe me, it wasn't easy. I paid sorely for my fling with you.'

'I'm sorry, Kath. I really am. Many a time I drove up here wanting to call and see you. I needed you so desperately. But common sense always prevailed. I knew you wouldn't have anything to do with me unless I left my wife, and that I couldn't do. I'd the boys to think about, you see.'

'What about when she died?' The words escaped Kath's lips without thought. She cringed inside. Now he would think she had wanted him to come back to her. And she hadn't! Well, not really. When she had learnt of his wife's death, she had feared he would come and open old wounds. For how could she ever forgive his treatment of her and his daughter? Well, he hadn't put her to the test and now he was too late.

Hope lit up his face at her words. Was there a chance she still cared? 'I thought too much time had passed. I thought you'd show me the door. If I'd dreamt there was a chance, I'd have come running.'

She didn't believe him and showed it. 'Huh! Why come now then?'

'Because now there's Liz to consider. She's a wonderful person and I want to get to know her.' He moved closer and she gazed into his face. Such an old face. Old and jaded. He had been a handsome man when first they'd met; now he could be any old man as far as she was concerned. He reminded her of her father, and she felt nothing for him. Nothing whatsoever. 'Kath, we could pick up the pieces. I feel as strongly attracted to you as ever.'

'Big deal! It's too late, Neville. Twenty-three years too late. I feel nothing for you now.'

'I made you care once, Kath, remember? I could do it again.' Tentatively he reached for her and, receiving no rebuff, gently drew her into his

240

arms. Her breasts were firm against his chest, the nipples hard. A good sign. He bent towards her and claimed her lips. They were soft and yielding. But only for a moment.

Startled at the emotions he aroused in her, she pushed him roughly away. 'No! I don't want this. I don't care any more. I'm too set in my ways. Too old for sex. You've probably had a string of women, but I devoted my life to Liz.'

He looked amazed. 'Are you saying there has never been anyone but me?'

Annoyed at her slip of the tongue, she cried, 'I mean no such thing! After the way you treated me, I couldn't trust another man again so I didn't get too involved, that's all.'

Disappointment clouded his eyes. He should have guessed there had been others, she was an attractive woman. 'Well, Kath, believe it or not there was never anyone else but you. But then, it was special between us. You're the only one I was ever tempted to risk losing my family over.'

'It didn't do me any good then. When it came to the crunch, I was the one you ditched.'

'It was the boys, Kath. I couldn't spoil their lives.'

'Hmm!'

'Look, come to the golf club. Let me get to know you again. Surely we can at least be friends?'

Wanting rid of him, she decided to string him along. She shrugged. 'Why not? I suppose we could be friends. But I warn you... Don't expect anything else. It's too late for us, Neville. Far too late. You had your chance and you blew it.'

241

Delighted at the chance to woo her, he pretended to agree. 'If that's how you want it, Kath, that's fine by me.'

'That's how I want it. Now I would like you to leave. I have to get ready for work.'

Reluctantly, he headed for the door. He wanted to hang on, persuade her to go out with him, but decided it was too soon to try; he must play by her rules or risk losing her altogether. 'You will come back to the golf club?'

'I said I would, didn't I?'

'Right! I'll expect to see you there in the near future.'

She saw him out and closed the door without another word. He stood on the pavement feeling at a loss. Somehow her promises didn't ring true, but only time would tell. If, in spite of her promises, she didn't return to Fortwilliam, he would cultivate his daughter's friendship. She had the right to know he was her father.

Kath stood with her back against the door and breathed a sigh of relief. She must never let him in again. She had thought all her feelings for him were dead but look how she had reacted when he kissed her. She was too lonely! This house was too big for her on her own. She was vulnerable. If Neville persisted, he just might penetrate her defences. For a moment there she had felt as if he was her husband returning after a long absence. Would that be such a bad idea? Could she learn to care again, just a little?

Danny was excited. A mate at work was selling his car and had offered it to him at a bargain price. But would he be able to persuade Bridget to spend half their savings on it? He very much doubted it, but it was worth a try. He eyed her across the dinner table. She seemed abstracted these past few days. Belatedly he questioned her.

'Is anything the matter, Bridget?'

She started as if stung and cried, 'No, nothing's the matter.'

'You seem a bit under the weather lately. Perhaps you should go and see the doctor?'

'Maybe I am a bit off colour. I'll get something from the chemist.'

They had viewed a couple of houses and he knew Bridget was anxious to move, but he couldn't let the chance of the car go by without at least trying. 'Bridget...'

He paused for so long that at last she prompted him. 'Yes, Danny?'

'Well, Frankie Muldoon is selling his car and gave me first refusal. It's in great nick. A wonderful bargain.'

Bridget gazed down at her hands clasped on the table in front of her and silently thanked God for his mercy. This was the answer to her prayers. Lifting her head, she gazed at her husband's eager face. She must show reluctance. Not give in too easily or Danny would be suspicious.

'How much is he looking for it?'

She didn't have to feign reluctance. The figure mentioned was half their savings and she gaped in disbelief. 'We can't afford that much, Danny.' She couldn't condone all that money being spent on a car while they were living in rented accommodation. Not even if it meant she'd been reprieved and they would not be moving to live up the Falls Road in the near future.

He left his chair and came to kneel at her side. 'Listen, Bridget, we'll never get another chance like this. I'll work all the overtime I can get. And, just think, there'd be no more bus fares. We could even go out for runs at the weekend. It would give you a break from being cooped up here every day.'

But she was not to be coerced. 'What about petrol money, eh?' she cried. 'It won't run on air, you know. And cars are always needing this and that done to them. Remember, our Patrick has one, and he's always moaning about the money it eats up. And he's single. We can't afford it, Danny.'

'Patrick's is an old banger. This car's in good condition. I had a mate who knows all about cars give it the once over. He says its going for a song, and if I don't take it he'll jump at the chance.'

'Then sing for it!'

He was on his feet in an instant, annoyed at her flippancy; his disappointment apparent. To appease him she cried, 'Danny, you know how much I'd love a car, but things are too risky at the moment. All this unrest in the city. If there's pay offs in Mackie's, you'll be one of the first to go. You know you will.'

'Ah, Bridget, we can't go through life always expecting the worst. You have to look on the bright side of things. If I get laid off, well, the car will have to go. It's as simple as that. And we might even make a few quid on it, into the bargain.'

Going to stand in front of him, she gently touched his face. 'This means a lot to you, doesn't it?'

He nodded. 'I know you're eager to buy a house up Iveagh, and I swear I'll double my efforts to get you one, but this car is a bargain, Bridget. We can't afford to pass up a chance like this.'

'Do you mean that, Danny? About doubling your efforts to move?'

'Of course I do,' he cried eagerly, picturing the car within his grasp.

'Even if it means going further still up the Falls Road? Maybe up the Glen Road? You see, I've gone off the idea of living in Iveagh. Will that be all right with you?'

He was flabbergasted. She had raved about Iveagh for so long. What had brought about this change? But he would promise anything to get the car. 'That's fine by me, love. We'll start looking up the Glen Road in a month or two. I'll lift the money out of the building society to-morrow for the car, all right?'

A sad nod of the head signalled her consent. All that money being spent and she had to go along with it because buying a house up Iveagh was unthinkable now.

A week later, Danny drove up to the door in a dark green Austin car. Bridget had been watching for him. With Martin in her arms she went outside to give the car the once over. It did look to be in good nick. Not that she was any judge of cars. It was also very clean inside. She nodded her approval.

'Come for a ride in it, love.'

'Don't be silly. Your dinner's in the oven and the flat isn't locked up.'

He was out of the car in a flash and ushering her into the passenger seat. 'Just a short drive. I'll lower the gas and lock up the flat. So no more excuses.'

Bridget had to admit she felt real proud as they drove along the Antrim Road and through Glengormley. Then a thought struck her and she cried in alarm, 'Danny, are we insured?'

'Of course we are. Why do you think I couldn't bring it home sooner? It's taxed and insured.'

'When did you learn to drive?'

'My Uncle Hugh taught me years ago. He said it's something you need to know if you want to get on. He was right, too. You're handicapped without a car.' Bleak thoughts of Liz's longing for a car brought pain to his heart for a moment. If only he had listened to her, how different things might have been. Now she was running around in a cute little number of her own.

Feeling Bridget's eyes on him he met them squarely. After all, she couldn't read his mind. 'We'll be able to take Martin to the beach at the weekends when the weather permits, and visit our friends in style.'

'Have you a licence?' Bridget was amazed at herself. How come they had never discussed these things before? Her fault, she should have asked. But then, he never asked her opinion of anything. Their one interest in common was Martin's welfare. And if he should ever find out about the rumours concerning the child? The

246

thought frightened her. What would keep them together then?

Danny was looking at her in surprise. 'I've a provisional licence. Do you think I'm daft?'

Her lips tightened. 'I don't know what to think. You never tell me anything.'

'What's got into you these days, Bridget?'

'Oh, forget it. You wouldn't understand.' All the pleasure was taken out of the drive as she pondered over just how little they had in common.

Danny looked at her averted profile and silently agreed with her. He would never understand the way her mind worked. Well, he hadn't married her for her brains. Some of the joy had disappeared from his day, though. Silently he turned the car and headed for home.

Outside the flat, Ian was about to enter the house when the car drew up. A glance at the driver and he stopped in surprise when he realised who it was. He lingered to admire it and congratulate Danny on possessing such a fine machine.

This was the first time Bridget had been in his company since the day she had witnessed him and Joseph on the landing. Aware that her brother-in-law still visited him, she had been avoiding Ian. Unable to meet his eyes, she muttered a greeting and when Danny opened the door she quickly thrust Martin into his father's arms and passed through the hall and into the kitchen to rescue her husband's dinner.

To her great dismay, she heard Danny invite Ian down later on for a cup of tea.

'Will that be all right with you, Bridget?' he called.

'Yes. Come down later,' she called hollowly.

Martin was in his cot fast asleep and Bridget was clearing up in the kitchen, hoping to avoid him, when Ian eventually came down. To her dismay he joined her.

'Danny's reading through the car manual so I said I'd offer to help you with the tea.'

'Oh ... fill the teapot, will you?' she said abruptly.

'Bridget, I have to talk to you.'

She stepped back in alarm. 'No! I don't want to know any sordid details about you and Joseph. The less I know the better.'

'Bridget, I need to talk to you. Explain how things stand.'

The look she turned on him was full of horror. 'Explain? I don't want to know what goes on between you two, I just don't understand these things.'

'Don't be silly. I don't mean that. Even so there's nothing going on between us. Please believe me, Bridget. I'm only trying to help him.'

'Leave him alone! That's the only way you can help him. Do you hear me? Leave him alone.'

'Leave who alone?' Danny stood in the door-way, a puzzled frown on his brow, looking from one to the other of them.

'I was going to ask you to come out for a drink, Danny, but Bridget seems to think it wouldn't be a good idea.' It was a lame excuse but the best Ian could think of on the spur of the moment. He stood tense. The ball was now in Bridget's court. What would she do?

He had said the wrong thing. It was Danny who cried out in anger. 'Bridget doesn't decide where I go.' He glared balefully at her and then back at Ian. 'If you fancy going out for a pint, that's all right by me. I haven't been in a pub for donkey's. It'll be a pleasant change for me.'

Still eyeing Bridget in apprehension, waiting for her to explode, Ian replied, 'I thought perhaps we could dander up to the golf club and celebrate you owning a car.'

Bridget wished she could let out all the frustration and contempt she felt. Howl accusations at him. But she was afraid of the repercussions. Had Joseph told Ian of his suspicions? Without a word she left the kitchen.

'Fortwilliam?' Danny asked in surprise. When Ian nodded he said, 'Well, let's go, then. I've never been to the golf club. Will we get in all right?'

Obviously Bridget didn't intend telling Danny about seeing him with Joseph. In a dilemma, Ian tried to back down. 'Yes, I'm an associate member, but I think I spoke out of turn, Danny. I know you hardly ever drink now and I don't want to cause any ill feeling between you and Bridget.'

'No woman is going to tell me what I can and can't do.' Danny was truly upset. What had got into Bridget? She had been in a surly mood during dinner and now this. She was asking for trouble. 'Let's go,' he said curtly and headed for the door.

It was almost midnight when they returned. Bridget had retired for the night and willed Danny not to ask Ian in. He did, but to her relief Ian refused. She feigned sleep when her husband eventually crawled into bed beside her.

'Bridget? I know you aren't asleep. Listen, love, I'm sorry but you shouldn't have put me on the spot like that in front of Ian. What on earth got into you?'

She rounded on him angrily. 'Put you on the spot? You made all kinds of promises to get the money for that bloody car and when the first test comes along you have to go out drinking. And at a golf club of all places! I bet the drink was twice as dear there.'

Glad to be able to refute this, Danny cried, 'That's where you're wrong. It was cheaper. Ah, Bridget, don't cry. I promise not to waste any more money on drink. Honestly!'

He gathered her close and she wept against his chest. 'Ah, now, Bridget. There's no call for this. I only had three pints.'

'You don't understand, Danny. I feel trapped here in this flat. I feel we're going to be stuck here forever.'

'I don't understand. I thought you loved it here, Bridget?'

'I did. But now we have Martin and I want to live within walking distance of my mam. If we move near her, I'll be able to get a job. She'll look after Martin for me. Or what if I've another baby? How will I manage then?'

'That's where the car will come in handy, Bridget.'

'Not for me. Not if you're working all hours. I'll be stuck here on my own.' She turned away in despair. 'I suppose I was too immature to get married. I feel as if I've trapped you too. You could have had a car long ago if I hadn't been so stupid and let you make me pregnant.'

'Wait a wee minute, Bridget. It takes two. I was every bit as eager as you. More so! Didn't I keep coming back, even though I was engaged to Liz O'Hara?'

To his dismay she howled all the louder. Great sobs that tore at her body. He gathered her close again, trying to smother the sounds. 'Hush, love. Ian will hear you upstairs.'

'Do you think I care about him? He's the cause of most of my worry.'

'Ian?' He drew back and looked at her in amazement. 'Unless he's changed his spots, I can't see him worrying you.' A thought struck him and he cried in alarm, 'Just because I went for a drink with him, you're surely not still thinking I'm a bit bent, are you?'

'No, of course I'm not. But would you have married me if I hadn't been pregnant?'

'How do I know? We are married and that's what counts. Everything else is water under the bridge.' He eyed her in bewilderment. 'I wish I understood how your mind works, Bridget.'

'So do I. So do I, Danny. Let's go to sleep or you'll be late for work in the morning.'

Gently, he wiped away her tears. 'Not just yet, Bridget. Give me another ten minutes, eh? I'll soon make you feel better.'

Resigned, she moved towards him. Even this

251

was a chore to her now. Something to be got over as quickly as possible. Why did men think sex was the answer to all a woman's problems? If only it was ... if only it was.

When she returned from town the following afternoon, Ian was sitting on the bottom stair waiting for her. Silently she allowed him to help her in with the push-chair and packages.

When he made no effort to leave, she reluctantly asked, 'Would you like a cup of tea?'

'Yes, please.'

He played on the mat with Martin until the tea was brewed, his eyes widening slightly when he saw there was only one cup and a plate of biscuits on the tray. 'Are you not having one?'

'I'll have mine later. I've a bottle cooling for Martin. I'll feed him first.'

Placing Martin in the playpen which his Uncle Peter had made for him, she sat down facing Ian and, brows raised, said, 'Well, did you not do enough damage last night?'

'Bridget, you know the last thing I want to do is cause trouble between you and Danny. I couldn't help the way things turned out last night, now could I? I was in a predicament. Didn't know what you intended to do. And thanks for not saying anything about me and Joseph.'

'Don't thank me. I don't want to encourage you, but I haven't any choice in the matter. Could you not just leave Joseph alone, Ian?'

'That's what I'm trying to explain to you, Bridget. I'm trying to save him from himself. I know what it's like at that age. You're all mixed up. If you meet the wrong company, you can be deceived and go the wrong way.'

Compassion smote her. 'Is that what happened to you?' she asked softly.

He smiled wryly. 'No, Bridget. You can stop feeling I've had a bad deal. I knew what I was for a long time before I admitted it to myself. But Joseph is different. At the moment he's in limbo. His hormones are all mixed up. If he wasn't so shy he would probably have a girlfriend by now and there'd be no problem. Instead he met me, and because I was stupid enough to be kind to him, thinks he's a kindred spirit. Feeling as he does at the moment, if I chase him away he might fall in with the wrong crowd and then he'd be lost forever. And that's the truth, Bridget.'

Exasperated, she bawled at him, 'Just leave him alone then.'

'You're not listening to me,' Ian cried in exasperation. 'You don't understand. He needs me to help him find his true self.'

'Are you telling me that kissing and hugging him, or whatever it is you do, is going to help?' she cried derisively.

'That doesn't happen often. And, believe me, when he does meet a girl he's going to hate me for it. But, you see, that satisfies him at the moment. Mostly we just talk. If he meets someone else and goes the whole way, he'll be lost. There'll be no turning back for him then, Bridget.'

She couldn't believe she was having this sordid conversation with him. Rising to her feet, she went to fetch Martin's bottle. Ian followed her into the kitchen and stood close behind her while she tested its heat.

'Bridget...' His voice was a whisper. Startled, she turned quickly and found herself right up against him. His pale blue eyes mesmerized her. 'Are you happy with Danny, Bridget?' he said softly.

'I don't know what you mean. Of course I'm happy,' she whispered back. Why am I whispering, she thought wildly.

'Are you, really happy?'

His breath fanned against her cheek and his aftershave smelt spicy and ... manly? She blinked, amazed at this thought. Suddenly she became aware that he was aroused. Breathless she gazed at him, noting the full sensual lips and wide-spaced pale eyes with passion in their depths. He held her gaze for some moments and it was as if he could see to the very core of her mind. To her horror she felt a stirring of interest which sent a tremor through her body, making her lean closer still, lips parted for his kiss. Backing slowly away from her, he broke the spell.

'See, Bridget?' His hands stretched wide in supplication. 'I can go either way. Believe me, I don't need a raw lad like Joseph. Think about it! I really am trying to look after his interests. Because I regard you and Danny as close friends, I don't want to abandon him. *You* could help, by introducing him to young girls.'

Ashamed and dismayed at the turmoil he had aroused in her, she gazed at him speechlessly. He grinned and turned to leave. 'I'd better go now because I really do find you very attractive,

Bridget. You are very sensual, you know, and if you're not careful, it could be your downfall. Don't pay any attention to Joseph's threats. He would never say anything to Danny. But if you have any doubts about Martin, it would be in your own best interests to tell Danny. I'll see you soon.'

Still in a daze, she fed the baby and changed his nappy, all the while reliving the emotions she had experienced in the kitchen. What kind of a person was she? For a short time she had actually been attracted to Ian. Strongly attracted. What if he had taken it further? How would she have been able to face him again? Of course many a girl, not knowing him very well, might be attracted to him. After all he was very handsome. But she knew what he was, and still had felt physically attracted to him. What if he had kissed her? Would she have allowed it? Hah! That was a gag. Hadn't she practically begged for it? What was to become of her if she couldn't control her emotions every time she met a handsome man? The knowledge that Joseph had told Ian his views on Martin frightened her. And it would be some time now before they could afford to move. How would she manage to get through the coming months?

With the passing of time Liz began to worry about her barren state. She longed for a child. They could give it so much. The business was thriving and this big bungalow was meant to house a family. The idea her husband didn't want children was beginning to bug her. Well, it was time to put him to the test; find out the truth. Choosing her moment carefully, she tentatively broached the subject.

'David, I'm beginning to get worried that I haven't conceived yet.'

It was a Saturday morning and they were sitting in the conservatory reading the morning papers. She sounded so woebegone he left his chair and joined her on the two-seater.

'What do you want to do about it, Liz?'

'I think perhaps I should go and see what the doctor has to say.'

He remained silent and she said, 'You don't want a family, sure you don't, David? Why won't you admit it?'

'Oh, but I do, Liz. I most certainly do. But, you see, I have a confession to make. Victoria and I tried for a child for a long time, but it never happened. The doctors could find nothing wrong with her, so it must have been my fault.'

'Did you not go for tests, David?'

He shook his head. 'No. I suppose I was a coward, but you see Victoria seemed contented with things as they were. I wanted a family more than she did. She thought children would tie us down, so I let it drift. What I'm saying is, what if we can't have any? Would you be heartbroken?'

The very idea of never having a child filled Liz with despair. He saw it in her eyes and, unable to bear it, rose quickly to his feet and left the conservatory. She gazed after him as he strode along the garden and disappeared round the side of the bungalow. I must go to him, she urged herself, reassure him. But her body felt leaden and she remained where she was, her mind in turmoil.

The need to talk to someone drove her up to Dunlewey Street. Kath was surprised to see her. One look at her drawn face and she ushered her daughter into the parlour. 'Sit down. I'll make us a cup of tea and you can tell me what's troubling you.'

Liz sat gazing blindly out of the window. Her attention was caught by a green Austin car drawing up to McGowans' door. To her surprise Danny got out and then, reaching into the back, lifted out a laughing child. Next Bridget climbed out of the car. Liz's eyes devoured the child. That should have been her son. If only she hadn't been such a prude, she and Danny would be married and parents by now.

Kath came in with a tray and, placing it on the table, joined Liz at the window to see what was holding her attention. All she could see was a green car outside McGowans' door. 'What's so interesting?'

'Danny just got out of that car.'

'And?'

'Bridget and the child were with him.'

'I don't understand?'

To Kath's amazement tears tumbled down Liz's cheeks. 'That should be my child!' she wailed. 'I've been so foolish, Mam. David can't have children. What am I going to do?'

Kath's breath caught in her throat but she willed herself to stay calm. 'Come on, drink up your tea and then tell me all about it?'

Weeping and wailing, Liz did as she was bid. When her words trailed off, Kath said sternly, 'You're not the only one, you know, Liz. Many couples face this predicament. All sorts can be done these days. Besides, if David never had tests he can't be sure the fault lies with him. It could be your fault, love. So don't go flying off the handle. Go to the doctor and get his opinion. That's the best advice I can offer.'

Liz wiped her eyes and smiled bleakly. 'You're right, Mam. It's just the idea that David never warned me he might not be able to father a child.'

'He loves you very much, Liz. He probably thought the longer you were married, the more understanding you'd be.'

Liz was not to be swayed. 'He should have told me,' she repeated stubbornly.

Bridget hadn't recognized the small car parked across the street but Danny had. He hovered near the window and when he saw Liz leave the house, quickly made an excuse to go out to the car.

Opening the boot he pottered about until Kath went indoors and Liz was about to enter her car. Then he retrieved a toy belonging to Martin and, closing the boot, glanced across the road. As if surprised to see her, he waved and crossed the street to speak to her. 'Long time no see, Liz. How are you?'

Aware he must see the signs of her recent outburst, Liz smiled brightly. 'I'm fine, Danny. And you?'

'Never better.' He eyed her car and nodded his

appreciation. 'That's a beauty, Liz. You did very well for yourself.'

She nodded across the street and said, 'You haven't done too badly yourself.'

'Well, it's only a secondhand one, but it's a start.'

'Actually, I meant your wife and child. He's lovely.'

'Oh, yes. Martin's a bit of a rascal at the moment. He crawls into all sorts of mischief.' Danny's eyes dropped to her flat stomach and he asked, 'No sign of a family yet then?'

'No!'

He drew back and blinked in surprise at her abruptness. 'I'm sorry. I didn't mean to pry.'

'Oh, it's all right. I didn't mean to snap at you. It's just I'm a bit touchy at the moment on that subject.'

He digested these words and, smiling wryly, teased, 'You mean, we could have been playing about and you wouldn't have become pregnant after all?' His voice filled with regret. 'What have we done, Liz?'

'What makes you assume it's my fault?' she snapped. Dismayed to have disclosed so much of her private affairs to him, she opened the car door and said curtly, 'Goodbye, Danny. I'll have to be going now.'

He watched the car out of sight, turning her words over in his mind. My, my? Was the infallible David firing blanks?

There was no sign of her husband when Liz returned to Somerton Road. Despondently, she trailed about doing unnecessary tasks, willing him to return. She had been unfair to him. After all, he had been there for her in her hour of need. If he had confessed then that he might never father a child, would it have made any difference? Would she have refused to marry him? Of course not. She had been only too eager to get away from the sight of Danny and Bridget together.

The child's laughing face sprang to mind. He really was a beautiful baby. Oh, if only she could conceive. The sound of the car drawing up to the door brought her from her musing. Making her way to the hall, she waited patiently for David to come inside.

To her consternation he went round to the back of the bungalow and entered through the conservatory. Slowly, she retraced her steps and found him in the lounge. He was pouring himself a whisky.

He gestured to the array of bottles. 'Want anything?'

She shook her head. 'David, I'm sorry I was such a fool earlier on. Can you ever forgive me?'

'It doesn't matter.' His voice was lifeless. 'After all, we do have a solution to our problem.'

'Now, David, I'd be prepared to try all avenues open to us before considering adoption.'

'Don't be foolish, Liz. I'm too old for adoption. Ten years ago I was on the borderline. I'd never be considered as a parent now.'

Confused at his reasoning, she asked, 'What solution do you have in mind then?'

'I once told you if our marriage didn't work out, I'd give you a divorce. I'll stand by my word.'

'I don't want a divorce,' she cried in a shocked voice.

A glimmer of hope entered his heart and some of the strain left his face. 'What do you suggest then?'

'I think we should visit the doctor and arrange to have all the necessary tests.' She shrugged slightly. 'Then we can take it from there.' She wished he wouldn't just stand there looking down his nose at her. He was so aloof and she needed to be held, to be reassured that he would do all that was necessary to set things in motion.

He nodded. 'If that's what you want. I'll do anything you say.'

'Thank you.' Sadly, she turned away. This was causing a great void between them and it was all her fault. When he had needed her reassurance, she could only think of life without a child. Now his aloofness kept her from throwing herself into his arms and begging his forgiveness.

He watched her leave the room and slumped down in a chair in despair. Obviously she didn't want him to touch her. Would she ever want him again? Had she no love in her heart at all for him?

Dr Williams heard Liz out in silence. 'You're being a bit premature, you know, Liz. You're not even married two years yet. My advice is to wait at least another six months, before you start putting yourself through the trauma of tests. You are a young woman. Why the big rush?'

'That may well be, doctor, but my husband is over forty. I don't want him to be an old man when we do eventually have children.'

261

'Look, give it another few months and if nothing happens come back to me and we'll investigate it further. OK?'

'I suppose so.'

Despondently, she left the doctor's premises. It was a beautiful day and she had walked to the surgery on the Antrim Road. On impulse she headed up towards the castle grounds. She had taken the afternoon off work and was in no hurry to be back home. A walk in the beautiful grounds of Belfast Castle would do her a world of good. She picked her way up a steeply winding path beneath trees rustling in the light breeze. Unused to all this exercise her legs soon tired. A spot back off the path dappled with sunlight caught her attention. Leaving the rutted path she sat beneath a large horse chestnut tree with her back resting against it.

The warm breeze fanned her face and teased her eyes closed. Her thoughts swung this way and that. She was happy with David. She liked the lifestyle being married to him afforded, and away from Danny she could forget him for long stretches at a time. But after seeing him with his son he was very much in her thoughts. She let her mind dwell on the past. It seemed strange to her now that she had refused to have sex with him because the priest had said it was wrong before marriage, yet a couple of months later had committed a greater sacrilege. Turning her back on the church she had, without a qualm, married David in a register office. In the eyes of the church and a great number of her friends and neighbours, she was now living in sin. But she'd had such a great need to get away from the sight of Danny and Bridget together, it had blinded her to everything else. Even the ecclesiastical laws she held precious.

Was marriage without children to be her punishment for doing this? At first she had given little thought to being cut off from the sacraments; had revelled in the luxury of her beautiful new home with plenty of money to spend, but now she wanted to storm heaven with novenas and rosaries begging for fertility yet felt that she hadn't the right to even ask for mercy no matter about divine favours.

What was to become of her if she couldn't have a child? Thoughts of Danny would not be stayed, they pushed to the forefront of her mind. Danny as she had last seen him, dark and virile, and passionate; a laughing child in his arms. She could actually feel his arms around her; feel the deep burning passion that had been ever constant between them from the day they met. Here in this quiet secluded place a deep longing for him filled her whole being. There was obviously nothing wrong with him. His son was beautiful.

The noise of someone coming helter-skelter down the steep path brought her eyes open and made her suddenly alert. This was a very remote spot. Few people came this way off the beaten track. Perhaps the soldiers who guarded the castle were having an exercise?

After some seconds the perpetrator of the noise came into view. A man hanging on to a pushchair that was propelling him along in a mad rush.

Danny McGowan of all people! Seeing Liz he managed to turn the runaway pram on to the grass eventually, bringing it to a standstill some distance below her. He gazed up at her, a grin of pleasure on his face.

Because he had been in her thoughts, Liz blushed guiltily. 'What are you doing here?'

Slowly, he manoeuvred the pram and sleeping child back until he was standing looking down at her. 'I come here quite often when the weather's good. I live along the Antrim Road there, you know?' He nodded back towards town direction.

'No, I didn't know.'

'So your ma didn't tell you? Well, well, I wonder why? Yes, I live quite near here. I've been to the doctor ... pulled a muscle in my back. He's given me a line off work for two weeks. I volunteered to take Martin to the clinic. You know, for his injections? And it's such a beautiful day, I thought I'd take him for a walk afterwards. I'm glad now that I did.' His eyes caressed her as he gingerly stretched his muscles. 'I'm afraid that bit of exercise didn't do me any good.'

He seemed huge, standing breathless above her, and she gestured vaguely to the ground. 'Why don't you sit down for a moment and catch your breath?'

He wheeled the pram to the coolest spot and settled the sleeping child into a more com-fortable position. Then throwing himself on the grass close to Liz, he scanned her face and neck and cleavage before speaking again. 'You look marvellous.' His voice was husky, his admiration evident. His proximity unsettled her and she moved slightly away.

'Don't be nervous, Liz. I'm not going to bite you.' He laughed wryly. 'That is, unless you want me to?'

Her eyes met his and the breath caught in his throat at the clouded pain in their depths. He moved closer still and clasped her hand. 'Liz? Are you all right?'

Suddenly, she was acutely aware of the danger of the situation. The child was asleep. They were in a small clearing, protected by trees. The chances of anyone else coming along here at this time of day was remote. It was fate that had led them here. It was meant to be, wasn't it?

Aghast at the path her thoughts were pursuing, she tried to pull her hand free but he clung on and throwing his other arm across her body, pinned her to the ground. 'Don't fight it, Liz. It was meant to be. Can't you see that? It's not just by chance we're here. Surely it was fate brought us together today?'

Amazed that he was echoing her own thoughts, she relaxed slightly. Immediately his lips claimed hers with a depth of hunger to match her own as they devoured each other.

At last he lifted his head and gazed at her in anguish. 'Ah, Liz, we're meant for each other. How could I have been so stupid?'

She tried to push herself free but he was not to be deterred. 'Listen, Liz. It's obvious we're meant to be together. Can't we meet? Just now and again, Liz. No one need ever know. No one would be hurt.'

'We'd know!'

'Don't you want to be with me? Did you ever really love me or was it all talk?'

At last she managed to free herself and rose to her feet. 'Of course I love you! But you spoilt all that. For us to meet would be wrong, Danny.' She examined the sleeping chubby cheeked child. 'You're very lucky. He's beautiful, so he is.'

Bounding to his feet he joined her by the pram. He had noted the present tense of 'I love you'. Now his arms circled her waist and he pulled her back against him, whispering urgently in her ear, 'I could give you a child, Liz. Think about it! No one would ever know.'

Struggling against the passion he was rousing within her, she cried aghast, 'I'd never do that to David.'

'It would solve all your problems. He would be happy in his ignorance. We could see each other. That would make me very happy. And you would be a mother.'

'You've been watching too many soap operas. Things like that don't happen in real life.'

'Oh, don't they? How do you know that, Liz? Many a man is blindly rearing someone else's child as his own. Think about it. The child that resembles neither mother nor father. They say it's a throwback, but is that always the case? Only the mother knows for sure.'

She appeared to have been struck dumb and he pressed on. 'Give it some thought. If you change your mind, let me know. I've to bring Martin to the clinic for a check-up next Wednesday. If the weather is good I'll come up here to this spot afterwards. Meet me, Liz. Even if it's only for a chat.'

When she related what the doctor had said, David eyed her keenly. 'Are you prepared to go along with that, or do you want me to insist we have tests done right away?'

Pleased to hear his intentions were good, she smiled wryly and said, 'I suppose another few months won't make any difference.'

'Do you know something, Liz? I'm terrified.'

Going to him, she put her arms around his waist and pressed her head against his breast. 'Don't be. Whatever will be, will be. But there will be no divorce.'

He pushed her gently away and gazed down into her eyes. 'Do you really mean that, Liz?'

'I mean it. There will be no divorce,' she said with conviction.

'Liz... Ah, Liz, my love. I hope I don't fail you.'

'It could be my fault, David.'

'That's hardly likely. Remember, Victoria and I were married a long time and nothing happened.'

'Perhaps it was her fault and she didn't like to admit it?'

'No, I don't think so.'

'That would account for the fact she didn't press you to have tests done. If she had been keen she would have insisted you go to the doctor. Was she a selfish person?'

He shook his head. 'No, Liz, she would do anything for anybody.'

'I'm not implying that she wasn't a good caring

267

person, but was she jealous where you were concerned?'

He closed his eyes and cast his mind back. 'Yes, I think you might be right there. We didn't socialise much. She preferred for us to be alone. I was the one who wanted children.'

She clung fiercely to him. 'Perhaps we will have a child, David.'

They went to Fortwilliam that weekend. Under duress, Kath agreed to accompany them. To be truthful, there hadn't been much coaxing to do. The memory of the music and twirling around the dance floor had weakened her resolve to stay away. This was a whole new way of life for her and she decided she would not let Neville spoil it. She decided it would do no harm to renew his acquaintance and take it from there.

He was late coming into the lounge and she was pleased to be twirling around the dance floor to a quickstep in Dick Kennedy's arms. When the dance ended he made his way over to their table.

'Hello, Kath. Nice to see you again.'

'Hello, Neville. I trust you are well?'

'Very well, thank you.' Dick had seated himself beside Kath and Neville addressed him. 'How are you, Dick? Is Irene not with you tonight?'

'Oh, you know what Irene is like, Neville. We had a bit of a tiff and she refused to come out with me.'

'Ah, well, the course of true love never runs smooth.' He eyed Kath closely as he said these words but she chose to ignore him.

David and Liz came off the dance floor and

more greetings were exchanged. At David's invitation, Neville drew up a chair beside Kath and joined the company.

When the music started again both men turned to her. To Dick's surprise, she graciously said, 'You will have to excuse me, Neville, but I have already promised Dick this dance.'

Well away from the table, he said roguishly, 'Have I missed out on something? Is my Uncle Neville making a pass at you?'

'I didn't know he was your uncle. But you're wrong. We've just danced together a few times.'

Dick was surprised to feel a twinge of jealousy and berated himself. Was he not practically engaged to Irene? 'He's too old for you anyhow, don't you think? You need someone younger.'

'Has there been no one on the scene since his wife died?'

'No, he and Olive were very close. It's been about eighteen months since she died. I suppose he must be lonely, living in that big house on his own.'

'Is he the faithful kind, then?'

'Very much so.' A puzzled look crossed Dick's face. 'Although mind you, there was...'

To Kath's disappointment the music ended and with a final twirl he led her off the floor and she never heard just what there was.

She enjoyed having two men fuss over her. Liz watched the antics of them with a twinkle in her eye. 'I think perhaps we're watching the beginning of a romance,' she confided in David.

'Wouldn't it be nice if she and Neville hit it off?'

'Dick is more her age, but then he's practically

engaged to Irene.'

'Still, he's a free man. Who knows what might happen?'

Liz gazed up at this good man who would do anything to please her and the memory of the episode with Danny filled her with shame. She pressed closer and David's grip on her tightened.

'Are you all right, love?'

'Yes. I'm fine.' She must not meet Danny again. Not even to talk as he had suggested. It was too dangerous. She must never risk hurting David.

Chapter Five

The weather broke over the weekend, showers and heavy mist clinging to the Cave Hill, and in its shadow the castle was barely visible. Liz was relieved. If this weather continued, Danny would hardly expect her to meet him. However, to her dismay it picked up again on Monday. Wednesday dawned mild and warm with the promise of a good day ahead. By noon the sun shone from a clear blue sky. Liz found it hard to keep thoughts of Danny at bay. She kept reminding herself that she had not agreed to meet him. If he wasted his time walking in the castle grounds, she was not to blame. She was up to her eyes in work at the factory and there was no way she could excuse herself. Besides, she assured herself, she didn't really want to meet him. A meeting that could lead to all sorts of problems.

Then to her great consternation fate took a hand. After lunch on Wednesday afternoon, when she was patting herself on the back, congratulating herself that any possible temptation had been averted, David approached her.

'Are you awfully busy, Liz?'

'Well, yes. But nothing that can't be put on hold for a while.'

'As you know, the joiners are coming to put the finishing touches to the new extension.' His lips tightened in a straight line. 'I'm afraid I'm far from pleased with their efforts so far. The window frames are a disgrace. They should have been with us hours ago and I want to be here when they eventually decide to show up. Meanwhile, would you go and see Jack Cunningham, Liz?' He gestured to a few sheets of paper he held in his hand. 'I want his advice on this new contract as soon as possible. I'm a bit worried about the penalty clauses in it.'

'That won't take long. I'll be back before you know I've gone.'

He leant across her desk and ran the back of his hand gently along her cheek. 'You needn't bother coming back, Liz. I've noticed you're looking a bit strained this past few days. It's such a beautiful day it's a shame to waste it, stuck in here. Take the rest of the afternoon off. Just phone and let me know what Jack says. Better still, give him the contract and get him to phone me when he has had a chance to go over it. That way you won't have to hang around listening to all the legal jargon. It will leave you completely free for a good soak in the bath and a lie out in the sun.'

'Are you implying that I've got BO?' she asked with a twinkle in her eye.

'Of course not. You always smell delicious enough to eat. I'm just picturing you in the bath.' He leant closer. 'I only wish I could join you. A rest will do you all the good in the world.'

'You don't understand, David. I'd rather come back...'

'You said there was nothing that couldn't be put on hold?' A raised brow questioned her.

272

'Well, no there isn't. But...'

He interrupted her. 'No buts! I forbid you to come back. Go home! Take a rest. Go on now, before I change my mind.'

Reaching for her cardigan, which was over the back of her chair, he held it ready for her and reluctantly she slid her arms into the sleeves. He wouldn't be so caring if he realized the temptation he was placing her in. She clung to him when he kissed her goodbye.

'Hey, what's all this about?' Concerned, he gazed into her big worried hazel eyes. 'Are you feeling all right, Liz?'

'Just a bit tired. I'll do as you say and go straight home.' Silently she repeated that vow. She would go home. After all, she hadn't definitely said she would meet Danny. He could cool his heels as long as he liked but she wouldn't show up.

She delivered the documents to Jack and, with his assurance that he would ring David as soon as he'd had a look at them, left his office, climbed into her car and determinedly headed for home. She took the Shore Road route so she wouldn't be tempted to crawl along the Antrim Road, hoping to see Danny.

The idea of a bath didn't appeal to her. It was too hot. She would have a cool shower later. Making herself a long cold gin and tonic on the rocks, she retired to the conservatory to read a magazine. Restlessly she thumbed through the pages. Really, she should have gone back in to work. This was such a waste of valuable time. Coming to a decision, she rose to her feet and entered the kitchen. She could at least have a special dinner ready for David when he came home. Relieved at having something to do to occupy her, she raided the cupboards.

All the ingredients she needed for a three-course meal were found and spread out on the big work table. Soon the main dish, a pork fillet stuffed with minced beef and herbs, was in the oven and the prawn cocktails for starters were in the fridge. She eyed the ingredients she had left out for an apple pie. It was too clammy for a hot dessert. What could she make for afters? Her roving eye caught sight of the big bowl of fruit and her problem was solved. With oranges, apples, bananas and kiwi fruit she could make a fresh fruit cocktail. They had finished the ice cream at the weekend. Knowing David's weakness for it with his dessert, she decided to go to the store along the Antrim Road.

A quick glance at her watch informed her it was just after four. It was hardly likely she would run into Danny this late. Even he wouldn't wait for hours. If she did bump into him it would surely be fate. She hadn't deliberately left work early. Nor had she planned to go to the shops. Arrested by a thought she paused in contemplation. Or had she? Had she unconsciously realized about the ice cream and, in a roundabout way, was using it as an excuse to go out? Oh, catch yourself on, girl. You're being paranoid, she thought. You're only going to the shop for ice cream, don't make a song and dance of it.

Pushing her feet into flat comfortable walking shoes, she gazed silently down at them for some moments. Why was she walking and leaving the car behind? With an impatient shake of the head she answered herself. For the simple reason the distance to the shop did not justify taking the car.

She was nervous as she walked the length of Antrim Road from Downview Avenue to the store. In vain she tried to keep her eyes ahead, but still she furtively scanned the far side of the road. I shouldn't have come out, she thought as she scurried along, endeavouring to keep her eyes fixed straight ahead. The sooner she got home the better.

Danny looked at his watch for the umpteenth time. It was obvious Liz was not going to show up. Had he really expected her to? Remembering the hunger in her last week he had to admit that he had. But then, she'd had a week to cool off. He had given up his vigil when Martin had become restless some time ago and returned home with him. Then, to his great delight, Bridget had asked him to fetch some milk from the store and unable to resist he had returned to the castle grounds, hoping to find Liz waiting there. That had been almost an hour ago so he had better get a move on. Bridget would be growing impatient.

Rising to his feet, he made his way slowly down to the Antrim Road, hoping as he rounded each bend in the path that he would come face to face with Liz. He was halfway across the road before he noticed her tall graceful figure striding along on the opposite footpath.

Quickening his step he reached the pavement

and approached her from behind. 'You're very late, Liz. I'd given you up for lost.'

A startled exclamation escaped her lips as she spun round. 'What do you mean, late? I'm going to the store for some ice cream.'

His eyes scanned the tanned contours of her face, seeing the golden eyes widen with dismay. 'So you had no intention of meeting me? Shame on you,' he chided her. 'I've been sitting up in the castle grounds for ages.'

'I didn't say I would come, Danny. You know I didn't,' she cried defensively. 'Where's Martin?'

'He became very restless and I left him at home. Just think, we would have been all alone,' he teased her.

Liz glanced nervously around and he sensed she was afraid of being seen with him. 'Let's not stand here. Come for a walk?'

At first she demurred, then with another nervous glance around her, allowed him to lead her across the road and up towards the castle; all the while her heart doing somersaults at the close proximity of him. The pressure of his fingers on her arm was like an electric current shooting through her. When they came to the secluded spot where they had met the previous week, he took her in his arms and, throwing caution to the winds, she entered them willingly. Wasn't this what she'd been hoping for? It was surely meant to be. This was fate, she convinced herself, and she had no control whatsoever over that.

Gently, he lowered her unresisting form on to the grass. The smell of the damp foliage, mingled with the perfume of wild flowers drying in the sun, assailed her nostrils. She lay contented, her senses swimming in a great surge of passion as she returned his caresses. Above them she could see the branches of the trees swaying slightly in the breeze; the clouds scudding across the deep blue sky. Slowly awareness of her position brought her back to her senses. What in the name of God was she doing lying here in Danny McGowan's arms? And out in the open like this! What if anyone saw them? Had she no shame? Clawing wildly at him, she at last managed to free herself and was soon upright. Panting and gasping for breath, she gazed down at him in horror. 'What the hell am I doing here?' she wailed. 'This is all wrong. I must be out of my mind.'

He sat up, arms around his knees, and eyed her warily. He felt thwarted. He had delayed far too long. But he was more experienced now and had wanted her to enjoy it; to encourage her to come back for more. Not like the last fumbling effort when he had failed her so miserably. Another minute or two and there would have been no turning back. She would have been his for the taking. 'It feels too right to be wrong, Liz,' he reasoned softly. 'You know that. It was meant to be. We won't be the only ones to play away from home, you know. No one need be any the wiser if we meet now and again.' He reached one hand towards her in invitation.

She waved it away. 'That doesn't make it right! *I'll* know.'

He rose to his feet and, resisting her efforts to hold him at bay, took her gently by the arms. She

277

trembled in his grasp as his arms circled her waist. His lips against her ear, he whispered, 'Right or wrong, it's meant to be. You know it is, Liz. I made a stupid mistake. I must have been mad. Don't make me suffer the rest of my life because of it. I need you. I need to know I can see you sometimes, to make life worthwhile.' His lips trailed over her cheek and gently covered hers, brushing them until she moaned deep in her throat at the naked passion he aroused in her. She enjoyed love-making with David so why did Danny thrill her so? Was this wild passion so raw because it was forbidden fruit? If she was reading a book and the heroine was wavering like this, Liz would be muttering under her breath, telling her to be sensible.

She squirmed in his arms. 'Look, Danny, I can't go through with this. It would be a mortal sin.'

His lips tightened. 'But you want to? At least admit that, Liz!'

'Yes, I admit I want to, but that doesn't make it right. It's still a mortal sin.'

'How can you talk about sin, Liz? Tell me something. Do you not feel it's a sin when you lie in *his* arms, night after night? What about all those sins, eh? After all, in the eyes of the church you aren't married, you know.'

'Being me, yes, sometimes I do worry about that. But I still feel married to David. He's my husband in every sense of the word, Danny. And in my own way I love him. Giving into this lust I feel for you would only make matters worse.'

She had managed to escape his embrace and was frantically brushing grass and twigs from her clothes. 'Look at the state of me. I must need my head examined.'

Since her marriage she had let her hair grow. It swung like a bronze curtain shot with golden highlights from the sun filtering through the branches above. Unable to help himself he grabbed her once more, sinking his face into its perfumed warmth.

Alarmed, she cried out, 'Stop it, Danny. Stop it at once!'

Knowing she wanted him and was afraid of her own emotions, he was tempted to compel her but knew she would never forgive him. She had to be willing. Reluctantly, he released her, and without further ado she headed down the path towards sanity. He dusted himself down and followed her more slowly, down the twisting path and on to the Antrim Road.

Here she faced him, flushed and unhappy. 'I'm sorry, Danny, for giving you the wrong impression, but I know now there can never be anything between us. I must run. David will be home soon.'

'You'll change your mind, Liz. I know you will,' he said confidently. 'When no baby is forthcoming, remember my offer. I'll be only too happy to oblige, and you can trust me to keep my mouth shut. Just remember that.'

Pleased to have given the joiners a really good rollicking about their unprofessional approach, and confident that all the shoddy work would be rectified and in the future done properly, David left them to get on with it. Leaving the newly

279

acquired security man to lock up when the workers left, he set off early for home.

As was usual these days when his mind was free from thoughts of work, he dwelled on their apparently barren state. Victoria and he had been contented enough without a family. In fact, she hadn't really wanted a child. But Liz was a different kettle of fish. If it wasn't to be, would she accept it? Could he keep her tied to him if he failed to give her a child? Would it be fair? She was a young attractive woman and would soon meet someone else. But how could he live without her? She was his all.

To his surprise, as he drove along the Antrim Road he caught sight of his wife, deep in conversation with someone. Intending to give her a lift home, he slowed and reversed the car until he had a clear view of them in the rear mirror. Dismay entered his heart when he saw her companion was Danny McGowan. Kath had confided in him that he lived somewhere about here, but she didn't know just where.

Whatever Danny was saying to her, Liz was disagreeing with him. Her head swung in denial and she turned on her heel and headed back along the Antrim Road. Danny following her at a more leisurely pace. What on earth was going on? Where was Liz going? How come she was with Danny in the first place? Afraid of what he might find out if he offered his wife a lift, David continued on his way. He must keep things in their proper perspective and not start jumping to conclusions. Liz was sure to explain everything when she returned.

Ten minutes later, when she turned down Somerton Road, Liz was dismayed to see her husband's car in the drive. Hurrying round to the back of the bungalow, she entered the kitchen. David was at the cooker. The cabbage was bubbling away in the pot and he was testing the potatoes.

'Ah, David, I meant to have your meal ready.' Her eyes went to the kitchen clock. 'You're home early, so you are,' she accused.

'Just a little. When I saw your car outside I knew you wouldn't be far away. And since the pork fillet looks about ready, I put a light to the cabbage and potatoes. Actually, I came home early because the picture of you soaking in a soapy bath played havoc with my imagination. I had an idea, I might join you.' Brows raised he asked, 'Did you bathe?'

'No, I decided to make a special dinner for you instead.'

'A wonderful idea, love. And don't think for one minute I don't appreciate it.'

He was tempted to broach the subject of seeing her with Danny, but sure she would mention it herself, waited patiently. When she did not volunteer the information, he asked casually, 'Where were you?' He was eyeing her covertly and noted the wave of colour that swept from jaw to hairline. Fear entered his heart. She looked so damned guilty. Where had she and Danny been, and more to the point, what had they been up to? She had yet to look him full in the face.

'I nipped out to the store to get some ice cream.

281

I'm doing fresh fruit cocktail for dessert and I know how you love ice cream with it. Remember we had the last of it at the weekend?' As proof she was telling the truth she removed a carton of soft-scoop vanilla from her shopping bag and, opening the freezer door, made room for it on a shelf, all the while avoiding his eyes. 'Look, I insist you go and sit down. I'll give you a call when everything's ready.'

'I don't mind giving you a hand.'

'I know you don't, but this is my treat. Please, read the paper or something?'

Seeing she was agitated, he nodded and retreated to the lounge. He was perturbed. Did her failure to mention Danny mean she was seeing him on the quiet? He found that hard to believe, Liz was such an honest person. But surely if her encounter with him was innocent, she would have said so? She might yet say something, he chided himself. After all, he had caught her on the hop. He must bide his time and not jump to wild conclusions.

Try though he might to put the picture of Danny and his wife from his mind, doubts plagued him. Danny was such a virile young man. They had looked good together. And she had looked far from happy. Just the way he'd expect Liz to look if she was doing wrong. If she were having an affair, would he be able to turn a blind eye to it? He thought not. Pray God he wouldn't be put to the test.

In the kitchen Liz sagged against the table, relieved to have time to pull herself together. Dear God, the way she was behaving she may as well have been having it off with Danny. What would it be like if she ever gave into his desires? It was something that must never happen. She would never be able to face David. She would be so weighed down with guilt he would surely guess and how could that bring happiness to any of them? Oh, how she wished she had never run into Danny last week.

By the time dinner was ready, Liz had her emotions under control. If her smile was a little strained when she called David to the dining room, she didn't realize it and his affable manner soon eased the tension. The meal was eaten in comparative silence. Unable to refer to her meeting with Danny in a casual manner, guilt kept her quite mute. David's tentative attempts to find out by indirect methods about her meeting fell on barren ground. Normally she would have guessed he was fishing for information and been horrified at the idea. However, her thoughts were in such turmoil as she wrestled within herself about whether or not to mention her meeting with Danny, that the gist of her husband's questions did not sink in.

Afraid he would get the wrong idea, she decided not to confide in him. This decision led to more unrest throughout the evening. Unable to settle and watch television, Liz excused herself and retired to bed early. David sat for a long time, gazing blindly at the screen. He felt so helpless. But then, he reasoned inwardly, his wife had not asked for time off work so the meeting could not have been planned. Well then, why had she not mentioned it? Perhaps it had slipped her mind? He grimaced at the stupidity of this idea. He was deluding himself. She had been like a cat on a hot griddle all evening. Still the chances were he was probably making a mountain out of a molehill. Easier in his mind, he locked up for the night. However, his anxiety soon resurfaced. His wife feigned sleep when he joined her, something she had never done before. Why start now?

Liz lay with eyes tightly closed and prayed her husband would be fooled. For the life of her she could not bear him to touch her. Tonight, with the memory of Danny's passion still fresh in her mind, she might find her husband wanting. In his arms she might be tempted to blurt out the truth and hope for his understanding, but after the way she had behaved would he believe that it had been just a few kisses? She couldn't risk it and sighed with relief when David apparently fell asleep. Somehow or other she had to lay Danny's ghost, once and for all!

'Where on earth have you been?' Bridget greeted her husband angrily.

He decided to confess at least part of the truth. After all someone might have seen him with Liz and Bridget might hear tell of it. 'I met Liz O'Hara at the store and we talked for a while.'

Her chin rose in the air and her eyes narrowed suspiciously. Since learning that the Atkinsons lived somewhere nearby, she had been dreading something like this. 'For an hour or more?' she asked plaintively.

'Oh, no. After I left her I met Dougie Brown

and couldn't get away from him. You know what he's like.' She should believe that. Dougie gossiped like an old woman.

Still unconvinced, Bridget scowled at him. 'Your dinner's in the oven. It's ruined, but don't blame me. It was ready ages ago.'

'I'm starving. I could eat a horse, let alone a well-cooked dinner.'

'Huh! I'm afraid it's more than well-cooked.'

'Is Martin asleep?' She nodded and he continued appeasingly, 'You look tired, love. Take a wee nap and I'll clear up the kitchen when I've eaten my dinner.'

She did feel tired. She always felt tired these days; tired and frumpy. With an abrupt nod she left him to it. Lying on top of the bedclothes in the darkened room she thought back over her married life. It consisted of looking after Martin, cleaning and cooking. One day like another; nothing exciting to look forward to. Her prophecy had come true. She spent long days alone with the child except for visits from her mother and the odd one from Marie. Still, she was in no position to complain. True to his word, Danny worked long hours to get enough money for a deposit on a house and their savings were rising slowly but surely. At least, she thought he was doing a lot of overtime. Were all those hours spent in Mackie's? She had never doubted this before so why now? And meanwhile she was bored out of her mind. The flat felt like her own private prison.

Now she was suspicious as well. Was Danny seeing Liz O'Hara? They both had cars and could easily make opportunities to meet at some out-of-the-way place. Was that why he hardly ever touched his wife nowadays? Tears seeped from her eyes and ran unheeded into her hairline and on to the pillow case. She felt so unwanted; had made such a mess of her life. At her age she should be out enjoying herself! All her mates were still going to the dances and pictures, and having a whale of a time. Her thoughts, as was usual when she felt unhappy, turned to Peter. If only she had met him first, how different things might have been. She wouldn't be bored married to him. Or would she? Did all married couples get into a rut. Even Peter rarely visited them now. That was her fault. She had acted uneasily when he was last around and he must have sensed it and been scared off.

Danny found he wasn't as hungry as he had thought. The sight of the chop, potatoes and vegetables congealing in a pool of gravy put him right off. With a grimace, he scraped the food into the bin and covered it with other rubbish. He didn't want Bridget to discover it and start a lament over the price of chops. Next he filled the sink with hot soapy water and began to wash the dishes. His thoughts were full of Liz. He closed his eyes and could still feel the contours of her body eagerly pressed against his; the silken feel of her hair against his cheek. Awash with desire, he lamented his own stupidity. Why couldn't he have waited?

He had to persuade her to meet him. Just now and again. For heaven's sake, some of the guys in work had mistresses and vowed it made all concerned happier. The secret was to keep the two lives separate; keep the wife happily in the dark. That shouldn't be too hard where Bridget was concerned, she was so gullible. He rinsed the milk bottles and opened the outer door to put them out beside the steps for the milkman the following morning. A glance around caused him to pause as he saw his brother hop off the bus further along the road and stride towards the house. Danny's watch showed him it was almost half-past six. A bit early for a visit, but then members of the family knew they were always welcome. Leaving the door slightly ajar for Joseph to enter, he returned to his work in the kitchen.

Unaware that Danny had seen him, Joseph crept stealthily past the open door and quietly climbed the stairs; relieved when he gained entry to Ian's flat unobserved.

A couple of minutes passed, and Danny went to the door and gazed along the road. He shook his head. He must have been mistaken. But that lad had looked like Joseph. He shrugged. Didn't they say everyone had a double? The likeness had certainly been uncanny. Closing the door, he went to wake Bridget and Martin. If the child slept any longer he'd be up all night.

Bridget was just leaving the bedroom with Martin in her arms. 'Well, were you able to eat your dinner?' she asked.

'Every last bit of it. It was lovely,' he lied.

'Huh!'

'How's about taking a run up to see the grandparents? After that nap Martin will be up till we're going to bed, so what about it?'

Her whole demeanour brightened. 'Would it be safe, Danny?' she asked tentatively. Trouble often broke out between the army and the youths on the Falls Road.

'We won't stay late. It'll be all right.'

She was touched that he was willing to take his car out at night. So many cars were hijacked then they rarely went out. 'You mean it, Danny?'

Ashamed to witness how easily pleased she was, he cried. 'Of course I do.' He really must make a bigger effort to take her out more often. After all she was his wife and the days must be long for her here on her own. He reached for his son. 'Here, I'll wash his face and hands and put on his shoes. Away you go and get ready.'

'Give me ten minutes to put on some make-up,' Bridget cried joyfully. 'And then we'll hit the road.'

They went to Leeson Street first. It being unusual for them to visit in the evening, especially during the week, Barney and Martha were overjoyed at their unexpected appearance. They had been worried about their daughter. As soon as she could, Martha warned her husband to watch his tongue, saying this might be the start of better times for Bridget.

Bridget could see her mother was having difficulty containing her excitement and after some chit-chat Barney invited his son-in-law round to the Clock Bar for a pint. Bridget opened her mouth to remind her father that her husband was

288

driving, but with a reassuring gesture Danny said, 'I'll just have half a lager.'

Her father was quick to back him up. 'Do you think I'd ply him with drink and him driving? We won't be long.'

When the door closed on them, Bridget turned to her mother with a wide grin. 'Well, now me da's got Danny out of the way, tell me what you're so excited about?'

'How did you guess?'

'It's written all over your face. Don't tell me one of the lads is getting married at last?'

'No such luck!'

'You shouldn't look after them so well,' Bridget chided her. 'I can't think what else would get you so excited.'

'Forget about the lads. I've given up all hope of them ever getting married.' Martha sat forward on the edge of her chair in her eagerness. 'I heard some good news today. If you hadn't come over tonight, I was coming over to your place tomorrow.'

Bridget looked mystified. 'Good news that concerns me?'

'Yes. The butcher's son is getting married.'

Bridget looked at her mother as if she was going senile then said gently, as if humouring her, 'Why would I be interested in the fact Jack McCann is getting married? You do mean Jack?'

'Yes, of course I mean Jack. Who else, for heaven's sake? They only have one son.'

Still mystified, Bridget said, 'I'm afraid I don't follow you, Mam?'

'Oh, I'm telling this all wrong,' Martha cried in

289

frustration. 'The bottom line is, the flat above the butcher's shop on the corner of the street will be vacant in a couple of weeks' time. Jack is buying a house.'

Bridget continued to look blankly at her mother. What on earth had this to do with her?

'What do you think, love? Will I find out more about it? I've been watching you, Bridget, and a blind man on a galloping horse could see you're not very happy stuck over there on the Antrim Road. Your da and I are worried sick about you.'

Comprehension dawned and Bridget laughed at her stupidity. 'You mean, you think I should go after the flat?'

'Why not? You'd be happier living over here among your own.'

'You're right, I'm not happy,' her daughter admitted. 'But don't you go blaming Danny. He's working all hours to get the deposit for a house. It's just I'm bored stiff.' She was already wondering how a move back to the Falls Road would affect her. The Iveagh Estate was a fair distance on up the Falls Road from Leeson Street. Why, if she hadn't frequented the 'dive' she might never have met Noel Gibson. Their paths might never have crossed. Chances were they would not meet again. So why not come back to live on the Falls Road? Because of the troubles, that was why. It was safer on the Antrim Road and she had Martin to consider.

She was silent so long Martha cried out in frustration, 'I thought you'd dive at the chance. It's not awfully big, but it does have a bathroom. It won't be empty for long, you know. As it is, it

290

might already have been snapped up.'

'Mam, would it not be foolish to bring Martin back here? I mean, it's quiet where we live. But up here there's trouble a lot of the time.'

'How do you think the rest of us manage, Bridget, eh? We keep our noses clean and our doors closed at night. That's how we manage. You'd be all right, so you would.'

Bridget came to a decision. If it was safe otherwise, she had to risk meeting Noel Gibson. After all, she couldn't run away from him for the rest of her life. Chances were she might never see him again. And all her family and friends lived on the Falls. She would be far happier here.

'You're right, Mam. It's too good a chance to miss. I'll mention it to Danny when they come back from the pub. I'm sure he'll be only too glad to move back here.' But would he? she asked herself. Would he want to leave the Antrim Road now he and Liz O'Hara had made contact? All would soon be revealed.

She put the idea of moving to him as soon as he and her father walked through the door, her eyes fixed on his face as she awaited his reaction.

'What do you think, Danny? Mam has heard on the grapevine that the flat above the butcher's shop will be vacant soon. She's willing to put a word in for us. Would you fancy moving back to the Falls Road?'

He looked at her blankly for a few moments and then slowly nodded. 'If it's what you want, love, I'm willing.'

'Great! Mam, will you make some inquiries and find out how much the rent is, and how much bond money will be required?'

'I'll go round first thing tomorrow morning,' Martha said, with a happy look in her husband's direction. 'As I said, it might already be promised to someone else, you know. But never venture, never gain.'

They delayed a short time until Danny reminded Bridget they still had to visit his home. 'If me ma finds out I was up here and didn't call over, she'd hit the roof. Not that she would care about seeing me. No, it's this little fellow she'll want to see.' He swooped Martin up in his arms and the child howled with delight. 'Come on, son. Let's put your coat on and go see Grannie McGowan.'

Joe was sprawled in an armchair in front of the fire when they knocked on the kitchen door and entered the house. He rose quickly to his feet, a delighted grin on his face, arms reaching for his grandson.

'Jane, Jane! Look who's here. It's young Martin.'

'And the other two as well, Mam, if you're interested,' Danny gaily sang out.

Jane descended the stairs in a noisy rush and the joyful look on her face as she reached for her grandson made Bridget realize how cut off from their only grandchild Danny's family were. It would please a lot of people if they came back to live on the Falls, but better not raise their hopes by talking about it until she was sure they were in with a chance.

After a lot of kissing and cuddling of her grandson, Jane insisted on making tea and retired to the kitchen, Danny warning her it would have to be a quick cup as they didn't want to be out too late.

'Is Joseph with you?' asked Joe.

'No. Why would he be with us?' Danny queried.

'He had a late class at school today and said he would go along to your flat for an hour or so afterwards.'

'He must have changed his mind. Hey, hold on a minute. I thought I saw him when I was putting out the milk bottles but he never materialized so I thought I was mistaken. Why, the little devil must have a girlfriend over there.'

Throughout this exchange, Bridget had been changing Martin's nappy. She didn't want to get involved in any conversation about Joseph. Now Danny called to her. 'Bridget ... does Joseph have a girlfriend over the Antrim Road direction, someone we don't know about?'

Without lifting her head she replied, 'Not that I'm aware of.'

'Queer,' murmured Danny.

He couldn't have picked a more appropriate word if he had a dictionary in his hand, Bridget thought grimly. If only she could speak out.

The door opened then and Joseph stood gazing at them in surprise. Let's see you get out of this, me lad, thought Bridget bitterly. They all looked at him expectantly.

'Is anything wrong?' he asked apprehensively, after a furtive glance in Bridget's direction.

'We were just talking about you,' his father volunteered, fixing a stern eye on him.

293

Joseph nervously licked his lips and his eyes once again swung to Bridget and away.

'I thought you said you were going to call up to the flat and visit your brother after school today?' his father continued.

'I meant to, but it was so late when I got away, I knew they would be at their dinner and didn't want to disturb them.'

Danny laughed aloud at this lame excuse. 'Come off it, Joseph. You know you're welcome anytime. You've been caught on, lad. Your secret is out. I actually saw you on the Antrim Road but when you didn't come in, I thought you must have a double. Come on, own up.'

Once more Joseph glanced at Bridget, eyes full of anguish. Her heart ached for him, but wasn't it better if it all came out in the open? Then, to her great surprise she found herself coming to his aid. Whether or not through fear of reprisals she didn't know. The words came out of her mouth without another thought. 'You'd better come clean, Joseph. They're convinced you have a girlfriend out near us.'

His relief was pitiful to behold and Bridget could not understand how everyone else failed to notice. 'Me, with a girlfriend? You've got to be joking.'

Exactly, you bloody queer! thought Bridget. But this lot can't see the obvious.

At this point Jane came through with a tray and the matter was conveniently shelved as Danny rose to relieve her of it.

On the journey home they discussed how

294

moving back to the Falls Road could help them financially. The rent was sure to be less, and Martha had hinted she would look after Martin if Bridget wanted to return to work. The very idea of returning to work filled her with joy. To be out and about. To mix with her old work mates again.

'Do you fancy the idea, Danny?'

'Well, it's a bit too close to your ma and da and mine for comfort, but if you get your job back we shouldn't be there long. We'll be able to save a fair sum every week.'

She was silent so long he gave her a sidelong glance. 'I know what you're thinking! Danny will get up to his old tricks again. With living so near to his old mates, he'll booze all the extra money away.'

'The thought had crossed my mind,' she confessed.

'I'm a changed man, Bridget. I promise to get you a house of your own as soon as I possibly can.'

She wanted to question him about Liz O'Hara. The thought of him and her together earlier that day really bugged Bridget. However, she thought better of the idea. If he wasn't interested in Liz any more, why put ideas into his head?

'Do you want to move, Bridget?'

She gaped at him in amazement. 'I can't believe I'm getting the chance.'

'It's just, well, I was wondering if our young Joseph was making a nuisance of himself and you didn't want to be moving too close to him?'

'What do you mean?'

'Has he been bothering you when I'm not there?'

'What are you suggesting? That I'm encouraging him?' Her voice had risen shrilly.

'No! Good God, no! Whatever gave you that idea?' Danny's brow puckered into a bewildered frown. 'It's just something wasn't quite right back there. Unfortunately me ma came in at the wrong time and got him off the hook. The way he looked at you... I got the notion he might fancy you and was pestering you and was afraid of you saying so. I know you wouldn't encourage him, Bridget. Give me some credit for heaven's sake. He's my brother! But I don't want him upsetting you.'

Silently, Bridget cursed Joseph. That was another reason she would be glad to move. Her brother-in-law was obviously still using them as a cover for his secret meetings with Ian. 'To be truthful, Danny, I hardly ever see him now,' she confessed abruptly.

'That's all right, then. So long as he isn't being a nuisance, that's all that matters.'

The thought of Liz had also entered Danny's mind. Perhaps it was all for the best. That she still cared for him he didn't doubt, and it sent a thrill through him when he thought about it. But he couldn't really imagine her playing the field. That sort of thing would be beneath her. Unless of course no baby came about. Then she might just take him up on his offer. Who knows? Perhaps even with David's blessing. A warm glow filled him at the good turn he would be doing them, and enjoying every minute of it into the bargain.

296

Not for one minute did he think of the harm it would do his own marriage should Bridget ever find out. After all, she was his wife!

A month later Bridget stood in her new home, in the midst of all her belongings, and her heart sang with joy. The flat was smaller than the old one but that was something she could live with. The rent was almost halved and the bond money was less than they'd received back from the other flat, so they had a bit in hand. Also it would be cheaper to heat and maintain. The future was beginning to look bright. No more scrimping and saving. No more doing without essentials. She was in her glory.

Martha watched her daughter and tears stung her eyes. So far Bridget hadn't had much of a marriage. With Danny working long hours and her unable even to afford the bus fare to visit her family, life had taken its toll on her. She had become thin and uncaring about her appearance. Probably had given Danny and the child the best of the food whilst she had gone without. And look at her now! She looked so happy at the very prospect of living in this wee flat. With a little help from her parents, things should change for the better.

Hugging her mother close, Bridget cried, 'Oh, Mam, this is wonderful. I'll never be able to thank you enough.'

Touched, but embarrassed by this show of affection, Martha pushed her gently away. 'Just be happy, love. That's all the thanks I need.' Surreptitiously brushing tears from her cheeks, she continued, 'Now let's get these boxes sorted out and get the curtains hung. You need a bit of privacy from passing buses.'

By the time Danny arrived home from work the curtains were in place, all the shelves and cupboards were stocked and the lesser pieces of furniture were pushed against the walls until Bridget decided where she wanted to put them.

He eyed the living room and nodded in approval. 'Very cosy. Very cosy indeed. You've obviously been busy.' He nodded down at the thick green carpet. 'That's a grand carpet, and everything spotlessly clean. I think we've done the right thing, Bridget.'

'I knew everything would be spick and span. Mrs McCann wouldn't want any talk about the state of the place. Mam wanted to send Dad and one of the lads round after tea to help you put up the bed and move the heavy furniture into place, but I told her your ones would be coming over to see the flat and your dad and Peter would give you a hand.'

'You're right, Bridget. They are coming over and we don't want to give offence. Make them think it's all onesided and we don't need their help. They'll be here soon, so how's about a bite to eat for your starving husband?'

'I've some spaghetti bolognese ready. I'll lift it while you're washing your hands.' Her voice was flat as she led the way into the small dining room. Why on earth could her husband not show her some affection? If only he would take her in his arms and show pleasure in their new home. But no, the days when Danny had shown spon-

298

taneous joy at any of their joint ventures had disappeared shortly after their honeymoon. Now the car was the only thing he drooled over. *They* were like a couple who had been married about fifty years. Well, there would be changes or she'd know the reason why!

Danny eyed her closely. 'Have I said or done something wrong?' he asked apprehensively.

'As if you could ever do or say anything wrong,' Bridget answered dryly.

For the life of him Danny couldn't be sure whether she was jesting or being sarcastic. As he washed his hands he pondered on all that had been said since he came home. He couldn't see where he had put a foot wrong. If he lived to be a hundred he would never be able to understand his wife. There was no pleasing her.

Liz sighed with relief when Kath passed on the news that Danny and Bridget now lived above the butcher's shop at the corner of Leeson Street. Knowing just how close Danny had lived to them, the past month had been spent in constant fear he would dare come near the bungalow. There had been a couple of times when David had answered the phone in the evening and the caller had apologized for dialling a wrong number and hung up. She had been terrified in case it was Danny trying to contact her. But then everybody dialled wrong numbers and David certainly had not seemed in the least perturbed. It was her own guilty conscience that was making her so uneasy. Was she actually trying to will Danny to get in touch with her? Did she really want him to? No!

She was dwelling too much on babies. That's what was wrong with her. Danny's offer sometimes made sense to her. Not always, but sometimes, when she was feeling a bit down. Even her mother was losing patience with her, reminding her she should be counting her blessings. In spite of her worries, she smiled when she thought of her mother. Kath had certainly blossomed. She was very fashion conscious at the moment, looking for quality and not quantity as had once been her habit.

Her hair was now cut and shaped by the best hairdresser in town and her figure needed no help. Her bust was full and firm, her waist neat and hips trim. She looked much younger than her forty-four years and, much to the chagrin of Neville, quite a few of the unattached men at the golf club were trying to get into her good books on a Saturday night. She never, ever sat out a single dance.

David confided in Liz that it had come to his ears Neville Barnes was also sprucing himself up. He worked out at a club in town a few days a week and had consequently lost a lot of weight. At Fortwilliam that Saturday night as he watched his mother-in-law and Neville waltz around the floor, David whispered in his wife's ear, 'You know something, Liz? I think we might see a wedding in the none too distant future.'

Liz had been watching Irene and Dick who were as usual bickering. She drew back her head and gazed up at her husband in amazement. 'I don't think those two will ever get married.'

A puzzled frown knitted David's brows. Then, following the direction of his wife's gaze he laughed aloud. 'I don't mean Dick and Irene. I mean your mother and Neville.'

To his surprise his wife retorted, 'I wouldn't be too sure of that either, if I were you. Mam hasn't a good word to say about Neville. I can't understand her attitude towards him. I'm surprised he continues to bother with her.'

Neville was thinking along similar lines to Liz. He gazed down at the woman in his arms and asked himself why he bothered trying to cultivate her friendship. Kath was so distant, he was getting nowhere with her. Then as he led her into a reverse turn her firm breasts brushed across his chest and he knew why. He wanted her. More than he had ever wanted her in the past and that was saying a lot. She was always in his thoughts, but he was no further forward now than he was at the beginning of their renewed acquaintance. She still refused to go out alone with him. Was it because she was afraid of her own emotions? Could that possibly be the reason? Or did she really feel nothing for him any more? Then the thrill of holding her, the memory of how things had been between them in the past, made him determined to be patient. He might still win her over.

He caught his daughter's eye and winked. Liz gave him a big grin and he once more bitterly regretted his decision to be no part of her life. Thoughtlessly, he said, 'Kath, do you not think it's time we told Liz the truth?'

She gaped up at him in surprise. 'I beg your

301

pardon? You promised me, Neville Barnes, that if I came to Fortwilliam regularly you would not tell her who you are. Well, I'm here, and I'm holding you to that promise.'

'Kath, to be truthful, I thought we would become close friends...'

She interrupted him. 'I warned you that wouldn't happen. You should have paid more heed to my words.'

'You won't give me a chance to show you how good a life we could have together. I've a lovely home and I'm not short a bob or two. Let's set a time limit. Let me take you out and about for ... say ... a month or maybe two? If I make no headway, I'll call it a day and leave you in peace. How's about it, eh, Kath? We're two lonely people. We could be happy together, I know we could.'

Big limpid blue eyes gazed up at him as she contemplated his proposition. It would be nice to be entertained. To be wined and dined. She would get a chance to show off all her lovely new clothes. It would be a waste of time, of course, but he didn't want to hear that, so why not give it a go?

'And what about Liz? If we don't make a go of it, do you promise not to tell her who you are?'

Confident that given the chance he would be able to win her over, Neville nodded eagerly. 'I promise.'

'All right, let's see how it goes then.'

Liz was surprised when her mother started dating Neville. They were out nearly every night

302

of the week and it was obvious Kath was having a whale of a time.

'Looks like you were right after all, David. There might be a wedding in the near future.'

'She could do a lot worse, you know, Liz.'

'There could be problems. Although Mam agreed to my marrying you outside the church, I can't see her doing it herself. She's one of the old school. Do you think Neville would consent to marry in the Catholic Church?'

David considered her words. 'To be truthful, if they had been younger, I don't think he would, but since there is no chance of children, I think he very well may.'

She eyed him intently for some moments. 'Would you have married me in the Catholic Church, David?'

'Ah now, that question never arose, Liz.'

'But if it had, would you?'

He shrugged slightly. 'I honestly don't know. I've never had much time for the teachings of Catholicism, but feeling as I do about you, I very well may have married you in the church.'

'But you promised me that any children we might have would be brought up Catholics?'

'I suppose I knew in my heart that the chances of my fathering a child were remote.'

'So it had crossed your mind even then, but you didn't consider it important enough to mention it to me?'

'I wanted you any way I could get you, Liz. You know that! You know I'm daft about you.'

'If we do have children, what then?'

'I am a man of my word and if we are blessed

303

with a child it will be reared a Catholic.'

Another long considering look was bestowed on him and then, rising to her feet, she made to leave the lounge. At the door his voice stayed her.

'Remember, Liz, if we should ever divorce you would be free to remarry in the Catholic Church.' A perplexed frown knitted her brow as she turned to face him. He continued, 'As far as your church is concerned you would be a free woman. It doesn't recognize our marriage.'

'I wish you would stop talking about divorce, David. I'm beginning to think it's what you want.'

'You know that's not true, Liz.'

'Huh! Do I?'

David gazed blankly at the door after she'd left the room. Another month gone and still no sign of a pregnancy. Liz was so intense when they made love now it was putting him off. He felt more used than wanted and was inclined to think she was thwarting her own desires. He dredged down into the depths of his memory and painfully uncovered the incident that Irene had sought to acquaint Liz with.

It was a very painful memory for him. At the time he and Victoria had had words about it and it was some time before he was able completely to forgive her betrayal, as he had seen it. They had been to the Opera House and returned to the bungalow for a late supper and a drink. Victoria and he had, at his instigation, been trying for a baby. They'd both had tests done, something he had not confessed to Liz, and were waiting the results.

His wife and Irene had spent a long time in the kitchen. When they rejoined the company, he had laughingly asked what dark deeds they had been plotting. To his great consternation Irene had answered him readily enough.

'I've been consoling Victoria in her great disappointment.'

'What disappointment?'

A puzzled frown creased Irene's brow and she glanced in bewilderment at his wife. Victoria made an abrupt gesture towards her as if trying to stop her.

David had repeated, 'What disappointment?'

Irene was flustered. 'Well, about your low sperm count and her poor chances of ever becoming a mother.'

Since Victoria had failed to tell him this devastating news, he felt gutted. There were three other couples besides themselves and as was usual in these cases, Irene's words fell into a lull in the conversation. An embarrassed silence ensued and Irene approached him and whispered. 'You must be very disappointed. I'm so sorry, David. I didn't mean to let the cat out of the bag. I thought you knew.'

Feeling as if he had been stripped of his manhood in front of their friends, he had mumbled excuses and retired to the bedroom, leaving his wife to entertain the guests. Soon they had all departed and Victoria had joined him.

Instead of the apology and sympathy he'd expected, she had been quite angry. 'There was no need to break up a perfectly lovely evening because of silly hurt pride.'

'My pride? You told Irene something as private as this before you even told me and you think my pride is hurt? Let me tell you something, there's more than my pride hurt.'

'Irene is my best friend. I never dreamed she would blurt it out like that. Besides, she thought you already knew.'

He wouldn't have believed she could be so callous about something so important to him. But then, had she ever really wanted a child?

He rubbed his hands wearily across his face as if to erase the bitter memory of that episode. He should have let Irene tell Liz his dark secret that night. It would have been easier on her to have known sooner. It would have been easier parting with her then. Now it would be like cutting off an arm or a leg. She was so much a part of him, he could not picture life without her. And to crown it all, she thought he wanted a divorce. How could she be so foolish as to think such a thing of him?

Neville and Kath had been going out for a month now and he felt he was fighting a losing battle. He had wined and dined her in all the fashionable restaurants and out-of-town pubs. Taken her to the cinema and Opera House. Had bought her expensive perfume and gifts. At first she had demurred and refused to accept them, saying she didn't want to be committed in any way. He had persuaded her he wanted her to have the gifts no matter how things turned out. Now, four weeks on, he was beginning to despair of ever winning her over.

They had been to a concert in St Mary's Hall and at the door of her home Kath turned to face him. 'Would you care to come in for a nightcap?'

He had been expecting the usual. 'Thank you very much for a lovely evening and good night.' So at her invitation his heart started to race as he eagerly nodded his acceptance. This was the first time he had been asked over the doorstep since his initial proposal of giving things a month's trial. He warned himself to be wary and not to take anything for granted.

Kath removed her coat and motioned him to do likewise.

'I'll pour us a drink and then we must talk.'

Neville sipped his drink in silence. She sat with her hands clasped around her glass, gazing into its contents. Her face, in the shadow of the table lamp, looked young and vulnerable. She really was a very attractive woman and he was an old man. How dare he even hope she might learn to care for him again?

He could see she was working herself up to some announcement and since he expected to be disappointed he sat in silence, awaiting the inevitable. He had no intention of making it easy for her by putting the words into her mouth.

At last she spoke haltingly, 'Neville, it's been a month now and you have to admit we're no closer...' Great blue eyes full of sorrow were fixed on his face as she prepared to let him down as gently as possible.

'That's not my fault,' he interrupted her.

'I know that! But I can't pretend to emotions I don't feel. I feel guilty as hell about wasting your time, so shall we call it a day?'

'Forgive me if I'm wrong, but I was under the impression you were enjoying yourself?'

'Oh, I was. I am. Don't doubt that for one minute. I've had the time of my life, but I don't want you to be deluded into thinking we're going anywhere.' Kath shrugged her shoulders. 'I'm sorry.'

Rage was boiling up inside him. She was certainly getting her pound of flesh. He warned himself to be cool. Noticing his hand was shaking slightly, he carefully set his glass of beer down on the coffee table beside him, relieved when not a drop was spilt.

'I seem to remember we agreed to one or two months?'

'You're only wasting your time and money, Neville.'

'Well, it's my time. Shall we give it another month?'

Her eyes widened, becoming anxious. 'Are you sure it's what you want? You're not getting anything out of this.'

'I have the pleasure of your company. At my age it's nice to squire an attractive woman around town.' He grimaced wryly. 'It gives my ego a bit of a boost.'

'I'll never marry you, Neville.'

At these words his brows drew together and he glowered at her. 'I don't recall asking you to.'

It was like a slap in the face, but Kath managed to greet the words with a wry smile. After all, this was good news to her. She didn't want to marry him, did she? 'Thank goodness for that! That's all

308

right then. If you're sure you want another month of my company, I'll be glad to oblige.'

Aware that if he stayed any longer he might not be able to control his tongue, and things might be said that would be irrevocable and put an end to their relationship altogether, he rose to his feet. 'I'd better go now, while the going's good.'

'But ... you haven't finished your drink.'

'That at least is one pleasure I can forgo. I'll give you a ring when I've something planned.'

About to open the outer door, he turned and looked down at her. 'Do you not think I at least deserve a good night kiss?'

Dutifully she raised an expressionless face. It was dark in the hall, only the light from the living room shining through. He gazed at her for some seconds. In the shadows, she looked like the young girl he had seduced all those years ago and the breath caught in his throat at the memory. Taking her in his arms, he gently brushed her cool lips with his. It was enough to set him off and he became rough, crushing his mouth against her, seeking some response. He would be damned if he'd let her treat him like this. After all, he had been here before and she had enjoyed it. So why not again? Gripping her close, he pounded his aroused body against hers. Alarmed, she tried to break free but his lips parted hers and to her amazement she felt excitement shoot through her. She pressed herself close and her lips moved hungrily under his. Her sudden capitulation took him completely by surprise and his grip on her slackened as he freed her lips to gaze at her in bewildered askance.

Immediately she broke free, turning away from him, her breath coming in short gasps.

'Kath?'

'I'm sorry, I don't know what came over me,' she admitted, hand pressed to her burning lips.

'You're not as indifferent to me as you pretend. That's what,' he said gently.

'You're wrong. I'm as surprised by my reaction as you apparently are.'

Moving closer, he said softly. 'Shall we give it a go? Can I stay the night, Kath?'

'*No*. If you stay it will finish us off for good. Can't you see I'm not ready for this yet?'

He thought about her words. Not ready for this *yet?* 'OK. Let's not rush it. I'm willing to wait. I'll pick you up at seven tomorrow night. All right?'

She nodded and he said, 'Get yourself on up to bed now, before I change my mind.' With these words he grabbed his coat off the rack and quietly let himself out of the house.

Kath stood all a-tremble, shaking her head from side to side in bewilderment. What had come over her? She didn't really want him. Maybe her body did, but then it had been so long since she'd had a man. In her youth she had been a very passionate woman. Had in fact been wanton. Neville had put paid to all that when he had refused even to acknowledge their child. Could she ever forgive him for that?

Mind in a turmoil, she rinsed the glasses. He must have been upset or he would never have left his beer, she thought wryly. One thing was sure. There would be no holding him at arm's length from now on. Did she want to? At her age she couldn't expect love to come along and sweep her off her feet. Still, it would be nice to feel some magic, like she had when she was young. She didn't want just to drift into an affair. Was it only the young who felt like that? She sighed as she slowly climbed the stairs. There was only one option left open to her, and that was to wait and see what another month's wining and dining brought about.

Neville's step was light as he walked to his car. He was relieved. Everything was going to work out all right after all. He could still get Kath to respond. Why hadn't he kissed her sooner? Because he was being the perfect gentleman, that's why. Things were certainly going to be different in future.

Liz's decision to go and see her mother was born out of desperation, the need to talk to someone who might understand her predicament. She saw so little of her these days; just Saturday nights at Fortwilliam when there was no chance to have a good heart-to-heart talk. At the end of the evening Neville usually whisked Kath off to a night club or whatever. As she passed the butcher's shop at the corner of Leeson Street her eyes ranged over the spotless white net curtains at the windows of the flat above it. How she envied Danny and Bridget their lovely son.

Her mother was delighted to see her and Liz scolded her. 'It's your fault we see so little of each other these days. Gallivanting every night of the week!'

Kath beamed happily at her. 'And enjoying

311

every minute of it.'

Her daughter's expression softened. 'I'm glad, Mam. You deserve to enjoy yourself.'

'What are you so desperate to see me alone for anyhow?'

Liz grimaced. 'I don't know where to start. It's all so complicated.'

'I've a bottle of wine. It's a good one. Neville brought it one night and I haven't had the opportunity to open it. This is as good an excuse as any. Wait until I pour some for us and then you can tell your agony aunt all the sordid details,' she said, with a grin at her own wit.

They drank one glass and Liz agreed with her that the wine was indeed very good, but Kath could see that her thoughts were elsewhere. The conversation had remained general. Kath started to replenish their glasses but Liz covered hers with her hand, reminding her mother that she was driving.

'Well, then, do you not think you should tell me what's troubling you?' Kath asked gently.

It all came pouring out in a gush. The fact that David had indeed been aware he was unlikely to father a child. How he had reminded Liz that if they were to divorce she could still marry in the Catholic Church as it didn't recognize their marriage.

'I'm beginning to think he regrets marrying me and wants a divorce,' she wailed. 'Who does he think I'd marry? Certainly not Danny. He's lost to me forever.'

'Let's get one thing straight, my dear. David does *not* want a divorce. He *loves* you.'

312

A suspicious look was bestowed on her. 'Have you two been talking about me?'

'When would we get the chance, eh?'

Head bowed, Liz said, 'I met Danny McGowan by chance some time ago, up in the castle grounds.'

'Oh?'

Ashamed, she met her mother's eyes. 'We got carried away a bit...'

'Ah, Liz, you didn't'

'No! No, not that. We just kissed.'

Thinking how she herself could easily have been carried away the night before, Kath's answer was heartfelt. 'Think God for that! Be careful, Liz. For a minute there I thought you were going to say you were carrying his child. Now *that's* something David wouldn't forgive.'

Hope dawned in Liz's eyes. Imagine her mother thinking along those lines. 'Would that be such a bad idea, Mam?' she asked tentatively.

Kath's face dropped in amazement. 'What on earth are you talking about?'

'Just think, if David can't give me a baby ... why not Danny?'

'Are you daft, girl? David would never hear tell of it. It would be the end of your marriage.'

'But he needn't know, Mam. Danny says I could trust him to hold his tongue.'

'You've actually discussed this with Danny Mc-Gowan?'

Liz grimaced at her mother's scandalized expression and admitted, 'It was his suggestion.'

'Was it indeed? And what if the child is the spitting image of him? Have you thought of that?'

313

She watched her daughter's face cloud over. 'No. I never thought of that.'

'Not only that,' Kath continued, 'think of his wife. The poor girl would be devastated if she ever found out. Besides, Danny would have you under his thumb for the rest of your life then. Why, you'd be open to all sorts of blackmail.'

'It wouldn't be like that. And Bridget needn't ever know.'

'Oh, no? Don't be so naive. Danny would be full of himself. You know what he's like. He'd be unable to hide what a wonderful guy he is. Take my advice. Put this silly idea right out of your head once and for all, and act your age.' Her daughter looked so despondent, Kath put her arms around her. 'Don't lose hope yet, Liz. Give it a bit more time.'

Silence reigned for some moments, and disappointed at her mother's reaction, she changed the subject. 'Are you going to marry Neville Barnes, Mam?'

'No, I don't think so.'

'He really likes you. Do you want to spend the rest of your life on your own?'

'I'll not be alone while you're alive, will I?'

'Of course not,' Liz hastened to assure her. 'I didn't mean that. You know David would love you to move closer to us, so why don't you? Every time there's shooting up here we worry about you.'

'I'm safe here, amongst my own, Liz. I'm happy the way things are at the moment. Maybe in a few years' time, I'll be glad to move closer to you. But meanwhile, I need my own space to decide

314

what I want out of life. For the first time I'm really enjoying myself. So, let's see what life has in store for us before we start rocking the boat, eh?'

Bridget hopped on to the bus at the bottom of Castle Street, happy and contented. She had managed to get her old job back in the Bank Buildings. They had been in the new flat a month, and this was her second week back at work. She felt as if she had never been away. With her bringing money in every week and Danny's overtime, the future looked rosy indeed. Someone took the seat next to her and glanced in her direction.

'Why, if it isn't Bridget Kelly,' a familiar voice said in her ear and laughing hazel eyes smiled into hers,

'Hello, Noel. How are you keeping these days?'

'Can't complain. Out of work at the moment, but sure, there are thousands like me.'

'You didn't stay on at school then?' Her eyes avidly raked his face. She was relieved to note that except for the eyes, her child didn't resemble him in the slightest.

'No, I wasn't really blessed with brains. Not like your brother-in-law Joseph. Now he should go far.'

'Do you see much of him now?'

'No. Very little in fact. I do, however, hear tell of him.'

Was it her imagination or was there some insinuation – in his softly spoken words? 'Oh, I see.' Bridget had no intention of asking him what

315

he'd heard. If there were rumours going about she didn't want to know. Joseph could look after his own interests. She hurried on, 'Are you engaged or anything like that, Noel?'

He laughed at the very idea. 'No, I love them and leave them.'

The way you left me, you bastard, Bridget thought bitterly. Glad to note that the bus was approaching Leeson Street and her stop, she rose to her feet.

He also rose to let her pass, enquiring, 'Visiting your mother?'

The closeness of brushing past him brought to mind the antics of them at the 'dive' and she blushed in shame. 'No, I live up here now,' she muttered. 'Goodbye, Noel.'

His jaw actually dropped. 'Have you and Danny split up?'

Smiling blankly as if she hadn't heard him, she jumped off the bus.

Her heart was thumping as she headed down Leeson Street to pick Martin up from her mother's. Noel's hazel eyes had thrown her for a minute. But how many people had hazel eyes? Liz O'Hara did, for example. Her mother came to the door with Martin and when she saw her daughter she let go of her grandson's hand. He raced on his little tubby legs to greet his mother. Sweeping him up in her arms, Bridget covered his face with kisses. No matter what, she would make sure her son didn't suffer.

'Hello, Mam. How was he today?'

'Boisterous as usual, just what you'd expect a child his age to be.'

'Are you able for him, Mam? I mean ... he isn't too much trouble for you, is he?'

'If it ever gets to the stage where I can't manage, I'll let you know. So don't you worry about me.'

'Thanks, Mam. I'll run on home and get Danny's dinner ready. See you in the morning.'

As she approached the corner, Peter got off the next bus and hailed her.

'Hello there, Bridget. How are you settling into your new flat?'

His grin was infectious and her worries dimmed as she grinned back at him. He was such an easy person to be with. The girl who got him would be very lucky indeed. 'Very well, thank you. It really is nice. I hear you have a girlfriend. Why not bring her to visit us on Saturday night and see for yourself the changes we've made?'

Peter had lifted his nephew high in the air when they met. Now he lowered Martin until he rested in his arms. 'Now who told you I had a girlfriend?' he asked, twisting his head about and chuckling as Martin pulled at his nose and mouth.

'You'd be surprised the things I hear now I'm back on the Falls,' she laughed in return.

'Do you know her?'

'I don't know. Your mother neglected to mention her name. Just that you were courting.'

'Ah. So it was me ma that told you. Well, her name is Teresa Quinn and I'll take you up on that offer. We'll come round about eight.' He threw the child up in the air and caught him again,

317

laughing as Martin squealed with delight. Setting him gently down on the doorstep, Peter chucked him under the chin and lifted his hand in salute. 'See you Saturday night then.'

Bridget stumbled up the stairs to the flat, nerves churning at her stomach. Teresa Quinn of all people. What on earth had she let herself in for? Teresa had been one of the crowd to frequent the 'dive' at the same time as Bridget had. And worse still, she lived up Iveagh, practically next door to Noel Gibson. Would rumours start up again? Should she put Peter off?

Tentatively she told Danny about Peter's proposed visit. Perhaps he had other plans made that would give her an excuse to put his brother off. However, Danny was delighted at the news. 'Why, that's great,' he enthused. 'It's about time he settled down and got married. I'll get in some beer and a bottle of wine. Maybe we'll have a game of cards, eh, love? Wouldn't that be nice?'

Mutely, she agreed with a nod of the head. She could only pray that everything would work out all right. Danny looked at her glum expression and lamented inwardly. Why had she invited Peter if she was going to be miserable about it? Would anything please this wife of his?

To Bridget's great relief, the 'dive' wasn't mentioned at all on Saturday night. Indeed, although they admitted knowing each other from going to the dance halls, and recalled past acquaintances, the girls seemed by mutual consent to want the 'dive' buried in the past and Noel Gibson wasn't mentioned at all.

318

During the course of the evening, Bridget found herself studying Teresa covertly. Petite and blonde, she was very pretty, but Bridget was recalling things said in the old days about Teresa that were far from complimentary. According to rumours, she had been fair game. It wasn't right. Peter deserved only the best. Then she chastised herself. Maybe Teresa was thinking the same thing about her. And with just cause. After all, Teresa hadn't had a shotgun wedding. Nor had she a child whose parentage she was unsure of. It could possibly have been all talk where Teresa was concerned, whereas Bridget herself had played about a bit. And how she regretted being so foolish!

Teresa had yet to see Martin as he had been settled for the night, fast asleep in his cot when they arrived. But what if Peter became serious about her and these visits became a regular habit? Teresa was sure to see him then. Bridget's eyes drifted in Peter's direction and she quickly looked away in confusion. He was watching her through narrowed eyes. Probably wondering why she was examining Teresa so closely, she thought with dismay.

Flustered, she rose quickly to her feet. 'Would anyone like a cup of tea? Or would you prefer a drink?'

Danny looked at her in amazement. 'I'm sure they'd prefer a drink, Bridget.'

Tentatively, Teresa said, 'I'd love a cup of tea, please, Bridget.'

Shooting her a thankful glance, Bridget said, 'See? Everybody isn't like you, Danny.'

To her dismay Peter rose to his feet. 'I'll give you a hand, Bridget. Give Danny and Teresa a chance to get to know each other.'

In the small kitchen, he seemed taller and broader than ever. He quite literally dwarfed her. 'What can I do to help?' he asked, his breath fanning her cheek.

'You go and sit down, Peter. There's not much room in here and I can manage quite well on my own, thank you.'

A twinkle in his eye, he reached around her to lift cups from the shelf, his body brushing hers as he did so. 'I noticed. Why do you think I offered to help?' he teased.

'Ah, Peter, behave yourself.'

Suddenly serious, his eyes held hers and he lowered his voice. 'Is Danny treating you all right?'

'Hush! He'll hear you. As a matter of fact, he's being a model husband.'

'Then why do you still look so sad?'

Her eyes widened in dismay. Did she look sad? 'I'm not sad. I've everything going for me at the moment.'

He shook his head. 'Have you? Have you really? Everyone else might be fooled, Bridget, but I can see the sadness deep in your eyes. If you ever need a friend to confide in, remember I'm here.'

She looked up at him and their eyes locked. 'I want to be your friend,' he said softly.

To her horror she heard herself reply just as softly, 'Just my friend?'

His gaze sharpened and he moved closer still, but before he could reply a shout from the living room reached them. 'Have you two gone to China for that tea?'

The spell broken, she shouted back, 'Almost ready, Danny.'

Aghast at what she had just said, she avoided Peter's eyes and started to pour the tea. 'Do you want a cup?'

'No, I'll join Danny in a beer. But remember, Bridget, I'm here if you ever need me.'

Again their eyes met and locked and she had difficulty looking away. 'Please carry the tray in for me, Peter.'

It was with apparent reluctance that he took the tray and left her alone. Afraid that her high colour might reveal her inner tumult she retired to the bathroom to cool down. Holding her hot cheeks in her hands, she faced herself in the mirror. What on earth had possessed her to say that to him. What on earth must he be thinking? She had better watch her tongue in future.

Although Peter seemed very fond of Teresa, Bridget derived great comfort from his presence and when he kissed her on the cheek as he said good night, she savoured his touch. Was it her imagination or had he lingered a while? She schooled herself not to show any response, but at the same time she thought, This is the way a woman should feel. Why couldn't Danny be like his brother? Why couldn't he show some affection and tenderness?

Still afraid that Teresa might see a likeness to Noel in Martin, she decided not to invite her back unless she had no other choice. To be truthful, after meeting Noel on the bus the other day, except for the colour of his eyes Bridget could not see any likeness to him in her son. She was convinced Martin really was Danny's child; a throwback, as Jane had suggested. Why should Teresa think otherwise? Unless she too had heard the rumours when he was born and those hazel eyes swayed her judgement?

There was one way to set her own mind at rest, at least. If Jane had a photograph of this cousin she thought Martin resembled and she let Bridget see it, that would settle it once and for all as far as she was concerned. She determined to put it to the test the next time she visited her in-laws.

It was a couple of weeks later that her chance came. They had been invited over to tea one Saturday and afterwards Jane went upstairs to hunt out some old photographs of Danny.

'She's trying to embarrass me, Bridget,' he warned her. 'You'll never believe the ugly wee twerp in them is me. Don't you dare laugh and take the mickey out of me.'

The next half-hour was spent laughing in good-natured banter as Danny and his brothers were displayed in sleeveless pullovers, long shorts and wellington boots, and in all kinds of un-complimentary poses. Bridget waited her chance and when at last, with a tear in her eye for times past, Jane started to put the photographs back in the old shoe box, asked, 'Have you any photographs of the relative Martin resembles?'

Jane paused and Bridget's heart missed a beat when she turned a bewildered look upon her.

Then her brow cleared and she laughed lightly.

'You mean my Uncle Willie's family? No, I'm afraid I don't. You see, when we were young, there weren't many families who were lucky enough to own a camera. Even so, Martin doesn't look a bit like him now he's lost his baby fat. To tell you the truth, I don't know who he takes after.'

Sorry she had spoken, Bridget kept her head down, very much aware that her husband was eyeing her closely. The box of photographs were put to one side and the evening continued without incident. It was when they returned home and she was bathing Martin that the question she dreaded was put to her.

Leaning his shoulder against the jamb of the bathroom door, Danny watched her in silence for some minutes. She wanted to scream at him to get on with it but willed herself to continue soaping her son, all the while talking lovingly to the child.

'Why did you want to see photographs of my Uncle Willie's family?'

She turned a bewildered look on him. 'What did you say?'

'I said, why did you want to see photos of my Uncle Willie's family?'

She widened her eyes as if in surprise. 'Because your mother says Martin is the spittin' image of one of your cousins, why else?'

During the course of the evening, Danny had been remembering words he'd spoken to Liz: 'Many a man is rearing another's child and is none the wiser.' Had Bridget pulled the wool

323

over his eyes? But then, the child had been full-term, so how could he be someone else's?

Unconvinced, he continued to watch them. Willing herself to be calm, Bridget lifted Martin out of the bath and, wrapping him in a big fluffy towel, turned to leave the room. Danny remained blocking the doorway for some seconds, his eyes searching deep into hers. She gazed back at him unblinkingly. Unable to stand it any longer, she cried impatiently, 'Are you going to stand there all night? He's no lightweight, you know.'

Although his eyes were still suspicious, without another word he stepped to one side. Bridget's hands shook as she dried her son and smoothed baby powder all over him. She was glad her husband hadn't followed them into the bedroom. If only she had kept her big mouth shut! Obviously Martin resembled no one on either side and, now she had aroused Danny's suspicions. And all because she had wanted her own mind set at rest. A fat lot of good it had done her. She was still none the wiser.

Later that evening when they were watching TV, Danny suddenly harped back to their previous conversation. 'It's strange, isn't it, that after being caught practically on our first encounter as it were, you haven't become pregnant again?'

He was watching her intently and saw vivid colour rush to her face. He was horrified by her reaction. Was Martin not his after all? Was *he* shooting blanks as well?

Bridget's lips tightened and her words were clipped when she replied, 'There's a perfectly good reason for that.'

'What do you mean? What reason?'

'I'm on the pill.'

Danny was on his feet immediately. 'What did you say?'

'I said, I'm on the pill.'

'But it's forbidden.'

'I know that. And I knew you would never agree to my taking it, so I saved you from having to take a stand. It's my choice. I don't want another baby right away.'

'It's a pity you weren't so careful before we were married!'

'What's that supposed to mean?'

'It means we would never have got married then, would we?'

She flinched but held her head high. After all it takes two to tango, and he had been every bit as eager as she. 'So, if I hadn't been pregnant, you wouldn't have married me. Is that what you're saying?'

He had seen her face crumple at his unkind words and felt remorseful. What was the use of lashing out now they were married? It was too late to do anything about it. Going to her, he tried to soften the blow.

'How do I know what way things would have worked out? After all, I was engaged to Liz O'Hara. You becoming pregnant changed things.'

'Do you still love her?'

Danny turned away. 'It's no use digging up the past, Bridget.'

She sighed. 'That means you *do* still love her.'

He swung back towards her. 'What difference does it make? We're married. We have a beautiful son. Aren't you happy with me?'

Happy? Her mind turned the word over. What exactly was happiness? Did she expect too much out of life? As Danny had pointed out, they were a family. They had to make the best of it.

'You're right, of course. We have a lot going for us.'

Going to her, he tilted her face to his. Her cheeks were wet with tears. 'Ah, Bridget, don't cry, love.'

His lips covered hers and she dredged up all the passion she could muster. It wasn't a lot but he didn't seem to notice. Taking her by the hand, he led her towards the bedroom. 'Let's have an early night, love.'

They undressed with their backs to each other as usual. Over his shoulder, he threw a question at her. 'Do you not think you should come off the pill now, love? Martin will soon be going to school and you'll need another child to occupy you.' Bridget wanted to laugh aloud at the very idea. She had no intention of coming off the pill. Not until she was sure she wanted to spend the rest of her life with Danny. She certainly had no intention of remaining in this flat but he seemed to have settled down into a routine. He liked being handy to all his favourite haunts. And their savings still were not growing the way they should. Danny was forever finding bargains. Always things he thought it would be nice to have, but which they didn't really need and hadn't the room for.

'I think I'll wait until we're in a house of our own.'

She heard the bed creak as he settled into it and joined him wearily. Remembering their passion in Raglin Street, she sighed for times past. At least it had been exciting then. Now it was a chore she was expected to perform. Like everything else around the flat. Danny's answer to everything was sex. But he was selfish and she didn't even enjoy it any more. She could well understand why marriages broke up.

The following Monday, Peter was waiting at the top of Leeson Street when she got off the bus on her way home from work. 'Look, Bridget, we have to talk. Give me your key and I'll wait in the flat while you fetch Martin.'

'I don't think that's a good idea, Peter. Say whatever you have to say here.'

'You're avoiding me. I've been to the flat twice and I know you were there. Why would you not let me in?'

'Because Danny wasn't at home and that's the reason you were there. Look, are you still seeing Teresa Quinn?'

'Yes, but not on a steady basis.'

'Bring her along on Saturday night. We'll be glad to see both of you.'

'If she's free I'll invite her along. If not I'll come on my own, all right?'

Her shoulders lifted in a slight shrug. 'We'll still be glad to see you.'

His look was pleading. 'Bridget, please give me the key and let me go on in. I just want to talk to you.'

'No! Danny is working late tonight, and I've a

lot of housework to catch up on. I'll have to run on now. Me ma will be wondering what's keeping me.'

He watched her stride off down Leeson Street, then turning on his heel crossed the road. He wanted to know what she had meant when she'd asked, 'Just my friend?' Did it mean that she was unhappy with his brother? Well, if she was, what of it? All marriages had their ups and downs. It was no concern of his. He had no right to interfere. Still he hated to think she was unhappy.

Saturday evening saw Peter at their door. The dates with Teresa had petered out and he was despairing of ever meeting the right girl. He was by no means in love with Bridget; at least he didn't think he was. But she was always there at the back of his mind when he went out on a date with a prospective girlfriend. He assured himself it was as if she was his sister and he worried about her. He felt that if he could be sure she was happy with his brother, his attraction towards her would die a natural death. Then he could get on with his own life. But meanwhile, he did worry about her. It was the sadness that lurked in the depths of those great dark brown eyes that bothered him. Was it all in his mind? Was it just his imagination playing tricks with him?

It was Danny who opened the door to his knock. 'Come in, Peter,' he said, and motioned towards the living room.

Peter could see that he wasn't expected and was about to make some lame excuse to leave when Bridget popped her head around the bathroom door. 'Hello, Peter. When you didn't send any word, I thought you weren't coming. Is Teresa with you?'

'I'm afraid Teresa and I have decided to go our separate ways. But as I'm at a loose end, I thought I'd still pop in and see you. I hope you don't mind?'

Her shrug was not encouraging. 'Take a seat. I'll be out in a few minutes. I'm just rinsing Martin's hair.'

Danny had been hovering in embarrassed silence. 'You've put me on the spot, Peter,' he whispered. 'I was on my way out. I'm meeting a few of the lads to go for a pint, you know how it is...'

A wet slippery figure hurled itself from the bathroom and hugged Peter's legs.

'Uncle Peter! Uncle Peter!'

'Martin! Come back here this minute. Oh, I am sorry, Peter. He's soaked you. The wee rascal took me unawares.'

Bridget attempted to wrap a bath towel around her naked son but he wriggled and twisted from her grasp and continued to cling on to Peter. Laughing, he took the towel from her and volunteered, 'I'll dry him. You fetch his pyjamas.'

Wrapping the now quiet child in the towel, he carried him into the living room and proceeded to towel him dry. He was very aware that his brother was a bit on edge. He got the feeling Danny was up to no good and refused to meet his eye; there would be no knowing man-to-man looks behind his wife's back as far as Peter was concerned.

Bridget, returning with the pyjamas, broke the tension. 'What Danny is trying to tell you, Peter, is that he has made arrangements to meet some of his mates in the pub. But sure, since you're at a loose end you can go along with him. You probably know them all anyhow.'

She waited for her husband to second this. As the silence stretched she turned a puzzled look on him. 'Isn't that right, Danny? Can't Peter go with you?'

He said heartily, too heartily for her liking, 'Of course he can. He's very welcome.'

Suspicious now, Bridget finished buttoning her son's pyjamas, kissed the tip of his nose and then slowly rose from her kneeling position. She eyed her husband. He looked guilty as hell and she immediately thought the worst. He must be seeing someone else. Could it possibly be Liz O'Hara? Would she risk losing all she had for Danny? There was a time when Bridget had thought anyone would risk their all for Danny McGowan, but not any more. And Liz was far from stupid.

It was Peter who broke the awkward silence. 'To be truthful, Danny, I'd rather not go out with the lads. You go on. I'll keep Bridget and Martin company for a while.'

'That won't be necessary, Peter,' she retorted curtly. 'You'd be bored stiff in no time.'

'I'd like to stay, Bridget. I don't see enough of this wee fellow.' He ruffled Martin's hair and his nephew cuddled close, grinning from ear to ear. 'Shall we get your train set out and play with it, Martin?'

'Yes, yes, yes!' The child slid off his uncle's knee and was jumping up and down in excitement.

'There, you see? Martin wants me to stay.'

Danny's relief was so palpable you could almost taste it. Bridget wanted to confront him there and then, but Peter's presence prevented her.

When her husband was ready to leave she followed him into the hall. 'Where are you really going?' she hissed.

'Like I said, out with the lads. Where do you think I'm going?'

'If I find out you're seeing someone else, Danny McGowan, I swear I'll kill you.'

'I'm not seeing anyone else. In fact, I'm offended you should doubt me. For God's sake, Bridget, how often do I go out?' He glanced at his watch. 'Look, I'll have to be shoving off or they'll think I'm not coming.' He bent to kiss her but she swung on her heel and left him puckering at thin air. With a wry grimace he let himself out.

The flat was so small, Peter couldn't help but overhear the whispered conversation between husband and wife. Seated in the middle of the floor he was slotting railway lines together watched by his excited, chattering nephew. When Bridget entered the room he stared her full in the face. She was very pale but looked composed.

'You don't mind if I stay a while, do you, Bridget?'

She flapped her hands wide in frustration. 'Does it really matter? Would it make any difference if I asked you to leave? Nobody pays any attention to me or cares what I think. Everybody walks all over my wishes. It's as if I don't exist!'

'If that's how you feel,' he said stiffly, 'I'll go.'

'Oh, for heaven's sake, stay. When you're finished there, put that train set away again. I don't want to be tripping over it. He has fifteen minutes and then it's his bedtime. Meanwhile I'll catch up on my ironing.' At the end of this outburst she stormed into the kitchen.

Fifteen minutes later Peter started to disconnect the train lines. It had been a waste of time; no sooner up than down again. Martin showed his disapproval by starting to wail. Peter didn't blame the child but he had no intention of getting any further into Bridget's bad books. 'Don't cry, Martin, and I'll ask your mam if I can read you a bedtime story. All right, love?'

The child continued to sniffle but nodded his head. Peter only hoped that Bridget would agree he could read the boy a story. She was unaware of him and he stood at the kitchen door and watched her for some moments. Her shoulders were slumped as if in despair. It broke his heart to see her so unhappy. 'Is it all right if I read him a story in bed, Bridget?' he asked tentatively. Without lifting her head, she nodded.

He was halfway through the fairy tale when she came into her son's room. She ignored Peter but, bending over the bed, said, 'I didn't get a good night kiss, Martin.'

He wound his arms around her neck and gave her a big slobbery kiss. 'Night, night, Mam.'

Eyes closed, she held him close for some seconds. 'Good night, love. Sleep tight.' Without a glance in Peter's direction she left the room.

By the end of the story, Martin was fast asleep.

Peter carefully tucked the bedclothes around him and quietly left the room. He didn't know what to do next. Should he stay a while or go? Did she really want him to go? He was delighted to find the decision made for him. In the living room, Bridget sat in one of the armchairs, a drink in her hand. On the small table beside the other arm-chair, a can of beer and a glass were waiting.

Sinking down into the depths of the chair, he said, 'Thanks,' and poured the beer. 'Cheers.'

She raised her glass in reply and said, 'Cheers. Is there anything you would like to watch on TV?'

'No, not really. I look at anything.'

'Good. Then we'll watch this.'

It was some kind of nature programme and normally he would have enjoyed it, but he was too aware of her sitting opposite him, huddled up in her armchair. Unhappiness seemed to permeate the very air around her. To his dismay, he became aware that tears were running down her cheeks. Not a sound came from her, but the tears were dripping off her chin on to her blouse.

He was on his feet at once and bending over her. Afraid to touch her; afraid of rejection. 'Bridget, don't cry. I can't bear it when you cry.'

A great sigh escaped her lips and she rubbed her hands wearily over her face. 'I'm sorry. I hoped you wouldn't notice. I can't help myself, I'm so miserable.'

Then he had the courage to reach for her but she pushed his hands away. 'Sit down, Peter. Now I've had a good cry, I'll be able to see things more clearly.' Rising to her feet, she headed for the door. 'I'll just rinse my face and then I'll be back to normal. I won't be long.'

Peter was annoyed with himself. He felt so stupid, delaying long enough to witness her breakdown like that. He should have left long ago. She must feel mortified. He'd leave as soon as she came back. Her voice broke into his thoughts. 'Would you like another beer, Peter?'

His eyes glanced quickly over her face; pale, weary, red-eyed. 'Perhaps you'd rather I left, Bridget? I didn't mean to embarrass you.'

'No, stay a while. I'll be glad of your company.'

He eyed her again; at least she seemed composed now. 'Then I will have another one, thank you.'

She'd brought him another can of beer. 'I'm sorry for making such a show of myself. You must have been mortified.'

Feeling awkward, he toyed with the glass. Should he or shouldn't he ask the question burning on his tongue? Throwing caution to the winds he did. 'Bridget, is our Danny seeing someone else? Is that why you're so unhappy?'

She sat down and looked him full in the face. 'I don't know, Peter. I honestly don't know. He doesn't really go out all that often on his own, just about once a week, and I've always believed he was with the lads. You see, there's no telltale sign in his behaviour that there's another woman involved, you know what I mean? But then, I'm a gullible fool, I suppose. It would probably be very easy to pull the wool over my eyes.'

'Don't talk like that, Bridget. You're no fool! Listen, I know you have brothers of your own you can turn to, but...'

She was shaking her head. 'I'm not really all that close to any of them. I mean, if Danny was violent towards me, they'd soon come running, but I couldn't confide in any of them about personal things. It would be too embarrassing.'

Peter moved to the edge of his chair and, reaching across, clasped her hands in his. 'As you know, Bridget, I haven't any sisters. I think that's why I'm so fond of you. Why I worry about you. I look on you as a sister and it hurts me to see you so miserable. I want you to know I'll always be here for you. Just remember, you're not alone.'

She gazed at him and sadness engulfed her. He must have been worried stiff by her asking him if he only wanted to be her friend. What on earth had possessed her? Anyone would think she was desperate to have an affair, when all she really wanted was stability for her and Martin. That's why Peter had wanted to speak to her, to make it plain his interest was brotherly. She, poor fool that she was, had thought she was warding off a possible affair. Just as well she wasn't in love with him. She would have been devastated to hear that his feelings towards her were strictly family.

'Thanks, Peter. I'll remember.' She returned the pressure of his hands. To her surprise his grip tightened. She gazed into eyes awash with desire and quickly withdrew her hands. Obviously his idea of brotherly love was different from hers. Still, he seemed sincere in what he said. She would just have to tread carefully.

Danny went down the stairs two at a time. He'd hated leaving Bridget in that state, thinking the worst of him, but hadn't any choice. If he'd delayed any longer his mates would go off without him. They were having a night out at the dogs and then back to Tom McNally's house for a game of cards. This gambling was becoming a habit. He knew it was a mug's game, but he had lost too much to stop now. Surely he was overdue a win? He had to have one soon or Bridget would do her nut when she saw how little there was in their building society account. Perhaps tonight Lady Luck would be with him. Once he had recouped his losses he'd stop. Dear God, please let tonight be my lucky night, he prayed.

Chapter Six

The scene from the conservatory window enchanted Liz. She would never tire of the beautiful lawns and flower beds decorating the grounds around her bungalow. The building and grounds lay behind a screen of bushes and trees, hidden from prying eyes, and even at this time of the year were still quite colourful. Far removed from the drab terraced houses on the Falls Road where the only view she had ever known was the houses opposite and neighbours' back yards adjoining their own. Autumn was her favourite time of year. In the autumn she had frequently walked in the Falls Park, in the crisp frosty air, when the trees were at their radiant best before losing their colourful foliage.

Already leaves were floating gently down from the stately chestnut trees in the garden, covering the lawn with a russet carpet. Their colours were magnificent, ranging from vivid orange to pale gold. A movement caught her eye and she rose on tip-toe to follow the trail of a squirrel as it scurried about. In her mind's eye she imagined a child chasing after the squirrel, sending the carpet of leaves into disarray. Picturing rosy cheeks and laughing eyes, pain touched her heart. They had so much here to offer a child, if only...

David broke into her reverie. Coming up

behind his wife, he circled her with his arms and nuzzled the hair away from the nape of her neck. She came back to reality with a reluctant sigh, not wanting to let go of the beautiful pictures in her mind. They were so real to her. Was make-believe to be her only taste of motherhood?

Relaxing against him, Liz whispered, 'Isn't it just beautiful out there, David?' She sighed. 'We're very lucky to live in such lovely surroundings.'

'Mmm. It's breathtaking up around the castle and Hazelwood at this time of year as well. Let's give Fortwilliam a miss and go for a walk, eh, love?'

'I'd love to do that, but unfortunately I told Mother we'd be there and I don't want to let her down. For some reason or other she doesn't like being alone with Neville these days.'

'Well, she's not committed to him. She doesn't have to be in his company at all if she doesn't want to. God knows there's plenty of men ready to fill his shoes.'

'I know that. I don't understand what her game is. Perhaps she doesn't want to offend him? But I did promise we'd be there.'

With a sigh, he withdrew his arms and went to draw the curtains. 'Well, if that's the case, it's time we were getting ready.'

They were late arriving at the club. The quartet was already playing music for those who wished to dance. The cabaret had yet to start. Liz could see how relieved her mother was to see them. After greetings were exchanged, Neville accompanied David to the bar for drinks and Liz questioned Kath.

'Is anything wrong, Mam?'

She grimaced. 'Not really. It's just that Neville's getting on my nerves – he's so possessive! He's scaring my usual partners away, the way he scowls at them. He acts as if he owns me, so he does. Do you know something? Dick Kennedy is the only one he can abide me dancing with. And that's only because he's his nephew.'

'Does that not please you? I mean, his intentions must be serious if he's behaving like that. You should be flattered.'

'His intentions *are* serious, but I've told him I'll never marry him.'

Liz was bewildered. Why was her mother leading him on then? And she was! There could be no other explanation for their frequent outings. 'You know, you could do a lot worse, Mam. He seems a very kind sort of man, and he has certainly treated you well.'

'Kind? Huh! He doesn't know the meaning of the word. As for treating me well...' Her eyes dropped and she examined her fingernails. Careful, girl, she warned herself. 'You just don't know the half of it, Liz.'

Thinking of all the expensive presents Neville had showered on her mother over the last couple of months, Liz was flabbergasted. What didn't she know the half of? Surely her mother shouldn't be accepting gifts from a man if she didn't care for him? About to question her further, she had to curb her tongue impatiently and her curiosity when Dick Kennedy ap-

339

proached the table. After courteously greeting Liz, he asked her mother to dance with him. Liz watched them take to the floor. They made a fine-looking couple. Her eyes scanned the lounge. No sign of Irene. She was coming to the club less often these days. Were things not working out between her and Dick after all?

The cabaret was very good that night, two boys and a girl, and the girl was a wonderful singer. Liz sat entranced. Suddenly her mother leant close and whispered in her ear, 'Can I have a word with you in private?' Annoyed that Kath wanted her to miss some of the cabaret, she retorted, 'Can't it wait until the break?'

'Please, Liz. It won't take long. I want a bit of advice.'

Reluctantly she rose and excusing herself, followed her mother out of the lounge.

The cloakroom was empty as she faced Kath – and no wonder! Everyone else was glued to their seats watching the cabaret. 'Well, what's so important it can't wait a few minutes?'

Her resentment was obvious and Kath was offended. 'Am I asking too much of my own daughter? Can't you afford me a few minutes of your precious time any more?'

Immediately, Liz was contrite. 'I'm sorry, Mam. It's just ... well, we don't often get such a good turn on. It seems a shame to miss it.'

'You're right, of course. What I want to ask you about is of no significance compared to that great singer. It can wait. Let's go back to the lounge and this wonderful cabaret,' her mother snorted sarcastically.

Before Liz was aware of her intentions, with a disdainful flounce Kath turned on her heel and left the cloakroom. Liz stared after her for some moments, then delaying to touch up her make-up, followed her.

To her surprise she found that her mother had not returned to their table. She caught sight of her across the floor at a table on the edge of the dining room where it joined the lounge. Head close to his, she was deep in conversation with Dick Kennedy.

'Where's Kath? Is she not feeling well?'

Neville sounded concerned and Liz gestured across the room. 'She's over there, talking to your nephew.'

To her surprise he immediately excused himself and, so as not to distract from the performance of the trio, quietly left the lounge and went along the landing to the outer door of the restaurant. Liz saw him enter and stand some distance away, watching her mother and his nephew for some minutes before he approached them. Even from a distance she could see her mother's resentment of the intrusion when Neville at last joined them.

'What was that all about, Liz?'

She turned to her husband in bewilderment. 'I've no idea, David. Suddenly everything was so urgent. Mam couldn't get me away quick enough for a quiet talk, and then when we reached the cloakroom she took offence and walked out on me. Look! She's off again. What on earth is she up to?'

David looked across the dance floor in time to see Kath leave the restaurant. After exchanging a

341

few words with his uncle, Dick Kennedy also left the room. 'Will I go and make sure she's all right?' David asked.

'No. Let her sort out her own troubles. Lord knows, she's old enough.'

Her husband's brows rose in surprise. 'Hey, that's not like you, Liz,' he scolded her gently.

She grimaced. 'You're right, of course. I am being a bit catty. It's just, well, she's carrying on like a young girl in love and it's unbecoming at her age.'

'She might not be young, Liz, but I know from experience that love can hit you just as hard when you're older.'

Her hand covered and pressed his where it lay on the table. 'I know, love, and I'm glad of it. Maybe she's had a disagreement with Neville and that's why she's acting so strangely. Perhaps she's trying to make him jealous. I'll go and see if I can find out what's going on.'

So much for wanting to listen to the trio, she thought wryly as she once more left the lounge. There was no sign of her mother or Dick on the upper landing, and she slowly descended the stairs. Someone was in the alcove under the stairs where the phone was. Surely her mother hadn't taken umbrage enough to resort to calling a taxi? Liz made her way slowly towards the alcove, her feet making no sound on the thick carpet. The shock of her life lay in store for her. There, in the shadow of the stairs, were her mother and Dick, locked in a passionate embrace. Unable to move, she stood gaping at them. Even as she watched, Dick raised his head and the breath caught in

Liz's throat at the look on her mother's face as she gazed up at him. Here was a woman in love. Or maybe infatuated? Slowly Dick bent his head and their lips met once more. They were oblivious to everything but themselves.

The intensity of the kiss amazed Liz. But why? she asked herself. Her mother was still young enough to feel passion. Still, it didn't seem decent for them to be acting like this where anyone might see them. After all, they were hardly teenagers who could be forgiven for getting carried away in public. For some seconds she stood stock still, praying they wouldn't see her. It would be too embarrassing for words. She needn't have worried. They were lost in a world of their own. Slowly she backed away, and once safely at the foot of the stairs hastily ascended them, her mind in turmoil. What on earth was her mother playing at? If it had been Neville Barnes in a clinch with her Liz would have understood. After all, he had been courting her this past couple of months. But Dick Kennedy? Why, he was practically married to Irene Brennan.

To her dismay, Neville had returned to their table. Unable to meet his questioning look Liz pretended to fix her attention on the trio. He was not to be put off.

Leaning across the table to get her attention, he enquired, 'Is your mother all right, Liz?'

She was in a quandary. What excuse had Kath given for leaving the table with Dick?

'Mmm? Oh, yes, she's fine.'

'And did they manage to catch Irene at home?'

343

'I beg your pardon?'

'Dick was going to phone Irene. It seems she wasn't at home when he called to fetch her earlier on. Your mother accompanied him because she was feeling the heat and wanted a bit of fresh air.'

Truthfully, she replied, 'Yes, they were at the phone so I didn't interrupt them.' A giggle threatened to escape her lips at the very idea of interrupting that kiss, but she managed to swallow it.

The trio were coming to the end of their act and had invited couples to take to the floor. Seeing she was a bit agitated, David rescued her. 'Would you like to dance, Liz?'

'Yes, please. Will you excuse us, Neville?'

'Certainly.'

As they passed the door of the lounge Liz saw her mother and Dick at the top of the stairs. They gazed raptly at each other for some seconds and then her mother headed for the cloakroom and Dick entered the lounge and approached the bar. To Liz's searching glance he looked like a man in a daze. And no wonder, after the antics of her mother! Who would have thought that she could act so wantonly in full view of anyone who happened to chance by? Unwanted memories of her own behaviour in the castle grounds with Danny McGowan haunted her then. Hadn't *she* forgotten where she was? But surely her mother couldn't feel that strongly about Dick?

She became aware that David had spoken to her. 'I beg your pardon?'

'I said, is Kath all right?'

'I don't really know. She's just gone towards the

344

cloakroom. Excuse me a minute, love. I must speak to her.'

She found her mother in front of the mirror, staring at her reflection, a dreamy expression on her face as she dabbed powder on her nose. Their eyes met in the mirror and a smile of pure bliss lit up Kath's face. Never had Liz seen her look so beautiful. Because of the others using the cloakroom, she had to wait impatiently to voice the questions hovering on her lips. At last they were alone.

She'd had time to think and decided to play it diplomatically. 'Mam, I've been looking for you. I'm sorry I was abrupt earlier on. What did you want to speak to me about?'

'It doesn't matter, love. It's not important any more. Everything has been resolved.'

'Mam, I saw you a while ago. Downstairs at the telephone...'

Colour flooded Kath's face then receded, leaving her deathly pale. 'Were you spying on me?' she accused. Her eyes widened in consternation as another thought struck her. 'Was anyone else with you?'

'No, I wasn't spying on you! Why on earth should I? As for anyone else seeing you ... well, I was alone, but whether anyone else saw you I don't know. You weren't exactly hidden from view, you know.'

Kath stood gnawing at her lower lip. 'I don't know what to do for the best,' she confessed.

'What do you mean?'

'As you already know, Neville has asked me to marry him.'

345

She was silent so long, Liz prompted her. 'And?'

Her mother replaced lipstick and comb in her evening purse. 'I can't say anything more at the moment. I must talk to Neville first.'

'Neville? What about Dick?'

'Dick understands. Look, Liz, I promise I'll explain everything to you later. Let's get back in there.' With these words she held the cloakroom door open and a disgruntled Liz was forced to precede her from the room.

Liz regretted not letting her mother confide in her earlier. If she had been a bit more understanding she might now know what was going on. She watched as Neville hovered possessively over Kath, saw her refuse dance after dance with him. Why was she doing this when she had just declared she must speak with him? Even from the dance floor Liz found her attention drifting to their table. To her great chagrin, when Dick approached the table and asked her mother to dance she was on her feet in a flash.

Her heart went out to Neville who looked so forlorn. 'Poor Neville looks lost, sitting there on his own. Let's join him, David.'

Neville was gazing after his nephew and Kath, a thunderous expression on his face. To Liz's surprise, when they reached the table he rose and said, 'David, do you mind if I have this waltz with your wife?'

David looked at her askance and at her nod of consent, agreed. 'Not at all. Be my guest.'

Not being stupid, Liz realized that Neville had

an ulterior motive for asking her to dance. Deftly he waltzed her through the dancers until they were shoulder to shoulder with Dick and her mother. Only then did he address her.

'You look lovely tonight, Liz. You really do resemble your mother. I've become very fond of her, you know.'

'Yes, I gathered that much.'

'Do you think she might one day consent to marry me?'

Embarrassed, Liz glanced wildly at her mother. She was startled to see that Kath was straining her ears trying to overhear what Neville was talking about. Embarrassed, she said softly, 'How should I know? Neville, do you not think you should be talking to me mam about it?'

'You saw the way she's avoiding being alone with me, Liz. And for the life of me, I can't understand why.'

'Perhaps she's letting you down lightly? Eh, Neville? Maybe she cares for someone else.'

His brows drew together and his eyes narrowed as he gazed blankly at her as if considering the possibility. He blinked and his eyes found and locked with Kath's. Loudly and distinctly, he said, 'Would you find the idea of me as a stepfather repulsive, Liz?'

Dick gripped Kath tightly as she sagged in his arms. Quickly he led her out on to the landing and to a chair. 'What happened, Kath? Are you all right?'

Relieved to see that her ploy had worked and that Neville and her daughter had followed them, she whispered, 'It was the heat. If I could just have a glass of water, please?'

At her request Dick hurried off to the bar, and Kath whispered to Liz, 'Leave us alone for a moment, love.'

Reluctantly, Liz stepped back into the lounge and Kath gazed imploringly up into Neville's face. 'Don't tell her! I beg you not to tell her. It can't do any good this late in life.'

'Talk to me then! Explain what's going on.'

'Here's Dick coming back. You're right, we must talk. Say you're seeing me home.'

Avoiding his uncle's eye, Dick gave Kath the glass of water and solicitously hovered over her. She sipped at it and when Neville said he was seeing her home, she gave Dick a defeated look.

He was quick to come to her aid. 'I'll see you home if you like, Kath?'

'No. Thank you for offering but I must talk to Neville.' She rose unsteadily to her feet and both men grabbed an arm to assist her. 'Will you phone a taxi, Neville? I must let Liz know I'm leaving.'

He headed towards the phone at the top of the stairs and Kath went in search of her daughter, leaving Dick utterly bewildered. Liz and David were standing just inside the door of the lounge. They anxiously came to her side.

'I'm leaving now, Liz.'

'You still look quite ill, Mam. Why don't you come home with us tonight? I'll be worried stiff about you on your own.'

'No, it's all right. Neville is seeing me home.'

'Is this what you want, Mam?'

She smiled wryly and shrugged. 'It's what must

348

be, Liz. I'll give you a ring in the morning. Good night, David.'

'Good night, Kath. Take care.'

'The taxi is on its way,' Neville informed her. 'About five minutes, they say. Don't worry, Liz. If I think she needs you, I'll give you a ring.'

'Thanks, Neville. We're leaving now ourselves.' Taking her mother in her arms, Liz whispered in her ear, 'Follow your heart, Mam. Don't let him force you into doing anything you don't want.'

'Sometimes we have no control over our actions, Liz.'

Thinking of her mother and Dick in the alcove earlier on, Liz had to smile, but she sobered abruptly when Kath said, 'Life's laid out for you. You rarely get what you want.'

'Remember your own very words to me! "Go for it!" You do likewise.'

In the taxi Neville put his arm around Kath's shoulders and to his relief she did not push him away. But neither did she encourage him by snuggling closer. The two months were almost up and he was determined to have it out with her. She had been avoiding him lately, refusing to see him. When he phoned or called at the house she wasn't there. He had expected great things after her passionate response almost a month ago, but all he had managed so far was a few kisses. He had decided to put up with this because he'd thought she needed time to make up her mind about him. He had been so sure he was winning her over. Certain she was about to accept his proposal. And then this past week she had been avoiding him, with the result he was not so sure of himself any more. Had he delayed too long? Tonight he had every intention of having it out with her.

At the door she asked, with a wry smile, 'I suppose you want to come in?'

'I should think so! We need to talk.'

Nodding in agreement she said, 'I thought as much.' She unlocked the door and entered the house. She knew he was going to pressurize her into marrying him and was a bit apprehensive. What should she do? Dick had yet to declare his intentions.

When she had removed her coat and hung it on the rack, she headed for the living room. With a hand on her arm Neville gently stayed her and turned her to face him. He didn't want her to choose a chair in the living room where he would be cut off from her. 'What went wrong, Kath, eh? Everything seemed to be going so well and I was sure you were going to consent to marry me, so what happened to change your mind?'

She was tongue-tied at his directness, but he was right. They had become very close to each other. She enjoyed his company and had been able to see a future together for them. She had made up her mind to accept his proposal of marriage; had been convinced they could make a go of it. Then Dick Kennedy had started to pour out all his woes while they were dancing. At first she had been annoyed with him and told him to pull himself together and get a new woman if he couldn't get on with Irene. Then, as she consoled him, a subtle change came over their relationship. She began to look forward to seeing him. Had even met him a couple of times in town for a coffee. Just to offer advice, of course. Until tonight they had never confessed to any feeling for each other. But they had been there nevertheless, ready to flare into life.

Dick had told Neville the truth. He had meant to phone Irene but someone was using the phone at the top of the stairs and they had gone down to the one in the hall. It hadn't been planned, but suddenly, close together in the shadowy alcove under the staircase, their eyes had met and the attraction that had been building up between them had proved too much to resist. They had entered each other's arms, regardless of who might see them. Luckily it had only been Liz. What if it had been Neville? All hell would have broken loose then! He wouldn't have been able to control himself. Not now when he considered Kath his property.

In a way it was all Neville's fault. If he, in his jealousy, hadn't prevented other men from dancing with her, she wouldn't have been in Dick's company so often and the attraction between them might never have blossomed.

She was quiet so long, he urged, 'Kath? Come back to me. Answer me, please.'

'You're right, Neville. I *was* going to accept your offer of marriage, but then I met someone else and I think I'm in love with him.'

'Someone else?' he exclaimed, his thoughts racing. Those times when he couldn't contact her, she had been with someone else? Who the hell was it? 'Who is he, Kath? Is it anyone I know?'

351

'Look, Neville, I'm cold and I'm tired. Let's go and sit down. There's a fire in the living room. I've a little brandy. Would you pour some for me? And have one yourself.'

She would have sat in the armchair but, taking her by the elbow, he steered her to the settee. He raked the fire that had been banked down into a blaze and poured two drinks, all the while his mind furiously working overtime. He was beginning to have a suspicion just who she thought herself in love with and it didn't bear thinking about. To lose her to his nephew would be unthinkable.

Sitting beside her, he twisted round so that he could look into her face. 'Kath, you say you *think* you're in love?'

Warily, she eyed him and nodded. 'Well now, do you not think you would *know* if it was love?'

'No. You see, there's complications. There's someone else in his life so we have never discussed our feelings for each other.'

He relaxed. It couldn't be Dick. He was a free man. 'He's married then?'

'Oh, no. I'd never be that stupid again.'

Utterly bewildered, Neville gaped at her. 'If he isn't married, what complications can there be?'

'He's engaged.'

Grim-faced, he uttered through tight lips, 'It's Dick, isn't it?'

'Yes,' she whispered.

Taking her hand between his own, Neville reasoned with her. 'Kath, do you not think it's a flash in the pan? Because you've been dancing so much with him?'

'To be truthful, Neville, I don't know what to think.'

'Has he said he loves you?' At her slight shake of the head he continued, 'I'd be the first to admit that my nephew is a bit of a charmer. But he can be fickle, you know. His wife divorced him because of an affair with a girl at work. He admitted to me he wasn't in love with this girl but the attraction was there and she was willing, so he couldn't resist her. He lost a very good wife because of it. He's had numerous girlfriends since, and now he's engaged to Irene Brennan. And, mind you, she won't let him off the hook without a fight, you can bet on that. Her pride won't let her.'

'She doesn't really care for him, otherwise she would accompany him to the club more often. He feels she's letting him down. Making a fool of him in front of all his friends,' Kath retaliated stubbornly.

'You could be right.' Neville's voice was sad. 'I must confess I'm blinded by jealousy. This is breaking my heart, you know, but I'm only trying to get you to see things in their true perspective. It could be quite messy, you know. Are you prepared for that?'

'I realise that, Neville. To be truthful, I didn't expect you to be so understanding. What about Liz? Will you keep our secret?'

'I confess I can't bear to lose both of you. If you don't tell her the truth, I'm afraid I'll have to.'

'She won't take kindly to it.'

'I'm afraid that can't be helped. Liz and I have become very good friends and I have to find out whether or not she will accept me in the role of father.' He sat silent for some moments. Then his great head with its mane of silver hair lifted and he looked at her sadly. 'I'll be going now. Give you a chance to think things through. Find out just how sincere Dick's intentions are; see if he returns your feelings. I'll phone you in a week's time.'

Cupping her face in his hands, he gently trailed his lips over it, just as he had when first they met. Then it had made her feel weak at the knees. An elusive sensual feeling invaded her body now as it had long ago. Before it could take a grip on her he broke the spell. 'Ah, Kath, I hope you do the right thing and choose me. I love you so much, and I know I can make you very happy.'

She realized that she must be fickle too. She wanted him to continue; wanted those lovely feelings to hold sway. As he turned away, she raised a hand to detain him. Unaware of her action he left the room without a backward glance. When the hall door swung shut behind him he stood on the pavement and there was fear in his heart at the ultimatum he had given her. Although lately he had felt quite young, he was aware he was a comparatively old man; Dick, at forty, was young enough to thrill her. Was there really any chance for him?

Kath sat for a long time, lost in thought. Was Neville right in his assumption that Dick was fickle? She imagined that marriage to Neville would be comfortable. She certainly liked his kisses and the feel of his hands. But, did she want to be comfortable now that Dick had awakened her slumbering passion? Given the chance, might Neville not also arouse the fire within her? She argued within herself. He had done so in the past. She hadn't given him a chance lately to find out if he still could. She sighed and for the first time wished she had not succumbed to Dick's kisses.

As they walked home in the crisp frosty air, Liz brought David up to date on all that had happened that evening.

He was astounded. 'Phew! Who would have believed it?'

Her laughter was sad. 'I know what you mean. It's like a soap opera, isn't it? I'm surprised at Dick Kennedy. After all, he's engaged to Irene.'

'Engagements are easily broken.'

'Don't I know that?' she exclaimed. 'Haven't I been there and had my heart broken too?'

'I'm sorry, I shouldn't have said that. But it's better to know sooner than later.'

'I feel so sorry for Neville. He has been so good and patient. He doesn't deserve this.'

'What makes you so sure she'll choose Dick? Perhaps he's just flirting a bit because Irene isn't around? I hope he doesn't break Kath's heart.'

'Huh! You didn't see the way they were devouring each other. It took my breath away.'

'Sometimes one can get carried away in the heat of the moment, but what seems irresistible at night can appear foolish in the stark light of day. Remember they were both drinking and tomorrow might feel differently.'

'I hope you're right, love, because I can't see

Dick making my mother happy, and my father caused her enough pain to last a lifetime. I think she would be better off with Neville.'

Unable to control her curiosity, Liz drove up to Dunlewey Street next morning to see her mother. Her hand was clasping the knocker when the door opened. Her mother stood there dressed in her best coat and hat, a surprised look on her face.

'What brings you here so early?' she greeted her. 'I'm going to ten o'clock Mass.'

'I'll come with you. Get into the car. We may as well drive up.'

As she manoeuvred the car around O'Neill Street and into the flow of traffic in Clonard Street, Liz confessed, 'It's nosiness that has me here so early. I'm near dead to know just what you were up to last night?'

'You mean with Neville? Nothing happened. He escorted me home and left within half an hour.'

'No, I don't mean with Neville. Though God knows you're torturing that poor man! You know what I'm talking about. Come on now, Mam. I saw you, remember, with Dick Kennedy, and you looked like you were enjoying yourself.'

'For heaven's sake, Liz, it was only a kiss!'

Seeing an empty parking space at the top of Dunmore Street, she quickly manoeuvred her car into it.

'That was handy.'

Caught up in the crowd, they crossed to the monastery in silence. Entering the hush and peace of the great church, Liz felt like she was returning home. As she knelt in prayer, the peace of the church seeped into her soul and she found tears on her cheeks. This was what was missing from her life. She found herself beseeching God's mother to intercede for her. To ask her Son to grant Liz a child; making all kinds of promises if it could be so.

After Mass they returned to the car and drove back to Dunlewey Street in silence, each absorbed in their own private thoughts. 'That did me a world of good, Mam,' Liz admitted when they were at last back in the house, sitting facing each other across the kitchen table, sipping coffee. 'Now tell me all about your romances.'

'What romances? You already know all there is to know.'

'Ah, come on now. How come you ended up in a clinch with Dick Kennedy? Under the stairs in Fortwilliam, of all places.'

Kath laughed aloud at this. 'A clinch? That's a new one on me, so it is. But then, I don't read romantic books.' She shrugged slightly. 'I don't really know. It just happened on the spur of the moment. I mean, we didn't go there to get into a clinch.' Laughter bubbled over at the expression, so foreign on her lips. At her daughter's stern gaze she brought her mirth under control and mumbled, 'I suppose you could say we were both a bit tipsy.'

'A bit tipsy? You're just playing for time, Mam. I want to know if you're in love with Dick or was it just the drink?'

A wry smile twisted Kath's lips. 'I don't

357

honestly know. And that's the truth. I had actually made up my mind to accept Neville's proposal of marriage, and then suddenly I found myself in Dick's arms and it was wonderful. It reminded me of how I used to feel about...' she stopped herself in time. She had been about to say Neville '...your father, all those years ago. But then, perhaps Dick is stringing me along the way *he* did.'

'What about Irene? Is he still engaged to her?' Kath nodded, and Liz said tentatively, 'She'll be devastated. I remember only too well what it feels like to discover the man you trusted has found someone else.'

'Ah, now, Liz. There's no comparison. You were young and vulnerable and very much in love. Irene is much tougher. In fact, even if Dick is attracted to me ... and mind you, he might not be. As you observed, we were both quite tipsy ... I can't see him standing up to her. Once she knows, she'll probably rush him to the altar and that will be that.'

'Did you tell Neville about your feelings for Dick?'

'Mmm.'

'How did he take it?'

'He thinks it won't last.'

'Could he not be right, Mam? Perhaps you're just infatuated.'

'He's given me a week to make up my mind.'

'Mam, he seems to love you.'

'Ah, Liz ... in my life it's a case of too little, too late.' She shook her head. 'Never mind. It will sort itself out in the long run, one way or the other.'

Bridget eyed Danny warily when he entered the bedroom carrying a cup of tea in one hand and a plate of toast in the other.

'Ah, you're awake. Good morning, love.'

Graciously she accepted the plate and watched closely as he set the cup down carefully on the bedside table. What was he up to?

'Danny, I hate to sound ungrateful, but what is this all in aid of?'

'I just thought you might enjoy a wee cuppa in bed before facing the world. It's freezing out there these mornings.'

Still doubt nagged at her. There was something fishy going on. In all the time they'd been married he had never before brought her breakfast in bed, but this past week, every morning as soon as the alarm went off, he was out of bed. It was so unlike him, she could not help but be suspicious.

'Whether it's cold or not I still have to get up and go to work, Danny,' she reminded him gently.

'I know. And God knows, I wish you didn't have to. Maybe one day I'll earn enough to keep us all and you won't have to work.'

Still plagued by doubt she nibbled at the toast. She heard the rattle of the letter box and Danny went downstairs to collect the mail. He came into the bedroom as usual and handed it to her.

'Nothing important, I'm afraid.'

She looked at the brown envelopes and sighed. Danny might shrug them off as unimportant, but she had to find the money to pay these bills.

At work, in the lull between serving customers, her doubts concerning Danny returned. Was he softening her up? Had he met someone else?

'Hello, Bridget.'

A delighted smile curved her lips when she looked up from her musing and saw it was Peter. He stood on the other side of the counter, a wide grin on his face. 'What brings you here?' She waved a hand around the lingerie displayed on models. Quite a few men nonchalantly bought underwear for their wives and girlfriends, but Peter did not strike her as the sort to enter this department willingly.

'To be truthful, I was thinking of something nice to buy my mother for Christmas and remembered you worked in this department. I've a few days off so I thought I'd do some early Christmas shopping before the rush starts. I came here for advice.' He eyed the brief 'teddies', all frills and bows, and all shapes and sizes of bras and knickers displayed, and shook his head in mock dismay. 'But I don't imagine this would be me ma's style.'

'Oh, we have some very nice things to suit the older lady. Was it underwear you had in mind, or would you like to see some pyjamas or a dressing gown?'

His eyes lit up. 'Now that's an idea. Pyjamas sound fine.'

The next fifteen minutes were spent examining all kinds of pyjamas. Cotton, silk and winceyette were spread on the counter for his appraisal.

'I think this cotton pair would be most suit-

360

able, don't you?'

Bridget nodded her agreement. They were pink, with a pattern of small flowers. 'We also have them in blue, lemon and pale green.'

'They'll do, Bridget. I've taken up enough of your time.' His eyes slanted in embarrassment to where a woman stood patiently waiting.

'Can I help you, madam?'

'I was wanting to look at some petticoats, please.'

'One moment, please.' Bridget pressed a bell on the counter. Immediately a young girl came from somewhere in the inner confines. 'Will you serve this lady, please, Helen? I won't be a minute, Peter. I'll fetch all the different colours for you to look at.'

Keeping his eyes averted from the scantily clad figures of the display models, he smiled wryly to himself. His mother was in for a surprise. Him buying her pyjamas? It was unheard of. But he'd wanted to talk to Bridget and was having difficulty getting in touch with her. Whether or not she was deliberately avoiding him he had no idea, but he'd had to resort to coming to the shop.

He chose the pale green with white flowers. 'Now, what about the size, Peter?'

'Ah, Bridget, I've no idea. What do you think?'

In her mind's eye Bridget imagined Jane McGowan's portly figure. 'I think she would take a size sixteen. Most women like plenty of room in pyjamas. Keep your receipt and if she's not satisfied with them you can always change them or get your money back.' She folded the pyjamas neatly and put them in a bag.

As she put the sale through, he asked, 'Are you due a break soon, Bridget?' He entered the shop at a quarter past twelve, hoping it was near her lunch hour. It was now a quarter to one.

Her surprise was evident but she readily volunteered, 'I'm free from one to two for my lunch break.'

'Will you have lunch with me then?'

She hesitated and he urged, 'I want to talk to you.'

She nodded her consent and he smiled in relief. 'I'll wait at the front of the shop until you're free.'

Bridget spent longer than usual in the staff cloakroom, renewing her make-up and brushing her hair until it shone. Examining herself in the full-length mirror, she was pleased with her reflection. Her figure had filled out and the dark blue suit that had previously hung on her now fitted like a glove. Pity Danny didn't seem to notice the change in her. She decided not to wear her outer coat. It was old and a bit shabby, and she wanted to look her best.

Peter watched her come through the swing doors of the building and his breath caught in this throat. Eyes followed her progress as she made her way towards him. He only hoped she would not be too upset at what he had to tell her. That is, if he got up the courage to do so.

'You look marvellous.'

'Thank you.'

'Any suggestions as to where we can go?'

'I know a little cafe. It's a bit out of the way but we're sure of a table. The food is good and the service is quick.'

She led the way down side streets away from the town centre and soon turned into small, brightly lit cafe. The conversation was general and they were awaiting the arrival of their lunch, chicken and green salad for her and chicken curry for him, before she sounded him out on why he wanted to speak to her.

'Now, Peter, out with it. I have this awful feeling I'm going to hear some bad news.'

'Shall we eat first?' he asked, loath to break the atmosphere of well-being between them. He gazed into wide, thick-lashed, brown eyes and thought how foolish his brother was to risk losing a wife like Bridget.

'Let's get it over with, shall we?' When he still hesitated, she laughed softly. 'Don't worry about it putting me off my food. I only had a bit of toast for breakfast and now I could eat a horse.'

Her eyes were clear and shining and soft brown hair framed a face pink-cheeked from the frosty air. It was the happiest he had seen her look for a long time and as he drank in the beauty of her, he wished now he had never come. He didn't want to be the one to burst this happy bubble. Suppose he was wrong? Why, it could spell the end of their friendship. He could pretend. Make up some pretext for bothering her. No, she would never believe him. Besides, if what he suspected was true, the sooner she knew the better.

Her colour deepened under his scrutiny. 'Peter?' He had delayed so long she was beginning to get worried. 'Surely it can't be all that bad? Danny only goes out on a Saturday night.

363

He swore he isn't seeing anyone and I believe him. Is he telling me lies? Is this what you want to talk about?'

The waitress arrived and he remained silent while she placed their plates in front of them.

'Thank you.'

'Would you like a drink?' the waitress asked.

Peter looked inquiringly at Bridget. 'I'll have a Diet Coke, please.'

'And I'll have a beer, thank you.'

The woman left the table and Bridget said softly, 'Well, Peter? Are you going to tell me you've been listening to rumours?'

'As far as I know, there is no other woman, Bridget. But yes, I've heard rumours.'

She looked down at the appetizing food on her plate. 'I think I will eat this first after all. Just in case,' she said wryly.

Glad of the respite he tucked into his curry. When their plates were clear he looked across at her. 'Would you like anything else?'

She glanced at her watch. 'No, thank you. I'd better be heading back. Please tell me why you're here?' If this was a ploy to get her to have lunch with him she would be very angry indeed. But then, hadn't he made it clear he only thought of her as a sister? And hadn't he admitted there was gossip? And it must be bad! Why else would he go to all this bother?

He cleared his throat. 'I hope to God I'm wrong, Bridget, or you'll never forgive me. But are you aware that our Danny is getting into a lot of debt lately?'

Her mouth opened in amazement. 'Why? Why

would he need extra money? Lord knows he gets plenty for his pocket. I just wish I'd as much to squander on myself every week.'

'He's borrowing all round him. Not much like, a few pound here and a few pound there. I could be wrong but ... well, I think he's gambling.' Peter shrugged. 'I'm sorry if I'm speaking out of turn, but I thought you should know in case it gets out of hand.'

The colour left her face as suddenly everything fell into place. The morning tea and toast was all a ploy so her husband could see the post before her. She had deliberately asked for a monthly statement from the building society. At the beginning she had wanted the thrill of watching their money mount up. Not that it was growing to her expectations. Danny had foxed her all right. Now she came to think about it, it must be two months since she had last seen a statement.

Anxiously, Peter leant across the table. 'Are you all right, Bridget?'

'Yes. Yes.' She glanced blindly at her watch. 'I must go now or I'll be late.'

She was on her feet and heading for the door. He rose to follow her but realized he had yet to pay the bill. He hurried to the cash register and fumed inwardly as the girl seemed to take ages. At last he was free to leave the premises but to his concern there was no sign of Bridget. What to do? Should he go back to the shop? No, he risked upsetting her further if he did that. Despondently he headed for the bus stop. He had done his best. Now it was up to Bridget. What would she do?

Helen Quigley watched Bridget covertly throughout the afternoon. In all the time she had worked alongside her, she had never known her to make a mistake. Indeed, she had been promoted to supervisor two months ago and had never put a foot wrong. Now, in the course of a few short hours, she had made two mistakes. Nothing important and easily put right when Helen brought her attention to them, but mistakes nevertheless.

'Are you feeling all right, Bridget?'

Looking for an outlet for her feelings, a sharp retort came to her tongue, but when she looked into the kindly eyes of her workmate it died on her lips. 'I confess I've had a bit of bad news, so I'm a mite upset.'

'It's five o'clock. Why not go home early? Surely you can trust me on my own for an hour?'

'Trust you? Why, of course I trust you. I don't know what I'd have done without you. Especially today,' she retorted.

Colour warmed Helen's cheeks at these words of praise. 'Go home then. Leave everything to me.'

'I think I will. I'll just nip up and tell Mrs Morgan I'm going. I know she rarely puts in an appearance, but with my luck today is the day she would.' On her return from the manager's office, she went into the cloakroom and returned dressed for outdoors. 'Thanks, Helen. Thanks for everything. See you in the morning.'

'You take care now, Bridget. See you tomorrow.'

Danny carefully tucked the bundle of notes away in an inside pocket. 'Thanks, mate.'

The big burly man's brows rose in surprise. 'Huh, I'm not your mate. And I'm not giving you that money. You'll pay it back with interest or I'll know the reason why.'

Outside the small office attached to a betting shop, Danny turned to his brother-in-law. 'I owe you one, Patrick. You've saved my skin. I'll clear all my little debts and put the rest in the building society. With a bit of luck Bridget need be none the wiser.'

Patrick Kelly looked far from happy. A bit of luck? Luck was sparse indeed where Danny was concerned. Patrick knew he wasn't really doing him a favour introducing him to a money-lender, but his brother-in-law had been so distraught, Patrick had consented to help him. It was all right borrowing ten or twenty pounds and paying it back at so much a week, but he had been horrified at the amount Danny had borrowed. He himself would have difficulty paying back such a large sum, even over the extended period. The interest would be astronomical, and he hadn't a wife and child to support.

'Do you know something, Danny? You'd be far better facing our Bridget's wrath and telling her the truth, than getting into all this debt.'

'Talk sense, man. Why, it'll be the end of our marriage if she ever finds out.'

With a sad shake of the head Patrick turned away. 'On your own head be it. I'll see you around.'

'See you on Saturday night. I got a bit extra so

I did.' Danny patted his coat pocket meaning-fully. 'I'll be there as usual.'

Dismayed, Patrick swung round to face him again. Would he never learn? 'Are you daft, man? For God's sake, cut your losses and get out. You can't afford to get in any deeper. I'll tell you something, Danny, I've never met anyone as unlucky at cards as you. Have you ever won?'

'That's just it! My luck's bound to change.'

'Don't count on it. I won't be there this weekend. I wouldn't be able to stand watching you ruin yourself.'

Danny watched Bridget covertly throughout dinner. She barely touched her food and was tight-lipped. Was a row brewing? What had he done wrong now?

With great difficulty she controlled her temper until Martin was in bed and asleep. Then, hands on hips, she addressed her husband where he lay sprawled on the settee watching TV. She stood silently until he became aware of her stance and turned his head to look askance at her.

'Is anything wrong, Bridget?'

'I was about to ask you that. Is there anything you should be telling me about?'

Slowly, he sat upright, his mind ticking over. What had she heard? Had Patrick thought it his duty to put her wise? Danny feigned ignorance. 'Explain yourself? I've no idea what you're talking about, Bridget.'

'You haven't been withholding the building society statements from me then?'

'Why on earth would I do that?'

He managed to look bewildered and doubts assailed her. After all, Peter had admitted he was only repeating rumours. She should have made sure of her facts before throwing accusations at her husband.

Danny was watching her closely and, glad to see her waver, patted the settee beside him. 'Come and sit down, love, and tell me what's on your mind.'

Dazed, her mind a jumble of conflicting thoughts, she sank down beside him. Her anxious eyes scanned his face. He really did look puzzled. Still, didn't she know Danny was a good actor? Hadn't she told him often enough he should be on the stage? And, Peter was usually a very reliable source of information.

Pulling her close, Danny said gently, 'Well, love, are you going to tell me what's wrong? What's this about statements?'

'We haven't had a building society statement for some time. You know how I love to watch our savings grow.'

'I think we've missed one statement, love. Just one. And you think I had something to do with that? Why would I, tell me that? After all, mail goes astray all the time.'

'I know, and I'm sorry for jumping at you like this.'

'Tell you what ... just to set your mind at rest, tomorrow morning why don't you phone the building society and find out the balance?'

'That's a good idea, Danny. I might just do that. I'll also make sure they continue to send out a statement each month.'

369

He was relieved to have thought of this idea. On the phone she would get the balance which would give him a breathing space. However, she would be watching for the next statement, but if he managed to win some money before then he knew he would be able to soft soap her. The only snag at the moment was the fact that their building society was very close to the Bank Buildings. What if she decided to call in on her lunch break? Then all would be revealed. She would find out everything and he'd be in deep trouble. But he'd cross that bridge when he came to it. For now he must lull her into a false sense of security.

'If you want I'll phone them, love?'

'There's no need. I believe you.'

Ashamed of doubting him, she moved closer and offered her lips in atonement. He was delighted. It wasn't often his wife made the first move. Gratefully he savoured the moment, drawing her closer as his passion rose. This was indeed a bonus. Ashamed of having doubted him, Bridget returned his caresses with intensity. When she next saw Peter, she would make a point of letting him know how wrong he had been. She must put a stop to these rumours once and for all.

Bridget didn't plan to go to the building society. Didn't she trust Danny? But as fate would have it, with extra staff in for the Christmas rush, she and Helen had the same lunch hour and decided to give food a miss and do some shopping themselves. Helen had to take some money from the building society; the same one as Bridget. Last night had been better than it had been for a long time between her and her husband, and she had decided to take Danny's word that everything was all right and hadn't phoned the building society. After all, he wouldn't be urging her to phone if he had anything to hide, now would he?

The queues for transactions were long, and as she waited for her friend, she decided it wouldn't do any harm to go to the inquiry counter and ask about their statements.

The girl on inquiries was very surprised to hear that a statement, maybe two, had gone astray. 'They come from head office, you know, Mrs McGowan. Do you have your pass book with you, and I'll check it out for you?'

'No, but I do know my account number.'

'Let's have it then and I'll see what I can find out.'

Some minutes later, the girl smiled at her. 'With the six hundred put in yesterday your balance is...'

'Six hundred put in yesterday? There must be some mistake! You must be looking at someone else's account.'

The girl checked the screen again, a worried frown on her brow. 'I don't think so. Mr Daniel & Mrs Bridget McGowan,' she queried, and gave the correct address.

'Yes, that's right.' Bridget whispered. 'What is the balance?'

At the figure quoted, Bridget nodded her head. 'That's about right. Look, could you send me out a copy of the last statement, please?'

The girl was sympathetic; she could see something was wrong. 'I'll phone head office right away and get them to send you out a copy today first-class post. You should receive it in the morning.'

'Thank you. Thank you very much.'

Bridget turned away from the desk in a daze and made her way unsteadily to where Helen, her business finished, was waiting for her.

Anxiously coming forward to meet her, Helen gripped her arm. 'Are you all right, Bridget?'

Forcing a smile to her lips, she nodded. 'Just a mix up in our account, but it's going to be sorted out. Let's go and spend some money.'

The toured the shops looking for bargains and Bridget knew she had put on a good show. Her friend was completely unaware of the resentment festering in Bridget's breast. Danny was so devious! Encouraging her to phone, knowing full well she would only be given the balance. He'd treated her like an idiot! But no more. By God, no more! she vowed.

Unwilling to face the row she knew must come, when she called to pick up Martin, Bridget lingered at her mother's that evening. Martha eyed her closely. Usually her daughter hadn't a minute to spare, but tonight she was messing about, wasting time.

'Is anything wrong, love?'

'No. What makes you think that?'

'The way you're hanging about here. Come on, if anything is worrying you, get if off your chest.'

Forcing a smile to her lips, Bridget assured her, 'You're imagining things, Mam. I'm just tired. Come here, Martin. Let's get your coat and hat on. I'd better get a move on, Mam. As you said, I've wasted enough time already.'

Martha saw her off and returned indoors, a worried frown on her brow. She had noted that the smile hadn't reached her daughter's eyes. What was wrong now? Was Bridget never to know any happiness?

Bridget was still in a state of shock as she prepared dinner for herself and Danny. He didn't deserve to come home to a meal tonight, she lamented inwardly. However, she did want Martin in bed and asleep before all hell broke loose, as she was sure it would. While the dinner cooked, she automatically fed Martin his dinner and got him ready for bed. From the beginning of her marriage she had vowed that the child would never be subjected to witnessing the rows between herself and Danny. She only hoped that tonight she would be able to hold her tongue long enough for Martin to have fallen asleep.

Danny eyed her covertly as they ate, very much aware that his wife was spoiling for a row but afraid to ask what was wrong. Couldn't he guess the reason for her sombre mood? He commented on how tender the meat was and praised the smooth gravy. This only added fuel to the flames burning in Bridget's breast. Any other night he wolfed down his dinner in silence and praise from him was hard to come by. Tight-lipped, she answered him with grunts and nods.

Every now and again, when he wasn't watching her, she threw baleful glances at him. How could he sit there enjoying his food, so unconcerned? Her dinner was choking her. Desperate to have a go at him but mindful of Martin, she managed to hold her tongue. All afternoon her mind had been tortured with thoughts of where he had obtained six hundred pounds. As far as they were concerned it was a fortune. And could he really have gambled so much without her being aware? Of course he could! Didn't some men gamble away fortunes in one go? Could he possibly have won this money back then? If only that were so and he had learnt his lesson, there might still be hope for them. But what if he had borrowed it from a money-lender? If so, she saw no future with him. He would always be a loser.

Their usual routine of her washing, him drying the dishes, was conducted in a silence charged with anger. He couldn't understand how the crockery remained intact under her assault but was afraid to speak in case he unleashed Bridget's wrath in his own direction. Rarely did she lose her temper, but when she did all hell broke loose. If she had visited the building society today, he'd be the first to admit that, in this instance, she had just cause to be angry. What excuse had he to offer her that was likely to be acceptable? None! He could never justify what he had done.

Without a word Bridget left him to finish off in the kitchen and went to make sure Martin was asleep. Looking down at the sleeping face of her son, she felt tears sting her eyes. She was working so hard and doing without small luxuries for herself so that they could move to a house with a garden for this child to play in. And by the looks of it, all to no avail. She had held her tongue so long she found she didn't want to speak out. The idea of a blazing row made her feel sick. It could only end in disaster. She saw her life in ruins. The money had been replaced! Would she not be better pretending she knew nothing of Danny's deception? After all, she could put an end to him touching their money by moving it into an account in her name only.

Her conscience would not let her take the easy way out. That money had come from somewhere. What was Danny up to? She had to find out. Wearily, she brushed the hair back off her brow and went to face her husband. Her legs felt so weak she was afraid they wouldn't hold her weight and sank down on to a chair facing him. Reaching across, she switched off the television.

Bewildered, he turned to her. 'Here, what do you think you're doing?'

'I went to the building society at lunchtime today.'

She saw him lick his lips and swallow before answering her. 'So?' he blustered.

'First of all, why did you take so much money out?'

He straightened up in his chair and a sneer twisted his lips. 'I thought you trusted me, eh? Oh, man but you put on a great show last night to prove you were sorry you doubted me. I really thought you meant it. You said you trusted me enough not to phone the society to get the balance. Then you go sneaking round checking up on me, behind my back. How can you blow hot and cold like that? What kind of a wife are you?'

She closed her eyes in frustration at the audacity of him. 'Danny! If you want me to stay on in this flat, you had better tell me everything. And I mean everything.'

The very idea of her leaving him brought him to his knees by her side. He tried to grip her hands but she warded him off. 'Don't touch me!'

He gripped his hands together on the arm of the chair as if in prayer and it took all her self-control not to lash out at his face with her fists. Her mind kept repeating, You conniving bastard.

'I can explain everything, Bridget.' His mind was in overdrive, seeking a plausible excuse that would satisfy her. 'I needed the money to help someone out of a fix. As you know, I paid it all back in.'

'Who were you helping?'

'A mate at work. I promised not to tell anyone about it.'

'Mmm. A mate at work? You must be very close to him. How come I wasn't aware of this friendship?'

'It wasn't a social thing, Bridget. He was in despair and I offered to help him out. He would have done the same for me.'

'Huh! Would he? So it had nothing to do with the fact that you're gambling every weekend?'

He sagged back on his heels and his jaw dropped in shock. Who had told her? Hell roast Patrick Kelly, it could have only been him. Why couldn't he mind his own bloody business? Still

Danny blustered it out. 'The money is all paid back so why not just drop this stupid interrogation? After all, it's my money. I work bloody hard for it.'

She stiffened in the chair. 'Oh, so it's *your* money now?'

He had risen to his feet and towered over her. It gave him courage to see her looking small and vulnerable. 'Yes, my money.'

'What have you ever gone without that gives you the right to claim that money is yours? Eh? Tell me that? During our marriage, what have you ever done without? And just what the hell do you think I'm doing every day in the Bank Buildings? Running some kind of bloody charity shop without wages?'

He shrugged. 'Well, if you put it that way ... it's *our* money. But I still have the right to do what I like with my half.'

Her eyes scorned him but she knew better than to argue at the moment. Once she started there would be no stopping her. It would all end in tears, with him promising all sorts. And her pride, her fear of everybody finding out how hard she was done by, would let him persuade her to give him another chance; to pretend all was well with them. Pride? To hell with that! She was fed up covering up for him; pretending all was well with their marriage. She didn't care any more who knew her marriage was on the rocks. Thank God, either of their signatures was sufficient to move the money. Tomorrow she would close down that account and put the money into one in her name only. Then just let him try to claim any of it!

She'd had enough. It was time to get out of this farce of a marriage. Watching all the different expressions pass over her face, Danny was at a loss to pinpoint just what she was thinking. Whether it would come out in his favour or not. In bewilderment he gaped after her when, without another word, she rose to her feet and left the room. A few minutes passed and he stood, ears strained, wondering what she was up to. When she returned she had a pillow and some blankets over her arm.

Throwing them on the settee she said tersely, 'I suggest you sleep here tonight. I need time to think.'

Unable to comprehend just what was happening, he was nevertheless relieved that apparently there was to be no great row. Grateful for the respite, he cried, 'You take all the time you need, love.'

Her lip curled scornfully but she bit back the ugly words ready to erupt and turned on her heel.

'Bridget,' he shouted after her. 'I've learnt my lesson, so I have. I'll never gamble again and that's the God's honest truth, love.'

Truth? He didn't know the meaning of the word! The urge to slam the bedroom door as hard as she could was very strong, but fearful of waking Martin she closed it gently, placing a chair under the door handle in case he thought to win her over with his idea of love-making. Tears coursed down her cheeks. She silently thanked God that so far she had managed to keep her own counsel. Tomorrow night when he came home she would be gone.

The minute the alarm sounded next morning Bridget was out of bed like a bullet from a gun and within seconds was down in the hall waiting for the postman. The building society had sent out a copy of the two previous statements. They confirmed her worst fears. This past couple of months her husband had been withdrawing fifty pounds, a few times as much as a hundred, every week. So much for him helping a mate out of a fix. Had he really thought he would get away with that story? How could he be so stupid?

They conversed little over breakfast, Danny only commenting on the weather and trivial matters, trying to gauge how the land lay. Bridget barely answered him. As soon as he left for work, she phoned in sick. Her greatest desire was to leave this flat and never return. She had no idea where she would go, but knew her mother would put her up for a few days while she arranged something. Packing as much of her own and Martin's clothes as she could in the suitcase and holdall, she left them ready in the hall. A glance at the clock told her it was time to take Martin to his grannie's. She would break the bad news to her before bringing round her bits and pieces.

Martha was waiting at the door for her. 'I was just about to come round. I thought you must have slept in or something. You'd better run away on or you'll be late for work, so you will.'

'Mam, I'm not going in today.'

Immediately Martha was all concern, anxious

eyes scanning her daughter's strained face. 'What's wrong, love? Don't you feel well?'

'I hadn't time to eat any breakfast and my head's splitting. Any chance of a cup of tea? Then I'll tell you all about it.'

Martha made the tea in silence. She could see her daughter was upset and dreaded hearing the reason why. 'Would you like something to eat, love?'

'No, Mam. I couldn't swallow anything. I would choke on it.'

Bridget sat gazing into her cup for a long time. Should she tell her mother everything? What if Danny talked her round? After all, he was her husband and he had talked her round to his way of thinking before. What if he persuaded her into staying with him? Then she would be ashamed to face her mother if she knew the truth. Aghast at these thoughts, Bridget's resolve deepened. No, under no circumstances must she let Danny sway her. Enough was enough!

Martha watched her and a great ball of resentment gathered in her breast against Danny McGowan. Her daughter had been looking so well lately. Today she looked haggard and careworn. How Martha now regretted forcing her into marriage with that selfish bastard. 'Well, love, tell me all about it?'

'I'm leaving Danny.'

Martha sighed, but it came as no surprise. Hadn't she guessed as much? 'I know you've a lot to put up with, Bridget, but so have other women. Marriage is a commitment. You can't just walk out when you feel like it. If it was just

380

yourself, I'd say good luck to you ... but you've him to consider.' She nodded to where Martin was playing on the floor. 'Besides, where would you go?'

Dismayed at her mother's reaction to her news, Bridget whispered, 'I was counting on you to put me up for a few days, Mam.'

'And I will, I will. But what next? You can't say here indefinitely.'

'Given time, I'll find somewhere, Mam. I just need a little space. I'm earning enough now to keep me and Martin.'

Martha leant across the table and gazed earnestly into her daughter's face. 'Now you listen to me, Bridget. You're going the wrong way about this. You've put a lot of money and effort into making that flat into a comfortable home. So why should *you* be the one to leave? Why should he sit there in comfort while you stay in cramped quarters? Eh? Because even on your wages that's all you'll be able to afford. A poky wee room somewhere. You should tell *him* to go. He has to support you and the boy. He has to pay the rent of the flat and give you so much every week to live on. So talk to him! Try to make him see reason. He won't want you coming back here, that's for sure. It would cause too much gossip and he would be afraid of running into your da or the lads in the pub. But if he leaves the flat for you and the child, it won't look so bad. Danny is very proud where outsiders are concerned and I think he'll agree to go and stay with his mother until you sort things out between you.'

'I don't think it can be sorted, Mam.'

381

'You don't know that, love. You loved him at the beginning and love doesn't just die.'

'Love? What is this great thing called love? That's what I'd like to know! I admit I thought Danny was wonderful at the beginning, and perhaps if he'd been good to me I might still have imagined myself in love with him. Now I'm not sure anymore.'

'Take my advice. Go in to work as usual and go home tonight and talk it over with Danny. Don't give him any excuse to put you in the wrong.'

Bridget digested her mother's words. She was right. Why should she be the one to leave; have all the hassle of finding somewhere else to live? Danny would have no trouble. Jane wouldn't turn her son away from the door.

'You're right, Mam. But I can't go into work now, I phoned in sick.'

'Go in at lunchtime. Tell them you feel much better.'

'I'll do that.' Going to her mother, Bridget put her arms around her and hugged her. 'What would I do without you, Mam?'

'You would manage. And remember, if it doesn't work out you can always come here.'

'Thanks, Mam.' She grimaced slightly. 'I'd better go and unpack the cases.'

Martha watched her walk up the street, her own heart wrung with pity. Wait until Barney heard about this! He'd want to break Danny McGowan's neck. She wondered what had happened; what the straw was that finally broke the camel's back? Her daughter had neglected to tell her.

Peter was devastated when his brother arrived home that evening with his suitcases and announced his marriage was over.

He stared in dismay at Danny. Had he been the cause of the breakup? He hadn't meant to cause a rift. He sat silent as his mother asked all the relevant questions.

'What do you mean, your marriage is over? Do you think you can just walk out on your responsibilities like that?'

'It was her put me out! I didn't walk out as you call it.'

'What on earth did you do? She didn't put you out for nothing.'

'Oh, but she did. A bit of an argument about money ... and she asked me to leave.'

A perplexed frown furrowed Jane's brow. 'I don't understand. It doesn't sound like you. You just packed your bags and left because she told you to?' Her chin lifted and she looked him straight in the eye. 'I don't believe you.'

'It's the truth, Ma. If I hadn't left, she threatened to go back to her parents. I couldn't bear the thought of Barney landing round, so I left.'

'You must be in the wrong then, or you wouldn't be afraid of Barney Kelly.'

'Look, Ma, are you going to let me stay or not?'

'You're not moving in with me again,' Peter warned. 'If you stay, you sleep on the settee.'

'That suits me fine.'

Jane was having none of this. His place was with his wife. 'Danny, I suggest you go back and make your peace with Bridget before it's too late.

You know rightly you wouldn't get a proper night's sleep on that settee.'

'So you're not going to let me stay?'

The bluster left her. No matter what the cause, he was homeless at the moment and she could not turn her own son away.

'You can stay. Just for a few days, mind.'

Peter rose to his feet in disgust. 'Remember, he sleeps on the settee.' The outer door slammed as he left the house.

Peter stood at the top of the steps leading to the landing outside the flat. 'Bridget, I know you're in there. Let me in, please.'

No answer. 'Look, Bridget, you can't stay there forever and I don't intend moving until I speak to you.'

A full minute passed and then the door was opened slightly. 'Peter, you and I have nothing to say to each other.'

'Just let me in for a minute. Please?'

Slowly the door opened and Bridget stepped reluctantly to one side to let him pass. She didn't want to talk to him. She could certainly do without his sympathy at this stage. It could only lead to complications and she had enough on her plate already.

She led the way into the kitchen. There would be no sitting down in comfort in the living room for a cosy chat. There had been too much interference in her marriage. She wanted a complete break from the McGowan clan.

The breadth of the kitchen table between them, she said tersely, 'Well, what is it you want?'

'I want to know if I was the cause of the breakup?'

'No. Rest assured, you were not.'

'You're making this very awkward, Bridget. Was Danny gambling? Is that why you put him out? Was it because of what I told you.'

She lost her cool then. 'Do you know something? You McGowans sicken me. Did Danny go crying to his mother?' Her fist struck her breast. 'Am I the big bad wolf? Because I'm sure he didn't tell you the truth. Tell me, do you wash all your dirty linen in public? Have you no secrets from each other?'

Tears threatened and to hide them she swung round to face the sink.

Peter was behind her immediately. 'You're wrong, Bridget. I've plenty of secrets. For instance, no one knows how I feel about you.'

Slowly she turned to face him. In the confined space he was too close for comfort. 'Hah! As a brother? That would hardly be frowned on.'

'I was deluding myself, Bridget. I care...'

She interrupted him. 'I don't want to hear any more of your declarations. Do you hear me? I've enough to worry about at the moment. Will you please leave now?'

'Bridget, have I not been good to you in the past? Was I not there for you when you needed a helping hand?'

'Yes, but...'

His hand reached out and tilted her face towards his. 'I'll never hurt you, Bridget. I'll play it any way you like.'

'Oh, Peter. I don't know what I want. I'm all

confused,' she wailed.

'I know it's early days, Bridget. For Martin's sake you might even be foolish enough to take Danny back. So I won't put pressure on you. Let's play it by ear. Eh, Bridget? Let me be your friend.'

She gazed at him, eyes brimming with tears. As they spilled over he cupped her face in his hands and brushed the tears away with his thumbs. 'Remember, I'll never hurt you, Bridget,' he promised. 'Now I'm going to make you a cup of tea. Is Martin down for a nap?'

She shook her head. 'Mam has him. I was afraid of a slanging match in front of the child.'

Peter filled the teapot and put it on to boil. 'You'll have to change the lock, Bridget. I know you can't change the downstairs one 'cause it also leads into the shop, but you must change the lock on the door of the flat.'

Her face stretched in amazement. 'Why?'

'Because our Danny will be drowning his sorrows and might come calling when you least expect him. Like in the early hours of the morning, for instance.'

'Oh, God. I never thought of that.'

'Would you like me to spend the night?'

'No! Oh, no.'

He had his back to her and a satisfied smile curved his lips. She was afraid of the attraction he held for her. 'Well, make sure you bolt the door, and if he does come, don't under any circumstances let him in. I'll get a new lock and change it over for you. Here, drink this up.'

Their eyes met as he handed her the cup and he

386

was glad to see a blush make her face rosy. She really was very lovely and he had made up his mind, sister-in-law or not, if he got the chance he would make her his. No matter what anyone said about living in sin.

Liz put the finishing touches to the Christmas decorations. She felt at peace with herself. In the New Year she and David were to start tests to find out why she wasn't conceiving. Please God, with a bit of luck it would prove to be something simple and this time next year she would have a baby in her arms.

It would be a very quiet Christmas this year, just the two of them. Her mam was cooking Christmas dinner for herself and Dick Kennedy. To everyone's surprise, Irene had broken off her engagement to him. Those in the know had thought she would fight tooth and nail for him but she chose to break things off quietly. Neville was being very understanding about it all. Liz couldn't believe it. Everybody was being so accommodating. For the past few weeks Neville had disappeared from the scene entirely, whilst Kath made up her mind about Dick. It looked very promising where he was concerned. It was obvious to all that he thought highly of her mother. However, Irene had started to come to the club again. Looking beautiful, she dressed to kill and had all the unattached men panting after her. She even made a point of flirting with David, much to his embarrassment. Dick always gave her a duty dance. On these occasions, Liz could see her mother was very uneasy. She supposed

Kath was still not really sure of him.

She smiled when she thought of how Irene could make even David turn hot around the collar. She certainly gave no one cause to pity her. Hadn't she announced to all that it was her decision to jilt Dick? And he hadn't refuted it. But then, being a gentleman, he wouldn't. Still, when Irene set her mind to it, couldn't she pick and choose?

What about Neville? There was sadness in Liz's heart when she thought about him, that big lonely man. It must be heartbreaking for him. Where would he spend Christmas this year? Probably with one of his sons. Perhaps they should phone and invite him over for his dinner on Christmas Day. Both she and David had no father figure in the background and Neville was like that to them; a much-admired father figure. She decided to talk it over with her husband when he came home from work.

David was all for it. 'I think that's a brilliant idea, Liz. But I don't imagine Neville will be spending Christmas on his own. Remember, he has sons and grandchildren. I can't remember how many but I'm sure he will spend some time with them.'

'His sons live a fair distance away. He might not want to travel, especially if we get the snow we're promised.'

David left his seat at the bureau where he was writing out Christmas cards and joined her on the settee. Putting an arm around her shoulders, he said, 'Ask him by all means, Liz. You really are a kind person, you know.'

Her eyes twinkled. 'Since Mam won't consent to join us, how about a mother figure as well?'

Realising that there was some kind of catch coming, he watched her from under lowered lids.

'I thought perhaps Irene might come if we ask her,' she teased. 'Who knows, perhaps she and Neville might hit it off?'

To her surprise her husband pushed her away and rose abruptly to his feet. 'Don't even joke about that, Liz.' Realising he was on his feet, at a loss he threw his hands wide in frustration. 'Would you like a drink?'

'No ... no, thank you.' She watched him walk to the drinks cabinet and changed her mind. 'On second thoughts, I'll have a gin with plenty of tonic.'

He grimaced slightly as he handed her the glass. 'You'll be wondering why such a strong reaction?'

'Well, yes.'

He sat down beside her and took a deep drink of Bushmill's before continuing. It crossed her mind as he gulped at the drink that perhaps he needed Dutch courage. But why? David wondered if he should tell his wife that the previous Saturday evening Irene had waylaid him in Fortwilliam and suggested he meet her somewhere private. She'd insinuated that she had information that would interest him. In spite of himself, his mind had unwillingly gone to his wife and Danny. Did Irene know something that could affect his marriage? If so, he didn't want to know. He had politely turned down her offer, causing a look of disdain to be bestowed on him.

With an indifferent shrug Irene had sauntered off. Should he confide this in Liz? Clear the air?

He found he was afraid he might get the wrong reaction. His excuse, when it eventually came, sounded lame even to his own ears. 'I have to admit, I hate the way that woman flirts with me.' The words sounded inane and he wasn't surprised to see his wife's scornful reaction.

'She's harmless, for heaven's sake. You should be flattered she admires you.'

He shrugged. 'I can't help how I feel.'

Noting the red tide that rose from neck to hairline, Liz said gently, 'I'm sorry I teased you. I didn't know you felt so strongly about it.'

'I didn't tell you, so you weren't to know.'

'No, you didn't,' she said slowly, wondering just why he hadn't mentioned how strongly he felt. He made no effort to explain further and after a short pregnant pause, she said, 'Let's forget it. I'll see if I can catch Neville on the phone and offer him Christmas dinner.'

She rose from the settee and he caught her hand and stayed her. 'Make it plain your mother won't be here. We don't want him to be disappointed.'

Weather permitting, Neville was playing Santa Claus to his grandchildren on Christmas Eve. He was, however, delighted to accept the offer to join them for dinner on Christmas Day. When Liz stressed that Kath would not be there, he laughed and assured her that he knew just where her mother was spending Christmas and with whom. He agreed to come to their home at two o'clock.

Neville arrived in a flurry of snowflakes as the weather promised by the Met Office at last arrived. 'Thank God that held off until I'd completed my Christmas duties to the family,' he said. 'And thanks for having me, Liz and David.'

'You're very welcome.'

Before they started the meal, he presented them each with a gift, a pair of silver cuff links for David and a beautiful brooch for Liz. She gazed down at the emeralds embedded in gold and her breath caught in her throat. 'Oh, I couldn't possibly accept this!' she exclaimed. 'It's far too expensive. Look, David, isn't it beautiful?'

He agreed with her. He also agreed that it was far too expensive a gift for his wife to accept.

'Now you are offending me. Who else would have invited a lonely old man into their home on Christmas Day? Please make me happy by accepting these gifts.'

Liz rose from her seat and, going to him, wrapped her arms around his neck and planted a kiss on his cheek. 'Thank you very much. I'll always treasure it.'

To hide his embarrassment Neville said gruffly, 'Hey, enough of that. That turkey is crying out to be carved and I'm starving.'

After dinner, dishes in the dishwasher and the remains of the delicious meal either disposed of or put away for a snack later on, they retired to the lounge. Liz regarded Neville over the rim of her glass. In repose there was a sad droop to his mouth and he looked tired. Determined to see that he enjoyed himself, she placed her drink to one side and addressed him brightly.

'Tell me, Neville, how did your stint at playing Santa Claus go?'

A smile brightened his face. 'It was wonderful. They're all too old for me really to pretend to be Santa any more, but the atmosphere was great when I arrived loaded down with parcels. They're wonderful kids. It's a pity I don't see more of them.'

Tentatively, David asked, 'Would you not consider moving house to be closer to them?'

'Actually, about a year ago I was considering selling up and buying a house near them, but then something happened that knocked all that on the head.' He eyed Liz and she immediately thought of her mother.

Her voice sad, she advised him, 'Neville, I think you would be foolish to hope Mam will change her mind. She's besotted with Dick. I must confess, I don't understand her. I thought she cared for you.'

He smiled slightly, but held her eye. 'Perhaps she's sowing the wild oats she should have sown when she was young?'

Liz gaped at him. 'Did she tell you she never sowed wild oats?'

'No, but it's obvious. She had you outside wedlock when she was barely nineteen. That must have been very hard on a lovely girl like Kath.'

Liz sat in stunned silence. What on earth was her mother doing with Dick Kennedy when she had thought enough of Neville to bare her very soul to him?

He was continuing. 'Liz, why did you not try to

392

trace your father? Did your mother forbid it?'

She sat bolt upright. This was going too far. He had no right to question her about her father. It was none of his business. Recalling her vow to see he enjoyed himself, she bit back the sharp retort that sprang to her lips and replied in an agreeable manner. 'For your information, he didn't want to know me. That's why I never made any effort to contact him. My mother never confided in me, but it was obvious from unkind remarks passed by neighbours that he was a married man. And since he didn't keep in touch, he obviously just washed his hands of us. So why would I want to seek him out?'

'You still feel very bitter towards him then?'

She shrugged. 'I can't help it. He denied me so much. You see, my mother's parents took it very badly, and besides not having a father I saw very little of my grandparents. But ... I suppose he had his reasons. I suppose he did what he had to do.'

'I'm saddened to hear all this, Liz. Your mother is so attractive, I'm surprised she has never married. She must have loved your father very much.'

'As I said, she never confided in me and by the time I was old enough to understand she seemed contented just to be with me. He certainly never made any effort to seek me out.'

'I'm sure he regrets that now, and I'm sure he looked after you in his own way.'

She shrugged. 'Why would he regret it now? But to be truthful Mam always had money when she needed it. And he bought us the house in Dunlewey Street, so he can't have been all bad.

There were, as you say, other men who came calling but Mam just wasn't interested.'

'I hope she finds happiness with Dick.'

David had listened to all these confidences in silence. He laughed aloud at these words. 'Do you really, Neville? Or are you telling fibs? I don't understand you. If I cared for someone, I wouldn't sit back and watch her go off with my rival. I'd be in there trying to win her over.'

'Ah, but you don't know the ins and outs of it. I made Kath a promise and so my hands are tied. And I'd be the first to admit that Dick is younger and more attractive than me. Why shouldn't she fancy him?'

'Neville, don't do yourself down. If you love Mam, fight for her.'

'If your mother and I were ever to hit it off, Liz, would you willingly accept me as a step-father?'

'Of course I would. I can't think of anyone I'd rather have.'

'Not even Dick?'

'Not even Dick.'

'Thank you, my dear. I appreciate that.'

Danny stood outside the flats on the Antrim Road in trepidation. Would Ian let him stay? He saw a corner of the curtain lift at the upper window and Ian peering out. A few minutes later, the door opened and he was motioned inside.

'Why the locked door?' he asked.

'The new tenants in your old flat feel safer if the outer door is kept closed,' Ian explained as he climbed the stairs to his flat. 'This is a surprise. To what do I owe the pleasure of your visit?' Over his own threshold, his eyes ranged over the suit-case in Danny's hand and his brows rose.

Danny gestured towards it. 'I was hoping you would put me up for a few days, mate.'

'Well now, Danny, that could prove a bit inconvenient at the moment.'

'Ian, please, I've no one else to turn to.'

'That bad, is it?'

'Yes. I know you'll be entertaining friends over Christmas but I'll make myself scarce. I promise you I won't cause any embarrassment. Those nights I'll stay at me mam's house.'

'Take off your coat and let's see if we can work something out.'

Gratefully, Danny parked his case. After hanging up his overcoat he followed Ian into the kitchen. Across the table, Ian questioned him. 'You haven't let that wee wife of yours down, I hope?'

'It's the other way about. She just won't listen to reason.'

'Mmm, I see.' He sounded sceptical. 'And why can't you stay with your mother?'

'It's too close for comfort. I'd be running into Barney Kelly all the time. Besides, our Peter is proving awkward. I really do think he has a soft spot for Bridget. He always takes her side. He doesn't want me back in the house.'

'Are you and Bridget going to separate? Has it come to that?'

'No, I'm confident that given time she'll see reason. I have to admit I've been very stupid. Still I never dreamt she would put me out of my own home just a week before Christmas. I suppose I should have stayed put. But, you see, she threatened if I stayed she would go to her mother's. So what could I do, but go?' A sob caught in his throat and he coughed in an effort to disguise it.

Ian sighed. His friend really did look wretched. His handsome face was haggard and his hair unkempt. How could he turn him away? A glance at the clock brought him abruptly to his feet. 'Look, Danny, I need a bit of fresh air. How about you and me walking up to the golf club for a drink?'

'It's freezing out there, Ian. Besides I'm broke.'

'Nevertheless, I have to go and I insist you join me. Come on, I'll treat you to a pint.'

Danny's face cleared as comprehension dawned. 'You've someone coming?' he guessed as he followed Ian's example and shrugged back into his overcoat.

'Yes, and if he finds you here all hell will break loose.'

'I understand.'

'No, you don't.' Ian disagreed with a laugh. 'Not by a long shot. Unfortunately, your sort never do.'

'What's that supposed to mean?'

'You're selfish, Danny boy. You think nobody has problems but you and expect everybody to rally round and help you. What if my friend had already been here?'

Danny shrugged his shoulders. 'That's simple. You wouldn't have let me in. But I would have come back later.'

'See what I mean? You only think of yourself.

What if it's someone you know?'

'No chance. I don't know any other ... I mean, you're the only one I know.'

'Don't be stupid, Danny. You can't tell by looking at a bloke, you know. I think you would be surprised at how many of "us" you know.'

As they faced the wind on their journey towards Downview Avenue, Danny pulled the collar of his coat up around his ears and the lower part of his face and snuggled down into it. Thus he failed to notice a figure turn tail away from the house in dismay and hover close by in the shadows of a garden wall. Ian saw him and shrugged his shoulders and spread his hands in Joseph's direction. With one last baleful look at Ian and Danny, Joseph turned and quickly headed for the bus stop. Trust his brother to spoil things for everybody.

Chapter Seven

Dutifully, two days before the Christmas break, Bridget met Danny and granted him access to Martin over the festive season. Still very annoyed at his deception, she was loath to meet him but realized he had a right to see his son. It was a bitter meeting, with Danny making snide remarks and Bridget trying to keep the peace, thankful that Martin wasn't with her to witness the slanging match. It left her feeling in the wrong, as if it was all her fault. Was it? Had she failed him as a wife?

They eventually agreed to one hour on Christmas Eve, two hours on Christmas Day, and two hours on Boxing Day. Danny tried to sway her to let him have the child longer but she remained adamant. She thought that even these short periods would be too long for Danny, knowing full well he would probably spend little time at home. He would be out celebrating and his son would be looked after by his family, but at least the grandparents would be delighted.

Her husband began his celebrations even earlier than she'd imagined. On Christmas Eve he had collected Martin as agreed, and with a disapproving sniff in Bridget's direction, carried him off. Watching him descend the stairs, talking lovingly to the child, she was suddenly filled with misgivings. He really did dote on Martin.

Suppose he did something stupid? She wondered just what her husband had in mind. Would he bring the child back as promised? Of course he would, she assured herself. Where on earth would he take him?

Still, for the next hour she was on edge and as time drew near for their return she hovered behind the net curtains, watching. It was with relief that she saw her father-in-law cross the Falls Road, Martin sitting on his shoulders. An embarrassed Joe McGowan was full of apologies for his son. 'I can't understand him, Bridget. He won't tell us why you put him out...' He hesitated, obviously hoping for some enlightenment. When she remained silent, he continued, 'But you can rest assured, we know what he's like. We don't blame you in the slightest. Am I out of place in asking what was so bad you had to put him out? He's in an awful state, you know. Doesn't seem to know what he's done wrong.'

'I'm sorry, Mr McGowan, but he knows full well. I can't tell you what it is. That's up to Danny. It's something he has brought on himself and there's no one else to blame. If it all happened to work out, he'd be embarrassed at you finding out. Know what I mean? If he can't sort out his own problems, well then, you'll probably know all about them soon enough. Until then I'm not saying a word. You know what he's like.'

To her dismay Joe saw this as a sign of hope. 'Do you mean there's a chance you might still get together?'

'I don't know. I honestly don't. Maybe, for Martin's sake, we might. But don't count on it. It all depends on Danny.'

A sad shake of the head showed Joe's despair. 'I'll come back for the child tomorrow afternoon and bring him over to his father. All right, Bridget?'

Relieved she wouldn't have to see Danny on Christmas Day she thankfully agreed. 'That will be fine, Mr McGowan. See you then. And Happy Christmas.'

Her mother had invited her round to tea, and later that afternoon as she was about to open the door to the flat she heard someone stumbling up the stairs. It could only be Danny, she thought in despair. If only she had left sooner. She would pretend to be out and perhaps he would go away.

The hour with Martin had made Danny feel homesick. What had he done that was so wrong? he argued within himself. Some women had to meet their men coming out of work on a Friday night to make sure they got their money before it was gambled away. For the sake of the kids, their wives put up with it. But not Bridget! The minute she got wind of it, she showed him the door. And he had let her! Imagine him being stupid enough to agree to leave. A week before Christmas too. The injustice of it all was eating away at him.

Determined to spend Christmas with his family, he had a few beers to give himself Dutch courage and climbed the stairs to the flat. He was convinced that given the chance he could make his wife see reason. It was only right and fitting that he stay the night and dress up as Santa Claus in an outfit borrowed for the purpose. A smile played around his mouth as he made to open the door. Did Bridget really think he was going to miss seeing his son opening his presents from Santa Claus on Christmas morning? If so, she must be even more gullible than he thought. He blinked in confusion when his key would not turn in the lock. Danny examined it intently. It was the right key and he tried again. An oath escaped his lips as comprehension dawned. The bloody bitch had changed the lock!

'You open this door, Bridget Kelly, or I'll knock the bloody thing down,' he threatened.

Her pretence of not being at home was shattered when a delighted Martin, cried, 'Daddy! Mammy, it's Daddy.'

Bridget rushed him away from the door. 'Hush, Martin.' But too late. Danny had heard him.

'That's right, Martin. It's Daddy come to see his wee son. Come on, Bridget, let me in, please,' he wheedled. 'Martin wants to see me.'

A warning voice reached him from beyond the door. 'Danny, you're drunk. Be sensible and get yourself away home to sleep it off.'

'I'm far from drunk, Bridget. I only had three pints. Anyhow I'll sleep it off here. I want to stay and be with my son when he opens his presents in the morning. I've every right to be with him.'

'Stay here tonight? Are you off your rocker?'

'I'll sleep on the settee.'

'Oh, no, you won't.'

'Don't be silly, Bridget. Do you seriously think you can keep me away from Martin tomorrow morning?'

'You'll see him in the afternoon, like we agreed.

Now take yourself off, Danny, before I phone the police.'

'They won't interfere in a domestic quarrel. Did you not know that, Bridget? I heard it for the first time yesterday. Yes, a mate in work was saying that the police wouldn't interfere between husband and wife.'

'Danny, I'm not going to open this door, so please go away.'

'Well then, you've been warned. Stand back, Bridget. I'm going to knock it down.'

He threw himself against the door but it was too sturdy and barely shook. He grunted and rubbed his shoulder as pain shot through it. 'Bridget, open up, or so help me God, I'll be back with a hatchet!' he threatened.

Clearing up after the delivery of turkeys and meat to customers, Jack McCann and his assistant heard the commotion and leaving the shop came to stand at the foot of the stairs.

'Hey, what's going on here?'

Danny waved a threatening fist in their direction. 'You stay out of this. This is between me and her. It's none of your business.'

Jack whispered to his mate, 'He appears to have had one too many. You know where he lives. Go see if his father or brothers are at home. And hurry!'

'Bridget! Let me in!' Danny's voice was getting shrill, out of control.

On the other side of the door Bridget held her son tightly in her arms and silently cursed her husband. Was it not bad enough that Christmas had been spoilt? Martin would have no caring father on Christmas morning, and now he was being frightened out of his wits by a drunken fool. Although, to be truthful, Martin seemed far from frightened. Agog with excitement was more like it. After all, it was just his dad on the other side of the door. He was probably wondering why she wouldn't let him in. Probably thought they were playing some kind of game.

She hurried into the bedroom and closed the door, hoping to drown out the sounds. Should she phone the police? She dithered. It would be so degrading if they came. And on Christmas Eve of all times. What if they kept Danny in overnight? No, she couldn't do that to him. To her relief, she heard the deep voices of her in-laws. A short time later she ventured out into the hall again. A light tap on the door and Peter assured her, 'It's all right now, Bridget. Dad has persuaded him to go home quietly.'

She opened the door and faced him. 'Thanks, Peter. I wish he would pull himself together. You'd think he'd see he's just making things worse...'

'I suppose in a way it's understandable. Every man must want to be with his family on Christmas Eve.'

'Are you saying I should let him stay here?' she cried incredulously.

'No. Oh, no, I would hate to think of him staying here. But then, I'm prejudiced. I do, however, think I should sleep here tonight, Bridget. You know, just in case he comes back later when there's no one in the shop to intervene.'

Bridget bit on her lip. If Peter stayed the night

the temptation would be unbearable. It would be lovely to have the comfort of his presence, but would it end there? She didn't think so. She was too lonely and too vulnerable and might give in to her feelings. 'I don't think that would be a good idea, Peter. I'm going round to me mam's for my tea anyhow. Our ones have presents for Martin so someone will help me back with them and I'll make sure they stay the night. But thanks all the same.'

'Tell you what, I'll nip over and make sure you have company before I make any plans for later on. OK?'

She shook her head. 'It's not necessary, Peter, but thanks anyway.' She would make sure she had company staying tonight. It would be too risky for him to stay. Attracted to him she might be, but she couldn't afford to make another stupid mistake; she had already made too many of those. Besides, she was after all, married to his brother.

Joseph had been in low spirits since Ian had agreed to let Danny stay a few days. There was no sign of a reunion between him and Bridget, and Joseph was wise enough to know that Ian wouldn't make a point of seeking him out. Oh, no; so far all the running had been on his part. Was Ian serious about him? It was about time he found out. Now, on top of everything else, his brother was making a spectacle of himself outside the flat. Joseph could picture the scene. The soldiers, stationed over near the library, would keep their distance; they never interfered in anything like that. Nevertheless they would have a good laugh at his brother's expense. And who would blame them? Joseph openly showed his disgust at the antics of his brother and when asked, declined to go with his father and Peter to his assistance.

His lip curled in scorn when Danny eventually returned to the house. 'You should be ashamed. Making a spectacle of yourself like that.'

Danny's eyes narrowed. 'Are you so lily white you have nothing to be ashamed of?'

Colour flooded Joseph's face. 'Just what's that supposed to mean?'

'Just what I say! There's something queer about you. You're too good to be true. What about this girl you're seeing? How come we've never met her? Is she a married woman?'

'You mind your own business!'

Danny raised a finger and wagged it in his brother's face. 'Bear witness. I will ... if you keep your nose out of mine.'

To everyone's surprise Danny stayed sober over the next two days. The time spent with Martin went all too quickly and he had to be restrained from going over and demanding the right to be with his son longer.

Listening to him vow to get his wife and son back, Jane questioned him. 'Why did she put you out, Danny? You never did say.'

'You wouldn't understand, Mam.'

'Try me.'

'No. The least said soonest mended.'

Peter sat glowering throughout this conversation. He longed to taunt his brother about his gambling but didn't want to open Pandora's box. 'What if she doesn't want you back? What then?' he taunted.

'She'll have to take me back, for heaven's sake. She's daft about me. She's just letting me cool my heels for a while. Huh! Thinks she's teaching me a lesson, so she does.'

'And no one will ever do that, will they, Danny? Teach the great Danny McGowan a lesson,' Peter cried derisively.

'Oh, shut your face! Mam, the atmosphere in here is terrible. I can do nothing right. So I'll take myself out of the way. I won't be home tonight. Ian Geddis is going to the golf club. He won't mind if I tag along. I'll stay at his place.'

'Remember you're at work in the morning. See you set the alarm clock.'

'I'll remember.'

Joseph couldn't believe his ears. He had intended visiting Ian tonight. He'd have to go early. Make sure he had a talk with him before Danny arrived. How come Ian never took *him* to the golf club? Or anywhere else for that matter. They'd have to come to an arrangement to meet elsewhere. It was so frustrating this happening just when Ian seemed to be cooling off. It was giving him an excuse to avoid Joseph.

Rising to his feet, he said, 'Mam, I'm going out tonight, too. But I won't be late. See you later.'

Danny could not let the opportunity to tease his young brother pass. 'Going to see this mysterious girlfriend, Joseph?'

'Mind your own business.'

407

'Why are you so ashamed of her? Is she very ugly ... or married?'

Alarmed that all their attention was now focused on him, he cried, 'No, I'm not ashamed. And she's not married, so there!'

'Why not hang on for a while and we can travel to the Antrim Road together?' Danny asked slyly.

Jane intervened. 'Leave him alone, Danny. He doesn't want to get too interested in a girl yet. Sure you don't, son? There will be plenty of time for that later on. Don't listen to him, Joseph. After all, he's no recommendation for marriage. You go on out and enjoy yourself.'

When Ian saw Joseph at the door, he was tempted to leave him standing there until he got fed up and go. He was beginning to think he had done the wrong thing where Joseph was concerned. The boy was not his problem after all, and he was such a clinger! If only he would meet some girl, but he wasn't even making the effort and certainly wouldn't meet one in Ian's flat. To Ian's dismay Joseph seemed to think himself in love with him. Still, there was hope for him yet. Joseph was far from being a homosexual.

Opening the door, he put the snib up and let Joseph enter the hall. Blocking the foot of the stairs he informed him, 'Danny's just phoned. He'll be here soon.'

'What about it?' Joseph cried resentfully and tried to push past Ian. 'I'm sick to the teeth of him. I don't care if he finds out we're friends.'

Fear gripped Ian's heart. He didn't care what anyone thought about him, but Joseph was a

408

different matter. Danny would blame him. Would be sure to think Ian had led his young brother astray. He'd blow a fuse and everybody would know the boy's secret. What would his parents think? The young lad would be in deep trouble.

'Look, you don't realize what you're saying. We'll have to have a quick word. Come on upstairs.'

In the living room he faced Joseph but before he could reason with him, the boy cried, 'Ian, don't send me away, please! You're the only true friend I have. I couldn't live without seeing you. Could I not move in here with you?'

'You're talking nonsense, Joseph. I thought I could make you realise how wrong you are. We're just good friends. Nothing else.'

'You're more than a friend. I love you.'

'No, you don't,' he cried in frustration. 'It's all in your mind. I want you to leave here and never come back. I'm fed up with trying to keep you on the straight and narrow.'

'What do you mean by that?'

'I mean, you're not a homosexual. You're just a mixed up kid and I thought I could save you from yourself by letting you come here. To keep you away from others like me, who might take advantage of you. I did honestly think I could keep you away from the wrong kind of people. Instead I've just deluded you into thinking that you're bent. Believe me, Joseph, it's not a world you would want to enter. Find yourself a nice wee girlfriend. Now please go and don't ever come back here, or you'll get us both into trouble.'

Pale-faced and shaking, Joseph accused him, 'You've met someone else. That's why you're telling me all these lies.'

'No. There's no one else. I just want to live my life in peace and I'm sorry if I've misled you. I'm also sorry to say this but you're becoming a nuisance.'

Tears filled Joseph's eyes and his lips trembled as he fought for control. 'Ah, Ian, don't do this to me. I promise not to be a nuisance. Just let me come now and again. I need to see you. Good God, my life's worth nothing if I can't see you!'

The sound of the door to the flat opening made Ian swing round in horror. When he'd brought Joseph upstairs he'd forgotten to release the snib on the door downstairs. 'Hello? Ian, are you there?'

'It's Danny.' Pushing Joseph down on the settee, he whispered tersely, 'Sit down and take that bloody stupid look off your face.' With these words he disappeared into the kitchen.

He emerged from the kitchen again as Danny entered the living room from the hall. 'Hello, Danny. You got in all right then? Joseph arrived a few minutes ago and knowing you were coming, I left the snib off for you.'

Danny looked from one to the other of them. 'I wondered why the door wasn't locked.' His gaze rested on his brother. 'What are you doing here?'

Joseph grunted. 'What do you think? The same as you. Visiting.'

Ian explained. 'He was visiting his girlfriend but she wasn't in. The silly boy should have let her know he was coming. But he won't interfere with our plans, unless...' Back to Danny, his eyes dared Joseph to take him up on his offer. 'Perhaps you would care to join us, Joseph?'

Much as he would have liked to defy Ian and agree to accompany them to the golf club, the idea of hours spent being picked on by his brother knocked that idea on the head. 'No, I'll have to be going home. I told Mam I wouldn't be late.' He rose to his feet. 'So, if you'll excuse me, I'll bid you good night. I enjoyed our chat. Perhaps I'll call and visit you again some time, Ian.'

'Feel free to drop in any time you're passing, Joseph.'

Ian felt heart sore as the young lad left the flat, he looked so lonely and unhappy. He would have to sever all connections with him; give him a chance to meet normal people. This ploy to save him from himself wasn't working.

There was a speculative look in Danny's eyes as he held Ian's gaze. He felt a bit uneasy but couldn't think why.

Ian returned the look, his eyes clear and innocent-looking. 'And how are you, Danny? You look a bit the worse for wear. I suppose you've been boozing over Christmas. Take a seat and I'll pour us a drink. It's a bit early for Fortwilliam.'

Still a little uneasy though unable to fathom why, he sat down. 'I'll have you know I haven't had a drink in three days. So there!'

'That's good news Danny. You've been a bit heavy on the drink lately.'

'Do you know this girlfriend of our Joseph's?'

'I've never met her.'

411

'Wonder why he doesn't bring her home?'

'Well now, would your mother welcome her? Would she want him to be serious about a girl?'

'No way.'

Ian shrugged. 'There's your answer then.'

'Does he call here often?'

Ian had no intention of starting to tell lies that he might become ensnared in later. 'Just now and again,' he said. That should cover a multitude. 'How are things between you and Bridget.' He breathed a sigh of relief when Danny went into a long tirade of complaints, his brother forgotten for the moment. Still, Ian thought, he felt sorry for Bridget. She was a nice person and didn't deserve all this hassle. But as they say, 'It's an ill wind that doesn't blow somebody good.' At least Danny's problems were keeping Joseph off his back.

A few days after Christmas, Neville invited David and Liz up to the golf club for a meal as a thank you gesture for having him at their house on Christmas Day.

They met in the foyer and as they took off their coats, Liz chastized him. 'You know, there was no need to invite us out, Neville.'

'It's my pleasure, Liz. I'm glad of the excuse to have your company for a few more hours.'

The lull between Boxing night and New Year's Eve was a quiet time in the club. No entertainment on in the lounge. In fact, very few people there at all. They took their time over the meal, discussing the quality of the food, the state of the country, and arguing as to who was right and

412

who was wrong in the latest conflict between the army and the locals. In the end, when the conversation became a little heated, David gave Liz a warning glance and they agreed to differ on that issue. He realized his wife had first-hand knowledge of some of the atrocities that had occurred on the Falls Road, but in mixed company one must control one's feelings.

After the meal they retired to the lounge for a quiet drink and a natter.

Neville looked over the top of his glass at Liz. 'Have you any news of your mother?'

'I visited her on Boxing Day and tried to persuade her to come and stay with us for a few days, but she refused. You know how stubborn she can be. She said that Dick was coming later on.'

'How did she seem?'

'To be truthful, I thought her a bit depressed and fished to try and find out if perhaps she and Dick had quarrelled. However, she assured me they hadn't and then clammed up. Once she does that I know I would be fishing in vain, so I arranged to meet her for lunch tomorrow. Perhaps I'll be luckier then.'

'Please give her my regards.'

'I'll do that. You know, we shall all be here at the club on New Year's Eve, Neville.'

David was quick to offer, 'You will join us of course, won't you, Neville?'

'It's very kind of you to invite me, but I don't think it would be a good idea, David. Let me give it some thought. Can I let you know ... say, tomorrow night?'

413

'Of course. But remember, you're very welcome.'

Neville smiled. 'I know that and thank you for caring. But, you see, emotions are inclined to run high at this time of year, and all kinds of announcements are made. I would hate to be there if Kath and Dick announced they were to marry.'

'I'll try and find out all I can tomorrow, Neville, and let you know,' Liz promised.

'Where will you go if not here?' David asked solicitously.

'I'll probably drown my sorrows in the Shaftsbury Inn.'

'Alone?'

He shrugged. 'Why not? No point in spoiling anyone else's fun, is there?'

David was scandalised. 'I forbid a friend of ours to spend New Year's Eve alone. I shall make sure that you're here.'

Liz was quick to back him up. 'Of course you must join us. But meanwhile I'll find out all I can tomorrow.'

It was when she was going to the cloakroom that she spotted Danny McGowan coming from the Men's Bar. She was so amazed, she stopped abruptly. Her action brought Danny's attention to her. A quick word to his companion and he headed towards her.

'This is a surprise, Liz. Though, I must say, a very pleasant one.'

A frown puckered her brow. Had he known that she came here? 'I didn't know you were a member, Danny.'

His head jerked back to where his companion waited. 'I'm not, but Ian is an associate member. We come now and again for a quiet drink.'

She glanced over at the tall fair-haired young man. He smiled and nodded in acknowledgement. Liz nodded in return. Her eyes ranged over Danny's face in concern. 'Have you been ill, Danny?'

A grimace twisted his mouth. 'I suppose you could call it a kind of sickness,' he agreed. 'Bridget and I are living apart at the moment.'

'Ah, no, Danny. I'm so sorry to hear that.' Her hand reached out in an involuntary gesture and she gently touched his cheek. 'What about the child?'

His eyes brightened at her action and he reached for her hand but deftly she withdrew it. 'He's with Bridget at the moment, but I see a lot of him.' His eyes travelled the length of her in a slow sensuous gaze. The long shift dress she wore hid nothing. 'No need to ask if you're pregnant. I can see you're not.' He leant closer and his voice became a caress. 'Remember, my offer still stands, Liz.'

She felt naked under his gaze and a hot flush suffused her face and body. To her shame a tremor of longing passed through her and she felt he must be aware of it. She was nothing but a wanton hussy, that's what she was, she railed inwardly. 'I'd better go now, Danny. I'm sorry to hear about your trouble,' she muttered, and hurried away from him.

His voice, low but insistent and full of longing, followed her. 'When are you going to stop running away from me, Liz?'

Upset and unhappy, she stood in the empty cloakroom and berated her own image in the mirror. Why did she always let him get the better of her? Why did her weak body betray her every time they met?

Poor Bridget. She must be in an awful state. Liz would never have believed that one day she would pity Bridget McGowan, but she did. It must be awful to be married to Danny and not be able to hold him. By the looks of it she herself had had a narrow escape. Have I? her errant heart cried. Didn't this just show she and Danny were meant for each other? He should never have married Bridget Kelly.

David had arrived at the bar to order a round of drinks when a glance towards the landing sent a chill to the core of him. There was Danny McGowan, standing as bold as brass. Full of misgivings David edged along the bar until Danny's companion came into view. It was Liz and she was caressing her ex-boyfriend's cheek, a look of deep tenderness on her face. He watched in horror as they whispered intensely together. What on earth had brought McGowan to Fortwilliam? Stupid question! Liz, of course. She must have told him she frequented the place. How else would he know?

With hands that trembled, he carried the drinks over to their table and said abruptly, 'Will you excuse me for a moment, Neville? I won't be long.' The need to be alone was strong. He felt betrayed and frightened.

On the landing there was no sign of Liz or her

old flame. Avoiding the Men's Bar he took the stairs in a rush. Once outside he gulped deep breaths into his lungs, watching the hot breath clouding on the cold air. He shivered and it wasn't just from the cold. Fear was rampant within him.

He had eventually convinced himself he was mistaken about Liz seeing Danny on the quiet. That time on the Antrim Road must have been a one off, he had thought. She just wasn't the kind of person to do anything underhand. He'd convinced himself. And now ... he had just seen proof with his own eyes. Wait a minute! He was jumping the gun. It might have been a totally innocent meeting. He must wait and see what Liz said about it. Still, that tender look on her face as she stroked Danny's cheek ... did that not say it all?

Neville looked in concern after the retreating figure of David. His friend had looked shattered. Neville noted that he'd headed for the stairs. Where was he going? Even more concerned, he went into the Men's Bar. From the window over looking the Cave Hill he saw David leave the club and pause to light a cigarette before striding to the edge of the green, to stand staring ahead of him, drawing deeply on the cigarette.

Liz returning to the lounge brought Neville's attention indoors and he quickly joined her. She looked pale and ill at ease. She and David must have had a tiff, but when? He had been with them all evening and would surely have noticed if anything untoward had happened. He decided to pretend not to notice anything was different; not to mention David leaving the clubhouse almost at a gallop.

'Do you mind if we leave soon, Neville? I have a bit of a headache.'

'Not at all, my dear. We'll go as soon as David comes back.'

'Back from where? Where is he?'

Neville improvised. 'He must have gone to the Men's Bar.'

Her head jerked up and her voice was shrill. 'The Bar? Why would he go there?'

Amazed at her reaction, Neville said, 'It's not unusual for men to dander in there, you know, my dear. But perhaps I'm wrong.' Relieved to see David enter the lounge, he said, 'Ah, here he is now.'

Liz relaxed back in her chair but avoided looking in David's direction. Had he seen Danny? She was afraid to look at him. Neither did he look at her and this confirmed Neville's belief that something wasn't right between them. He said brightly, 'Liz would like to go home after this drink, David. She has a bit of a headache.'

A slight shrug was all the answer he received. Good Lord, this wasn't like caring David Atkinson who thought the sun shone out of his wife's backside. It must be more serious than he'd thought. 'Shall I order a taxi?' he asked tentatively.

David rose to his feet again with alacrity. He was sick at heart and found he couldn't bear to look in his wife's direction. 'You sit there. I'll ring for it, Neville.'

418

Concerned at the disharmony between these two lovely people he held so dear, Neville tried to console Liz. 'Whatever has upset you two, don't let it spoil your evening, Liz. If David has annoyed you, I'm sure he didn't mean it. Be kind to him.'

Blank eyes met his. 'I don't understand. David hasn't annoyed me.'

Taken aback, Neville stressed, 'Well, if I may say so, you don't seem your usual self, Liz.'

She made a great effort to pull herself together. David mustn't notice she wasn't herself or questions would be asked; questions she couldn't answer. 'I'm fine, Neville. Just a headache. A couple of Aspirin and I'll be as right as rain.'

Deciding to give them a chance to make up their differences, he finished his pint and declined to share their taxi, saying he would have a game of snooker before going home. After bidding them good night, he left.

In the taxi, Liz stole glances at her husband. His face was stern and he seemed lost in thought. He was keeping his distance. Was that deliberate or because he was preoccupied? Should she mention seeing Danny at the club? She decided against it. David would be sure to think he was there at her invitation. What would happen if Danny made a habit of coming to the club? It would cause so much tension it didn't bear thinking about. Once inside the house her husband disappeared without a word into the kitchen. She gazed after him, wondering what to do.

With an effort David controlled his voice. It

reached her calm and clear. 'Would you like a cup of tea, Liz?'

Relieved that he sounded normal, she quickly made her excuses. 'No, my head is throbbing. I'll take a couple of tablets and go straight to bed.'

He stared blankly in front of him; his teeth gnawing at his lower lip. So his wife wasn't going to mention seeing her old flame at the club? Where did he go from here? Should he confront her ... or play it by ear? Chances were he wouldn't get a chance to do anything tonight. He wasn't a betting man, but he would be willing to bet all he had that his wife would feign sleep tonight. Well, he was so angry she wouldn't have to. He'd sit up so late she wouldn't have to pretend. Turning the kettle off, he left the kitchen and headed for the drinks cabinet.

Contrary to all his expectations, Liz was still awake when he clumsily entered the bedroom an hour or so later. He had drunk a lot of whiskey and was unsteady on his feet. Oh, she pretended to be asleep but he wasn't fooled. 'Forgive me, my love,' he said sarcastically. 'I hope I'm not disturbing you?' He undressed and slipped naked into the bed beside her. Liz lay with her back to him, so rigid he wanted to lash out at her in anger. Suddenly the rage within him could be contained no longer.

Reaching for her he pulled her round towards him. 'Come on now, Liz. Why the pretence? Don't you want me to make love to you?'

David was a moderate drinker at most times, but to her horror she realized he was very drunk tonight. Very drunk indeed.

'You're drunk!' she exclaimed, her voice shrill with disbelief.

'No,' he contradicted her. 'Just what you Falls Road ones would call tipsy.'

'Let me go, David. You're hurting me. You'll regret this in the morning.'

'I'll have a lot of regrets, Liz, but I don't think this will be one of them.'

'David ... please.'

'Can't you bear for me to touch you, Liz? Eh? But then, you've been in the presence of your one true love tonight, isn't that right? Am I so very different from bloody Danny McGowan? What's he got that I haven't? Here, let me help you.' He grabbed her hand and put it against his face. She snatched it away. 'Ah, so it's only Danny who can evoke the tenderness I saw you bestow on him this evening. And in full view of anyone who happened to notice. Huh! Like mother, like daughter, eh, Liz?'

'David, that's unfair. You don't understand. He's unhappy. It meant nothing.'

'Liz, I was there, remember? I saw how you looked at him. Besides, I do understand. I understand perfectly. You've been seeing him on the quiet, haven't you? I'm just surprised you invited him to come to the club. Did you expect me to turn a blind eye to that?'

'I have not been seeing him! Neither did I invite him to Fortwilliam.'

'Well, I can believe you didn't invite him. But he came all the same. He knew where to find you. And how would he know if you hadn't told him? Eh, Liz?'

'I've never mentioned Fortwilliam to him. He came with a friend.'

David's lips tightened and the pressure of his fingers on her arms hurt her. 'Come on now, Liz. Do you expect me to believe that? That's the second time I've seen you with him, you know. And each time you've looked very cosy.'

Colour flooded her face and she was glad of the dim beside light. 'You're hurting me.'

'Do you say that to Danny?'

'He never hurt me physically.'

'Ah, so you *are* seeing him?'

'What on earth's got into you, David?' she wailed in frustration. 'You're twisting my words. I never said that.'

'You don't have to. I'm not blind. Just stupid and trusting.' A harsh laugh escaped lips white with suppressed anger. 'You see, Liz, I thought you wouldn't do anything underhand. Now I find that when you're in heat, you're just like any other little slut!'

She struggled to free herself but he only gripped her tighter. 'Let's have some of what Danny's been having on the quiet these last few months. I'm your husband, I deserve some loving.'

Tears poured down her cheeks and she lay like a corpse as he made rough love to her. Her feelings for Danny had spoilt her marriage. How could things ever be the same between her and David again?

Kath tut-tutted with impatience when her daughter at last arrived at the restaurant where

422

they were to have lunch. 'What on earth kept you? I've been standing in this foyer for ages.'

'Don't exaggerate, Mam. I'm only ten minutes late. The traffic was terrible.'

'You don't look too good.' Kath observed, as they followed a waiter to their table. 'Had you a late night?'

'Snap! You don't look your best either, Mam. And no, I hadn't a late night. Neville invited us to dinner at the club but we were home early.' She didn't add that she had spent a sleepless night in the spare room. The memory of her husband's actions the night before was tearing her apart. He had taunted her about Danny. Said some unforgivable things. As she had foreseen, he had thought the worst. In a way she didn't blame him. Danny was the last person you'd expect to frequent a golf club, and she didn't blame David for believing he had come at Liz's invitation. Coming from David, though, the cruel taunts had hurt. He seemed to think she had been seeing Danny on the quiet for some time. And hadn't she almost? Hadn't she even considered having Danny's child and palming it off as her husband's? How could she have been so naïve? How could she plead innocence with all this guilt on her conscience?

The waiter put an end to her tortured thoughts by offering a menu to each of them. They selected their courses and ordered a bottle of wine to drink while they waited.

Silence reigned until their wine arrived, and Liz forgot her own misery when she took a good look at her mother and saw she really did look ill.

Pouring them both a glass of wine, she raised her glass in Kath's direction and said, 'Cheers, Mam.' Then, leaning across the table, questioned her. 'Have you been ill?'

'A bit of a tummy upset. Nothing to worry about. But it did take a lot out of me.'

'You should have phoned. David would have fetched you over to stay with us.'

Reaching across the table, Kath squeezed her daughter's hand. 'I know that, Liz. And it's great to know you're there for me, but I needed time to myself. I needed to get things sorted out in my mind.'

'What kind of things?'

'Oh, this and that.'

'And did you get them sorted?'

'Not yet, I'm afraid.' A wry smile accompanied the words.

'How do you feel at the moment? I mean, are you ready to stomach this meal?'

'I certainly am! I've eaten hardly anything since my Christmas dinner. I'm starving.'

They drew back as their starters were placed in front of them and silence fell as they got started. Kath, true to her word, was hungry and scoffed the lot in record time. With a contented sigh she dabbed at her mouth with her napkin and sat back in her chair. She watched her daughter push her egg mayonnaise about the plate. Very little of it reached Liz's mouth. At last she pushed it aside with a sigh of regret.

'I thought I was hungry, too, but I'm not.'

'What's wrong, Liz? You seem upset.'

Upset? Her heart was breaking. But this wasn't

the time for self-pity. Her mother obviously needed a sympathetic ear. All thoughts of David must be banished for the time being. To divert her mother's attention, she asked, 'Did you know that Danny and Bridget have separated?'

Kath's eyes widened slightly. 'No, I didn't,' she said slowly. How had she missed that bit of gossip? 'Who told you?'

'He was at the golf club last night.'

Kath looked scandalized. 'He went there to tell you about it?'

'Of course not. He was as surprised to see me as I was to see him. He was with some friend.'

'Don't you believe it! He must know you go there. What else would bring him to Fortwilliam?'

'He seemed genuinely surprised, Mam.'

'Huh! Did David see him?'

'I'm afraid so, and thought the worst. He never said he saw him and of course I hoped he hadn't and didn't mention Danny was there ... so, can you blame David?' She shrugged.

'No, I certainly don't blame him. But you explained, of course?'

Thinking of the episode in the bedroom, Liz squirmed in her chair. 'It didn't quite work out like that.'

'You mean, even when you got home you didn't tell him that Danny was at the club?'

'No.'

'Oh, you foolish girl! His mind must be working overtime. What happened?'

Liz recoiled slightly. She could never tell her mother the things David had accused her of. The pain was still too raw. Pushing her own worries to the back of her mind, she gave her full attention to her mother.

'Forget about me. I'm just a bit down in the dumps at the moment. I'll tell you all about it some other time. Tell me, will you be springing any surprises on us on New Year's Eve?'

Kath saw her withdrawal and allowed her to change the conversation. 'What do you mean? What kind of surprises?'

'Like announcing you're getting married.'

A harsh sound left Kath's lips. 'No fear of that. I've been very disappointed in Dick Kennedy.'

'Ah, Mam, didn't he come up to scratch? He seems besotted with you.'

'Perhaps. But you see, Liz, he's been two-timing me with the beautiful Irene.'

'How do you know?'

'He told me.'

'He admitted he was seeing Irene as well as you, and you didn't show him the door?' Liz's disbelief was apparent.

Kath was shaking her head. 'That would be too straight forward. He said she phoned him because she was lonely and he went round to spend a few hours talking with her. It happened twice, he said.'

'And you don't believe him?'

'Oh, I believe he went round, but I don't believe it was at her instigation and I don't for one minute think it was just for a chat. I'm not a bloody fool, you know.'

'Ah, now, Mam. You don't know that.'

Kath shrugged. 'Maybe it's because your father

426

let me down that I can't trust another man. Besides, Dick is a randy bugger. He can't keep his hands to himself. He certainly wouldn't just sit and talk.'

'Do you love him, Mam?'

Again that bewildered shake of the head. 'I don't know. I really don't. I'm confused. I think maybe I was hungry and he excited me. I certainly enjoyed his company.'

Their main courses arrived and Kath was glad that Liz was so preoccupied with her affairs she seemed to have forgotten her own. She watched her daughter get through her meal in no time, and then look in bewilderment at the empty plate.

'You will be at Fortwilliam to see the New Year in, won't you, Mam?'

'Well now, I don't know about that. Dick thinks we're going, but if Irene is there, who knows what she will do?'

'What on earth *can* she do?'

Kath shrugged. 'Take Dick away from me in front of everybody?'

'Now you're being melodramatic.'

'You think so? She hasn't forgiven me for taking him from her in the first place, you know. She'd be delighted to get her own back.'

'For heaven's sake, Mam! Dick is a grown man, not a child. He chose you, remember?'

'There's more of the child in Dick than you would imagine. If Irene hadn't got on her high horse and thrown his ring back at him he'd be still with her. He can't make decisions for himself. He'll always take the easy way out.'

'Well then, convince him he wants you more than anything else in the world.'

'That's just it! Do I want a man as weak as him? A wimp, for heaven's sake.'

'Well, you're the only one who can decide that. What about Neville?'

Kath's expression sharpened. 'What about Neville?'

'Is there no hope for him?'

'Do you think I could ever face him again after the way I behaved? No fear. He would think I was deliberately getting my own back, so he would.'

'What do you mean, getting your own back? What did he ever do to you?'

The sweet trolley stopped near their table. 'Liz, do you fancy a dessert?'

'No, I've had enough, thank you. And stop changing the subject.'

'I'm not. Since you don't want a dessert, could we go home, please?'

'If that's what you want.' Kath called for their bill and Liz reached for the bottle of wine. Her mother moved it to one side.

'I think you've had enough to drink. Remember, you're driving. You go straight home and have a rest. I'll call a taxi.'

'Mam, I'm not drunk. I'll take you home.'

Kath hesitated and Liz cried. 'Don't you trust me to get you home safe?'

'Of course I do, you've only had two glasses of wine. But should you not go home and patch things up with David?'

'I'll see you home first. Then I'll go and see if he will listen to me. Although, to be truthful, I'm

428

not very hopeful.'

In Dunlewey Street, before leaving the car, Kath turned to her daughter. 'You realise that Danny and Bridget being separated doesn't change the situation as far as you're concerned, don't you?'

'Of course I realize that! Do you think I'm daft or something? I'm not after a separation. But you don't know the things David accused me of. He thinks I'm the lowest of the low. I don't think he wants to be married to me anymore.'

'The things he accused you of, are they true?'

'Of course not!'

'Had he reason to think they might be?'

'No! Well, I don't think so.'

Seeing her hesitation, Kath's heart sank. What had this usually sane daughter of hers been up to? 'Go home, Liz. Clear the air,' she advised. 'David's not an unreasonable man. He will believe you. That is, if you have nothing to hide.'

Her daughter remained silent, and with a sigh Kath climbed out of the car. Liz's voice stayed her. 'Are you coming to the golf club on New Year's Eve?'

'As things stand between you and David, will you be there?'

Her daughter grimaced. 'I don't know. But if the worst comes to the worst, we can accompany each other. I'll give you a ring.'

As Liz drew away from the footpath, Kath gave her the thumbs up sign. Why not? Why not indeed? She silently agreed.

The house was quiet; no classical music playing

softly in the background which David favoured when alone. Liz wandered about the empty rooms in a pensive mood. David had been so sure she had been seeing Danny on the sly. He must have a very good reason for doubting her. She felt guilty because she *had* thought of betraying him. Wasn't that as bad as the actual deed? The fact that she had even considered having Danny's child and letting David believe it was his filled her with horror now. How could she argue her case with all this guilt in her mind and heart? And there was certainly no way she could admit her thoughts to him, her mixed up reasoning, and expect him to understand and blindly trust her.

She was relaxing in a warm soapy bath, hoping to ease the soreness in her limbs, when she heard her husband let himself into the house. It was some minutes before he tapped on the bathroom door. 'Is it all right if I come in?'

She sank down under the level of the suds. Not because she was shy but to hide the dark blue bruises his lovemaking the night before had left on her arms and legs. 'Yes.'

He stood in the doorway unable to meet her eyes, looking the picture of misery. 'Liz, there is absolutely no excuse for my behaviour last night so I'll not ask your forgiveness. I'll pack my bags and move to a hotel until you decide what you want to do.'

'David, look at me.' Sheepishly, his eyes met hers. 'Do you want to go?'

'Of course I don't.'

'Then you're being very silly. I don't want you

430

to move out. Let's forget it happened, eh? Surely we can put it all behind us?'

He gaped at her, unable to believe his ears. Slowly moving to the side of the bath, he gazed down at her. 'You mean that?'

She nodded and rising up out of the water a little, gently touched his arm. He gaped in dismay at the livid bruises on her arms. 'In the name of God, Liz, did I do that?'

She nodded mutely, and he threw himself on his knees by the edge of the bath. 'Ah, Liz, I didn't mean to be so rough. I can't believe I treated you like that. I'm so ashamed of myself. You know I've never hit the bottle so hard before! It was the drink.'

'I know that, David.'

'How can you forgive me for that?'

'Because I care deeply for you.'

She cared deeply. Well, he would have to settle for that. It was better than the lonely life he had been picturing ahead of him. But first he must find out if she intended seeing Danny McGowan again. In the lonely hours of the morning, when Liz had left their bed to sleep in the spare room, he'd discovered he would be unable to handle that. He couldn't bear to picture her with a young virile man. Now he asked tentatively, 'What about Danny McGowan?'

'I haven't been seeing him, and that's the honest to God truth. I only bumped into him a few times. A couple of times on the Antrim Road. As for last night in the club ... I got the shock of my life when I saw him.' It was on the tip of her tongue to tell him that Danny and Bridget were separated but she stopped herself in time. Then he really would think that Danny had sought her out to tell her that. And he hadn't!

David gazed into her eyes and believed her. But then, he wanted to believe her. He reached for the bath sheet and slowly Liz rose from the water. The bruises on her thighs caused him to mutter, 'I'm sorry. Oh, God, I really am so sorry,' as he wrapped the towel around her and sweeping her up in his arms carried her from the bathroom.

Kath was disconcerted to find Dick waiting in the house for her. 'Hello. I didn't expect to see you today. Is Irene too busy to talk to you?' she asked slyly.

'There's no need to get on like that, Kath.'

'No?'

'No need whatsoever. I came to find out if you intend going to Fortwilliam with me to see the New Year in?'

'You must be psychic. I've just been making plans to go with Liz.'

'Why not go with me?' He sounded outraged but was that a note of relief too she detected in his voice? She wasn't sure.

'I thought perhaps Irene might need you to accompany her?' she queried.

'Well, she did mention it, but of course I said no, I said I'd be taking you.'

'How very gentlemanly of you, Dick,' she said dryly. 'Don't you worry about me. I'm going with David and Liz. Feel free to take Irene if you like.'

'Are you sure, Kath? You see, she's so alone...'

Kath interrupted him. 'There's no need to make excuses, Dick.'

'If I do ... take her, it won't mean anything. It won't change things between us, you know.'

'I don't think there is an "us" any more. Do you, Dick?'

'Of course there is,' he blustered, but again she thought she heard an underlying relief.

'No, that's where you're wrong. I think you'd better go now. You can't burn the candle at both ends and get away with it. Especially if I'm at one end,' she said sarcastically.

'Kath, don't be like this.'

'Never worry, Dick. I don't intend making a scene. It was nice while it lasted. We can remain friends but that's as far as it will go between us from now on.'

He came to stand in front of her. 'You mean that, Kath? No hard feelings?'

'No hard feelings,' she agreed.

He bent his head to kiss her but she turned aside and his lips landed on her cheek. 'Goodbye, Dick. And please leave the key on the hall table on your way out.' Slowly he withdrew from her, and with a last solicitous look left the room.

She heard the key rattle in the glass dish on the hall table before the door closed gently. For her it signalled an end to their love affair. It had been nice while it lasted but would she really miss him?

With the closing of the door, the strength holding her erect ebbed from her body leaving her limp as a rag doll. She sank weakly on to the settee. She had made the wrong choice there. But then perhaps she would have found Neville wanting too. Now she would never know. But what difference did it make? She had been alone for so many years it shouldn't make any difference. It did, however. She now knew and wanted the comfort of a man's presence in her life.

Barney and Martha always had a bit of a 'wee do' for special occasions and the New Year was no exception. Having previously missed some of these family affairs because of Danny's reluctance to go, Bridget was now excited about the coming event. Friends and neighbours always ended up in their home and a bit of a dance and a sing-song finished the night off.

She had to work on New Year's Eve but the store closed early and she hurried home to help prepare a buffet meal for the party. Going to the flat first to change out of her work clothes, she was dismayed to find Peter sitting on the top stair. That was the worst of the street door leading to the butcher's shop where Jack Mc-Cann was clearing up. It had to be kept open during working hours.

'What are you doing here?' she greeted him. Her manner was abrupt and she made no effort to open the door to the flat.

'Are you avoiding me? I've been trying to get in touch with you. I came to see if I could persuade you to come out with me tonight. Or if you can't get a babysitter, I could bring some wine and beer and we could have a quiet evening in the flat.'

434

'I'm sorry but I've already made plans of my own. Thanks all the same.'

'You're going out?'

'Not exactly. Mam always has a bit of a party on New Year's Eve. As a matter of fact, I'm in a terrible hurry, Peter. I've to help prepare the buffet for tonight. You'll have to excuse me.' She brushed past him and unlocked the door, turning to bid him farewell.

He forestalled her. 'Let me come in for a minute, Bridget.'

'There's no point. I'll not have time to make you a cuppa. I'll not even have time to talk to you. I'm just going to change out of these clothes then I'm off round to my mam's.'

'I'll make you a cup of coffee while you change,' he offered eagerly.

'Oh, all right.' She gave in ungraciously and entered the flat. He was close on her heels. Entering the bedroom she closed the door and swiftly changed into trousers and top.

She wished Peter would leave her alone. She was managing all right without Danny. Their savings had been transferred into an account in her name only and so far Danny had not objected. Of course, he might not know of the changeover yet. If so, it was a good sign he hadn't tried to lift any more money from the building society. If only he would get himself sorted out he could return to her and Martin. She didn't want a broken marriage. The parents on both sides would be so upset. Bridget wanted them to be a family again.

However, her body was hungry for love and

Peter was so attractive. He awoke longings in her that frightened her. With a sigh she powdered her nose and brushed her hair.

The coffee was ready and he had pulled a low table close to the settee. Very intimate-looking. Ignoring the place beside him, she lifted her cup and stood, leaning her arm on the mantelpiece as she sipped at the coffee.

His eyes travelled the length of her and she felt colour wash her cheeks. When they locked on hers she saw raw desire within him and licked her lips as her own emotions started to rise. He was quick to recognize her response and his face lit up. He rose eagerly to his feet.

This will never do, she thought wildly. She was giving him false hope. Or would a good snog clear the air? Show their feelings up for what they were – pure lust? But what if it made them want more? She couldn't take that chance.

Carefully placing her cup on the mantelpiece, she said, 'Sorry, Peter, I'm afraid I haven't time to finish that. But thanks for making it for me. I'll have to be going now or Mam will think I'm skiving.'

He was close beside her in an instant. 'Bridget, don't do this to me. You want me as much as I want you. Don't keep me at arm's length like this. What harm would it do?'

'For heaven's sake, Peter, talk sense. You're my brother-in-law! What if we became closer and Danny sorted himself out, eh? How would we be able to meet as if nothing had happened?'

'You'd consider going back to him?'

'What choice have I got? There's Martin to

consider.' His nearness was making her nervous, but she had to pass him to get to the door.

'Look at me, Bridget,' he demanded, and at the same time reached for her.

Reluctantly, she looked into his eyes and was lost. His lips were on hers, soft and oh, so gentle. She closed her eyes and gave herself up to the tenderness of his caresses. He held her closer still and the kisses became more urgent. It brought her back to her senses.

'No! No, Peter. This will never do. I want to patch up my marriage and if we give into this lust I'll never be able to face Danny again. Can't you see? This is why we can't be friends.'

'Ah, Bridget, come on. You want me as much as I want you.'

'That's because I'm lonely.'

'What harm would it do? Don't get me wrong, mind. If I thought our Danny could make you happy, I'd leave you alone. But why deny ourselves? We both know he's in love with someone else. Do you think if she was willing, he'd say no?'

'I can't say what he would do.' Her voice was sad. 'Who knows? Maybe Martin would influence his actions too. Danny loves him.'

'What if he were ever to doubt that Martin was his?'

Shock, like an electric current ran through her body. White-lipped, she pushed Peter away.

'Don't look like that! You know I'd never say anything.'

'Did you listen to the rumours too?'

'No. Teresa Quinn told me.'

'Just what exactly did she say?'

437

He shrugged, sorry he had opened his mouth. 'Just that it was rumoured Danny might not be Martin's father.'

'Is that why you keep hounding me? Do you think I'm an easy lay?'

'I think nothing of the kind!' he cried indignantly.

Brushing past him, she snatched her coat and headed for the door. 'You had better go.'

'Bridget, honestly, I do respect you.'

'Show it then. Come on. I've got to go.' With an abrupt flick of the hand she motioned him out and locked the door. He descended the stairs ahead of her and waited on the pavement. Jack McCann was driving off in his van as Bridget paused to lock the outer door. One of Peter's mates happened to be passing and stopped to talk to him.

Glad of the respite she said, 'I'll run on, Peter. Mam will think I'm lost. See you again. Thanks for calling in.'

She raced down Leeson Street her mind in turmoil. Who else had heard the rumours? How come she hadn't been aware of them? Why had no one told Danny about them? One thing she was certain of. If she took him back, she would have to tell him the truth. She couldn't live with this hanging over her head. Too many people knew. But what if Danny wanted proof and a blood test showed Noel Gibson was the father? What then? Her blood chilled at the very idea of her husband's reaction.

Bridget worked alongside her mother and sister

438

making sandwiches. All the savoury dishes had been prepared earlier that day and spicy aromas permeated the air. The neighbours would also bring pies and bottles of spirits or beer so there was never a shortage of food and drink. Some of the joy had gone out of the occasion for her, but with a determined effort she shrugged her worries to one side. Tonight she intended to enjoy herself. Martin was fed early and Patrick ran him over to Marie's house where Marie's sister-in-law and her friend were baby sitting and had offered to take Martin as well.

It was quite late when they at last finished and Marie retired upstairs to change into her party wear. Bridget returned to the flat to change into her glad rags. The staff got first look at the sale goods, and that afternoon she had purchased a new dress. The 'little black dress' designed for all occasions, the one she had always wanted to possess, had been reduced sufficiently for her to buy it without feeling too guilty. She spread it lovingly on the bed and touched the sequinned top. It was very brief. The top would leave her shoulders bare and if she wasn't careful probably half her bosom as well. The layered lace bottom came to just below the knee and had a split up the front. She already had black suede shoes and matching purse and had bought fishnet stockings to complete the outfit.

Showered, her freshly shampooed hair caught up on top of her head in curls with just wispy bits trailing her face and neck, she applied light make-up. Next she stepped into black french knickers, a strapless bra, suspender belt and the fishnet stockings. She stood in front of the cheval mirror and admired her figure before donning the dress. It was shapely. Firm bust, narrow waist and rounded hips. Pleased with her reflection, she stepped into the dress and carefully pulled it up into place. Her breath caught in her throat as she gazed at her reflection. The dress left nothing to the imagination. She felt beautiful and sexy. As she thought of her father's reaction to her appearance, she was tempted to change into something more subdued. But then, all the women would be dressed to kill. Why shouldn't she look her best? Because she would be a woman on her own, that's why! Other women would resent their husbands looking at her.

Well, what about it? Did she want pity because her husband wasn't up to scratch? No! She would wear the dress and to hell with what anyone thought. She pulled the wispy bits of hair more into play around her face and reaching for her coat and purse left the flat; locked the door and descended the stairs.

Martha Kelly's heart missed a beat when her daughter entered the living room and shyly removed her coat. Bridget looked like a film star. Why, oh why, hadn't she waited? Looking like that she could have had her pick, but it was too late for that now. Much too late. Danny McGowan had seen to that. Hell roast him!

'You look beautiful. Doesn't she, Barney?'

Barney thought she looked a bit underdressed. After all, she was a married woman with a young child. Her chin rose in the air and her cheeks

440

burned with hot colour as she defied his expected reprimand. Sensing that she expected censure from him, he bit his tongue and agreed with his wife. Why spoil his daughter's night with his old-fashioned ideas? His reward was a smile of pure happiness.

Marie, who until that moment had felt quite daring in a figure-hugging red velvet dress, was not so complimentary. 'You look like a high-class pro, so you do!' she exclaimed in disbelief. 'If you sit down in that dress everybody will see your knickers.'

'Well, they're clean so I'm not bothered. May I also say how pretty you look tonight, Marie?' Bridget asked sarcastically.

With a defiant toss of her head, she hung her coat in the hall and went to answer a knock on the door to admit the first of the party guests.

It was half-past eleven when she noticed Peter McGowan arrive. The cheek of him, gate crashing! she thought, temper rising. He made his way through the swaying dancers and handed her a bottle of Bushmill's. 'I was talking to your father earlier on and he invited me to call in and see the New Year in here, if I was at a loose end. So here I am.'

Mollified, she asked, 'What about your own family? Should you not be with them?'

'A couple of aunts and uncles are with Mam and Dad reminiscing about the good old days long before I was born. Joseph is already in bed and as far as I know Danny is at some golf club or other.'

This floored her. She had been thinking of

Danny sitting at home lonely and miserable. But then, knowing Danny as she did, wasn't that a foolish thought?

'Would you like to dance?'

She wanted desperately to dance but none of the married men had offered to partner her and her brothers had yet to arrive from their individual haunts. The living room wasn't all that big, really, there was only room to sway about. Aware of the danger but unable to resist the chance to go with the music, she put the bottle on the sideboard and entered Peter's arms.

He drew her as close as he dared. 'You look marvellous.'

'It's kind of you to say so.'

He put his lips close to her ear and whispered, 'That dress is very sexy. It suits you.'

'Mmm.'

'You don't know the effect it's having on me.'

She was close enough to have an idea just how he was reacting. 'Don't I?' she asked with a demure smile.

He laughed and put his cheek against hers. 'I wish you were a free woman, Bridget.'

She pondered these words. She had often wished she had met him first, but had thought he only wanted an affair. So why did he wish she was free? She decided it was time to find out.

Drawing back in his arms, she gazed up at him. 'Why do you wish that?'

He looked bewildered. 'Then we could get married.'

'Huh! You expect me to believe that? You're only after one thing, Peter McGowan, and we both know what that is. Don't we?'

His lips found her ear again and he whispered fiercely, 'Believe me, I'm crazy about you.'

'Huh!'

'Why are you so cynical, Bridget? Don't you believe me?'

'It's safe for you to say that.'

Bewilderment clouded his face. 'Why do you say that? I love you.'

Those magic words that made all the difference to a woman. The words she had waited in vain to hear her husband say. They worked their magic and she pressed closer. He steered her from the living-room into the kitchen. It was almost as packed in there. However everyone was preoccupied with their own partner, and no one paid any attention to them. The door to the yard was slightly ajar. Peter looked askance and she found herself nodding, grabbing a shawl off a shelf on the way out. It was freezing cold outside and no one else had faced the biting cold night air. They were alone.

Pulling the door closed, he cuddled her close and kissed her fiercely. She responded eagerly.

'Hey, where are you, Bridget?'

The door was pulled open and the light shone full on them. Patrick Kelly surged forth. 'What the hell are you doing with my sister?'

Bridget realized how bad it must look. When she had put her arms around Peter's neck her dress had slipped down and her breasts were almost bare. Tugging it into place, she faced her brother. 'It's none of your business what we're doing,' she whispered furiously. 'And for heaven's sake, keep your voice down! There's no need to let the whole street know.'

Patrick scowled at Peter. 'Are you not ashamed of yourself? She's your brother's wife, for heaven's sake.'

'It's not what you think, Patrick.'

'Oh, no? Do you think I'm stupid or something?'

In spite of the shawl clutched around her, away from the warmth of Peter's body Bridget's teeth were chattering. Patrick removed his jacket and put it around her shoulders. 'Come inside before you get your death of cold in that scrap of a dress. It's not decent, so it's not.' His eyes ranged over her scanty attire. 'It's almost twelve. Dad sent me to look for you. It's as well he didn't come out himself or there would have been blue murder. Has me da seen you in that yet?'

Through chattering teeth, she whispered, 'Yes, he has but he's not as big a prude as you. Even so, Patrick Kelly, I'm my own boss and I'll wear what I like. Peter didn't drag me outside, you know. Besides, it was only a New Year kiss.'

'Huh!' He lifted a leg. 'Here, pull the other one. How long has this been going on? When I think of the state Danny was in when he kept losing at the cards. He was afraid to tell you, so he was. That's why he borrowed money from D.K. Muldoon. No wonder he gambled so much. He was afraid of losing you.'

Bridget was about to enter the kitchen. Now she gripped her brother's arm and pulled him back outside. 'That Shylock? Is that where Danny got the money?'

Patrick realized he had put his big foot in it. 'I thought you knew, Bridget? I thought that was why you threw him out.'

'Was it you, my own brother, started him gambling?'

'He wanted to come. How was I to know how unlucky he'd be? If Danny bet on a one-horse race he'd lose.'

'You bastard! We were doing all right until this happened. There was hope for us until I found out he'd gambled half our savings. I'll never forgive you for this, Patrick Kelly. Never!'

'Here, you can't blame me for his weakness...'

'Oh, get out of my way.' Roughly she pushed past him and Peter quickly followed. Twelve o'clock was chiming, church bells were ringing and everybody was kissing and hugging as the New Year was welcomed in. A smile plastered across her face, Bridget wished this one and that one all the best. Her mother and father, fervent in their wishes to her, brought the tears even closer to the surface. Then the buffet table was uncovered and Peter was there between her and the crowd. 'Let's get you out of here for a while. Where are the coats?'

'All the coats were taken upstairs out of the way. They're on the bed in the front room,' she said dully. 'I'll fetch ours.'

'I'll come with you.'

At the top of the stairs she said. 'Wait here.'

Ignoring her words he followed her into the bedroom. Closing the door, he gently gathered her against his breast and held her as the tears fell. When the storm subsided and only little sobs

445

were left, he kissed her face, her lips, her neck and bosom. 'I love you, Bridget. Come what may, I intend to look after you. You know, I remember reading once that a marriage could be annulled if one of the party was tricked into it.'

She pulled back and gaped up at him in horror. One moment he was kissing her and saying he would look after her; next he was accusing her of trickery. 'I didn't trick Danny into marriage! I really thought Martin was his. I still do! I nearly died when Joseph threatened to tell Danny about the rumours he'd heard when Martin was born.'

'Our Joseph?'

'Your Joseph. You all seem to think he's a saint...'

Bridget clamped her lips together. She had said enough. It wasn't fair to divulge the boy's secret just because she was unhappy. After all, he hadn't given her away.

'Our Joseph threatened you with exposure, is that what you're saying?'

'Look, I've had all I can take for one night, Peter. Let's join the crowd and get something to eat.'

He could see she meant it and reluctantly let go of her.

'You go on downstairs, I want to freshen up a bit.' When he would have demurred she insisted, 'I mean it. I've had all I can stand. Away on down.'

Downstairs, he discovered he was hungry and lifting a plate helped himself to some of the food. Sitting where he had a view of the stairs he waited patiently for Bridget to appear. It was a

446

full hour before she came down, pale but composed.

'Where on earth did you get to?' It was her mother, peering anxiously at her. 'Are you all right, love?'

'I was taking a wee rest, Mam. Everything suddenly got to me.'

'I know what you mean. It's only natural that you should miss Danny and wish he was here. If only things were different... Shall I fill a plate for you, Bridget?'

'Would you, Mam? You know all my favourites. But don't overdo it, I'm not very hungry.'

'Away and sit beside your da. He's been anxious about you too.'

Avoiding Peter's eye, she made her way to where her father was sitting, a pint of Guinness in his hand. He began to rise, offering her his chair, but she gently pushed him down again. 'I'll sit here on the floor beside you.'

'Are you all right, love?'

'Just a bit sad.'

'I understand. I hope you didn't mind me inviting Peter over?'

'No. Why should I? Everybody seems to be enjoying themselves.'

'Yes, it has been a success, I'm happy to say. Your mother goes to a lot of bother for these wee dos. I wouldn't like anything to spoil it for her.'

'Here, love. Eat that all up.' Her mother handed her a plate. 'What would you like to drink?'

'What about this?' It was Peter with a glass of orange juice.

Without meeting his eyes, she accepted it and

447

placed it on the floor beside her. 'Thank you.'

There was nowhere for Peter to sit. Everyone was eating and every available space was occupied. He hovered hopefully about and was rewarded. Barney stood up. 'Sit here, Peter. You can keep it warm for me. I'll have to organize some more music for a dance and a sing-song.'

Peter motioned for Bridget to sit in the armchair. Giving him a narrow look she moved into the chair her father had vacated. Peter perched on the arm and smiled down at her. She scowled back.

Leaning down, he whispered in her ear, 'I love you.'

'Oh, give my head peace, for heaven's sake,' she growled, but he thought she was pleased nevertheless.

Kath was a bundle of nerves when David called for her on New Year's Eve. She slipped into the car beside him and gave him a nervous smile.

'You look wonderful.'

'Get away with you! I look like the old hag I am.'

'You know that's far from the truth, Kath. You're a very attractive woman.'

Her face clouded over. 'I couldn't hold on to Dick.'

'Perhaps in your heart you didn't really want to?'

She pondered his words for some moments then smiled. 'Do you know something, David? I think that you might very well be right.'

Fortwilliam was packed. A table had been

reserved for them on the edge of the dance floor and was set for their meal. This way their seats would be secured for the cabaret.

'Look at the style in here tonight, Mam. And all that jewellery would dazzle your eyes.'

'And the queen of diamonds has just come in,' Kath said dryly. 'A bit overdressed, don't you think? Or are my claws showing?'

Following the direction of her mother's eyes, Liz saw Irene. She had paused just inside the door and was smiling all around her. Her eyes swept the lounge and came to rest on Kath. The sweetness of her smile made Liz want to puke. Taking her by the arm, Dick led her across the floor to a table in one of the alcoves. She nodded in their direction as they passed by. Liz was proud of her mother. Kath smiled and nodded in a friendly way, as if it didn't bother her that Dick was Irene's escort.

'Thank goodness she's sitting behind us. I won't have to look at that false smile all night,' Kath said wryly.

'Are you all right, Mam?'

'I'm fine. Don't you worry about me. I don't intend to let *her* ruffle my feathers.'

The waitress arrived with the menu and David asked her to return later as they were waiting for another guest. Only then did Kath realize the table was set for four. She looked inquiringly at her daughter.

'Neville Barnes is joining us,' Liz said tentatively.

'Does he know I'm here?'

'No. He thinks you'll be coming with Dick. He

449

might not come but we'll wait a little longer. You see, Mam, he has this idea in his head you might even announce your engagement tonight. I didn't tell you in case I put you off.'

'He won't want to sit with me, Liz,' Kath lamented. 'I've treated him so shabbily. I think I should go home.'

Her mother looked so shaken Liz found herself hoping Neville wouldn't come. She had been unable to get in touch with him but they had booked a place at the table just in case. Now, seeing her mother's distress, she wondered if she had done the right thing.'

'Oh, my God, there he is now! I'm away to the cloakroom.' Kath was so agitated, she would have cleared the table in her haste to get away had Liz not managed to grip the cloth and save it.

David returned at that moment with a tray of drinks. He stood gazing after Kath in amazement as she hurried through the restaurant towards the far door. 'What on earth's going on? Where's she off to in such a hurry?'

'Neville has just arrived and Mam's in a tizzy.' Liz shook her head in bewilderment. 'It never took a feather out of her when Dick walked in with Irene, but one look at Neville and she did a runner.'

'Hello, Neville,' David said loudly to warn his wife of his presence.

Had Neville heard her? She swung round, only to gape in horror. Neville was accompanied by a tall slim woman. No wonder her mother had done a runner.

'Hello, Liz. I hope you don't mind my bringing

my friend Betty along?'

'No, not at all.' She nodded in the woman's direction.

'Betty, this is Liz and David. Two very good friends of mine.'

'You're very welcome, Betty.' David, always the gentleman, stood and shook her warmly by the hand. 'If you'll excuse me a moment, I'll get the waitress to set another place at the table. Then I'll fetch you a drink.'

Neville looked apprehensive. 'Is your mother joining us?'

'I think so.' But would she when she saw Neville had a partner with him? Liz thought wildly.

'Is Dick ill?'

'No, he's here. He's over there with Irene Brennan.'

Stricken was the only word Liz could think of to describe the look on Neville's face. He turned to one side and muttered something. She wasn't sure but she thought he said, 'In the name of God, what have I done?'

He seemed to get a grip of himself and remembered his manners. Pulling out a chair from the table, he said, 'Forgive me, Betty, please sit here.'

There was a perplexed frown on her brow. 'Are you feeling all right, Neville?'

His smile was bleak but he assured her, 'Yes. Yes. I am.'

David arrived back with the waitress, and Liz took the opportunity to excuse herself and headed quickly for the cloakroom.

It was empty. No sign of Kath whatsoever.

451

Quickly, she retraced her steps along the corridor and descended the stairs. She found her mother huddled in one of the chairs close to the door, her coat on and her handbag clutched on her lap.

Sitting beside her, Liz clasped her hands. They were icy. 'What are you doing sitting down here, Mam?' she asked gently as she tried to rub some warmth into her cold fingers.

'I'm going home. I've phoned for a taxi but they're busy at the moment. God knows how long I'll have to wait.'

'Mam, there's no way I'll let you go home to see the New Year in on your own.'

'Liz, I saw him! I saw him with that tall, attractive woman.'

'Well, what's it to you? You sent him packing, remember. So why worry?'

'Liz, I can't go back up there. Can't you understand? I'll be the odd one out. Everybody will be pitying me. I couldn't stand that. I couldn't bear to watch him with that woman.'

A shadow falling across them caused them to look up. Neville said, 'Can I talk to your mother alone, Liz?'

She looked askance at Kath. With a slight nod she gave her assent and Liz withdrew and slowly climbed the stairs. Looking apprehensively back, she saw Neville take the chair she had vacated and put an arm around her mother's shoulders. It wasn't shrugged off and Liz thought in bewilderment, wonders will never cease.

'Kath, what do you think you're doing?'

'Look, Neville, don't rub salt in the wound. Just

go back up to your friend.'

'Are you worried I've a new lady friend, Kath?'

'Worried? Why on earth should I be worried?'

'Then it's not me you're running away from, but Dick?'

'That's right. I made a right fool of myself with him and he preferred Irene. Now I can't bear to see him with her. I thought I didn't care any more, but I do.'

'Come back upstairs then. Pretend you don't. We'll all support you. Betty is a very nice person, you'll like her.'

'I'm sure I would, but I'd prefer to go home.'

'Kath, you can't spend New Year's Eve alone.'

For the first time since he'd sat down she looked him in the face. 'That's good! Coming from you, that's very good. While Liz was growing up I spent a lot of New Year Eves on my own, while you were probably enjoying yourself with your wife and sons. Many a New Year I've greeted with tears of loneliness.'

He looked crestfallen. 'What can I say, Kath, but how sorry I am?'

'Oh, it wasn't all your fault. Away back upstairs to your friend. I'll be all right.' A note of relief tinged her voice as she said, 'Here's my taxi now.'

Rising quickly to her feet, she gazed down at him. 'Happy New Year, Neville.'

He also rose to his feet. He felt he was missing something but was at a loss to know just what. 'I'll see you out to the taxi.'

'That won't be necessary.'

'Nevertheless, I will.'

He opened the cab door for her. 'Thank you,

453

Neville. And I really do wish you and this Betty all the best.' She offered her cheek for a kiss. He gripped her chin and turned her face towards him. Whispering 'Happy New Year,' he kissed her lips. Kath stood motionless but he continued kissing her until at last her lips moved under his and she responded. Breathless they drew apart and she saw joy in his eyes. Then he took out his wallet and stuffed a note into the grinning cab driver's hand.

'Sorry, mate. The lady has changed her mind.'

Doffing his cap, the driver said, 'Good luck to you, sir.'

Offering Kath his arm, Neville said, 'Will you be warm enough to take a short walk? We must talk before we go back in.'

She nodded, afraid to remind him that he had a very attractive woman waiting inside for him. 'What about you? You've no overcoat.'

He laughed ruefully. 'I'm in a fever,' he confessed.

Silence reigned as they made their way along Downview Avenue, each engrossed in their own thoughts, wondering what the outcome would be.

At last he asked tentatively, 'Are you really upset about Dick?'

Turning her head aside, she muttered, 'No.'

'I can't hear you?'

'I said, no, I'm not.'

'Then why were you running away?'

'Why do you think?'

'You'll have to help me here, Kath. I'm afraid to think, in case I'm wrong.'

She stopped walking and they faced each other on the pavement. 'I was running away from you and that attractive woman you arrived with.'

'You were jealous?'

'You want your pound of flesh, don't you?' He nodded and she continued, 'I can't explain. I hoped you wouldn't be here tonight because I was ashamed of how shabbily I've treated you.'

'And...?'

'I was completely gutted when you walked in with her!' Kath gave an embarrassed laugh. 'The way I've been carrying on lately, poor Liz must think I'm going round the bend.'

'You haven't answered my question, Kath. Were you jealous?'

'I thought I had. Yes, I suppose you could say I was jealous. I wanted to tear her hair out! Does that satisfy you?'

Neville laughed aloud. 'It will do for starters. Come here.' Gripping her shoulders, he pulled her into his arms and kissed her soundly. 'I suppose we'll have to go back to the club, but I'm seeing you home. Do you hear me?'

'Yes,' she said humbly, but joy tinged the laughter that escaped her lips.

Back upstairs a small table had been placed on the edge of the floor, close to theirs and set for one place. Liz eyed it. If her mother came back and had to sit there, the target of all eyes, she would surely do another runner. The waitress was once again waiting to take their order. 'What's happening, Liz?' David asked. 'Is Kath coming back? Can we order?'

'I don't know.' She looked at the young girl. 'Could you give us another few minutes, love.'

'Sure. No hurry.'

Once again Liz eyed the table. As if reading her thoughts, David said, 'Don't worry, if Kath comes back, I'll sit there.'

She glanced apprehensively at Betty who gave her a big smile. 'Don't worry about me either. Neville has put me fully in the picture. I guess I can tell you the truth. I was going to spend the evening alone as my husband was called away on urgent business but Neville kindly asked me to accompany him here. He said I'd be doing him a favour.'

'Oh, so there's nothing between you and him?'

'Nothing at all. John, my husband, and Neville are close friends. Am I right in thinking I'll be in the way now?'

'Not at all!'

'Liz, is Kath with Neville?'

'I think so, David. Mam was waiting for a taxi downstairs. Then Neville came down and asked if he could have a word in private. I left them together. I hope he can persuade her to stay, but I doubt it.'

'I'll nip down and see what's happening.'

Finding the hall empty, David was slowly climbing the stairs again when there was a knock on the outside door. He retraced his steps and opened it.

'David, sorry about all this, but at least I've persuaded Kath to stay.'

His answer was heartfelt. 'Thank God for that! Now maybe we can order our meal.'

Liz stared in amazement when her mother and Neville crossed the floor behind David. Her eyes questioned her husband. With a slight shrug, he made her aware that he was no wiser than herself.

'Sorry for the hold up, friends, but we can order now.' Still holding Kath's hand, Neville drew her forward and introduced her to Betty. 'Betty, this is my very dear friend, Kath O'Hara. Kath, Betty's husband and I are old friends.'

Rosy-cheeked, Kath sat on the chair he pulled out for her. 'Sorry for creating a fuss but I was a bit upset,' she confessed.

'All's well that ends well,' David said, and catching the waitress's eye beckoned her over. 'We're ready to order at last.'

During the course of the evening, the two men divided the dances between the three women. It was while she was sitting out a dance that Liz received the shock of her life when Danny McGowan appeared by her side.

'Hello, Liz. May I have this dance, please?'

'No, indeed you can't! What are you doing here?'

'I've just arrived but I'm hoping to enjoy myself. I'm surprised your husband leaves you sitting on your own. He's asking for trouble. Just one dance, Liz, for old times' sake.'

'No, I'm too tired.'

'You're afraid – admit it! Afraid to dance with me.' He leant closer and his voice became intimate. 'You're remembering what it feels like to dance with a real man instead of one old enough to be your father. Isn't that right, Liz?'

She realized he was a bit tipsy. Obviously Fortwilliam was not his first port of call. She wondered how she could get rid of him without drawing attention to them. 'Danny, please leave me alone.'

'I just want one dance, Liz. Is that asking too much?'

'As a matter of fact, it is. Please go.'

David couldn't believe his eyes when he glanced across the floor and saw Danny bending over Liz. He was dancing with Kath at the time and with a muttered, 'There's Danny McGowan, pestering Liz,' ushered her off the dance floor and over to the table.

Danny straightened up and faced them. He nodded to David and greeted Kath. 'Hello, Mrs O'Hara. I trust you're well?'

'I was until I saw you.'

'I was just asking Liz to dance with me, for old times' sake, but I think she's afraid to. Afraid her husband might object.' Danny smirked slyly at David as if he was the big bad husband. He rose to the bait.

'Liz has no reason to fear me.' He turned to his wife. 'Why not dance with Danny, Liz?' Desperately, he silently willed her to refuse; to tell him to shove off.

Confused, she rose to her feet. Why was her husband urging her to dance with Danny? Would it prove something to him?

Disappointed, David watched them take to the floor. Kath watched him and her heart ached. Didn't Liz realise what she was doing to this

458

man? She should never had consented to dance with Danny.

Gently, she took his arm. 'Let's sit this one out, David.'

On the dance floor, Danny drew Liz as close as he dared. 'This brings back memories of happier times, eh, Liz?' he whispered in her ear.

Straining her body away from his, she muttered, 'You can stop chancing your arm! I'm no longer interested in you.'

'I don't believe you, Liz.'

'It's true. You couldn't hold a candle to David. I just wish I'd discovered it sooner.'

He jerked her closer. 'I know you love me, Liz. Aren't you considering having my baby?'

He was only slightly drunk but it was obvious he didn't care who heard him. And to think she had ever contemplated trusting him. She must have been daft. They were shoulder to shoulder with Irene and Dick. Horrified to see that Irene was straining to hear their conversation, Liz whispered fiercely, 'For heaven's sake, shut up! People can hear you.'

'That doesn't bother me, Liz. I don't care who knows, I love you. And no matter what you say ... I know you love me.'

They were close to the entrance to the lounge and, abruptly pushing him away, she headed for the door. He was on her heels. Out on the deserted landing, she swung round to face him. 'Get out of here! Do you hear me? Leave me alone.'

'You don't mean that, Liz.'

'Oh, yes, I do.'

He moved closer, peering into her face. 'Promise you will meet me and I'll go now. Meet me just one more time, Liz. You owe me that,' he pleaded.

She glanced helplessly around, seeking a way to escape him. To her dismay, David was there within earshot, with Neville and her mother, but made no move to come to her aid. Had he heard Danny? It sounded so damning; as if they had been meeting regularly. After a bewildered glance at her husband's failure to intervene, Neville spoke. 'Are you all right, Liz?' Thankfully she ran to him and he put a protective arm around her shoulders.

'I think you had better leave the premises before you're thrown out, young man,' Neville advised in the voice of authority.

'Huh! Who the hell are you? What gives you the right to interfere in our affairs?' Danny growled.

'The right of a father. That's what!'

His words passed over everyone's head but Liz's. To say she was flabbergasted would be the understatement of the year. She gaped up at him. Had she heard him right?

Annoyed that this young bounder had made him reveal such a well-kept secret, Neville released his hold on her and moved threateningly towards Danny. Then Kath was at his side, a restraining hand on his arm.

'It's all right, Neville. Let him go. He's not worth getting banned for.'

A worried Ian put in an appearance. 'I wondered where you'd got to.' Taking Danny by the arm, he apologized on his behalf. 'I'm sorry if he's made a nuisance of himself. I'll see he causes no more bother.' Knowing he was out of his depth, Danny allowed himself to be led towards the Men's Bar, saying over his shoulder, 'You know where to find me, Liz.'

She never heard him. All her attention was focused on her mother. 'Mam? I don't understand...'

Giving Neville a wry smile, Kath took her daughter by the arm. 'It's time I told you the truth, love.'

'I'm sorry, Kath. It just slipped out.'

'It doesn't matter, Neville. It's time she was told anyway. But not now. Later. It's almost midnight.'

It was almost four o'clock before the party broke up. Once again hands were joined and 'Auld Lang Syne' was sung, at the end of which Bridget found herself locked in Peter's arms.

'I think it's about time I got that New Year kiss, don't you?'

She gazed up at him, eyes dark and mysterious-looking. Their kiss was soft and tender. 'I'm seeing you home.'

'No, you're not.'

'I am. I won't take no for an answer. Get your coat.'

'Bridget, I'll walk you round to the flat.'

Patrick had been watching them all night. Every time she looked around, he was there. Now she rounded on him fiercely. 'No, you won't. Peter is seeing me home.'

'Over my dead body!'

461

'The way I feel about you at the moment, Patrick, I'd gladly arrange that.'

'I'm only thinking of you, sis. You've had a fair amount to drink.'

'I won't take advantage of her,' Peter growled.

'Huh! You expect me to believe that, after that demonstration earlier on? No, I'll see her home.'

'No, you will not!' Bridget cried indignantly. How dare Patrick dictate to her? 'Let's go, Peter.' Thrusting past her brother, she made her farewells and left the house.

It was bitter cold outside and arm in arm they walked briskly up Leeson Street. Bridget was inwardly furious with her brother. Why couldn't he mind his own business? If he hadn't interfered, Peter would not be seeing her home now. She was nervous. The heat of his body against hers was exciting. She wanted him. There she was admitting it! But what difference did it make? She was a married woman.

At the door she gently released her arm from his and moved away from his tempting presence. 'Thank you, Peter. You have been very kind to me.'

She had to laugh aloud when he stared at her in amazement. 'I'm sorry, I shouldn't laugh. I've given you the wrong impression. Blame our Patrick! He was so arrogant, he got up my nose. I didn't mean to lead you on.'

'I don't find it very funny, Bridget.'

'No, you're right. It isn't. And I really am sorry. I apologize again.'

'I think you at least owe me a nightcap.'

She opened her mouth to protest but shut it

again. He was right. She was in his debt.

Peter watched her wrestle with her conscience and released a silent sigh of relief when she nodded and turned to open the door. Full of confidence, he climbed the stairs behind her.

Determined to send him packing as soon as possible, Bridget headed straight for the kitchen, saying over her shoulder, 'Coffee or tea?'

He followed her. Before she knew what was happening he had her in his arms. She tried to demur but he covered her mouth with his hand.

Against it she said softly, 'Our Patrick said you would take advantage of me.'

She was joking, but he released her at once and the hurt on his face dismayed her. Before she could draw breath he was at the door. 'I'll see you around, Bridget.'

'Peter! I was having you on. Please wait.'

He hesitated, hand on the doorknob. Tentatively she approached him. Hands on his chest, she gazed up at him. 'I didn't mean to offend you.'

He remained stiff and unyielding. 'It's all right. We've both been drinking. It's better I go.' In fact, he had been careful and had drunk less than usual. He'd wanted her to enjoy their union. Wanted her to want more.

'Peter? Don't be offended, please.' She raised herself on tip-toe and pressed her lips against his. 'I know it's wrong but I do want you,' she muttered.

He drew back and looked down at her. 'Are you sure about this, Bridget? It's not just the drink talking?'

'I've been on orange juice most of the night, so it definitely isn't the drink.'

When he swept her up in his arms and headed for the bedroom, she laughed with joy. Tonight was theirs; the devil take tomorrow.

Chapter Eight

The festivities laid on by the club committee to welcome in the New Year passed in a blur for Liz. She was utterly confused and unhappy. How could her mother have the gumption to keep her in the dark so long once she knew that Neville was their friend? They had both known and said nothing to her. She felt a complete idiot. Had David also known? Now her mother had confessed to her that it had been no idle threat Neville had made to Danny. He really was her father. She had promised to explain everything the following day. A bit late for that, wasn't it?

Her eyes drifted to where they sat holding hands. Her mother and *father?* She examined his face and could see no likeness in it to herself. But then, she was the picture of her mother. Hadn't he unwittingly noticed the resemblance at their first meeting? In repose he looked old; much older than her mother. Well, he *was* much older. Was this how she and David would look in years to come? Still, she had to admit, Neville and Kath looked good together. Happy and fulfilled.

It was hard to take it all in. And it was going to be awkward. How could she possibly act normally towards him? Would he expect her to be all over him now, call him *Father*, when he had failed to acknowledge her birth all those years ago? Why should she? Why indeed. She had managed

465

without a father all these years so why bother with one now? But they had already become good friends, that was the snag. It felt more of a loss than a gain.

To Liz's surprise, Kath was acting like a woman in love; making cow's eyes at him and hanging on his every word. But hadn't she, not so long ago either, put Dick before Neville? Hadn't she apparently had an affair right under his very nose? Her father must be a very understanding man where her mother was concerned. Words he had once said sprang to mind. 'Perhaps your mother is sowing her wild oats.' Liz had been surprised at how well he understood Kath. Hah! Didn't he know her only too well? Hadn't he been the cause of her downfall?

From across the room, David watched his wife battle silently with her doubts, conflicting expressions flitting briefly across her face. He could see she was bothered about something. However, he felt unable to talk to her after this latest carry on between her and Danny, because of the jealousy that consumed him. Should she not be seeking him out and defending herself if she had nothing to hide? Instead she was sitting there, waiting for him to make the first move. He remembered how, barely a week ago, he had forced himself on her because of his jealousy. Did she not realize he was afraid of this terrible rage that was eating away at him? The ugly marks on her body had yet to fade completely. That must never happen again. He must be very careful not to lose control again. Better to keep his distance for a while, he thought.

Danny McGowan's appearance tonight had brought back all those doubts he'd unwillingly harboured against his wife. She had denied seeing him, and he, fool that he was, had believed her. They had apparently put it behind them. But surely she must be having an affair with Danny when he could so blatantly ask her to meet him one last time? Meet where? No venue had been mentioned. So a meeting place must already be arranged. Liz must know just where to go. And how would she know that if they weren't lovers? How often had they met on the sly? Who else knew about them? And who else had heard Danny's request tonight? As far as he could recall, as well as Neville and Kath, Dick and Irene had been within earshot. He hated the thought of those two having this knowledge. Still, if they had heard, they were certainly not gloating over it. To avoid his wife, he had been in their company for some time now and it had not been mentioned. Indeed, Irene could not be more friendly or caring. For the first time ever he felt drawn to her.

Liz caught his eye and he could see that she was bewildered by his attitude. Unable to face her, he glanced away. Well, what did she expect? He was only human. Tears stung Liz's eyes at her husband's apparent indifference. Did he not realize the knowledge that Neville was her father had come as an awful shock? Hadn't she told him that she had no desire ever to meet the man who'd abandoned them? Now, instead of supporting her, David had been dallying in the company of Irene and Dick for the past fifteen

467

minutes, leaving her sitting alone. Not that she was really alone. Her mother and Neville were at the same table, but wrapped up in each other. Betty had made her excuses directly the New Year was in, saying she would get a taxi home before the rush began and insisting that Neville remain with Kath.

It was so unlike David! Why was he acting like this? Surely he hadn't taken what Danny had said to heart? Could he not see that the man was drunk? Liz thought she had convinced him that there was nothing going on between them. Did he still not trust her? What else could she do?

Unable to bear the anguish any longer, she rose blindly to her feet and grabbed her purse. With a muttered excuse in her mother's direction, she left the table and made her way from the lounge. What a start to the New Year! This was one New Year's Eve she would not forget in a hurry. She would ring for a taxi and go home. She would hardly be missed, she thought bitterly. Grabbing her coat from the rail, she almost ran down the stairs, oblivious to the surprised looks that followed her.

When Liz scurried from the room, Kath rose and made to follow her. Neville's hand stayed her. She turned a worried gaze on him. 'Liz is having trouble coming to terms with the fact that you're her father.'

'I can see that, but if we're to be together...' His eyes sought reassurance. She responded at once with a nod and a squeeze on his arm, and he continued, 'She had to be told, Kath.'

'I know that, but I think it was the way it came

out. It must have been a terrible shock. Especially since you've become very close friends. It's my fault. I should have prepared her once I realized you'd met. But I never dreamed we would come together. You see, I was so sure I could never forgive you. So if we hadn't made up our differences, I thought it was better she didn't know.'

'I don't agree with you there. Once I knew she was my daughter, you must surely have known it was inevitable I would one day risk her scorn and introduce myself.' His grip on her hand tightened. 'You're not having second thoughts, I hope?'

'No. Nor am I likely to.' Kath returned the pressure of his fingers as she confessed, 'I nearly died when I thought I'd lost you for good. I couldn't believe my eyes when you walked in with Betty.'

'Well, as you now know, she was just helping me out.'

'I honestly don't know what I was thinking of, carrying on with Dick Kennedy like that,' Kath said ruefully. 'You must have been hurt?'

'I was. Very. But all's well that ends well. I don't really deserve a second chance but I thought if you went and sowed some wild oats you might eventually change your mind where I'm concerned.' Earnestly, he vowed. 'And it worked, Kath. That's the main thing. I promise I'll make you happy. I've a lot of making up to do. I'll serve you until the day I die.'

'I trust you to, Neville. But now I must go and try to make my peace with Liz.' She brushed her lips across his and went in search of her daughter.

After scurrying about looking in all the obvious places, and some not so obvious, she returned and approached David. Ignoring Dick and Irene, she addressed him. 'Sorry for interrupting, but do you happen to know where your wife is? I've searched high and low and can't find her.'

'The last time I saw her, she was sitting with you and Neville.'

Kath fixed a stern eye on him. 'Have you two quarrelled?'

'No!' He spoke abruptly unable to meet her eye. Guilt was beginning to plague him. He had seen his wife leave the lounge in obvious distress and hurt pride had prevented him from following her. 'Perhaps she decided to go home. Is her coat still there?'

'You're not much help, are you?' With a dismissive wag of her hand Kath turned away but her words reached him. 'I think you could spend your time more profitably than sitting here with these two, don't you?' For the first time in their acquaintance she found David wanting. He was being selfish. Her daughter needed him and here he was, sitting with his old friend Irene. The wonderful Irene who during the evening had appeared to be losing interest in Dick now she had him in tow again. Was she hoping to snare David at last?

A crowd was waiting for taxis but her daughter was not amongst them. Kath decided Liz must be walking home. After all, it was no great distance, but it was late and they should follow suit and make sure she was all right. Accompanied by Neville she set off to walk the short distance to the bungalow. It was in darkness when they arrived and there was no reply to their urgent knocks.

'Where on earth can she be? I hope she's all right, Neville.' Kath's voice was fraught with anxiety.

'Of course she is.' He sounded more confident than he felt. It was a wee bit dicey at the best of times for a woman out alone at this time of night, but tonight there would be a lot of drunken revellers about and anything could happen.

They turned, startled, as Liz's voice came out of the darkness. 'How on earth did you get here before me? Did you manage to jump the taxi queue?'

'Thank God you're safe! We were getting worried. We walked from the club. How come we didn't pass you?' Kath peered into the dim light at the figure behind her daughter and was amazed to see Danny McGowan. 'What are you doing here?' she asked suspiciously. Where had they been that she and Neville had passed them unnoticed? Worse still, what had they been up to? Really, it was very remiss of David, leaving his wife alone when he knew Danny was in the vicinity, and her in such a vulnerable state.

'Danny kindly walked me home. I'm just going to ring for a taxi for him.' Without further explanation, Liz opened the door and entered her home. They all trooped in behind her. She ushered them into the lounge and reached for the telephone.

She replaced the receiver in its cradle and faced them with a sigh. 'It will be at least half an hour before one comes. Can I get you a drink while we're waiting?'

Not once had she acknowledged Neville, by so much as a glance. They all declined and Liz abruptly said to Kath, 'Mam, can I have a word with you?'

Kath followed her into the bedroom. 'Are you going home with Neville tonight?'

'I had intended to. Why?'

'Can I spend the night at your house?'

'Liz, you'd be better having this out with David.'

'Mam, I'm fed up to the teeth having to explain myself every time somebody says something out of place. I need some space to think. Decide what to do.'

'All right. But I'll come with you. Neville will understand.'

'I would prefer to be alone. I'll share Danny's taxi.'

'You're playing with fire, girl, going home alone with him.'

'Who cares? I've been too good for too long, and where has it got me? Marriage to a man old enough to be my father. A man who doesn't trust me. If I had listened to Danny in the first place none of this would have happened. I would never have married David. I would never had met my *father.* And I wouldn't be expected to accept everything with a smile, like some simpleton who knows no better.' The fire went out of her and wearily Liz indicated the door. 'If you don't

472

mind, I'd like to be alone while I pack a bag.'

Affronted at being dismissed so airily, Kath stiffly left the room and rejoined the men. They waited in uneasy silence; Neville glowering at Danny from under bristling brows and warning himself not to make a scene, Danny eyeing the luxurious surroundings. That David bloke must really be loaded, he thought enviously.

The arrival of David heightened the tension. He stopped on the threshold of the room and gaped at Danny in disbelief. 'What the hell are you doing in my home?'

Kath rose hurriedly to her feet to defend him. 'He's waiting for a taxi, David.'

He rounded on her. 'Can he not speak for himself? Does he always hide behind a woman's skirt?'

Danny shot to his feet at this accusation. 'I walked Liz home. Anyway, where were you? It's too dangerous for her to be out alone this late, you know. When we got here, she kindly offered to phone for a taxi for me.'

Well aware that he had neglected his wife's welfare, David's face flooded with colour. He jerked his head towards the outer door. 'Wait outside for it. Or I won't be responsible for my actions.'

'I'll wait with you, Danny.' Liz's voice came quietly from behind him.

Slowly, David turned to face his wife. His face blanched when he saw she had changed out of her evening attire and was dressed for outdoors. A small overnight bag was at her feet.

'Where do you think you're going?'

473

'I'm going to Mam's.'

'Oh, I see. You're going home with Kath?'

'No, you're wrong. Mam is staying with Neville. But I need some time alone. That's why I'm going to stay in Mam's house tonight.'

'You're leaving here with *him?*' David's voice was clipped with anger and his eyes blazed.

'I'm sharing his taxi, yes.'

'If you leave now with him, Liz, don't come back. Do you understand?'

She flinched as if he had struck her. Then nodded that she understood. Lifting the hold-all she walked tight-lipped to the door, opened it and left. With an apologetic shrug at Kath, Danny followed her.

David laughed, a heartbreaking sound. 'I didn't handle that very well, did I?'

'No, you didn't,' Neville agreed with him.

'Go after her, David,' Kath urged.

'What's the use? It's him she wants. He's all she's ever wanted. I've been living in a fool's paradise.'

'I think you're wrong, David. I think she cares deeply for you. More deeply than even she realizes.'

'That's not enough any more, Kath. Besides, we're embarrassing Neville, discussing our private affairs in front of him.'

'You don't know yet?'

'Know what?'

'Neville is family. He is Liz's *father.* I thought you heard him say so tonight?'

David blinked in astonishment. 'No. No, I didn't. Does Liz know?'

474

Kath nodded sadly. 'Neville let it slip out tonight in the midst of that scuffle with Danny. That's why she's so upset. It's not because of Danny, it's because she feels betrayed. And I don't blame her! You didn't help any, taking yourself off like that to sit with Irene. What on earth were you thinking of?'

Wearily David sank down on a chair and buried his head in his hands. 'I didn't know. I've been so blind. But when that fellow asked her to meet him one last time, something died inside me. I couldn't find anything to say to her. Then when I saw him here in my home...' Words failed him and he shrugged. 'It was the last straw. Now, if you don't mind, I'd like to be alone.'

Kath looked at Neville. Her eyes asked if it was safe to leave him. He nodded, and they quietly withdrew.

Danny cautiously opened his eyes but quickly closed them again as daggers seemed to stab at his brain. Dear God, what had happened? Where was he? He felt as if he had been run over by a bus.

The nurse on duty had seen his eyes flicker and, leaving her chair, hung over the bed. 'Danny, can you hear me?'

A slight nod and a whisper answered her. 'Water.' His lips hardly moved and he groaned as he felt the restriction in his jaw.

Gently she raised his head and placed the straw left ready in a glass of water, to his lips. His face was a mess; stitches in his cheek, and his eyes almost lost, so swollen were his features. His

475

lower lip was also stitched. Slits appeared where his eyes should be as he peered into her face.

'Don't try to talk, Danny. Your jaw is cracked. You'll have to be careful for a while. Who on earth did this to you?'

A slight shake of the head, caused him to wince, but indicated that he had no idea.

His eyes closed and he feigned sleep as memory came rushing back. He recalled that Ian had met a friend at Fortwilliam who was going back to the flat with him. So, as promised, Danny was to make himself scarce and go back to his mother's house. Ian had escorted him out of the club and right out on to Downview Avenue. He had no intention of leaving Danny hanging about in the lobby waiting for a taxi. Anything could happen. Warning him of all the ills that would befall him should he try and make contact with Liz O'Hara, he had left Danny to hail a passing taxi.

Annoyed because Ian had prevented him from seeking Liz out to wish her a Happy New Year, Danny glared resentfully after him for some moments. However, he knew better than to return to the club. In this mood Ian could be ruthless. Utterly disgruntled, he had started to walk along Downview Avenue towards Shore Road, reckoning it would be easier to get a taxi there than on the Antrim Road. A figure passed him practically running. It was Liz!

Unable to believe his luck, he started to run after her. 'Liz? Hey, Liz, hang on a minute.' His voice brought her to a standstill. Slowly she turned to face him.

'What on earth are you doing out alone at this

time of the morning?' he asked incredulously.

'I'm on my way home. I live down here, remember?'

'Where's your husband?'

'He was held up and as I'm very tired, I decided to go on home. It's no distance after all.'

He could sense she was upset and curbed further questions. 'I'll walk you home then.'

Too dispirited to object, she fell into step with him. The pavements were coated with frost and he offered her his arm. Side by side, they covered the rest of the distance to Somerton Road in silence. Danny was trying to gauge what his chances were. She obviously wasn't her usual self. Where the road joined the avenue she stopped.

'You needn't come any further.'

'Liz, I can see you're upset. Was it because of me? Did David take exception to what I said? Did he take his spleen out on you? I didn't mean you any harm. You know that, don't you?'

She laughed, a harsh sound. 'Believe it or not, my husband has hardly spoken to me since you put in an appearance. And, to crown it all, I was introduced to my *father* tonight for the first time. It never rains but it pours!' To her horror all the pain and frustration of the evening brought sobs to her throat, threatening to engulf her.

'Liz, sweetheart.' Sick at heart, she allowed Danny to hold and comfort her. His tenderness made her cry all the harder.

He led her away from the light of the street lamp and into the shadowy entrance of a drive-way. There, hidden from view by a hedge, he

477

kissed her tenderly. 'Hush, love. It will be all right. So, that big man who threatened me, is he really your father?'

'Yes. I've known him for ages and Mother never told me the truth. I feel so betrayed and mixed up. Why did they keep me in the dark? I'm so unhappy about it all. As for David, I can't understand what's got into him.'

'Hush, love. Everything will be OK. I'll look after you.'

His lips trailed her face and throat. She closed her eyes and pictured David with Irene. She had looked stunning tonight. They really did look well together. Did he realize now he had made a mistake? It must be obvious to all that Irene would make him a more suitable wife. Was he deliberately looking for an excuse to get rid of Liz? The way she had been behaving about Danny, she could hardly blame him. Still, she had been so sure that he loved her.

She savoured the sweetness of Danny's kisses and felt the tension leave her body as she relaxed against him. It was nice to be wanted. They remained locked in each other's arms for some time, forgetful of everything but the comfort derived from each other. However, when Danny became more passionate, she pushed him away.

'No! I don't want this. Good night, Danny.'

He gave in gracefully. 'No, you're right. Not now. I'll see you to your door.'

Too weary to argue with him, she had allowed him to accompany her and he had ended up in her beautiful bungalow, the opulence of which kept him speechless for some time. Then, how it came about he didn't know, wonder of wonders she had actually shared a taxi with him to Dunlewey Street. At the door she had been adamant he couldn't come in, not even for a moment. When the door closed on her he stood for some time gazing sadly at it. Things could have been so different if only he had behaved himself. Locked in hopeless thoughts, he slowly crossed the street to his mother's. While searching his pockets for the door key, he became aware of a rush of heavy footsteps and movement near him. They must have been lying in wait for him in the shadows, three big thugs who took it in turn to punch and kick him with hob-nailed boots. He tried to defend himself but didn't stand a chance against three of them.

When Danny awoke he was lying on the pavement close to his mother's door. How long had he been out? He had no idea. Gingerly, he touched his face and winced in pain. His hand was covered in blood. He licked a lip that seemed to by lying open. He must look awful. He couldn't go to his mother in this state. The shock might prove too much for her. He thought of Liz across the street but rejected the idea of going to her. She must never know of the trouble he was in; why this had come about. Pulling himself painfully to his feet, he tested his limbs. Thank God, no bones appeared to be broken although his chest felt as if a knife was stuck in it. Clasping his arms across his rib cage to try and ease the pain, he started on his painful journey down the street. He would have to depend on Bridget caring enough to take him in.

After all, she was still his wife. He took it easy, a couple of steps at a time, but knew he would never make it to the flat. He must go to Liz after all. If he could make it across the street, she wouldn't turn him away.

Liz was still downstairs making a hot drink when Danny pounded on her door. At first she hesitated to open the door so late at night. Suppose someone had seen her enter and knew she was on her own? On the other hand, suppose a neighbour was in trouble and needed help? Turning out the kitchen light, she entered the dark hall and made her way to the door. Cautiously she peered through the bull's eye. At first she didn't recognize the bloody face on the other side. Then the door was thrown open and she caught him as he practically fell inside.

'In the name of God, Danny, what happened? Did you walk in front of one of the army jeeps? Or ... did they do this to you?'

Consciousness kept coming and going as she helped him out of his coat. Boiling some water, she gently bathed the bloody mess that was his face.

'Danny, you're in a bad way. I'll have to get an ambulance.'

'No. Please ... wait ... until morning.' The effort to talk was so painful he almost passed out.

She assisted him upstairs, every step obviously agony to him. An hour passed and as the pain in his chest increased with every breath he drew, she swept aside his objections and rang for an ambulance.

She lay on the bed beside him and held him

until they came some time later and carried him out on a stretcher.

Danny eventually drifted off to sleep again and awoke in a cold clammy sweat some hours later. A weak sun lightened the room and he realized he was in a hospital ward. He hadn't dreamed up the nurse earlier on, then. His mother and father sat by his bed.

'Who did this to you, Danny? Was it Barney Kelly? Did he hear about you and Liz O'Hara?'

It hurt too much to speak so he shook his head in horrified denial.

'Who did it then?'

'Leave him be, Jane. Can't you see he's in no fit state to answer you?'

'Your jaw's cracked, Danny, and you have a broken rib,' his mother told him.

He grimaced. Could they not see he needed rest? His father's next words got his full attention.

'Danny, the police have been. They're coming back later.'

Seeing the terror in his eyes, Joe cried, 'What's the matter, son? Are you in some kind of trouble?'

He motioned with his hand that he wanted to write. Joe rifled through his pockets and dug out an old envelope and a stub of pencil. Gratefully, Danny took them and wrote with a hand that shook: *I don't want the police involved. I fell down some stairs.*

'Ah, now, Danny, nobody's going to believe that. It's obvious somebody gave you a good hiding. That's why the hospital informed the police. The question is, who and why? Was it un-provoked or did you deserve it?'

'Don't talk daft, Joe!' Jane cried incredulously. 'Nobody deserves to be left in this state. They could have killed him.'

Her husband looked sceptical but let the matter drop.

It was Peter who had opened the door to Liz early that morning. She looked haggard and drawn.

'Can I come in, Peter? I've some bad news. I'm staying at Mam's and I've been watching for some sign of life over here.'

Silently he stood to one side, he could see she was in a right state. Jane came from the kitchen and they both stood silently waiting to hear what they knew would be bad news.

'Danny was at Fortwilliam Golf Club last night and we shared a taxi to Dunlewey Street. I was sleeping at my mother's, you see.' Liz ignored Jane's scornful grunt and continued, 'He saw me safely into the house and I assumed he was coming over here. Ten minutes later he came pounding on my door. He was in an awful state ... somebody had beaten him up. I phoned for the ambulance and they took him to the Royal.'

'Have you two been carrying on?' Jane cried angrily.

'No, Mrs McGowan. It was nothing like that. We just shared a taxi.'

'If you aren't carrying on, how come our Danny started going to this golf club in the first

482

place? It's not his scene, so it's not. Eh? Bridget found out about it, didn't she? That's why she put him out of the house. I bet it was that Barney Kelly fella that beat him up. He idolizes Bridget so he does.' Liz gaped at Jane in horror as everything was twisted out of all proportion. Peter came to her rescue.

'Give over, Mam. Liz has just brought us the news. Our thoughts should be with Danny. Wake me dad and get over to the hospital. I'll go and tell Bridget.'

Liz left the house with him. 'Peter, please believe me, Danny and I are not seeing each other. If it was Bridget's father who beat him up, it wasn't because of me.'

'I believe you, Liz. Me mam got hold of the wrong end of the stick as usual. Thanks for taking him in last night and coming over this morning. We're indebted to you, so we are.'

Flushed rosy with sleep, Bridget looked lovely in her pink dressing gown. Hair a tousled cloud of curls and eyes shining with love, she was obviously delighted to see him. Her greeting was joyous and Peter wouldn't have been human if he hadn't pushed the bad news to the back of his mind and responded passionately to the warmth of her kisses. She looked so happy and fulfilled, he hated having to tell her about Danny's plight. He was aware it was going to make a difference to the plans they had tentatively made in the aftermath of their love-making the night before. The kisses intensified and they ended up in bed again.

Stretching luxuriously, Bridget thought, this is the way it should be. This feeling of oneness. The only snag was, Peter wasn't her husband. With a hint of regret in her voice, she said, 'Back to porridge. First I must shower and then go round and collect my young son. He'll be back from Marie's by now.'

'Bridget...'

Something in the tone of his voice warned her and she was immediately on her guard. 'What? Is anything wrong?'

He nodded.

'Well, tell me, for God's sake!'

'It's bad news I'm afraid, Bridget. Danny is in the Royal. He was beaten up last night.'

Her hand pressed in anguish against her lips muffled her reply. 'Is he badly hurt?'

'I don't know, but I think he's pretty bad.'

Her face crumpled up and she wailed. 'You mean, while we were...' Her hands fluttered about... 'You know? While I was being unfaithful, he was lying somewhere alone and wounded?'

'No, he wasn't alone. He was with Liz O'Hara.'

'Liz O'Hara? What was he doing with her?'

Peter shrugged. 'Your guess is as good as mine. Apparently he shared a taxi home from some golf club or other with her last night. She took him in and phoned the ambulance.'

Bridget sat in stunned silence for a while, digesting all she had heard. Then she was on her feet and heading for the bathroom. 'You'd better leave, Peter. I must get ready to go to the hospital.'

Tentatively, he tried to catch hold of her but she

pushed him away. 'Bridget, this doesn't change anything, you know,' he cried.

'Doesn't it? Well, you're wrong there, it changes everything,' she assured him sadly. Imagine her thinking she could be with Peter. Fool! She was a stupid fool.

After a shower, with some make-up on, she felt ready to face what the day might bring. She arrived at the hospital as Joe and Jane were leaving. To her dismay, Jane blamed her for what had happened.

Thrusting her face close to Bridget's, she hissed, 'This is all *your* fault. This wouldn't have happened if you hadn't put him out of the house in the first place. Imagine, cutting a man off from his own child at Christmas. You should be ashamed of yourself, Bridget Kelly!'

'Control your tongue, woman,' Joe admonished her. 'This is nobody's fault but his own.' He knew guilt when he saw it and it had been etched across his son's face. He didn't for one minute think Barney Kelly had had anything to do with his son's wounds, so what kind of trouble was Danny in? Now he assured Bridget, 'He won't be able to say much because his jaw's cracked, but he'll be glad to see you. Goodbye, love.'

She gave him a grateful smile. She had already been blaming herself for making Danny leave the house, and Jane's words had touched a raw nerve. Now she ignored her mother-in-law and entered the small ward where Danny lay.

Her breath caught in her throat and tears stung her eyes when she saw the state of him. 'Ah,

Danny, Danny. What have they done to you?'

He held out his hand and she gripped it tightly. 'Danny, did Shylock Muldoon do this? If it was him, mind you, I'm telling the police.'

Danny's lips clamped tightly together. Trust Bridget to open her big mouth. Thank God his da was already away home.

Groping for the pencil stub, he scribbled, *'Don't tell anyone. They'll kill me if you do. And don't, for God's sake, involve the police.'*

A hand reached over her shoulder and took the old envelope from her hand.

'Just how much do you owe Shylock?' Peter's voice was full of contempt.

It was Bridget who answered him. 'Six hundred and fifty pounds plus interest.'

'Jesus! And just how do you intend paying that back?'

Danny's eyes beseeched Bridget. Although her heart was breaking at the loss of so much money, she came up trumps. 'I'll see he gets it.'

Angrily, Peter rounded on her. 'Are you mad?' He jerked his head in Danny's direction. 'You'll get no thanks from him. He'll never change, you know.'

'I said I'd pay the money. Half of the savings are his anyway. But this will be the last time I help him out. Do you hear that, Danny? The very last time. How long will you be in here?'

Feverishly, her husband looked about for something else to write on.

Removing a small address book from her handbag, Bridget opened it at a blank back page and handed it to him.

He scribbled quickly and returned it to her. *'I can come home in a couple of days, if I've somewhere to go?'*

Peter read it over her shoulder. 'What about Liz O'Hara?' he asked. 'Weren't you with her last night? Won't she take you in?'

'Hush, Peter,' Bridget admonished him. Without another word he turned on his heel and left the room. She held her husband's eye. 'Will Liz take you in? Have you been seeing her?'

A shake of the head denied this.

Bridget sighed. 'If you have nowhere else to go, you can come to the flat for a few days until you feel better,' she said. 'But then I trust you to leave me and Martin in peace. Do you hear me? Don't for one minute think everything will be back to normal, 'cause it won't. I'll lift the money out of the building society and get our Patrick to pay off your loan.'

He grabbed gratefully for her hand but she eluded him. 'I'll have a word with the doctor on my way out. I'll be back later.' Her shoulders were slumped and her steps dragged as she left the ward. What was going to become of them all? The doctor was unavailable, but the staff nurse confirmed Danny's words. He'd had concussion and they wanted to keep an eye on him, but barring complications he should be out in a few days.

Sick at heart Bridget made her way across Grosvenor Road to Dunville Park. She intended taking the short cut through it and then the entry that ran along the back of Dunville Street and cut up Cairns Street towards her mother's house. The park was very run down nowadays, the fountain a dirty grey and long devoid of the cascade of water that used to fall from the raised centre in a continuous stream. The summer houses were badly in need of a coat of paint and looked neglected. But today the frost had transformed all that. It gave her a lift to see the fountain looking majestic in its white coat. The summer houses looked like the quaint winter chalets seen on the winter holiday programmes on TV. The trees lifted silver branches towards grey skies and the grass was stiff and crunchy under her feet. Another time she would have sat down on one of the frost-covered benches to admire all this false beauty. Today her thoughts were too sad to allow her to linger.

Last night, lying in Peter's arms, the future had looked as bright and clear-cut as the park did today, but she admitted to herself it had all been a foolish dream. Today she had returned to earth with a thump. She had no intention of staying with Danny as his wife, but stay she would and make a pretence of happiness for their child's sake. But what about Liz O'Hara? Was she back in the picture? What was she doing in Danny's company last night? And if it were true, where was her husband? Had Danny somehow managed to come between them? If he had, what about Peter? It had been bad enough before she had tasted the joy of his touch. Never before had she known such excitement; such fulfilment. Oh, if only she hadn't! Because now, the loss would be unbearable. How could she possibly live without him? But even if Danny had won Liz round and left the way open for her, could she blatantly live in sin with his brother? Their parents would be up in arms about it. There was no getting away from that and, to be truthful, she wouldn't blame them.

As she turned into the entry, a hand cupped her elbow and drew her to a standstill. Peter turned her round to face him. He was quite breathless. 'Bridget, I nearly missed you. I was waiting at the corner. I couldn't believe my eyes when I saw you leave the park.'

'I'm taking the short cut to my mam's.'

'I realize that. Listen, Bridget, you know this changes nothing? I won't let you change your mind.'

'Ah, Peter, you're being foolish. If Danny comes back I'll have to try to make a go of it. Surely you understand that? I've Martin to consider.'

'You weren't thinking of him last night.'

'That's below the belt, Peter. Last night I was in a fool's paradise. Today I'm back in the real world and it's far from pleasant where I stand.'

'Are you serious about paying Danny's gambling debts?'

'I've no other choice. And he is entitled to some of the money. But by the looks of him, he's going to be off work for a while. I only hope he doesn't lose his job, for I don't know how we'll manage if he's put on the dole.'

'Don't take him back. Bridget, I beg you not to take him back. He can have my room at home. I'll kip on the settee. Me ma will look after him.

There's absolutely no reason for you to take him back.'

'It wouldn't work, Peter. If he wasn't in the flat, the temptation to be alone together would be too strong for us.' She smiled slightly as she reminded him. 'Remember, I've no back door for you to steal in and out of. Folk would soon twig on and everything would become one big sordid mess. We wouldn't be able to look at each other without feeling some shame. At least my way, no one will know how we feel about each other.'

His heart soared. The temptation would be too strong! She did really care after all. 'Bridget, I know. And I don't care who else knows. I love you and that's all that matters as far as I'm concerned, and you know that I'd always treat Martin as if he were my very own flesh and blood. No matter who his father is. You'd have no fear on that score. I'll not be able to stay away from you. Don't you understand? I can't bear to think of *him* in the flat with you. What if he tries it on?'

She laughed at these words. 'Ah, Peter, I feel the same. But I married him, remember? For better or worse, Danny is my husband. Look, I can't stand here all day talking, I'll have to go now. I've to collect Martin. Me mam will be wondering what's keeping me.'

'I'll come with you.'

'It's better if you don't.'

'I insist...'

They were at the steps in the entry that led up to Cairns Street when he swung her into his arms.

490

'Peter, don't start anything. Someone might come along and see us.'

'I only want to hold you, Bridget. I get such comfort just from holding you close; knowing that you care.'

'I know what you mean.' She relaxed against him. He was right. It wasn't just a matter of sex any more. Just being together was enough. Reluctantly, she pushed him away. 'I must go, Peter. I've to go to the building society and all.'

'I'll come with you. It's not safe carrying all that money about on your own. Now, give me one last kiss.'

They climbed the steps and she stopped in dismay. What on earth was wrong? Benny's shop on the corner was all locked up.

'Ah, Peter,' she cried in dismay. 'I forgot. It's a bank holiday. The building society won't be open today.'

'Don't look so upset, Bridget. Another twenty-four hours won't make any difference.'

They collected Martin and explained Danny's situation to Martha, asking her to let Barney and the rest know what had happened. Martha was distraught. Who would do something like this she lamented.

'Ask our Patrick when you see him,' Bridget retorted, and regretted the words the minute they left her mouth. 'Forget I said that, Mam. See you tonight.'

They left Martha gaping after them in consternation. Surely Patrick hadn't hit Danny? Unlike his da, he was a big softie. Besides, why would he?

They took Martin with them when they went to see Danny that afternoon. A plaster covered the stitches in his cheek and the swelling was starting to subside. Nevertheless, he was still a sorry-looking sight. Martin sat on the bed and examined his face.

'Did you fall over, Daddy?'

It was a bit easier for Danny to talk now. 'Yes, love,' he managed to whisper.

'Where did you fall, Daddy?'

'Outside.'

'Mammy will kiss it better. Won't you, Mammy?'

'Yes, love.'

Danny eyed his wife intently in silence. He resented his brother hovering in the background. Had he no sense of decency? Why didn't he leave them alone?

Bridget understood, and answered his thoughts. 'It's a bank holiday.'

His face dropped in dismay and she tried to reassure him, 'I'll get it during my lunch hour tomorrow and Patrick will take it to Muldoon tomorrow night.'

Danny had to be content with this. Time dragged as they tried to make positive conversation. They talked about lots of things yet said nothing. At last Bridget could stand it no longer. 'Look, Danny, we'll run on now. You need to rest that jaw. How long will you be off work, do you think?'

He shrugged. 'Who knows?'

'Will you find out? You'll need to send in a sick note.' Lifting Martin up, she held him close to his father. 'Give your dad a big kiss, Martin.' The child being in her arms saved her from doing likewise and she could see this pleased Peter. 'See you tomorrow, Danny.'

Peter arranged to meet her the following day to take the money off her. They met outside the building society. 'How much should I take out, Peter?'

'Seven hundred.'

'Will that be enough? Surely the interest will be steep?'

'If it's any more, I'll put it to it. I intend going along with Patrick when he returns it. After all, if Muldoon's getting it all back at once, he should be satisfied. If not, perhaps a little threat about going to the police will help him see reason.'

Still she hesitated, a worried frown on her brow. 'Peter, I don't want him, or any of his cronies coming after you too. It's not your fight. I couldn't bear for you to get hurt.'

'Go on. Seven hundred.' With a little push he sent her in the direction of the door. He and Patrick were big guys. Surely if Muldoon got his money and a bit of interest, he wouldn't bother with any more beatings? Not quite convinced, he shrugged. They could but try.

Liz was in the kitchen washing the breakfast dishes when she heard her mother's key rattle in the lock. She waited for Kath to make her presence known. When the silence stretched she slowly entered the hall. David stood there, stiff and awkward-looking, just inside the door.

'I'm sorry for intruding. I suppose I should

have knocked, but Kath insisted I take her key and come and see you.'

Liz nodded and waited to hear more. Her husband, who always looked spruce and shining, looked wretched today. She wanted to go to him and take him in her arms and smooth the anxious lines from his face, but her feet wouldn't allow her to take the necessary steps. He had made no effort to approach her. If he wanted it that way, wanted to be free of her, she would not cling on but make it easy for him. He couldn't seem to find any words so she broke the silence that was becoming oppressive.

'Would you like some tea or coffee?'

'No, thank you. What I have to say won't take too long.'

Again the silence stretched but Liz decided to wait him out this time and stood passive. At last he spoke. She was surprised when all he said was, 'I think I will have a cup of coffee after all. If you don't mind?'

'No. It's no bother.' Nodding towards the parlour door, she said, 'Wait in there. I won't be long.'

David wasn't usually at a loss for words. Had he come to suggest they should divorce? Was he regretting not recognizing Irene's worth sooner?

Liz's heart was heavy as she prepared the tray. How had she let it come to this? Was it all her fault? Tears of self-pity threatened but she fought them back and was in control of her emotions when she carried the tray into the parlour. David had been prowling restlessly about the room. He took the tray from her and placed it on a small occasional table before sitting down. She poured the coffee and took the seat facing him.

'Liz...' He sat forward on the edge of the chair and his voice was entreating. 'I didn't mean it when I said you couldn't come back. It was just my hurt pride talking. Of course I want you to come home.'

'Didn't you mean it, David? After all, I did come back here with him against your wishes.'

'I know that! But I also know he lives on the Falls Road. I was being very unreasonable. He wasn't actually here with you.'

She wanted to grasp at this chance to put things right, to pretend Danny had left her at the door, but her conscience wouldn't let her. Enough lies had been told. 'What if I tell you he was here in this house with me last night? What then, David?' Why was she punishing herself like this? she thought, distraught. There was no need for him to know.

David smiled slightly. 'I wouldn't believe you.'

Still she turned the knife in the wound that was her heart. Had she not just vowed there would be no more lies? 'He was here, David.'

He went white and the hands resting on his thighs clenched into knuckled fists. For a minute she feared him, he looked so angry. He quickly regained his composure. 'All night?'

'No. Most of it.'

'Just one more question, Liz. So that I can get this straight in my mind and there's no chance of a misunderstanding. Did you go to bed with him?'

Trust David to phrase that question wrongly.

He could have asked if she'd had sex with Danny, or if anything had happened between them. But no, always the gentleman he avoided crudeness and asked if she had gone to bed with him. She thought of how she had lain on the bed beside Danny for hours, holding and comforting him until help arrived. What could her answer be but yes?

Aware that she should be putting him in the picture, explaining everything that had happened in detail, she resisted the impulse and forced the word 'Yes' out through lips that felt frozen. If he wanted to be free of her, why stand in his way. Why waste time explaining? Better to get it all over with, quickly.

White-faced, he was on his feet at once and reaching for his coat where it lay over the arm of the settee. 'That says it all then, doesn't it?' He shrugged and his lips twisted into an ugly grimace. 'I told Kath I'd be wasting my time. That Danny was all you wanted.' He stood at a loss for words for some moments. 'I will, of course, keep the promise I made to give you a divorce if things didn't work out. I will keep my word, Liz. You will be well provided for.'

He paused at the door. 'I don't know how you feel about the news regarding Neville? Kath seems to think you're upset. Is that right?'

She wished he would go. She was having difficulty holding back the tears. 'Yes.'

'Look, I want you to understand that I didn't know about him being your father until after you left last night. Had I known, perhaps things might have worked out differently. Knowing how you feel about your father, I realize it must have come as a terrible shock. I should have been there for you. Might have been able to soften the blow. However, we both know Neville's a decent bloke.'

'Decent blokes don't walk out on the mother of their child.'

She looked so woebegone he wanted to throw all ill feeling to the wind and take her in his arms and comfort her. Instead, he merely said, 'We don't know all the circumstances, Liz. Perhaps he had no other choice.' She remained silent. 'Well, look, if you want to stay at the bungalow, I'd be happy to move into a guest house until we see how things work out.' After all, the ball was in Danny's court now. He would want to look after her.

'That won't be necessary, thank you.'

Ah, well, he hadn't really expected her to jump at the offer. She would want to be on the Falls Road near Danny. To hide the hurt that was tearing him apart, David switched the conversation back to her father. 'I thought you liked Neville,' he said gently.

Her head reared back and her voice strengthened as she assured him, 'As a friend he was all right. As a step-dad I would have accepted him. But as a *father I* despise him.'

'Ah, Liz. Don't cut him out of your life as well. Don't make Kath choose between you and him. She would probably choose you but live to regret it. Why, she'd be heartbroken. And heaven knows, she deserves some happiness.'

'I know she does! No one knows that better

than me. But I can't accept Neville in the role of father. I just can't!'

Still he hovered at the door. She willed him to come to her; to take her in his arms and make everything right. Obviously the vibes weren't strong enough. He didn't, but merely said, 'Let me know if you change your mind about the bungalow. And, Liz, take a few days off work. No reason for the staff to know yet. Let's get used to being separated before the tongues start wagging, eh?'

Work? She hadn't given it a single thought. How could she ever go back and work alongside him the way things were?

She nodded and at last he left. After he'd gone she sat for a long time, her coffee growing cold. David hadn't even touched his. She couldn't believe her marriage was over. She hadn't done anything wrong except in her mind. But wasn't that as sinful as the deed itself?

Kath arrived late-afternoon. Since David's departure, Liz had spent the time aimlessly wandering about the house, asking herself if she should go and see Danny. In the end she'd decided against it. The footpaths were treacherous outside, and she had no boots or flat-heeled shoes here. Besides, she would hardly be welcome there anyway. She was at the parlour window waiting for a glimpse of Peter, to inquire after his brother, when her own mini drove up to the door, Neville behind the wheel. After a short discussion her mother left the car and approached the house.

Kath held out her arms to her daughter when Liz opened the door but she pretended not to notice and walked away down the hall, leaving her mother to follow.

In the living room, they faced each other. 'So, you've decided not to accept Neville?' Kath declared.

'Why should I?'

'Why not? He's your father.'

'The man you told me you despised.'

Kath had the grace to look shamefaced. 'I know. I was bitter and mean. He did his best for me over the years. You know we never wanted for anything, Liz. I took it all and never once thanked him. Even when I met him at Fortwilliam and he did everything he could to please me, I still couldn't find it in my heart to forgive him. That's why I never told you about him. That's why I made a fool of myself over Dick Kennedy. I was stupid. I've made a lot of mistakes, Liz, I admit that. Can you not find it in your heart to forgive me?'

Liz remembered David's words and decided not to put her to the test. 'I do forgive you. And I hope you and he will be very happy together. I mean that sincerely, Mam. Just don't expect me to welcome him as my father. I've managed without a father all these years so why should I need one now?'

'To please me?'

A shake of the head was all the answer she got.

'We brought your car up for you. David thought you would probably need it.'

'Thank you.'

Kath removed an envelope from her handbag. 'He asked me to give this to you.'

'I don't want it.'

'Liz, it's money!'

'I guessed as much. But David has always been so generous. I've plenty of money.'

'He will be angry if I take it back.'

'That's your problem. You shouldn't have interfered in the first place. Let him do his own dirty work in future.'

'Huh! There are times when I could gladly wring your neck, you're so stubborn. David is a good man.'

'There's no need for you to remind me of that, but I think you had better go now. Thanks again for bringing my car.'

Slowly, Kath returned the envelope to her handbag. 'What makes you think I'm going anywhere? I live here, remember?'

Liz's eyes widened in dismay. 'I thought you and Neville would be living in his house?'

'Not right away. Actually we intend getting married first. Besides, I have a job to go to tomorrow. And another thing – I'll have to see about putting this house on the market. Meanwhile, I'd better go out and send your father on his way.' She paused, hoping her daughter would relent and offer to drive him home. Liz remained stiff and unyielding. With a sigh, Kath went to inform Neville of his fate.

Jane buttoned her coat and pulled a woollen hat down around her ears. She dreaded going outside in this weather. Everything was white with frost and the footpaths were like glass. She looked over to where Joseph was sitting, his nose stuck in a book. 'I wish it would snow and get it over with,' she sighed.

'It's too cold for snow, Mam.'

'Joseph, I don't suppose you'd consider accompanying me over to the hospital?'

'Ah, Mam. You know how our Danny always picks on me. He can't say a civil word where I'm concerned.'

'He won't be able to talk much, son. He can hardly open his mouth. Come on, love. I'm nervous when it's icy outside.'

Reluctantly, he marked and closed his book. 'Mind you, if he starts on me I'm leaving, OK?'

Relieved that she had persuaded him, she waited patiently while he got ready. At the corner of Linden Street she nodded her head in the direction of the greengrocer's and thrust some money at him. 'Here, away in there and get him a bunch of grapes or something.'

'Mam, if he can't open his mouth, he won't be able to eat anything!'

'Maybe you're right. I never thought of that, son. Get him a bunch of flowers then.'

'Huh! You're going to carry them, mind.'

When he reappeared with two bunches of flowers, she almost swallowed her tonsils. 'Two bunches? Do you think I'm made of money or something?'

'I paid for one of them.'

Completely taken aback, Jane could only accept her change in silence. Wonders would never cease. Joseph spending some of his precious pocket money on flowers for Danny? That was a turn up for the book.

During the afternoons there were never many visitors and Danny, bored to tears, was pleased to see them and gratefully received the books his father had sent over. 'How are you feeling, son?' Jane asked solicitously.

He had been told that the hairline crack in his jaw was minor and if he didn't abuse the injury by talking too much, it would heal quickly. Saving his jaw from unnecessary movement, he reached for pencil and paper and informed her of this, adding that he was coming along fine. 'Thanks,' he mouthed the word to Joseph, as he accepted the great bunch of bronze and yellow chrysanthemums. A young probationer came along and exclaimed at the colourful bouquet.

'Aren't they gorgeous? They must have cost you a bob or two. I'll put them in a vase for you.'

A voice from the other end of the ward hailed her. Thrusting the flowers into Joseph's arms, she ordered him, 'Take these to the sluice room. Second door on the left out there. I'll come as soon as I can.'

The look on the lad's face was comical and Jane laughed aloud. 'She'll not bite you, son. She's only a wee slip of a lass. Away and do as you're told.'

Reluctant as usual to put himself out of joint, Joseph made his way along the corridor and found the sluice room.

He stood gazing about him. What was he supposed to do now? Two great big empty sinks but not a vase in sight. The door swung inward, almost knocking him off his feet.

'Oh, sorry.'

It was the same petite nurse, but this time he looked at her more closely. Dark auburn curls escaped from her cap and bright blue eyes begged his pardon. She was very pretty. 'I am so sorry. Are you all right?'

He felt the heat creep up his neck and across his face and inwardly cursed it. 'I'm fine.' He thrust the flowers at her and turned to leave. Her voice stopped him.

'I know you, so I do. You were in the same class as my brother at St Comgall's School. My friend Rosie used to fancy you.'

Joseph was flabbergasted. Some girl fancied him when they were at school? Huh! He didn't for one minute believe it. Throwing open a cup-board door, she pointed to a high shelf. 'Could you get that big vase down for me, please? How I wish I were tall.'

'You look just right the way you are.' He reached up and handed down the vase she had indicated, blush deepening at the audacity of himself. Imagine saying something like that to a stranger! And a female at that. He had never had the nerve to chat up girls at school.

'It's nice of you to say so but don't men prefer taller girls? Especially a tall fellow like you.'

He shrugged. 'Not all of them. When I was younger, small girls appealed to me.'

'Really? Rosie is small too. Would you like me to introduce her to you?'

'No! I'm not interested in girls.'

Her eyes swept him from head to toe. 'What a

503

pity. So it's true? You do have aspirations towards the priesthood?'

'What on earth gave you that idea?'

Opening the wrapping paper, she separated the flowers and started arranging them in the vase. 'You were so quiet at school, I guessed you were going to become a priest. Rosie thought you were just an arrogant so and so who thought you were better than anyone else.'

Joseph recalled his lonely, shy years at school and felt like weeping. Had he really come across like that? 'You couldn't be further from the truth on both counts,' he stiffly informed her, and left the room. Cheeky bitches! he thought. What right had they to label him like that? If they were really interested, why couldn't they see through his shyness and befriend him? It would have made such a difference to him. Anyway, it was too late now.

Back in the ward he discovered Ian had called in on his way to work and his spirits soared. 'Hello, Ian. How are you?'

'I'm fine, Joseph. How about yourself?'

'As well as can be expected in the circumstances.' Joseph gave him a knowing look and Ian felt like hitting him. If he continued like this, people would notice and start talking.

Stifling his anger, he forced a cheerful note into his voice. 'Well, Danny, I'll have to be going now or I'll be late for work. I'm on the early shift tomorrow. I'll call in to see you on my way home. And, for heaven's sake, don't fall down any more stairs. You're ugly enough.' He punched him playfully on the shoulder. 'Goodbye, Mrs

504

McGowan. Goodbye, Joseph.'

'I'm sure Mam and Danny would like a few minutes alone. I'll wait outside for you, Mam. Goodbye, Danny. I'll come back again tomorrow.'

Words trembled on Ian's lips but he clamped them together and turned away before he said something he might regret. Joseph had become a right pain in the neck. Somehow or other, he would have to get shot of him.

Both Danny and his mother gave Joseph a funny look. Was he doting? What on earth would they want to be alone for? He ignored them, determined to have a word with Ian before he took off. It was so hard to get hold of him nowadays. Ian strode quickly down the corridor, his face set in angry lines. Joseph had to hurry along to keep up with him. Outside the building, Ian rounded on him in anger.

'Will you kindly keep away from me? I've met a friend and I don't want you giving him or anyone else the wrong idea. So stay away from me and the flat. Got that?' With these words he quite literally flew away from this young man who was becoming such a nuisance.

Joseph was speechless. Ian had met a new friend? He watched him stride away through a blur of tears. This was all Danny's fault. Ian had been lonely for too long. He had sought company and met this new friend. That wouldn't have happened if Danny hadn't given Bridget cause to put him out of the flat. Joseph and Ian would have drawn closer then; their relationship would have blossomed. He had a good mind to go back in and give his brother a piece of his mind for spoiling his only true friendship.

'Is anything wrong?' It was the nurse, dressed in cape and outdoor shoes, obviously going off duty. 'My friend Rosie will be coming on duty soon. Would you like me to hang around for a while and introduce you?'

'No!'

His abruptness brought embarrassed colour to her cheeks. 'Oh, well. I was only trying to do you a good turn. Forget it!'

Stiff with offence, she turned to leave but he caught her arm. 'I'm sorry. I'm not used to small talk.' He groped about in his mind for something to say and came up with, 'What's your brother's name?' So inane. She must think him a right twit.

Mollified, she answered him. 'Same as yours, Joseph. Joseph McNally.'

'Of course. I remember him well. What's your name?'

'Sally McNally.'

'I don't suppose you'd come to the pictures with me some time?'

Surprised at his own audacity, he was prepared for the brush off and when she said, 'I'm sorry, but I'm not off duty again for another week,' was ready to retaliate with a snide remark.

'It's all right. I...'

Luckily, she didn't give him a chance to finish. 'Unless ... are you free tonight?'

He blinked in astonishment. 'Yes. Yes, I am.'

'There's a good show on at the Ritz.'

'Where do you live, Sally?'

'Peel Street.'

'I'll be at the corner at seven o'clock. Is that all right with you?'

'That will be fine.' She gave him a tremulous smile before hurrying away.

Joseph gazed after her in a daze. He had asked a girl, a very pretty one at that, to go to the pictures with him, and she had agreed.

Jane arrived at the entrance and he apologized for leaving, so abruptly. 'I was wanting to catch that young nurse before she went off duty,' he said by way of explanation.

'What did you want to catch her for?'

'What do you think, Mam? I asked for a date and she said yes.'

'Oh, did you indeed? Well, remember you have exams to study for and don't get too involved.'

'Mam, since I spent my spare cash on flowers for Danny, could you lend me some money?'

About to refuse, she saw how intense he was and changed her mind. 'All right. But don't think you can make a habit of it. In future don't ask anyone out unless you can afford it.'

'Thanks, Mam.'

On the walk home doubts were beginning to set in. He shouldn't have opened his big mouth. After all, she might not turn up and that would be another blow to his already bruised ego.

Kath and Liz had eaten their evening meal in comparative silence. As they were washing the dishes, Liz asked casually, 'Are you seeing Neville tonight?'

'I had invited him here but because of your

stubborn attitude towards him, he thought better of it. He wants to give you a chance to change your mind. And since we didn't want to leave you to mope about here on your own, I decided to stay in tonight.'

'Mam, I'm not moping! You should have said. I would have taken myself out somewhere.'

'Huh! With Danny McGowan? Do you think I'd be responsible for pushing you into his arms.'

'Of course not. He's in hospital.'

'In hospital? What on earth's wrong with him?'

Reluctantly, Liz recounted the episode of the night before, ending with. 'I would rather you didn't repeat this to David.'

'You mean, you didn't tell him?'

'It's none of his business.'

Kath fell silent for a short time, choosing her words carefully. She didn't want her daughter to get the wrong impression. David had refused to discuss their affairs and she didn't want to say anything that might lead Liz to think otherwise. However, she had come to her own conclusions. 'It seems to me it's very much his business. Does David think you spent the night with Danny?'

'He certainly does.'

'And did you not put him wise?'

'Why should I? It's what he wanted to believe. You saw him last night, fawning all over Irene Brennan. The beginning of a new year and he had no time for his own wife; wasn't in the least bit interested in me. He just wanted to be with *her*. That showed me where his true interest lies. He must surely know now that he's made a terrible mistake where I'm concerned. He's even offered to give me a divorce.'

Kath slumped against the sink, her mouth agape. 'He actually said he wanted a divorce?'

'Not exactly, but it meant the same thing.'

'Liz, you have to tell him the truth, before it's too late. He's not in the least bit interested in Irene. Or anyone else for that matter.'

'How do you know that, Mam. She's a beautiful woman after all.'

'Huh! she's not all that good-looking, for heaven's sake. If she scraped all that muck off her face you wouldn't say that.'

'Mam, I hate to remind you, but she did get Dick back,' Liz cried indignantly.

'That was below the belt, Liz. And you know I didn't really try to keep him. My heart lay elsewhere.'

'I know, Mam. I'm sorry.'

'David is under a misapprehension. He thinks you want Danny McGowan. Do you, Liz?'

'Look, Mam, I've been through all this before with David. It all boils down to a matter of trust. He doesn't trust me and what good is a marriage without trust? He doesn't believe a word I say. It will be better if we divorce. Besides, do you not think they're well suited for each other?'

Seeing tears trickle slowly down her daughter's cheeks, Kath gathered her in her arms. 'No, I don't think they look suited. And deep down in your heart, neither do you. Ah, Liz, you're your own worst enemy.'

'Promise me, Mam, you won't tell David anything I've told you?' Kath hesitated and Liz gripped her arm tightly. 'Promise me?'

Reluctantly, Kath agreed. 'All right, I promise. But you're being very foolish about all this, so you are.'

The following night, Peter and Patrick entered the lion's den with trepidation. Shylock Muldoon was a small man, but employed big, well-developed muscle men to look after his affairs. He greeted them cheerfully enough.

'Well, what can I do for you gentlemen?'

'It's about my brother-in-law's loan, Mr Muldoon. You know, Danny McGowan?'

'Oh, let me see...' He thumbed through some pages of a ledger. 'Ah, yes, Danny McGowan. I hear he had a nasty accident the other night?'

'Yes, he did.'

'Too bad. Fell down some stairs, I hear?'

'I believe that's what the police were told.'

'I'm sure it will teach him to be more careful in future.'

Peter wanted to puke at the way Patrick was handling the situation. However, Patrick had at first refused to allow him to accompany him. Only after Peter had sworn to hold his tongue did he relent.

'I think he will be very careful in future, Mr Muldoon.'

'He borrowed a lot of money from me, Patrick.'

He withdrew an envelope from his pocket. 'It's all there, plus fifty pounds interest, Mr Muldoon. It's every penny my sister could gather together. Is that enough?'

The money was shaken from the envelope and carefully counted. 'He has had this money a couple of weeks. Do you think fifty pounds is enough, Patrick?'

'It's all she has, Mr Muldoon. Peter here is Danny's brother. He and myself helped to make up the money,' Patrick lied. 'She hadn't enough.'

Muldoon's small beady eyes raked over Peter's face. 'Indeed?'

How Peter kept his tongue still he didn't know. He wanted to yell, that it was bloody daylight robbery and the police should hear about it. Instead he allowed himself a nod of the head in agreement. Two of Muldoon's thugs had come in and stood menacingly by the door.

'Well now, I know your Bridget and she's a canny wee girl. Bring me another twenty-five next week and we'll call it quits. Good day, gentlemen.' He dismissed them with a wave of the hand as if shooing a fly away.

Peter opened his mouth to remonstrate but Patrick gripped his arm warningly 'I'll be back next week with twenty-five pounds. And thank you very much, Mr Muldoon.'

Outside the premises, Patrick expelled his breath and said, 'For a minute there I thought you were going to blow it.'

'Huh! I'm sorry I didn't speak my mind. You were a right crawler in there. "Thank you very much, Mr Muldoon," he mimicked. 'You should have threatened him with the police, not let him order you to bring him another twenty-five pounds. It's disgusting so it is.'

Patrick looked amazed. 'I don't believe I'm hearing this. You don't live in the real world.' Thrusting his face close to Peter's, he explained,

'Believe it or not, we got off very lightly in there, so we did. Muldoon must be in a good mood. He had the upper hand, you know. If we'd started making threats, the interest would have kept going up and up. And he would have got it eventually. One way or the other. You just make sure your Danny puts an end to his gambling habit. He has no sense of responsibility.'

Peter's lips clamped together. He knew Patrick was right and he had no intention of defending his brother. In spite of himself the words escaped him. 'He's married to your sister. *You* weren't thinking of her when you introduced Danny to the card sharks. You must have known he was a novice at the game. Did you make money out of him as well? Eh, Patrick? Tell me that.'

Patrick's face convulsed with rage. With a roar he launched himself at Peter, almost knocking him off his feet. 'Why, you bastard! All you McGowans are the same. Irresponsible.'

Regaining his balance, Peter retaliated, 'Irresponsible? You didn't even warn Bridget. If I hadn't told her, all their savings would have been lost by now.'

'You? It was you told her? Why, you lousy home breaker, you...'

Fists flew and noses were bloodied before a couple of passers by managed to pull them apart. Disgusted with himself for allowing the scuffle to happen in a public place, Peter pressed his handkerchief to his nose and, turning on his heel, walked away.

Patrick's voice, thick with rage, followed him. 'You stay away from my sister, do you hear me?

Or it won't be just your face next time.'

Jane McGowan burst into tears when she saw the state of Peter's face. 'What on earth's going on? First Danny, now you. Who did this to you?'

'It's only a scratch, Mam. I was tidying up some of Danny's affairs.'

'So you know who beat him up?'

'Yes.'

'Was it the soldiers, son?'

'No, it wasn't.'

'Well, who ever did it can't just get away with it. You'll have to go to the police and tell them.'

'Mam, he was gambling heavily and got into the clutches of auld Muldoon. That's why Bridget put him out of the house. He gambled away most of their savings.'

'Ah, son, wait until your da sees you. He'll make you go to the police.'

'No, I won't.' Joe stood in the doorway, looking from one to the other. 'I heard what you said, son, and it must end here. You can't win against the likes of them loan sharks. Our Danny was a fool to get involved with them.'

Peter looked at him gratefully. 'I knew you would understand, Dad. I'll go and clean myself up.'

Washed and ready to go out, Peter examined his face in the mirror. Not too bad. The black eye had yet to come to its full beauty and his lip was only slightly grazed. Patrick Kelly was probably a sight sorrier-looking than him. He examined his grazed knuckles with satisfaction. He had enjoyed the feel of them crunching into Patrick's face. All his frustration had been behind those punches. He hated the way the guy was always hanging about, watching him with accusing eyes. Could he not see how unhappy his sister was? He wondered how Bridget would feel when she heard about the fight. At the moment she was at war with Patrick but the fact remained, he was her brother.

Well, he would soon know. Bridget had left the bottom door on the latch so he could enter the flat unobserved. Now he slipped in, released the snib, and climbed the stairs. What frame of mind would Bridget be in? Danny was being discharged from hospital in the next few days. He would gladly give up his bedroom if only she would refuse to take Danny back. She opened the door and gazed at him in dismay.

'Ah, Peter, I'm sorry you had to get involved. Did Muldoon's henchmen do that?' She entered his arms and gently touched his grazed lip.

He held her close and shook his head.

'Then how ... I don't understand?'

'Patrick and I had a fisticuffs after we left Muldoon's office.'

'What about?' She withdrew her comforting closeness and turned away in despair. 'As if I need ask.'

'I have been warned to keep away from you.'

She sighed. 'That won't be hard to do. Danny will be home tomorrow.'

'Tomorrow?'

She sighed deeply. 'Yes, they need the bed.'

He reached for her but she eluded him and

514

quickly entered the kitchen. 'I haven't eaten yet. Are you hungry?'

'A sandwich would go down well.'

'I worried all day about you. How did it go?'

'Muldoon asked for another twenty-five pounds next week and Patrick agreed.'

'That's not too bad. It will be worth it to be free of him.'

'If I'd been allowed to speak, I would have refused to give him any more. But Patrick made me promise to keep my mouth shut.'

'He did right! Muldoon had the right to demand interest. That was quite a large sum he loaned Danny.'

'I can't believe my ears. He was getting it all back at once. He doesn't deserve any more interest at all, for heaven's sake.'

'Look at it from his point of view, Peter. He loaned Danny all that money thinking he would probably double it or more by the time Danny finished paying it off. It was lucky we had the money in the building society or we would be in debt forever.'

'Lucky? Our Danny doesn't deserve you, Bridget. He should be left to stew in his own juice.'

'Ah, come off it, Peter. He's your brother! Would you like to see him get another beating?'

'No, but he should be left to pay it off a bit every week.'

'At that rate the interest would be colossal. We would never have a house of our own.'

'What do you mean – a house of your own?'

'Here, bring this tray through. I'm starving. We

can talk later.'

'Is Martin asleep?'

'Mam's keeping him tonight, so that I can get the flat ready for Danny coming home. You see, he'll have to get a taxi home from the hospital. I can't afford to take the time off work.'

'There is nothing wrong with his legs. What's to ail him walking home? He'd be here in ten minutes. How long will he be off work?'

'He has a sick line for a week. Hopefully that will be long enough.'

Peter watched her closely as they ate. He wished he could read her mind; find out just what else she had in store for him. It was after they had cleared the table that she broke the bad news.

'Peter, come and sit down. I want to talk to you.'

'You needn't bother talking, Bridget, if you're thinking of putting me off. I won't hear tell of it.'

'Peter, you know in your heart that there's no hope for us. I must try and make a go of my marriage. It's not something you can just walk away from.'

'Do you want to be miserable for the rest of your life, eh, Bridget? Think about it.'

'I have! I've thought of nothing else these past few days. But I think if we get a house away from here – you know, somewhere up the Falls or Glen Road – maybe Danny will settle down.'

'You really believe another house will make all that difference? You're kidding yourself.'

'I have to give it a try.'

'What about Liz O'Hara? Has Danny explained

what he was doing with her at that hour of the night?'

'No matter what he was doing, wasn't I doing likewise?'

He heard the tears in her voice but hardened his heart. 'Well, don't expect me to hang around,' he threatened. 'I'll have other fish to fry.'

He grabbed his coat and took the stairs in such a rush that for a moment she thought he had fallen. Tears poured down her cheeks as she pictured life without him. But she hadn't any choice in the matter, had she? Was she being foolish? No. Marriage was forever.

Liz chose the day David returned to work to collect her clothes and a few personal belongings from the bungalow. She stood at a window and stared out at the beauty of the garden, resplendent in its winter cloak. How she would miss living here. It was heartbreaking leaving all this peace and tranquillity to go back to streets patrolled by army jeeps and armed soldiers. Should she take David up on his offer to move into a guest house? But would that not put him out of his own home, maybe drive him into Irene's arms all the quicker? No, that would never do. She must make other arrangements and find her own accommodation.

Even so, there was no hurry. It would be some time before her mother's house was sold. Would David sell the bungalow and live in Irene's home, a big detached house on the front of Antrim Road? Liz hoped he would. The idea of him and Irene living here together filled her with sorrow.

But then, he would probably get it redecorated, like he had for her. Still, she considered it her and David's domain and it devastated her to think of Irene's intrusion.

Suddenly she squirmed. She must have eaten something that disagreed with her. These cramps and the feeling of nausea she had been having lately weren't natural. She would call in and make an appointment to see the doctor on her way back.

A short time later, after a final tour of her beautiful home, she left the keys to the bungalow on the hall table where David would be sure to see them, looked around for the last time and, heart breaking, stepped outside. Passing the route to the castle where she had been foolish enough to dally with Danny, she berated herself. Why on earth had she not sent him packing at the beginning? How could she even have contemplated having his child? What on earth had got into her? She had wanted the best of both worlds. Poor David. He must have known about those meetings between Danny and herself and thought the worst. And could she blame him?

At the doctor's surgery, Liz was pleased to learn that if she waited a short time he would be able to see her today, save her from having to come back. It would be good to get something for the nausea.

After a short wait she entered the room and he smiled kindly at her. 'I suppose you're eager to get started on these tests we've planned?'

A fist seemed to squeeze her heart when she realized those tests would be no longer necessary. Perhaps it was just as well they would not now take place. It was obvious that David had never wanted a child. Still, no need to explain her marital problems to the doctor. She might very well break down. Smiling brightly, Liz said, 'Well, actually, I'm here with a different complaint, doctor. I seem to have picked up some bug or other and feel quite ill at times. The sickness comes and goes.'

'Hmmm. Tell me more about it?'

She described in detail how she felt.

'I'll have to examine your tummy.' He nodded to a screen in the corner. 'Would you go behind there and loosen your clothing? No need to strip. Just expose your tummy. I think I know what's wrong with you.'

'That sounds ominous,' she said, a worried frown on her brow. She watched carefully as he examined her, but his expression remained inscrutable.

Quickly she dressed and was soon back facing him across his desk. He smiled at her. 'I can't be certain at the moment because you're not far gone but I feel confident you and David can forget all about the tests.'

She gazed at him in silence, digesting his words. At last comprehension dawned. 'You mean, I'm pregnant?'

'Well now, as I say, I can't be certain. When did you have your last period?'

'I'm two weeks late. But that isn't unusual. I often run late.' He must be mistaken. Hadn't she time and time again thought she was pregnant, only to be disappointed when the period finally arrived?

'Have you ever felt ill before?'

'No. Never this kind of sick feeling.'

'I think we can be pretty sure you're carrying a child, Liz, but come back when you've missed another period and I'll make arrangements for you to see a gynaecologist. Meanwhile, take plenty of rest and look after yourself. And ... congratulations.'

He beamed at her and she found herself grinning back. It really was wonderful news. 'I'll give you something to control the sickness,' he said.

Remembering the Thalidomide tragedy years ago, Liz was on her feet at once. 'I'd rather not, doctor, if you don't mind. Now that I know what's wrong, I'll suffer in silence. Sickness is a small price to pay for being blessed with a baby. Good day, doctor. And thank you very much.'

She sat for a long time in the car park, trying to control her excitement; unable to take in the fact that she might be pregnant. Just what difference would this make? Did she want to keep her husband in a marriage when he didn't want children? First she must wait until she was sure, then she would decide what to do. Come what may, this baby would be the most wonderful thing that had ever happened to her. Dear God, please let it be true that I'm pregnant, she prayed.

David's heart plummeted when he saw the keys lying on the hall table. He had hoped Liz would phone and then maybe he would have been able to persuade her to have dinner with him so that

520

they could discuss everything in detail. It was like a slap in the face, the final goodbye, seeing her keys lying there. She was making sure he got the message she was finished with him. How would he be able to bear it? Never to hold her again. He dreaded that big lonely bed waiting for him every night. His first wife's death had been hard enough, but Liz was still very much alive. And he needed her, desperately.

He headed for the drinks cabinet but stopped himself in time. Drink was not the answer to his problem. He could lose himself in work during the day, and must build up a social life to take care of the evenings. Deciding to eat out, he was heading for the shower when the phone rang. It was Irene.

'Hello, David. I wondered if you and Liz would care to join Dick and me for a meal at the golf club?'

He hesitated, but only for a moment. It was better than being alone. 'I'm afraid Liz is staying with her mother for a few days but I would love to join you. Save me from cooking for myself. What time?'

'About seven-thirty. See you there.'

A smile curved Irene's lips as she replaced the receiver. She was right! David and Liz had quarrelled on New Year's Eve. And Liz was staying with her mother? That was a sign something serious was wrong. That young lad Danny something or other must be the cause of it all. But surely she had misunderstood him? She could have sworn he said Liz was going to have his baby. Well, Irene intended to get to the bottom of this. Perhaps if she played her cards right David would turn to her for comfort. Then, who knows what the outcome would be? She hummed happily as she prepared for her evening with David. A pity Dick would be there, but that couldn't be helped. If things went according to plan, she would get rid of him later.

During the meal, David put on a brave front; keeping the conversation going in spite of Dick's glum responses. Afterwards, when they retired to the lounge and Dick went to the bar for the drinks, he found he had failed miserably. Moving closer to him, Irene placed a hand on his arm.

'You seem very unhappy, David. I hope all is well between you and Liz?'

'Of course it is. Her mother's putting her house on the market and Liz is helping her sort out furniture and things. Kath is marrying Neville Barnes.'

This floored Irene. Kath getting married? Had she got the wrong end of the stick again? She intended finding out. 'Oh, I thought you and Liz had quarrelled on New Year's Eve and that's why she's staying at her mum's?'

Remembering how he had sought her and Dick's company then, and let Liz go home alone, David was at a loss for words. Pride brought the lies to his lips eventually. 'Not at all. We had a misunderstanding regarding that young lout Liz was dancing with, but everything's fine now. Never better,' he stressed.

Irene's lips tightened. She knew when she was being put off. 'Then Liz isn't really expecting his baby?'

David went so white she thought he would pass out. 'What? What did you say?'

Dick had returned to the table and, alarmed at David's reaction to her words, Irene turned to him for confirmation. 'Dick, do you remember when we were dancing close to Liz and that young man on New Year's Eve?'

He eyed her warily. What was she up to now? 'Yes.'

'Well, can you remember what they were talking about?'

Dick scanned David's white face and muttered uneasily, 'Not really. Something about a baby.'

'Dick, think! He said Liz was going to have his baby, didn't he?'

'I don't know about that, Irene. All I heard was the mention of a baby.'

David had heard enough. He knew he should stay and put on a brave front but couldn't stomach it. 'If you will excuse me, I think I had better go home. I don't feel too good. Thanks for asking me to join you, I'll be in touch.'

Irene watched him walk unsteadily across the floor. He obviously didn't know about the baby. Was she wrong? One thing was for sure. Right or wrong, she had opened a right can of worms.

It was a bitter cold night and David had taken a taxi to the club. Now he decided to walk home. It was starting to snow and he lifted his face to the large cold white flakes, glad of their cooling effect. He felt he was burning up. How could Liz do this to him? She should have been honest! Told him she was expecting Danny McGowan's child. He had gone up to see her and she had

523

deliberately kept him in the dark. Let him find out from Irene. This was something he could never forgive. Their marriage really was over. He must stop deluding himself that there was any hope of a reconciliation.

Once home from hospital, Danny's recovery was slow but sure. He still looked battered, but his rib-cage was bound with bandages and the broken rib was knitting together healthily. To Bridget's great relief, being foreman and therefore able to take it easy for a while, he would probably be back at work within the week. He had been a bit put out to discover that she had decreed he should occupy the double bed on his own. She had borrowed a camp bed from her sister and this she had put alongside Martin's cot. He had offered to sleep on the camp bed but Bridget knew he would soon worm his way in beside her some night. That was something she would never let happen, no matter how cold or uncomfortable she might be.

Whilst covertly watching his reaction, Bridget had informed him that Liz was back living with her mother. He had appeared unconcerned though Bridget felt he was very much interested. She wasn't surprised when he said, airily, 'I must call over and thank her for rescuing me the other night.'

All she could do was wait and see what the outcome of the visit would be, and make her final decision then.

Kath watched in concern as her daughter tried in

vain to hide her morning sickness. Unable to bear the uncertainty, one morning she collared Liz coming out of the bathroom.

'Are you pregnant?'

Ruefully, she confessed, 'I think so but I didn't say because I won't know for sure for awhile yet. I've to go back to the doctor in another week.' A joyous smile covered her face as, confident of her mother's delight, she said, 'Isn't it wonderful? I'm afraid to believe it. It's like a miracle.'

The grin slipped at her mother's reaction. 'It's Danny McGowan's, isn't it?' Kath's voice was full of censure. 'I didn't think that you'd be daft enough to go through with it. How could you, Liz? How could you do this?'

Liz was so surprised, she was speechless. How could her mother think that? Then her conscience pricked her. Why not? Hadn't she told her mother of Danny's offer? Hadn't she tried to sway her into her way of thinking? What would David think when he heard? Would he also believe it was Danny's?

'Well, I'm not sure yet that I am pregnant but...'

Kath interrupted her. 'Believe me, you are. I hoped against hope I was mistaken. But I know the signs when I see them and I think you have been a very foolish girl. This is something David will never forgive, you know.' With these words, Kath entered the bathroom and the door closed behind her with an angry click.

Liz blinked tears away at the unfairness of it. Her mother hadn't even given her a chance to defend herself. Her head lifted and her chin thrust out. What did it matter who thought it was

Danny's child? She knew it was David's and that was all that mattered.

As the day wore on, Liz softened and relented towards her mother. After all, she had every right to think as she did. Later that afternoon she tried to explain just who the father of the baby was. To her great dismay Kath didn't want to listen.

'Look, Liz. I'm very sorry, but it's none of my business. I just don't want to know all the sordid details. I'm so disappointed in you. I also feel guilty. When you discussed the idea with me, I should have done more to put you off the silly notion. But I never really thought you'd go through with it. Now your marriage is really over, and will Danny leave his wife for you? I very much doubt it. Remember, I learned that the hard way.'

'This will come as a surprise to you, Mam, but I don't want Danny to leave his wife. I...'

'Just as well! Because, believe me, he won't,' Kath angrily interrupted her. She was distraught. Was her daughter to share the same fate as herself – a lonely life rearing a child on her own? Oh, but she could wring Liz's neck, she was so angry with her. She quickly left the room before she said something irrevocable. Liz was going to need her help in the months ahead.

Danny McGowan was the last person Liz expected to see when she opened the door that afternoon.

Her eyes scanned his face. Although multi-coloured and somewhat bruised, it didn't look too bad now the swelling had gone down. 'What

526

are you doing here?'

'Can I come in for a moment? I just want to thank you for rescuing me the other night.'

'Well, you've thanked me. There's no need to come in.'

'Are you all that frightened to be alone with me, Liz?' he taunted her.

With a disdainful flourish she motioned him in. 'You can get that idea out of your head right away. I've no interest in you whatsoever. Now, say what you have to say and then get out.'

Danny was baffled by her attitude. He didn't understand. Hadn't she been glad to let him kiss and cuddle her the other night? 'What on earth are you playing at, Liz?'

'Look, Danny. I'm not playing at anything. I just want to make it clear to you, once and for all, I'm not in the least bit interested in you any more. Get it?'

'Why are you living here then? Have you and David not separated?'

'That's none of your business! But in case you're still harbouring the thought I might need your help where a baby is concerned, forget it. I'm pregnant.'

'Is it David's?'

'Of course it's David's.'

'I don't understand.'

'You're not meant to. Now, if there is nothing else, I've a lot to do.'

He dithered, at a loss for words. 'Are you sure about this, Liz?'

'I was never as sure of anything in my life before.'

'If you change your mind, you will let me know?'

'I won't change my mind,' she assured him.

'But if you do, you will get in touch with me, won't you?' he persisted.

'I won't.' He opened his mouth to argue and she cried in frustration. 'All right! If I change my mind, I'll let you know. Now get out.'

'Now don't you forget, Liz. And congratulations. I know how much this baby means to you.'

Tears smarted in her eyes as she closed the door on him. Congratulations! Apart from the doctor, he was the first to say that to her. If only her mother could feel happy for her and congratulate her, things would be more pleasant around the house. But one thing Liz had made up her mind about. No matter what happened, she had no intention of explaining to anyone again who the father of her child was.

Chapter Nine

After much deliberation, Liz decided to seek a meeting with David to tell him about the baby. When all was said and done, it was his child. It was only right he should be given a choice as to what he intended doing about it. Even if he hadn't wanted a child, surely the fact that she had conceived would make some difference? After all, she was his wife. It wasn't as if it was a one-night stand. It was to be expected in marriage, even if he did think himself infertile. He was wrong and now it could be proved. But there would be none of that nonsense about having blood tests. He would have to take her word for it, or else...

Or else what? She would love to have been able to discuss the matter with her mother, find out her opinion. However, to her great dismay Kath was still silent and unforgiving so Liz had decided to continue keeping her in the dark as to the father's true identity. After all, even if the baby was Danny's, her mother had no right to sit in judgement of her. Annoyed at her attitude, Liz just could not find it in her heart to tell her the truth.

It saddened her that her husband had not been in touch with her since New Year's Day. It showed how little he cared. Still, he had to be told. In some trepidation she phoned him. It was a Sunday evening and he answered on the second ring. She could hear classical music playing softly in the background. Pictured him reclining in his big comfortable chair, legs spread out, eyes closed, giving himself up to the music. How she wished she could be there with him, wallowing in the tranquillity. When she spoke, she could actually hear him sit up to attention. He returned her greeting cordially enough but when she asked him to meet her in town for lunch the next day, there was a long pause.

Taken aback, she said, 'If you're too busy, it doesn't matter. I understand. However I would like to see you sometime in the near future. I've something important to tell you.'

Another pause, shorter this time. 'All right. Let's meet tomorrow. Where would you like to eat?'

She mentioned a select restaurant in the town centre and he said he would book a table and see her there at one o'clock.

Slowly, with a hand that shook, David replaced the receiver in the cradle. Tomorrow. He was seeing Liz tomorrow. Rising to his feet, he went to the big ornate mirror that hung above the mantelpiece and examined his image. God, but he looked awful. Old and haggard. No wonder Danny had won hands down. It was two weeks since Irene had dropped her bombshell about the baby. Only hard work had kept him from losing his sanity altogether. He had informed the staff that Liz would be away for some time as she needed a break. Their sly comments about the patter of tiny feet nearly broke his heart. How different things would be if only the child were his; how joyfully he would revel in their good-natured banter. He neither confirmed nor denied the rumours that were rife. They would know soon enough that he and Liz were to divorce.

He had eaten a snack in town during his lunch break each day and avoided the golf club. Irene had visited him a few times on different pretexts and had eventually lured him back to Fort-william, to the cabaret nights. Tonight, for the first time, he had relaxed his guard and indulged in some whiskey; seeking solace in the amber nectar, from the misery that threatened to engulf him. And tomorrow his wife wanted to meet him. Wasn't that always the way? He had remained relatively sober since learning the truth; tomorrow he would probably have a hangover. He replaced the top on the bottle and returned it to the cabinet. He would have a long hot soak in the bath and maybe get a full night's sleep for a change. Tomorrow! He was seeing her tomorrow. He couldn't believe now how nervous he felt.

David watched Liz enter the restaurant and pause to scan the crowded room. All eyes gravitated towards her. And no wonder. She looked beautiful in a russet-coloured coat and matching fur-trimmed hat. Her eyes sparkled and her cheeks were glowing pink from the frosty weather. He lifted his arm to get her attention. Acknowledging him with a nod and smile, she slowly made her way across the floor to where he sat at a window table, her progress followed by admiring eyes.

Her beauty only increased his sense of loss. He now regretted agreeing to meet her. It could only make him feel worse. Didn't he already know what she wanted to tell him? Wasn't he already aware that it was Danny McGowan who had put that glow in her countenance, that bounce to her step? However, when she had phoned the night before, in spite of everything, the chance to be alone with her one more time overrode all the bitterness he harboured against her for what she was putting him through.

David stood up as the waiter hurried forward and pulled out a chair for her. 'You look wonderful.'

'Thank you.' Her eyes swept over him. He was his usual spruce self. Pale grey suit, snow white shirt and conservative silk tie. However, on closer inspection his pale, drawn face caused her to cry in concern, 'You don't look too good. You're much too thin.'

She removed the hat and, placing it on the window-sill, loosened her hair with her fingers and a shake of the head. The pale midday sun filtered in, showing the translucency of her skin and setting alight the bright chestnut highlights in her hair. He longed to feel its silky softness under his hand. Even his cheek, if only... Realizing that she was looking at him questioningly, he brought his wandering thoughts back to reality.

'I beg your pardon?'

'I said, you're much too thin. Are you not eating?'

'That's probably due to not getting any good

home cooking these days.' He smiled wryly. 'I have a snack in town most days. But don't worry about me, I'm managing all right. Wine?'

'No. I'll forgo that at the moment, thank you,' she said, a faint, secret smile curving her mouth.

He nodded. He knew her well enough to know she wouldn't drink while pregnant but had felt obliged to ask. After all, he was not supposed to know her big secret.

'What about a soft drink?'

'I'll have a glass of water if I may, please?'

'Certainly.' A flick of his fingers brought a waiter to the table. 'A jug of iced water please.'

She loved the way he could command attention, even when the place was crowded. As she perused the menu, she wondered how to break the news to him. How would he react when he heard he was to be a father? She stole a glance at him and met his eyes. He looked away before she could put a name to his expression. Was it regret? Even if he regretted their marriage and didn't want a child, she knew he was a good enough person to want to do what was best for his own flesh and blood. But would he consider their getting back together again? Why should he, after all? She had brought him nothing but unhappiness. But perhaps for the baby's sake, he might take her back. Or in the circumstances was that expecting too much? Had Irene got her hooks into him good and proper this time? Would he not want his life cluttered up with all the disruption a baby brought with it, broken nights and constant worry?

If only she hadn't taken his love for granted. If

only she could win a second chance to show him how much she really cared. To tell him she loved him! Not once had she said those precious words to him. She had taken all he gave, and in return all she could think about was Danny McGowan. How had David put up with her for so long? No other man in his right senses would have been so understanding.

They discussed work as they ate. He brought her up to date on the day-to-day running of the factory and how the new workers were faring, his comments about the funny antics of some of the staff making her laugh. Liz lamented how sad she would be not to be able to return to work. To her concern, he let this pass without comment. She had hoped this would give her the opening to explain about her condition. However, he just nodded his agreement without even asking the reason why. Was he glad she would not be returning? Could he not even bear to work alongside her any more? No other opportunity presented itself. They had almost finished their dessert and still she had not broached the subject that had brought her here today. Seeing a slight frown furrow her smooth brow, David decided to help her out.

'You were wanting to tell me something important, Liz?'

He watched her lick her lips and her mounting uncertainty was clearly visible. 'If it makes it any easier, Liz, I know what you're going to tell me. You're pregnant, aren't you?'

Her bright tawny eyes widened in surprise. 'How did you know?'

He dragged his eyes away from the beauty of hers. 'Irene told me.'

'Irene Brennan? But how did she know?' Her bewilderment was apparent.

'That night on the dance floor, she heard Danny say you were having his baby.'

It was so unexpected Liz was dumbfounded. Irene was certainly going all out to get him, telling lies like this!

Before she could refute it, David continued, bitterly, 'I have to tell you that hurt, Liz. I went to see you and you never mentioned it to me. You should have told me you were expecting Danny's child. Instead you left me to hear about it second-hand and from Irene, of all people. That was very cruel of you, Liz.'

At last she managed to untangle her tongue. 'David, you've got it all wrong! When you came to see me, I didn't even know I was pregnant.' She could see he didn't believe her and her heart sank. 'Honestly, David.'

He shrugged, as if in disbelief. 'Well, it's none of my business anyway, Liz. Is Danny still separated from his wife? Are they going to divorce?'

She was in such a bemused state, she didn't know which way to turn. How did he know that Danny and Bridget were living apart? Kath must have told him. No wonder he had been so quick to believe the child was Danny's. He probably thought Liz was the reason Danny and Bridget were living apart. There was obviously no doubt whatsoever in his mind about the baby's parentage. And after the antics of her, why would there be? Tears stung her eyes, but pride came to her rescue. She could not tell him the truth now. He would think she was trying to coerce him into taking her back. Would think she wanted the best of both worlds, the prestige of being his wife while she raised Danny's child.

'Whether or not they divorce remains to be seen.' She groped about in her muddled mind for something to say to change the subject. Anything at all. 'Any sign of Dick and Irene getting married?'

'She isn't seeing him at the moment. They have agreed to part for a while.' David smiled grimly. 'Dick will be sorry he was stupid enough to let Kath slip through his fingers. I hear she's going to marry Neville. Have you resolved your grievances with him yet?'

'Not exactly. However, we're on speaking terms. They have been to see St Paul's parish priest and he's agreed to marry them. Just a quiet ceremony during Easter week.'

David looked pleased. 'I'm glad they are to marry in the Catholic Church. Kath must be so happy.'

'Probably. We haven't talked much about it. *She* blames me for our break-up.'

'And you think it was *my* fault?' he asked, eyes widening in surprise.

'Do you not agree we were both to blame?'

For the life of him David could not see what he had done wrong. Nevertheless, he found himself nodding in agreement. If it helped her for him to shoulder some responsibility, he would certainly play along.

Liz squirmed inwardly; she had put him on the

spot and out of pity he had agreed with her. How she wished herself far away from this place! Away somewhere quiet where she could get things straightened out in her mind. Irene and Dick weren't seeing each other. So was David seeing her instead? And was Irene fawning all over him, making him feel wanted? The idea of him and Irene together made her feel quite ill. She blinked back tears and with difficulty forced herself to finish her dessert. Pushing her plate to one side, she smiled weakly across at him. 'The meal was lovely, thank you. Now I've told you how things stand, I must be on my way.'

'Won't you have a cup of coffee, Liz?' he exclaimed in dismay.

She shook her head and was reaching for her hat when he caught hold of her hand. 'Liz, can we not go somewhere more private and have a coffee?'

His touch was sending little tremors of excitement coursing through her body. Gently, she released her hand. 'No, I'm full to the brim, thank you.' She couldn't bear to be alone with him. Not now she knew how much he meant to her and how little he cared.

At a loss as how to keep her with him any longer, he said, 'Well, if you need any help, anything at all, you know where to find me. For your sake, I'll try and hurry the divorce through. When is the baby due?'

'About August.'

'Don't worry about money, Liz,' he said gently. 'I'll see you're all right.'

She looked into his caring eyes and wept inwardly. Through her own obstinate behaviour, she had lost this wonderful, kind man. What a stupid fool she was. 'I know you will, David. Thank you.'

'Have you the car with you?'

'No, I got a lift down. I'll call a taxi.'

He rose to his feet at once. 'There'll be no need for that. I'll drive you home.' He beckoned to the waiter. 'My bill. At once, please.'

'No. You go on back to work. I know how busy you must be. It's not necessary to see me home, I'll be all right.' Liz just wanted to escape all this kindness and concern. Her emotions were all on edge and she was afraid of losing her self-control.

'I insist.' David paid the bill and escorted her from the restaurant.

How could she sit beside him in the close confines of the car without pouring out what was really in her heart? Throwing herself on his mercy? That would never do. The last thing she wanted was to make him feel duty bound to take her back because of the child, and live in a loveless marriage. He deserved his chance of happiness with Irene. While he had shown no desire whatsoever to be close to her, she longed for the comfort of his arms. She couldn't bear to live on those terms with him. She turned to him in despair, an excuse on her lips. 'David, I'm meeting someone.'

He had taken her arm and was leading her towards Rosemary Street where the car was parked. Immediately he removed his hand and widened the space between them as if she had suddenly developed leprosy, his steps slowing to a halt. 'Oh, I see. Well, that hits that idea on the head then.' They faced each other and his eyes drank in every detail of her features, as if seeing her for the last time. 'It was nice seeing you. And I hope you will be very happy, Liz, whatever you decide to do.'

'Thank you. I hope you find the happiness you deserve with Irene.'

He watched her walk away and his heart went with her, leaving a hollow feeling in his chest. Did she really think he wanted Irene? Hardly. He had told Liz often enough he wasn't in the least bit interested in her. Of course, at the moment anyone could be forgiven for thinking otherwise. He knew there was talk about them at the golf club. It even boosted his ego to think that he and Irene were regarded as a couple, poor fool that he was. Though Liz would not know about that. And, to be truthful, Irene was being very kind to him. She was going out of her way to see he didn't sit at home moping over his loss. Nor was she making any demands on him. They were just good friends and he needed her company. He suppose it helped to ease Liz's conscience to think he had someone to turn to. Meanwhile, the light was going out of his life.

Jane gaped at Danny in dismay. 'You're going to buy a house up Andersonstown? You'll never be able to afford it, son.'

'We've worked it out, Mam, and with both of us working, we'll manage all right.'

'Do you not want any more family?'

'All in good time, Mam. We're still young.'

'It was bad enough when you were over on the Antrim Road, but if you move to one of those new estates up Andersonstown, we'll never see Martin.'

'You will, Mam, I promise I'll bring him down every weekend to see you.'

'Mmm. If Bridget lets you.'

'Of course she will. Mam, Bridget is a good wife and mother. I'm very lucky she took me back. We had a big deposit saved towards a house and I blew most of it gambling.'

'She must have driven you to it, son. You were never that way inclined before.'

'Look, Mam, I can't let you put the blame on Bridget. I'm the one who was at fault. I never really put any effort into keeping our marriage together. But I've learned my lesson now. From here on I'll treat her with the respect she deserves.'

'Huh!' Jane was not to be appeased. In her eyes her sons could do no wrong. 'She shouldn't have led you into a shotgun wedding in the first place.'

'Now, Mam, you know very well it takes two. Besides, we haven't got a house yet. We could still be here this time next year for all we know.'

'What about Liz O'Hara?'

Danny's eyes narrowed and his face became guarded. 'What about her?'

'She has that bloom about her. I'd bet my last penny she's pregnant.'

'What's that got to do with me?'

'Well, you've been knocking about with her lately, haven't you? Is it yours?'

'Mam, she's a married woman! Why shouldn't

she be pregnant? And I wasn't knocking about with her, as you so crudely put it.'

Jane's look was sceptical. 'I haven't seen any sign of her husband lately. Don't you think that strange, son? Just Liz and Kath and that big man they say Kath's going to marry.'

Danny seized the chance to turn the conversation away from himself. 'That big man happens to be Liz's father,' he said, and had to laugh at the expression on his mother's face.

'I don't believe you!' she gasped.

'Cross my heart and hope to die.'

'Well, what do you know? After all these years he's going to make an honest woman of Kath. She's a fool, taking him on. I'd have chased him so I would. She's in her prime while he's over the hill. She'll spend the rest of her days looking after him.'

'Well, she's marrying him, so she must love him. Look here, Mam, this was told to me in confidence. Sure you won't spread it about?'

'Not a word will pass my lips.'

He laughed aloud at the pious expression on her face. 'Not that it will make any difference,' he conceded. 'Kath won't be worrying about the neighbours. He has a bungalow somewhere over near Belfast Castle, I hear, so I suppose they will live over there.'

'Never!'

'Yes, I would think so.'

'What about her house?'

'She'll probably sell it.'

'Son, would you not put an offer in for it?'

For a moment Danny was taken aback. Why

541

hadn't he thought of that? He found himself considering the idea. Could he persuade Bridget? Then he thought of Peter, forever lurking in the background, and shook his head.

'You'd have no trouble getting kids minded if you lived there. And the schools are handy and everything.'

'Mam, Bridget wouldn't hear tell of it. Act your age. Live facing her mother-in-law?'

'I wouldn't interfere, son,' Jane cried earnestly. 'You tell her that. Tell her I'd mind my own business, but I'd be there if she needed me.'

He laughed again at this. 'You, mind your own business? You wouldn't know how. Look, I'll have to run away on. I'll see you at the weekend.'

Her parting words followed him, giving him food for thought. 'Think about it, son. Those parlour houses are big and airy. You could do a lot worse.'

Peter waylaid Bridget during her lunch hour one day. 'You're avoiding me, Bridget. It's not fair. I must speak with you.'

'Look, Peter, I've made up my mind. All the talking in the world won't change it. So please leave me alone.'

'Me ma says you and Danny are looking at houses on Andersonstown Road.'

'That's right.'

'You can't move away up there. Why, I'll never see you.'

'That's one of the reasons I'm moving.'

'You're running away, Bridget. Do you not miss me at all? I sure as hell can't stop thinking of you.'

'Of course I miss you!' Her expression softened as she gazed at him. 'We're very lucky, Peter, that we had those few precious times together...'

He interrupted her angrily. 'Don't talk rot! They just went to show that we're meant for each other. Can't you see that?'

'Look, Peter, I'll have to go. I've a lot to do before I go back to work. I'll see you later.'

Before she could move away he gripped her arm and pulled her close. 'Are you and Danny ... you know?'

His touch was weakening her resolve. She wanted to move closer; find comfort in his embrace. If only things were different and she could spend the rest of her life with him. But that was not for her. She'd have to put a stop to this once and for all. But how? Make him believe that everything was wonderful between her and Danny? 'Yes, of course we are. We've decided to do our best for Martin's sake. I've got to give it my best shot, Peter.'

'How can you, Bridget? How can you let him touch you, after all he's put you through?'

'Talk sense, Peter. He's my husband, for heaven's sake. It's just an act after all! Part of married life. It can be quite exciting at times,' she lied.

'I don't believe you! What about us? We were special! Can't I see you sometime?'

'It wouldn't work, Peter.'

'Bridget, please, I beg you, don't do this to me.'

'Peter, you're a wonderful person and there's plenty of girls will be only too glad to have you.'

'I only want you.'

'You'll soon change your mind.'

'I won't, you know. There was a time when I convinced myself my feelings for you were just brotherly, but not any more. I love you, so I do. Nobody else can take your place.'

Tears filled her eyes and he wished they were anywhere but on Royal Avenue. 'Peter, please leave me alone. I've enough to put up with, without you badgering me.'

'But I can't help myself. Surely you don't expect me to stand back and let you ruin all our lives?'

'Our lives won't be ruined. Can't you see? This is a second chance for all of us, and we're very lucky to get it.'

Seeing he was getting nowhere, Peter changed tack. 'What about Liz O'Hara? She's pregnant and separated from her husband. Can that have anything to do with Danny wanting to move away up Andersonstown?'

Bridget's eyes widened. 'Who says she's pregnant?'

'Oh, me mam. She says she can read the signs.'

'What makes you think Danny's running away from her? Surely you're not suggesting...'

'No. No, not really. Liz isn't the sort to stray.'

Immediately Bridget's chin rose in the air and she backed away from him. 'Oh, and I am, eh? Is that what you're saying?' she hissed. 'Was I an easy lay? Well, was I? Is that why you're hounding me?'

'You're deliberately twisting my words, Bridget!'

'Well, let me tell you something, Peter McGowan. No matter what, for Martin's sake,

I'm going to try and save my marriage. He's more important to me than you or anyone else, and he loves his daddy. What you said just now makes me more determined than ever. Goodbye, Peter. And please don't pester me again.'

Neville was in the living room waiting for Kath when Liz let herself into the house. Unaware of his presence, she removed her coat and hat and went straight into the kitchen. Running cold water over her wrists to reduce the feeling of faintness that threatened to engulf her, she wept, sore and hard, at the hurt that gripped her. The sounds brought Neville to his feet in alarm, and into the kitchen.

Dismayed to see the state she was in, he cried, 'Liz, what's wrong?'

She swung round in surprise and blinked at him. 'Nothing,' she gulped. 'I didn't know you were here. Where's Mam?'

'She's upstairs. Liz, tell me what's wrong? Let me help you, please.'

'You can't. Nobody can help me. Nobody cares what happens to me.'

'Ah, Liz, you know that's not true. Besides, it can't be all that bad. Aren't you expecting a much-wanted child, eh, love?'

His sympathy was too much to bear and the tears fell faster.

At a loss what to do, afraid to approach her in case of rejection, he stood helpless, watching her fight for self-control. Her hand made a slight movement towards him and that was all the encouragement he needed.

In two strides Neville was with her. Gathering her close to his chest, he muttered, 'There, love. Cry it all up. You'll feel better for it.'

Kath descended the stairs quietly and stood in the doorway astonished at the sight before her. Over Liz's shoulder, with a slight movement of his head, Neville motioned her away, Quietly, she retraced her steps upstairs. She was nonplussed. Liz couldn't say a civil word to Neville since finding out he was her father, and to see her now crying her eyes out in his arms simply amazed her. Then she was back on her feet. What on earth was she doing sitting up here? Something awful must have happened for her daughter to be in such a state. Quickly she descended the stairs again.

Neville's voice reached her from the kitchen. 'I'm making Liz a cup of tea. Would you like one, Kath?' He stood in the centre of the kitchen, a finger pressed warningly to his lips. 'Go easy on her. She's very upset,' he mouthed.

'Yes, I'd love a cup, please.'

She joined Liz where she sat huddled over the fire in the living room, her hands pressed between her knees as if for warmth. 'Are you cold, love? Here, let me put some more coal on the fire.' Kath busied herself with the coal shuttle and tongs. Then, glancing at her daughter, appeared to notice for the first time that she was upset. 'Liz love, what's wrong with you?'

She blew her nose noisily and rubbing one cheek after the other with the back of her hand, grimaced. 'I don't know what came over me, Mam. I suppose it's the old hormones playing up.'

546

'What happened, Liz? Something must have bothered you, for you to be in this state.'

'Ah, you know how it is. It just suddenly hit me that I'm the only one who cares about this baby. But I'll make sure it doesn't suffer because of any failing on my part.'

'What do you mean? Is Danny McGowan not going to leave Bridget, after all?'

'No, he's not,' Liz cried in frustration. 'At least, not that I'm aware of.'

'Well, you can't say I didn't tell you so...'

'No, I certainly can't! And, Mam, strange though it may seem, I don't want to have anything to do with him.'

'Huh! A bit late in the day for that, isn't it?'

'See what I mean?' Liz placed a hand gently on her stomach. 'Poor little mite. This baby is your grandchild, and you can't bear the thought of me having it. Furthermore, the way things stand, it will probably be the only child I'll ever have. Therefore, your only grandchild. No matter who the father is, you should be happy for me.'

'Ah, Liz, I am. Honestly.'

'Well, I wish you'd show it sometimes! I've felt so alone this past few weeks.'

'God, Liz, you should have said. I didn't realize you felt this way.'

'Huh! No, you were too busy punishing me because in your opinion I'd sinned.' She glared at her mother and cried indignantly, '*You* of all people.'

Kath was flabbergasted. There was no need for this kind of talk. Liz should watch her tongue. She was about to retaliate when Neville entered the room and gave her a warning glance. Setting the tray on the table, he handed a cup of tea to Liz. 'I think your mother was just sad that you and David are divorcing,' he said soothingly. 'But believe me, Liz we'll both be very glad and proud to welcome this baby into our lives.' He handed Kath a cup. 'Isn't that right?'

'Of course it is.'

'Neville?' Liz's voice was low and tentative.

He bent closer to hear. 'Yes, dear?'

'Will you ever be able to find it in your heart to forgive me? I've been so rotten to you lately.'

Reaching for her free hand, he clasped it between his. 'Ah, Liz, I don't blame you in the least for being annoyed with me. I certainly haven't been a real father to you. But I do promise to be the ideal grandfather.'

'You wouldn't mind if it was Danny's child?'

'Not in the slightest. No matter who the father is. This is *your* baby. My grandchild, and I'll do all I can for it. I'll even spoil it rotten.'

'Thank you, Neville. My baby won't have a proper father, and to think I was trying to deny it a grandfather as well is preposterous. I must need my head examined.'

'Drink your tea, love and then take a lie down. You'll feel all the better for it.'

'What do you think brought all that on?' They had persuaded Liz to go upstairs to rest and now Kath questioned Neville. 'Did she say anything before I arrived on the scene?'

'Not a word. Who was she meeting for lunch today?'

She shrugged. 'I haven't the foggiest idea.' She shook her head in annoyance. 'I could kick myself! I didn't mean to give the impression I didn't want the baby. I just couldn't believe she would really play away from home with Danny McGowan. I thought she was too sensible a girl to go through with it. But she should have known better than to think I would hold it against the wee baby, whoever its father is.'

'She's very hurt and upset. I'd love to know who the hell she had lunch with. I imagine he or she is the cause of Liz's distress. They've a lot to answer for. I'd wring their bloody neck if I knew who it was.'

'Now don't you be getting all hot and bothered about it. It was probably Danny. I think he's back with his wife. Perhaps he told her so today and that's why she's so upset. And, to coin a phrase, "Now she's left holding the baby".'

'She can't cut herself off from everybody like this, Kath. She hardly goes out of the door. We'll have to get her out and about. There's a cabaret on in Fortwilliam on Saturday night. Do you think maybe she would like to go?'

Sadly, Kath shook her head. 'And see David with Irene? No. It's bad enough Danny letting her down. But to be confronted with the fact that Irene is chasing after David as well, and that he's not exactly fending her off ... that would really break Liz's heart.'

'Sorry, I never thought of that. Do you think there's any chance of Liz and David getting back together?'

'How would I know? He's certainly keeping his

distance. Oh, Neville, what are we going to do?'

'There's nothing we can do, love, but be here for her when she most needs us.'

Bridget returned to the car with Danny, feeling depressed. They had hoped that the house they had just looked at would be suitable for their needs. At least she had. In her heart she knew Danny didn't want to leave the Lower Falls. Well, he could stop worrying for a while. The house was too big and the upkeep on it would be too much for them. And it would take a fortune to furnish. The new housing estate itself was beautiful but apparently all the smaller houses had been snapped up.

'I'm beginning to think we're doomed to spend the rest of our days in that flat,' she lamented.

He put an arm around her. 'Don't worry, love. Something suitable will turn up, you'll see.'

She stiffened and was about to reject his advances, as she had done since his return to the flat, but the worry that was forever nagging at the edge of her mind these days surfaced, sending her once more into despair. Despondently, she remained in his embrace.

She had been so sure that remaining with Danny was the right thing to do, to give Martin a stable home with the father he adored. But what if her suspicions were true? Oh, if only she had stayed on the pill. But she had been so disillusioned, so sure her marriage was over, vowing she would never let a man near her again, that she had come off it. Now she had been proved wrong on both counts. She was such a weak person, always ready to take the easy way out. What a mess everything was! Was there no end to all her troubles?

Unable to believe his luck, that she wasn't pushing him away, Danny gave her a squeeze. 'Me mam was saying Mrs O'Hara is getting married and her house will be going on the market. She actually suggested we put in an offer for it. In the present climate around here we'd probably get it cheap. She won't want to take what the Housing Trust offer her, so if we bid a bit more she'd probably let us have it.'

He waited for her to blow a fuse at the idea. To his surprise, Bridget appeared to mull it over in her mind. 'I don't know, Danny. I don't fancy living across the street from your mam.'

Delighted that she was even considering it, he said tentatively, 'Mam says she won't interfere with us.'

'And you believed her? Catch yourself on, Danny!'

'I'll warn her off, Bridget. Make sure she doesn't interfere. It's a parlour house and in great nick. You'd love it. And with St Finian's School just around the corner, there'd be no problem getting Martin in there. Shall I get me mam to have a quiet word with Mrs O'Hara? Find out all she can? We might even save on estate agent's fees as well, if we can do a private deal.'

Bridget sighed deeply. She had so wanted a garden for Martin to play in. But after all, plenty of children were reared with just a back yard to play in, and there were always the parks to take him to. Besides, it looked like she wouldn't have

551

any choice. 'Let me think about it,' she said despondently.

She remained quiet on the journey home. Danny dropped her at the door of the flat as he usually did and drove over to leave the car outside his mother's house, away from the main road. As she climbed the stairs Bridget knew what she must do. She must let Danny coax her into bed tonight, just in case she was right. She would demur, explain that she had come off the pill while they were apart. Knowing him, he would say they must take their chances. Tomorrow she would go back on the pill, in case her suspicions were wrong. What a conniving person she was becoming! If she was pregnant they definitely would not be able to afford a house up Andersonstown Road and she would have no one to blame but herself. And it looked like she would end up living across the road from Peter.

In the lead up to Easter, Kath kept Liz busy with preparations for the wedding. Her daughter was to be matron of honour. It was with trepidation that she broke the news to her that Neville's family would not be attending. The excuses made sounded plausible enough, but Neville was not all that convinced. He knew full well their views on Catholicism and deep down had expected them to boycott the wedding as a sign of their disapproval. If their loss was the price he had to pay for marrying Kath, then so be it. They had their own lives and it was her he wanted to spend the rest of his life with. Although disappointed, he still respected their views.

The refusal did however create the problem of who would be his best man. Kath's brief affair with his nephew Dick ruled him out, so David was the obvious choice.

Tentatively Kath broached the subject with her daughter. 'Liz, would you object if we asked David to be best man at the wedding?'

'Don't be silly, Mam. It's your day. You ask whoever you like. It makes no difference to me.'

'Are you quite sure?'

'Yes, Mam, I am. David has been very considerate. I hope we can remain good friends.'

'I have something else to ask you. How would you feel about us selling this house?'

'Are you putting me out on the street, Mam?'

'Don't be silly. You know that will never happen. But you've seen Neville's bungalow. There's plenty of room there for you and the baby, and the garden would be the ideal place for a child to play. We would so love to have you share it with us.'

'Mam, I've already said no. I don't want to live with you and Neville.' Her thoughts went to another bungalow with beautiful gardens and she turned away to hide the tears that sprang so easily to her eyes these days.

'Then Neville says you are to have this house. It's your inheritance. But if we sold it we could buy you one somewhere away from all those dreadful tanks and soldiers. Somewhere comparatively peaceful. I mean, it can still be quite nasty about here, and you'd be on your own with a baby. What do you think, love?'

'I don't want to think of moving until after the

birth, Mam. I'm quite content here for the moment. Nobody bothers me. Even so, let's get the wedding over first, eh?'

Kath sighed. In spite of her daughter's words about not wanting to have anything to do with Danny, Kath didn't believe her. Why else would she wish to remain here in Dunlewey Street, if not to be near him? And why was he dragging his feet? If he still loved Liz, why didn't he leave his wife? Though married men seldom did. But she agreed with her daughter, 'Just as you wish.'

Eyeing her mother covertly, Liz asked apprehensively, 'Mam, David will hardly bring Irene with him, will he?'

'Why should he? He knows she's no friend of mine. I for one haven't invited her, and I'm damned sure Neville hasn't either,' Kath said with a grim smile.

'If David agrees to be best man, will he not expect to bring her along?'

Kath was looking worried now. 'I never thought of that. I'll warn Neville to sound him out first. I couldn't bear for that woman to be there. I'm sure David will understand.'

'It's going to be a very quiet wedding, isn't it, Mam? First Grannie and Grandad aren't well enough to attend, and now Neville's family are crying off. But at least it's in church.' Going to her, Liz hugged her close. 'Ah, Mam. I hope you have many happy years ahead of you.'

Her mother laughed at these words. 'Well, Neville's no spring chicken, but hopefully we will have some time together.'

To say Kath was surprised when Jane McGowan stopped her in the street and congratulated her on her marriage plans would be putting it mildly. They had never been on intimate terms before. She soon realized, however, that there was an ulterior motive behind Jane's well wishes. After a few pleasantries she asked if Kath was thinking of moving house?

'Well, yes. I will be moving eventually.'

'When you do, could my Danny have first refusal?'

'I'm surprised he wants to buy my house.'

'Why not? It's a lovely house from what I hear.'

'Well, yes, but...' Kath laughed before continuing. 'Bridget living facing her mother-in-law? You and her must get on very well together?'

'Yes, we do,' Jane agreed, and actually believed her own words. 'But it's more for convenience' sake I'm asking. You know, being near the school and all. And if Bridget wanted to keep on working she wouldn't be short of baby minders.'

'Well, if Neville and I can persuade Liz to live with us, we shall certainly put the house on the market. I assure you, if we do, you will be the first to know, Jane.'

She nodded her thanks, her mind avidly digesting this piece of information. Liz living with her mother? It sounded as if she and her husband were parted for good if Kath was trying to persuade her to live with them. What on earth had gone wrong there? Had her Danny been the cause of the split?

Joseph was sitting at the window and heard their

555

exchange of words. He watched his mother covertly for some moments before inquiring casually, 'Is Danny thinking of buying Mrs O'Hara's house?'

'You were obviously listening to what doesn't concern you.' Jane gazed at him suspiciously. 'Why all this interest?'

He shrugged his shoulders. 'No reason. I'm just making conversation.'

'Huh! You making conversation? That'll be the day.'

'See? There's no pleasing you, Ma. I can't do right for doing wrong, as far as you're concerned.'

Later that evening he made his way over to the flat to visit his brother. It was Bridget who came clattering down the stairs to answer his knock. She eyed him suspiciously. 'Hello, Joseph. To what do we owe this honour?' She motioned him in and up the stairs in front of her. 'Danny is out at the moment but he won't be long. Take a seat.'

He remained standing and she watched in surprise as his face flushed bright red. 'Bridget, I would like to take this opportunity to apologize to you.'

'What for? Threatening to break up my marriage?'

'You know I wouldn't have really said anything, Bridget.'

'How was I to know that? There you were, having a sleazy affair with Ian in that flat above me, and because I showed concern and was really worried about you, mind, you dug up dirt about me.' He opened his mouth to speak but she held

556

up a hand to stop him. 'Let me finish, please. I spent many sleepless nights because of you, Joseph McGowan. And do you know what was the worst of it? Although I held my tongue where you and Ian were concerned, you told him those lies about me.'

'Ian?'

'Oh, yes, he came down to assure me I had nothing to worry about. That you would never say anything. But the way I saw it, if you told him, who else did you tell? Eh, Joseph, who else? Or was it just pillow talk between you and him?'

His colour deepened even more at this insinuation. 'Bridget, you've got it all wrong! There was never anything like that between me and him. We were just good friends. You must believe that.'

Her brows rose towards her hairline. 'Oh, and why would I? Remember, I saw you two together and you didn't deny it then. In fact, when I showed concern, you blackmailed me. Because that's what it amounted to, you know, blackmail!'

'I'm sorry, Bridget. I was way out of line. My only excuse is I was very unhappy at that time.'

'Huh! So you wanted me to be unhappy too, is that it? What kind of a person are you?' She turned away in disgust but he heard her muttered words. 'As if I don't know.'

'Honestly, Bridget, there was nothing between me and Ian. I wish you would believe that.'

She swung around to face him again. 'Like you believed me when I said there was no truth in the rumours you heard? And there *is* no truth in what you said about Martin.' She had to convince him of this.

The door downstairs slammed shut and Bridget whispered savagely to him, 'Let's get all our accusations out into the open. Clear the air once and for all, eh, Joseph? You tell Danny about the rumours you heard and I'll tell him about your friendship with Ian.'

Danny breezed into the room and looked from one to the other of them. He could feel the tension and eyed his brother through narrowed lids. 'This is a surprise, Joseph. What brings you here?'

'Actually I heard rumours that...' He heard Bridget's low gasp of dismay and saw the colour fade from her face. Realizing he had chosen the wrong words and she thought he was going to spill the beans, he hastened to add '...you and Bridget might be buying Mrs O'Hara's house and wanted to put in a word for a friend of mine, for this flat.'

'Anybody we know?'

'No, it's a wee nurse I'm dating. I met her when you were in hospital. She lives in Peel Street with her parents, but she's looking for a place of her own.'

'Oh, what happened to the girl over on the Antrim Road?'

Joseph's eyes darted to Bridget. Would she tell Danny there never was a girl? She remained silent and after a pause, he said, 'That's all over.'

'Are you serious about this wee nurse? Does me ma know you're courting?'

'She knows I'm seeing someone, yes.'

'What do you think, Bridget?' Danny's eyes scanned his wife's pale face. 'Could we put a word in for somebody we don't know?'

Bridget came out of the shock Joseph's words had plunged her into. First she had thought he was calling her bluff. Next he was admitting he was courting a girl. Aware that Danny's interest had been aroused, she smiled pleasantly and warned, 'Joseph, it might be a while before the house is empty. Your friend could have a long time to wait. I can't believe it! You, courting? Sit down. I'll make a cup of tea and you can tell us all about her.'

He smiled at her obvious surprise. 'Yes, strange though it may seem, I've got myself a girlfriend. A very pretty one, too. But I can't stay. I'm meeting her soon. Can I tell her you'll consider putting a word in for her?'

'Well, if we get the house, we'll put a word in, but that doesn't mean Mrs McCann will agree. She might have other plans for it. Meanwhile, bring this girl to meet us.'

'That would be wonderful, Bridget. Thanks for all your help. I won't forget your kindness. 'Bye for now.'

The door closed on him and Danny eyed his wife. She felt the colour heat her face and entered the kitchen to escape his gaze. He followed her. 'Bridget, you would tell me if our Joseph was being a nuisance, wouldn't you?'

'Of course I would,' she cried in anger. 'I don't know where you get your ideas from.'

He shrugged, at a loss to explain the vague doubts that still troubled him. She sighed in relief when he left the kitchen without further questions.

On the Wednesday of Easter week, Kath and Neville were married in St Paul's church. It was a short ceremony as, Neville being non-Catholic, no Nuptial Mass was said. So long as they received the blessing of the church, Kath was happy. Jane McGowan and some other neighbours were in the church to see her wed. Her friends from work also turned out to wish her well. After the ceremony David took some photographs outside and then they departed for Belfast Castle where he was treating them to lunch before the newly weds set off on their honeymoon. For the next two weeks they planned to tour the West Coast.

It was late afternoon when they left the castle. The farewells were tearful. Liz hugged her mother close. 'You see and have a good time! Do you hear me?'

'Of course I will. Your dad will see to that.' Putting her mouth close to her daughter's ear, she whispered, 'Liz, be kind to David. He can't help it if you threw him into Irene's arms.'

She drew back wide-eyed and questioned her mother. 'Does that mean he and Irene are seeing each other?'

'Well, as you know, Neville and I don't go to the golf club very much now but I've heard rumours.'

'Thanks for the warning, Mam. I'll handle him with kid gloves,' Liz promised dryly, and smiled brightly. No one, not even her mother, must guess how much she hurt.

They waved the car out of sight and then David

turned to her. 'It's a beautiful day, do you fancy a drive out towards Cushendun?'

Her head was shaking long before he'd finished speaking and he cried bitterly, 'I won't bite, you know.'

Startled, she replied, 'I'm sorry. I didn't mean to offend you, but it's been a hectic week and I tire easily at the moment. I really am exhausted. I just want to go to bed.'

Immediately he was contrite. 'I'm the one who should be sorry, Liz. I'm a thoughtless fool.'

'You weren't to know.'

'Liz ... will you please come back to the bungalow with me? I have a proposition to put to you.'

She opened her mouth to protest but he urged, 'It's such a nice day and you can rest in the garden. I'll make you a long cold fruit drink. Please? I won't keep you long.'

Reluctantly, she nodded. It would be agony going back to the bungalow now she no longer lived there, but she couldn't say that to him. She left the car on feet that dragged and entered the beautiful cool hall. Her heart ached as she passed through it and out through the conservatory. To think this used to be her home. How had things gone so terribly wrong? In the back garden she removed her coat and hat. David placed them carefully on a nearby bench and insisted on removing her shoes. Kneeling by the chair, he eased them gently off her feet. She looked down on his bent head so close to her and longed to reach out and touch him. With a great effort she resisted the impulse. Once he was sure she was settled in the shade of the chestnut tree, he rose to his feet and smiled down at her. 'I won't be long. Any particular flavour?'

She smiled. 'One of your famous fruit cocktails will do nicely, thank you.'

Mixing different fruit juices in two tall glasses with ice, David let his mind dwell on the events of the morning. At first he had been surprised and dismayed at Neville's asking him to be best man and his first thought had been to refuse. However, when his friend had explained about his sons boycotting the wedding, David had felt obliged to agree. He was far from happy at the prospect. The idea of seeing Liz and Danny together had filled him with dread and he was not in the least looking forward to the occasion. To his surprise, when he and Neville arrived at the church, Danny was nowhere to be seen.

It had been wonderful, wallowing in the closeness of Liz again, her perfume filling his nostrils. She looked beautiful in the outfit bought for the occasion. It consisted of a loose silvery grey dress and matching three-quarter-length jacket. A large picture hat shadowed her face and she carried a posy of roses. He could have described her in detail from memory. On the other hand, if anyone were to ask him what colour the bride had worn he would have had to plead ignorance. As the morning progressed an idea had entered his head. He examined it from all angles and decided it was worth a try. Now he must see how Liz reacted to it.

After removing his jacket and tie David returned to the garden. Liz was asleep. Sitting in a chair close by, he sipped his drink and took this chance to feast his eyes on her. The sun filtered through the branches of the tree, causing her eyelashes to cast long shadows on lightly tanned cheeks. The bump that now showed as she reclined wasn't very big. How he wished it was his child! Pregnancy suited her. She had simply bloomed. He wondered how she would take the proposition he was about to put to her. Of course, he would have to tread carefully. Danny might be still very much in the picture. Perhaps his wife was in ignorance of Liz's baby, or maybe she was determined to hold on to him at all costs. David felt frustrated. He had no one to turn to, to ask how things stood. Whatever the reason, he just had to find out if Liz had a future planned that included Danny.

He heard a car enter the driveway and draw up to the front of the bungalow. In an instant he was on his feet and passing quickly through the conservatory, closing the door behind him. At all costs he had to ward Irene off and get rid of her before Liz awoke.

To his dismay, quick though he was, he was too late. He reached the front door in time to see Irene disappear round the side of the bungalow. Trust her not to ring the bell for admittance. Agitated, he followed her.

'I told you I was going to Neville's wedding today,' he whispered accusingly.

'I was passing and saw the car, so I called to see how things went. Why are we whispering? Are you angry with me?' She rounded the side wall and saw Liz. 'Ah, I see. Why is she here?'

'She's still my wife. We're not divorced yet.'

'What about this Danny person?'

'He doesn't seem to be in the picture anymore.'

Irene's eyes widened as she digested his words. She whispered furiously, 'Surely you're not considering taking her back and rearing another man's child?'

'Why not? I wouldn't be the first man to do so.' Too late he realized she was the last person he should be telling this.

'What about us?'

'Now, Irene, be fair. You know there is no us.'

'You've been leading me on! Taking up all my time. And all the while you were hoping to get back with her?'

'Irene, I wasn't leading you on. I value your friendship. And you know we're just good friends. I never said anything to make you think otherwise. I never made any promises.'

'But ... let me get this straight. You do intend to ask Liz to return?'

Liz awoke to the sound of voices. Irene and David were whispering together a short distance away. She couldn't make out what they were saying but she could see they were both agitated. Carefully, she struggled to an upright position. David was at her side instantly.

'Don't disturb yourself, Liz.'

'Have I been sleeping long?'

'Just a few minutes.'

'I think it's time I was going.'

Lifting the fruit drink he had left on the table, he handed it to her. 'Drink this first. It will revive you. Irene is just leaving.'

To prove him wrong, she sat down on the chair

he had vacated. 'Hello, Liz.'

She acknowledged the greeting with a slight nod.

'My, but pregnancy agrees with you. You look wonderful. Danny must be very proud of himself.' She cast a covert glance at David and saw his lips tighten angrily. 'That drink looks delicious. May I have one please, David?'

He could have seen her far enough, but was too much the gentleman to refuse her request. With a rueful glance at Liz, he reluctantly headed indoors.

Irene ran an eye over Liz's attire. Now she was sitting up, her bump was hidden by the folds in the well-cut dress. It was a first-class creation and had probably cost an arm and a leg. Irene had to admit that Liz certainly carried it off perfectly. 'I believe Neville and your mother were married this morning?'

'Yes, they were.'

'They got a lovely day for it. I offered to accompany David, but he said you wouldn't like that.'

'It had nothing to do with me. My mother and Neville didn't want you there.'

'I can see their point. They probably thought that without me around, you would be able to win David back.'

'What makes you think I want him back? I'm just glad that in the circumstances, we have remained good friends.'

'I'm glad to hear that. Because, you see, David and I have become very close. You won't be surprised to hear another wedding will soon be in the offing?'

Liz felt as if a knife was turning in her heart but she managed to smile sweetly. 'You've waited a long time for him, Irene. I hope you make him happy.'

Irene's smile was just as sweet as she got her barb in. 'I certainly won't spring another man's child on him, that's for sure! I'm too old for that. But then, so is David. He's not a family man. I think we're well suited. We should be very happy together.'

He caught these last few words as he approached them. What mischief was she up to? 'Here you are, Irene.'

'Thank you, David.'

Liz found she couldn't force any more juice down a throat that ached with unshed tears. With a hand that shook, she placed the glass on the table and, pleading fatigue, reached for her shoes. To her dismay her feet had swelled in the heat and the shoes would not go on.

Glad of the excuse to make her linger, David said, 'Come inside where it's cool. The swelling will soon go.'

Stay and watch Irene fawn all over him? No way. Liz rose determinedly to her feet. 'No, I really must go now, David. Can I ring for a taxi?'

'I'll drive you home.'

'No! That won't be necessary.'

'Be sensible, Liz. You can't go home in a taxi without shoes. I'll see you home,' he insisted grimly.

Irene gave her a languid wave. 'Goodbye, Liz.' A warm intimate smile was directed at David.

566

'I'll stay here until you come back. Then I can prepare some dinner for us.'

'Goodbye.'

Lifting her shoes and purse, Liz avoided the conservatory and picked her steps carefully down the side of the house. David followed, carrying her coat and hat. She stood silently while he unlocked the car and put all her belongings on the back seat. Then he assisted her into the passenger seat. 'You know, this isn't necessary,' she lamented. 'You shouldn't leave Irene on her own.'

'I would love to tell you exactly how I feel about her at the moment, but the words would be unsuitable for your ears. I do, however, want you to know that she is not in the habit of cooking meals for me.'

The journey was conducted in silence. Liz felt despondent. She could not rid herself of a picture of Irene cooking a cosy meal for two. (In Liz's beautiful kitchen.) Then they would probably have a drink and listen to classical music. And then what? Would she spend the night, in the bed Liz and David had once shared? How Liz envied her.

David was also thinking about Irene and cursing her for spoiling his plans. He now realized he had been very foolish to spend so much time in her company.

Arriving in Dunlewey Street, Liz turned to face him. She had no intention of prolonging the agony. 'David, I forbid you to get out of the car. Irene is waiting for you.'

'But you can't possibly open the door with your

hands full. I'll see you to the door at least. You go ahead and open it. I'll bring your belongings.'

Unlocking the door, she made no effort to invite him in. Reaching for her belongings, she clasped them close to her breast. 'Thank you very much. You have been very kind.'

'Liz, can I not come in for a moment?'

'No, I'm tired. I need to rest.'

'Can we have dinner some night?'

'No! Again, thank you for looking after me so well today but don't keep Irene waiting on my account. Goodbye, David.'

At a loss how to persuade her, he reluctantly turned away. He had just entered the car when he heard someone hail her. To his great chagrin, it was Danny McGowan. Without another glance, David put his foot down and zoomed up the street and around the corner. He could not bear to see her admit Danny to the house. So much for his proposition. It looked like Danny was still in the frame after all... David smiled grimly to himself. He had deliberately kept one of her shoes. An excuse to visit her and return it. What a fool he was!

Liz kept Danny standing at the door. 'Hello, Danny.'

'How did the wedding go?'

'Very well. It was a lovely service.'

'Was that David who dropped you off?'

'Mmm. As if you didn't know. Look, Danny, I'm tired. I'll see you around.'

'Can I ask you something?'

Her eyes narrowed and she became wary. 'Fire away.'

'Why are you and David living apart?'

'That is none of your business.' The door closed in his face with a decisive click. He stared at it for some seconds. If their marriage was over, was it his fault?

Wearily, she climbed the stairs and removed her new outfit carefully. Only then did she give into her feelings and collapse on to the bed. Burying her face in the pillow, she gave way to her anguish. It was because she was exhausted, she told herself. It was only natural she should feel so depressed. She would feel better after a good cry. This time, there was no one to witness her shame and offer comfort. The tears rained down until she fell into a fitful sleep.

It was a week later that David called to return the shoe. He had decided he couldn't just sit back and do nothing. There was too much at stake. He would play it by ear; find out if she had any plans for the future. Liz smiled when she opened the door and saw the shoe in his hand. 'I thought I must have left it in the car. But you shouldn't have bothered, I'm in no hurry for it. I don't wear high heels at the moment. I bought those especially for Mam's big occasion.'

'I was afraid you might think you'd lost it.'

'No, I was pretty sure I'd left it in the car.' To his great delight, she stood aside and motioned him in. 'I was just about to make myself a cup of coffee, will you join me?'

'I'd love to.'

Over the coffee, all their shared interests came to the fore and they chatted happily for some time. At last there was a pause and David said diffidently, 'Am I keeping you back?'

'No. But if you're in a hurry, don't let me keep you.'

'I'm not in any hurry. I just thought you might be expecting Danny?'

Liz was silent for some moments, then confessed, 'I don't see much of him.'

'Why's that?'

She shrugged. 'He has his own life, I have mine.'

'Has he left you in the lurch, Liz? Sorry! I didn't mean that the way it sounds. I mean, has he not come up to scratch? Surely he doesn't deny he's the father?'

She had to smile at these words. 'He doesn't deny anything. Really, David, it doesn't matter. I'd prefer not to discuss Danny, if you don't mind.'

'I just want to know if you're planning a future with him?'

She moved restlessly. 'No, I'm not. And, David, I don't wish to discuss it any more. Please respect my wishes!'

'Liz, I'm not asking out of idle curiosity. Please hear me out.'

At a loss how to make him change course, she sat silent. He took this as permission to speak. 'If you and Danny are not planning to marry or live together, I suggest you return to the bungalow.'

He could not see her expression. Dusk had fallen while they'd talked and her face was in shadow. She did, however, give a slight start of surprise but remained silent. He willed her to say something. Give him some idea how she felt. But in vain; the silence lengthened. At last he continued, 'Liz, don't think I would expect anything from you. You would have your own room and privacy. We're good friends and the bungalow is big enough for both of us to live together without getting under each other's feet ... and we could remain married. I would of course treat the child as if it was my own. Give it my name. No one need be any the wiser. Would you not consider it? It would be better than living here on your own.'

Tears threatened as she took in his words. They could live together but she would have her own room. Was it that bad? Could he not bear to be near her any more? And why? Why was he suggesting this if he wasn't interested in her? She couldn't comprehend his reasoning.

Tentatively, she asked, 'You mean, I would be a housekeeper to you?'

He hesitated; he hadn't quite meant that but half a loaf, as they say... 'If you want to put it that way. Why not?'

'I don't think that would be a good idea, David. No matter what, you would always resent the child. It would be an intrusion into your peaceful life and I couldn't bear that. Even if we didn't live as husband and wife, you would come to hate my presence for coming between you and Irene. If I hadn't married you in the first place, you and she would have been married long ago. She has been very patient. She deserves some reward.'

'Irene doesn't enter in to this.' His tone was abrupt.

'No? I heard you were very much a pair. And, I must confess, Irene confided in me that you were to marry.'

He straightened up in indignation. 'I never asked her to marry me!'

'Maybe not, David,' she said gently. 'But you must have given her that impression else why would she tell me? She would know I'd find out if it wasn't true. You can't let her down.'

'I didn't ask her,' he repeated, but didn't sound so sure now. His conscience plagued him. Had he, in his misery at the loss of Liz, led Irene to believe he would propose to her? Hadn't he been glad of her company these past months? Still, marriage had never been mentioned. Irene had got the wrong end of the stick. Wasn't he still married to Liz? 'I don't think I ever gave her that impression.'

She heard the doubt in his voice. 'It makes no difference, David. My child might not have a proper father, but you will be glad to hear he will have a proper grandfather. Neville and I are friends again. He is going to take care of us. Once the birth is over I have promised Mam and him that I will look for a suitable house. He'll look after me and his grandchild. Meanwhile I will live here. So there's no need for you to worry about me. By all means marry Irene, and I really do wish you all the happiness your deserve.'

He did everything in his power to talk her round to his way of thinking. Afraid to use declarations of love, he unwittingly used all the wrong expressions and got nowhere. Liz was adamant that she didn't need a job as housekeeper. He felt he had not the right to ask her to be anything more. She seemed happy enough at the idea of him marrying Irene, so must care very little for him.

Liz sat for a long time after he had gone, going over his proposal. She was bewildered. If he didn't want children, why was he asking her to return? He'd be taking on, as he thought, the responsibility of another man's child. A man he despised. He obviously didn't want any sexual favours or he wouldn't be insisting on pushing her into a room of her own and offering her the job of housekeeper. Did he not want to admit the failure of his marriage? Was that the reason behind all this? Was saving his face the reason behind his proposal? As for him rearing the child as his own, that would never work. She would be forced to tell him the truth. And since he didn't love her, he would soon feel trapped. If only, in spite of all she had done, he had trusted her a little more, they might still be together. But she couldn't let him, out of a sense of duty towards her, give up his own chance of happiness.

Kath returned from her honeymoon radiant. 'It was wonderful, Liz. We stayed in first-class hotels. A few nights here, a few nights there. It was an eye opener as to how the other half live. Wait till we get the photographs developed. You wouldn't believe the scenery if I tried to explain it. Especially around the Ring of Kerry. It was breathtaking.'

'I'm glad you enjoyed yourself, Mam. Where's Neville?'

'He's getting your present out of the boot. How did you manage?'

'I was grand, so I was. You mustn't worry about me being here on my own, Mam. I like solitude. And you shouldn't have bothered about a present for me.'

'It's not really for you ... it's for the nursery. I do wish you would come and live with us. We could have yon big room at the back of the bungalow turned into a nursery. No matter what you say, I'll worry about you here on your own.'

'Look, Mam. I promise that as soon as the baby is born, I'll look for a house somewhere quiet. Perhaps over your direction. OK?'

'Will you come and stay with us this weekend? Just to please your old mum?'

'Well, since the weather is supposed to be good, why not? It will be a nice change to sunbathe in your garden.'

A loud thud sent her into the hall. A huge box took up all the floor space at the foot of the stairs. A breathless Neville greeted her. 'I think we had better unpack this, Liz, or we'll never get it upstairs.'

'What on earth is it?' Eagerly, like an excited child, she started ripping off the outer wrapping paper. Underneath was a plain brown box.

'Careful now. Don't tear it open. We'll need the box should it have to be returned,' Neville warned.

At last it stood there in all its glory: a big rocking horse carved in hard wood, painted in vivid colours and with real horse hair for mane and tail.

'Oh, it's absolutely beautiful! It must have cost the earth.' There were tears in her eyes as she thanked them. 'Thank you, Mam. Thank you, Dad.'

A wide grin of delight spread over Neville's face at these words. He turned away so she wouldn't see the tears in his eyes. She had called him *Dad*.

The weeks passed and Bridget's worst fears were realized. She was pregnant. She tried to convince herself that it might possibly be Danny's, but knew in her heart it wasn't. Hadn't the signs already been there? The tender breasts; the brown nipples? That's what had driven her back into his arms. No one, not even Danny, must know for another month at least. At Easter she would announce that she was to be a mother again. By then it would be taken for granted by everyone that it was her husband's. Everyone? What was she thinking? There was one person likely to have doubts, and he would need some convincing. Peter was no fool. What kind of a woman was she? Two children apparently to men other than her husband. But she didn't feel like a bad woman; hadn't deliberately conned Danny into marriage. She had believed Martin was his. Still believed it! Indeed, she felt more used than wanton. Her parents would be devastated if it became known. As for Peter, he must not get so much as a hint that this one was his or he would make it known to one and all. He would be proud and do everything in his power to per-suade her to leave Danny.

There was no way now she could contemplate

life facing her mother-in-law. See Peter every day? No! It would be impossible to live like that. It would drive her round the bend. To Danny's great bewilderment and concern, she began to talk again about moving up to Andersonstown, even though she knew they could ill afford it.

'Talk sense, Bridget,' he entreated. 'You saw the houses. They're well beyond our reach. Why this change of heart, eh? I thought it was all settled. I thought we were going after Mrs O'Hara's house as soon as Liz was ready to move out?'

Suddenly she longed for him to say he loved her. It would help make it worthwhile. If he really loved her, she would do all in her power to make their marriage work. 'Danny, tell me the truth now. Are you sorry you married me?'

'Ah, Bridget. For God's sake, let's not go over that again. We're married, and as far as I'm concerned, I'm contented with you and Martin. What more can I say? What about you? Are you not happy with me?'

They eyed each other. As far as he was concerned, at this moment their future hung in the balance. If she admitted she was unhappy with him, dissatisfied with their life together, he would not keep her tied. He would willingly offer to release her from their marriage. But it had to be *her* wish. What she really wanted. Then he would feel free to make a bee line for Liz. Try and rekindle the passion she used to feel for him. Probably in vain. But, on the other hand, she was separated from her husband, and who knows, perhaps that's the way it was meant to be? Fate! A second chance for them. He felt his pulse suddenly quicken at the very idea. Otherwise it was his duty to do all in his power to make a success of his marriage. Especially if what he thought was true and Bridget was expecting again. That much he owed her. He waited breathlessly for her reply. It was in the lap of the gods.

She was in a dilemma. This was her chance. Should she grab the bull by the horns and confess about the baby? Admit Peter was the father? Her mind ranged over all the implications. There would be talk. The finger would be pointed at her. And where would she and Peter live? They would have to move far away, to escape wagging tongues. Danny would be incensed. There was no love lost between him and his brother. He would demand custody of Martin. In the midst of all this, Joseph would probably think it his duty to divulge the earlier rumours he had heard and she would be branded a wanton hussy. Danny could very well get custody. It would all snowball out of control. The scandal would bring shame to both sets of parents. No, she couldn't do it. She wasn't brave enough; she was too ashamed. The moment for honesty passed as quickly as it had arisen and she said lamely, 'I suppose I'm as happy as can be expected, living here with no prospect of a decent home.'

He expelled his breath on a long drawn out sigh. For a moment there, as he'd watched all the conflicting emotions flit across her face, he had... He didn't finish the thought. He'd been wrong. They were to remain married. So be it. 'Look,

Bridget, I'll ask Liz to let you see over her mother's house. I know you'll love it. It's big and airy.'

'I so wanted a garden for Martin to play in,' she lamented.

'Be fair, Bridget. I'm doing my best. We had no gardens to play in and it didn't do us a bit of harm, now did it?'

Wearily she shook her head. Couldn't he understand that she wanted better for her children than what they'd had. However, there was no reasoning with him. He always had the last word. Was this how she wanted to go through life? Making do, just to please Danny?

'Besides,' he continued, 'we're better off than our parents were. At least we have a car. We'll be able to take our kids to the parks and seaside. Bridget, is it not time you were telling me the truth?'

Wide-eyed, she drew back in alarm and gulped deep in her throat. 'What do you mean?'

'I'm not stupid. I hear you being sick in the mornings. That's why I'm surprised at you, wanting to move up to Andersonstown. If, as I suspect, you're pregnant, we really won't be able to afford it with two children.'

She could only stare at him in dismay.

'Don't look like that! Is it because I insisted we risk it even though you weren't on the pill? Are you blaming me? Is that it?'

'No. No, I'm not blaming you.'

'Don't you want another child, Bridget?'

'Yes, but not just yet. The flat's too small. That's why I'm so anxious to move.'

'Why didn't you tell me?'

'Because I don't want everybody to know until I'm showing. And that goes for your mam! She can't keep her big mouth shut.'

'All right. I won't say a word.' He joined her on the settee. Putting an arm around her, he drew her close against him. 'Come here, love. Let me make you forget all your troubles for a while.'

'Mam will be coming with Martin any minute now,' she objected fretfully.

'She's not here yet. We'll get plenty of warning.'

At that point, the doorbell rang. 'That will be her now.' Thankfully she escaped his embrace and went to answer it. It was Peter. 'What do you want?' Bridget whispered furiously.

'Just confirmation you're not moving far away?'

Danny's voice reached them. 'Who is it, Bridget?'

'It's your Peter.'

Without answering Peter's question she turned and climbed the stairs. How could she live in this perpetual state of tension, never knowing when he was going to pop in?

Danny scowled at his brother, annoyed at his interruption. 'What do you want?'

'What a way to welcome your brother. Am I not allowed to visit you two any more? You'll be glad of me when you need some decorating done.' His eyes swung from one to the other of them suspiciously. 'Have I interrupted something?'

'Yes, as a matter of fact you have. And we're not contemplating doing any decorating at the moment. To be truthful, Peter, I'd rather you didn't come round unannounced. When we buy

Mrs O'Hara's house, I don't fancy the idea of you popping in and out whenever the notion grabs you.'

'So you're not going up Andersonstown after all?' His eyes were on Bridget's face. 'You're actually going to buy Mrs O'Hara's?'

His relief was apparent, at least to her. She could feel his hidden excitement. What difference did he think it would make where they lived? Hadn't she made it plain that it was all over between them?

'No, we can't afford it. What with...' Bridget caught her husband's eye and slightly shook her head 'one thing and another,' he finished lamely.

In despair, she left them to it and entered the kitchen. At this rate her secret wouldn't be a secret very long. Then Peter's mind would be working overtime.

Martha Kelly knew all was still not well between Bridget and Danny. Although her daughter put on a happy front, she could sense her unrest. When at Easter Bridget confided in her that another baby was on the way, Martha could not hide her dismay.

Bridget smiled wanly. 'I thought you would be pleased. You always said have your family close together and they help rear each other.'

'That's when you're happy and have a kind, caring husband,' Martha retorted.

'Mam, Danny really is trying hard to please me. It's just ... well, I've changed, you see.'

'Well, that's just too bad, dear! Because you're really tied down now with two kids.' She turned aside to hide her disappointment.

Behind her back, Bridget grimaced wryly. 'I've more news. You're just going to love it too.'

She paused so long, Martha swung round and cried in frustration, 'Are you going to tell me? Or will I start guessing?'

'Would you like to sit down, Mam?'

'Ah, come on! It can't be all that bad.' Suddenly she straightened to attention. 'Don't tell me it's twins?' she cried in alarm.

'No, it's not twins.' Bridget smiled slightly and added, 'At least not as far as I know.'

'Thank God for that! Tell me what it is then.'

'OK. Danny is thinking of doing a deal with Mrs O'Hara to buy her house.' Bridget waited for the explosion.

It never came. Martha was too gobsmacked. She groped for a chair and sat down. Gaping at her daughter, she wailed. 'Don't tell me you've agreed to go along with it?'

Bridget shrugged. 'Why not? If I agree, at least I'll be able to go back to work soon after the birth. And in a few years' time we'll be able to sell the house at a profit and move somewhere better. Mam, it's the only chance we have. We can't stay in that flat with two children.'

'Ah, Bridget, I worry about you.' Martha gave a woeful shake of the head. 'You know, I thought you were on the pill. Because it's against all our beliefs, I didn't say anything. But in my heart I was glad! I hoped you had the courage to shape your destiny in spite of being married to Danny McGowan.'

Shamefaced, Bridget admitted, 'I was on the

581

pill but I came off it at Christmas when I thought my marriage was over.'

'Why didn't you go on it again?'

'I did, but it was too late.' Bridget turned away from her mother's searching gaze. Over the years she had sometimes thought Martha had second sight. She always seemed to know what was going on in your mind, especially if you were doing something wrong.

A frown on her brow, Martha let her thoughts range back over the past months. She remembered how attentive Peter McGowan had been. She had made him welcome in their home. Had thought him a lovely lad, caring for his brother's wife and child over Christmas. Patrick had never been too keen on him. Without just cause, she had thought! Now she wondered if he had known something she hadn't? Surely Bridget couldn't have been so stupid... 'Bridget, it is Danny's child, isn't it?'

Feigning offence, Bridget swung round and faced her. 'Of course it is! Who else's? How could you think such a thing, Mam?' Martha remained silent and Bridget added, 'Now you can see why we must buy Liz's old home. Not an ideal choice, considering, but I hear it's a bargain at any price.'

'Well, don't come crawling back here looking for sympathy when you find you can't stand Jane McGowan's interference. That old bitch would get on anybody's nerves.'

'I think I'll be able to handle Jane. After all, I'll be in my own house this time. I'll be my own boss. I'm not worried about her.'

As if her daughter had said the words, 'It's

Peter I'm worried about,' Martha heard them clearly in her own head. But some things are best left unsaid. The less she officially knew the better. She rose to her feet. 'On your own head be it. I've a little sherry. I'll pour us a drink. I for one need it.'

Bridget received a vastly different reception to her news when she confided in Danny's mother.

'That's wonderful news, Bridget!' Jane enthused. 'I'm sure Danny's over the moon. And if you get Kath O'Hara's house, you'll not want for someone to look after the kids. Your mother and I will manage between us.'

'Manage what between you?'

They both swung round to face Peter. 'I thought you were away to the pictures,' his mother exclaimed. 'Did your date let you down?'

'Never mind about that. What will you and Mrs Kelly manage between you?'

'Bridget is expecting another baby. Isn't that great? Martha and I will look after the kids when she returns to work.'

Bridget managed a laugh. 'Imagine! Return to work, and I'm hardly started yet.' She felt her cheeks redden as Peter's eyes scanned her figure.

'Just how far on are you?' Jane asked. 'When is it due?'

'I haven't been to the doctor yet,' Bridget lied. 'Time enough for that. I'm only a couple of months. Look, I'll have to run on now, Danny will wonder where on earth I am.' She was annoyed. She had deliberately chosen this opportunity to tell Jane her news because Danny had mentioned seeing Peter waiting for a bus.

'I forgot my wallet. That's why I came back, Ma. If you must know.' Peter climbed the stairs, and Bridget quickly made her farewells and left the house.

He was right on her heels. 'So, you're expecting another baby?'

'Yes.'

'But you don't know when it's due?'

'I've only missed a couple of months.' She thought she sounded convincing and added, 'No point in going to the doctor too soon, you know. Even so, it's none of your business.'

'No, Bridget?' He stopped and, blocking her way, peered into her face. 'Are you quite sure of that?'

Her heart was racing but her brows drew together as if puzzled. 'I don't know what you're on about, Peter.'

'You listen to me, Bridget Kelly! Don't you take me for some kind of a sucker. You might succeed in pulling the wool over Danny's eyes, but not mine. I'll be counting the months, and if it is mine, I won't keep quiet. Dear me no! I'll make sure everybody hears about it. Just you bear that in mind, Bridget! Now you will have to excuse me. My friend is waiting.'

He left her and strode across the Falls Road. She watched him approach a young woman who was waiting outside the Dolphin fish and chip shop. The girl was petite and pretty. The answer to her prayers? She *would* convince him he wasn't the father, and perhaps then he would get married and leave her alone. A great feeling of

584

desolation engulfed her. Was that what she really wanted? She gave herself a slight shake. Whether she wanted it or not, she had made up her mind. She had finally decided that her future was with her husband and children, and no one was going to come between them. No matter what! Even if she was going to be living opposite her in-laws. With this thought in mind her face was set in grim resolute lines as she headed back to the flat.

June had been a scorcher of a month, and July looked like being the same. Liz was glad to spend her weekends with her mother and Neville. She was quite big now and felt awkward and ungainly. At the bungalow, her every wish was their command and she revelled in all the attention she was getting.

Stretching luxuriously, she smiled across at her mother. 'I've been thinking, Mam. Perhaps you should consider putting your house on the market. You won't want it standing empty too long in case squatters move in.'

'What if it's sold before the baby arrives?'

'That's hardly likely.'

Looking embarrassed, Kath confessed, 'Liz, look, I didn't mention this before because I didn't know how things stood between you and Danny McGowan. You're so tight-lipped about him and I didn't want you to feel hurt.'

She paused so long Liz sat up to attention. 'What has he got to do with it?'

'Are you still in love with him, Liz?'

Bewildered, she cried, 'Look, Mam, obviously

585

something strange is going on here. What didn't you tell me?'

'Danny wants first refusal on the house.'

'He came to you? You should have told me.'

'It was his mother who asked. I didn't know what to do for the best. I must confess I showed Danny and Bridget over the house one day while you were down here. It was the day I went up to fetch some things for you. I met him in the street and he kept hinting how much Bridget would like to see the house, so I told him to bring her over. She fell in love with it. I didn't see any harm in it. I hope you don't mind, Liz?'

Liz did mind. She minded very much. Not about Bridget and Danny looking over her home. She resented the fact that her mother had omitted to tell her. She was pregnant, for heaven's sake! Not some invalid who had to be shielded from bad news.

'Liz, say you don't mind?'

'Why would I mind?' she lied. 'It's your house. I just wish you had told me about it, that's all.'

'I didn't want you to think I was pushing you out. Shall I have a word with Mrs McGowan? Or would you prefer me to put it in the hands of an estate agent?'

Liz sat silent for some moments. 'Yes, go ahead. Talk to Mrs McGowan. The baby should be born before everything is settled. Anyway, it's time I was looking about for a house of my own. Meanwhile, if the baby decides to come early, can I move in here with you? Another four or five weeks at the most, should do the job.' She patted her bulge gently.

Relieved that her daughter didn't seem perturbed about Danny, Kath couldn't contain her excitement. 'Don't look for a house yet, Liz. Stay here until you've regained your strength after the birth,' she urged. 'We would be delighted to have you and the baby here with us. Then we can all go house hunting together.'

Liz smiled at her happiness. 'All right, Mam. But, mind you, I want a home of my own in the not too distant future. Believe me, I'm not going to sit in the corner of someone else's house, wondering if I'm getting under their feet.'

'You know it wouldn't be like that.'

'Nevertheless, I would like a place of my own.'

Kath gave in gracefully. 'All right. Have it your own way. In the meantime, I'll go and see Jane McGowan tomorrow and get things set in motion. She will be so relieved.' Tentatively, she added, 'I don't know whether or not you know that Bridget's expecting another baby?'

'No. How would I know, Mam? Nobody tells me anything.'

'I only heard recently, and I didn't know whether or not Danny had already told you.'

'Why would he tell me, eh? It's none of my business, Mam. Believe it or not, I never see anything of him these days.'

Bewildered, Kath asked, 'So, you really don't care about him any more?'

'I don't care what he does, where he goes, or anything else about him. I wish you would believe that.'

'OK. Will I have a word with Jane then?'

'By all means, do.'

587

'If we can agree a price, we may as well cut out the middle man. Save a bit of money. Oh, I'm so happy. Wait until Neville hears this. He'll be over the moon.' Her happiness was so obvious; she was quite literally beaming. 'It will be wonderful to have you staying here. Even if it's only for a short time.'

Neville added to her mother's pleas and Liz found herself agreeing to move in with them right away. A price had been agreed on the house and wheels were set in motion for the trans-action. With this in mind Liz returned to Dunlewey Street two weeks later to pack the remainder of her clothes and personal belong-ings. Everything else had been attended to. Most of the furniture had been sold. The best pieces were in storage for her new home. Danny and Bridget may as well have access to the house, to come and go as they please. Even decorate if the notion took them. It was only a matter of time before the house was theirs.

As she made a final tour of the house, she pondered her life. Wasn't it strange? It amazed her to think of Danny living here, in her old home, with Bridget.

She tried to imagine what life would be like if she had married him; not to have known David. It would have been a great loss, that was for sure. But then, she wouldn't have known any better. He would have just been her boss, probably married to Irene, and she wouldn't have known this devastation that threatened to tear her apart. Would never have known his goodness; his wonderful, tender lovemaking. She, would have been living in total ignorance. How could she have been so blind as ever to compare Danny with him? David was in a class of his own and she hoped he got all the happiness he deserved. As her baby had grown bigger within her, so had her longing for David. He had not returned to try and sway her to come back to the bungalow. Had he done so, in her great need, there was no way Liz could have resisted him.

She now bitterly regretted turning down his offer but he had taken her unawares. If she had gone back as he'd suggested, perhaps she could have made him fall in love with her again? It would have been worth a try. Had he decided it wouldn't be worth the effort after all? Was that why he hadn't returned? Were he and Irene already planning their wedding?

Packing clothes, shoes and handbags into suitcases, she dragged them from the bedroom and left them at the top of the stairs. Neville would collect them later if she asked. He would be angry with her for hauling them about but Mrs McGowan had asked her mother if Danny and Bridget could measure up for curtains this evening and Liz wanted to leave everything neat and tidy.

To her great concern, the baby suddenly started moving around. This was the time of day when it was usually quiet. It must have been all her activity that had started it off. He or she seemed to give a huge kick that turned it right over and she actually felt it dropping down in the womb. It was like nothing she had ever experienced before and Liz felt suddenly afraid. She prayed it would not settle in its favourite position on a nerve or she would never make it home alone. At the clinic that morning she had been told the head was not engaged and it was very likely she would go the full time. That was still a few weeks away. But the pains intensified and slowly it dawned on her that she could very well be in labour now, no matter what had been said at the clinic.

Panic set in. Having nowhere to sit, she made her way painfully to the top of the stairs and sank down on the top step. Head in her hands, she drew deep breaths and tried to calm herself. Perhaps she had just strained herself pulling the cases about and a rest would put things right. But no. She sat for some minutes but realized her pains were still coming and growing more severe. Even if she could make it out to the car, she would be unable to drive safely. Thank God the phone wasn't cut off yet. She must ring her mother and get Neville to collect her. But first she had to get downstairs to the phone. Cautiously, she leant on the suitcase to lever herself to her feet. It was too near the edge and rocked perilously. Liz grabbed wildly at the banister and for some seconds managed to regain her balance. Her relief was short-lived. A sharp gripping spasm of pain doubled her in two. Her fingers automatically released their hold on the rail and she toppled headlong down the stairs.

For the umpteenth time Kath looked at her watch. 'I wonder what's keeping Liz? She should have been home ages ago.'

'The phone hasn't been turned off yet, Kath. If she needed us she'd have rung.'

'You're right, of course. I'll wait for a while. She does so hate for me to fuss over her.'

Another half-hour passed before Kath headed for the phone. 'I'm sure something is wrong, Neville. I'll give her a ring. Remind her it's almost dinnertime.'

The phone rang on and on and at last she hung up in despair. 'There's no answer,' she informed her husband unnecessarily.

'She's probably on her way home, Kath. Sit down. She'll be here any minute now.'

Fifteen minutes later, she was on her feet again. 'That's it! Neville, please humour me and run me up to Dunlewey Street.'

A bit perturbed himself now, he only pretended reluctance. 'She'll be angry, you know. And what about the dinner?'

'I don't care whether she's angry or not! As for the dinner, to hell with it! I'll lower the gas.'

Turning into Dunlewey Street Neville cried in relief, 'There's her car. She's still here.'

'Then why didn't she answer the phone?' Kath was out of the car before it had come to a standstill and, running to the door, banged on it loudly.

No answer and no sound from within. Crouching down, she peered through the letter box. 'Neville! She's lying in the hall,' she screamed. 'Oh, why didn't I bring my key? Jane McGowan has one. Go over and get it, love. And for God's sake, hurry.'

A few minutes later they were inside. Kath threw herself on her knees beside her daughter, fear gripping her when she saw Liz's ashen features. 'Oh, sweet Jesus, she must have fallen down the stairs.' She felt for a pulse. 'Thank God, she's alive. Phone for an ambulance!'

The sound of their voices penetrated Liz's brain. Forcing her eyes open, she looked groggily at her mother. What on earth? Where was she? Slowly memory returned and she grabbed thankfully at Kath's arm. The action brought a groan of pain from her lips. 'Ahh! Thank God, you're here, Mam. I fell down the stairs.' Then she pawed wildly at her stomach and a wail of misery burst from her lips. 'Mam! The baby isn't moving. Is it dead? Mam, is it dead?'

Frantic with worry, Kath tried to sound reassuring. 'I'm sure it's all right, love. Don't move too much. We've sent for the ambulance. It should be here any minute.'

The paramedic was able to set Liz's mind at rest when he examined her. 'I can hear a heartbeat. Listen.' He removed his stethoscope and held it to her ears. 'Hear it?'

Tears of relief poured down her ashen cheeks as she listened to the fast pulsating beat of her baby's heart. 'Yes. Yes, I do. Thanks be to God!'

'And as far as I can see you have no broken bones.' With a reassuring pat on her shoulder the young man said, 'Let's get you to the hospital.'

Soon she was in bed and an intern was examining her. The pains had eased off and he explained that although labour appeared to have stopped, they would like her to remain in hospital for a few days to keep an eye on the baby. Liz assured them that she would do anything they asked of her. Reconciled to perhaps a stay in hospital until the birth, she made a list of all she would need in the way of night clothes and cosmetics.

Kath made a special trip to deliver the things and Liz was grateful. 'Thanks, Mam. What would I do without you? It will be great to get into my own nightie.'

'How do you feel? Any more pains?'

'Not so far. I could be in here until the baby's born, Mam. You'll be run off your feet before it's all over. Where's Dad?'

Kath gave a wan smile. 'He's parking the car. By the way, I saw Danny today and he sends his regards.' Her lips thinned in anger. 'I must say, he didn't seem unduly concerned when I told him about the false alarm.'

'Mam, please don't expect anything from him.' Liz smiled over her mother's shoulder. 'Hello, Dad.'

The following afternoon there was cause for concern. The baby appeared to be in slight difficulties.

When made aware of it, Liz was assured there was no immediate danger and that they were keeping a close eye on it. Fearfully she asked, 'What do you mean, slight difficulties?'

The Sister under whose care she had been placed explained, 'Remember you told us the baby seemed to give a big kick, turn over and slip down in the womb?' Eyes fixed apprehensively on the woman's face, Liz nodded slowly in reply. 'Well, it was obviously preparing for the birth. Not all babies are so dramatic, mind you. Some take weeks to make their way down.' She smiled kindly at Liz, patting her gently on the shoulder.

Big haunted eyes gazed back at her. 'Trust me to be different from everyone else. But please tell me what's wrong?'

'I'm sorry, dear, I shouldn't be rambling on like this. Believe me, your baby is fine at the moment. There's no immediate cause for alarm. However, we think the sudden movement has looped the umbilical cord around its neck ... loosely, mind you. But if we let you go into normal labour, it could possibly tighten and cut off the baby's oxygen supply. Now we could be worrying unnecessarily. It might right itself. The birth could go without a hitch. But rather than risk any complications, the gynaecologist has proposed that we do a caesarean section. And the sooner the better. How would you feel about that?'

'Do whatever is necessary to save my baby's life, please.'

'Right! I'll get you prepared for surgery. But first we need your husband's written consent.'

'I'll sign anything that has to be signed. My husband doesn't enter into this.'

'We do need his permission, Mrs Atkinson – you see – the baby or yourself could be at risk, so the father has the right to know!'

Liz had given the hospital her mother's number in case of emergencies. Kath had been summoned earlier and now arrived breathlessly at the beside, followed closely by Neville. When Kath was put in the picture she asked to speak to her daughter privately for a few minutes.

'Liz, no matter what the consequences may be, you must let me send for Danny.'

'No! Leave him out of this.'

'Liz, be sensible. He has to be informed. It can't be helped if it causes an uproar.'

She gripped her mother's arm. 'Mam, there certainly would be an uproar if you sent for him, because he's not the father.'

Kath gaped at her some seconds in amazement, then cried, 'Then who in the name of God is?'

'Who do you think?'

'David?' At her nod of assent, Kath cried in exasperation. 'What have you been playing at, girl?'

'Mam, he never wanted children and when he was so easily convinced ... just like you ... that Danny was the father, I let everyone believe it.'

'Dear God! Well, he'll certainly have to know now, that's for sure.'

'No, he will not! There must be some way round this.' She fell silent for some moments. 'Mam, if I tell them I don't know who the father is, will you ask Neville, as my father, to sign that stupid piece of paper?'

'Liz, love, what if the baby dies? David would never forgive you.'

Frightened now, she whispered fiercely, 'Don't say that, Mam! It won't die. They told me there's little danger. That's the reason they're doing a caesarean. Even so it won't make any difference to David. He doesn't want to be tied down with a child. I'm the one who longs for it. I'll rear it myself. I don't want him sent for, and that's final!'

Kath buried her face in her hands and rocked in despair. It was grey and strained when she lifted her head once more and looked at her daughter. 'You're doing the wrong thing, Liz, but I'll speak to the doctor. See if we can work something out.'

Neville was in the corridor. 'The doctor was called away on an emergency,' he explained. Then, noticing her pallor, cried in concern, 'What's wrong? Is Liz all right?'

Drawing him away from the door of the ward, she hurriedly told him of their daughter's request.

His lips tightened. 'Does she think Danny won't come? Is that it? I'll bring that swine here by the scruff of the neck if I have to,' he threatened.

'That wouldn't do any good, I'm afraid. You see, it isn't his baby.'

She watched Neville's face go slack with surprise. 'Not Danny's? Then who is the father?'

'Who do you think?'

'David?'

'Yes, David.'

'I don't understand.' Neville pushed his own confusion to one side and concentrated on what really mattered. 'But surely there's no problem then? You know he will do all in his power to help her. I'll fetch him right away.'

He turned to go, but Kath caught hold of his coat to stop him. Annoyed at the delay, he gazed at her. 'She doesn't want David to know.'

Puzzled and confused, he shook his head. 'I'm all mixed up. Tell me, Kath, have I missed something here?'

'I know just how you feel, Neville. I'm exactly the same. I can't figure out why she has kept him in the dark all these months. She said he was too ready to believe that it was Danny's ... so she let him.'

'Listen, Kath. No matter what she says, David has the right to know. I'm going for him now.'

'You're right. She might not forgive us. But he does have the right to know. Get him here. And hurry, love.'

So that no time would be wasted, Neville phoned David at work and, telling him there was no time for explanations, instructed him to come to the Royal Maternity Hospital at once.

David was in the car and on his way within minutes. If it was the maternity hospital, Liz must be involved. He wished his friend had been more explicit. Was Liz or the baby in danger? He had been counting the weeks. Surely she had another few to go? The roads were busy but at last he turned into the gates of the hospital and followed the signs to the car park.

Neville was waiting for him at the entrance to the maternity wing. 'Thank God you're here! Hurry, Liz needs you.'

'What's wrong, Neville?'

'Liz will explain. I must warn you she didn't want you sent for. So be prepared for the worst.'

David's steps slowed to a halt. 'Liz doesn't want me here?'

'I'm afraid not.'

'I don't understand.'

'Neither does anyone else. But believe me, David, she needs you. Come on, let's get a move on. They're preparing her for surgery.'

The word surgery galvanized David into action again and they arrived breathless at the door to the ward. Giving his son-in-law a slight push, Neville remained outside.

Liz was lying, eyes closed, hands clasped on her chest as if in prayer. Kath was sitting by the bed. When she saw David she whispered in her daughter's ear and with an encouraging smile towards him, left the ward.

Liz couldn't believe her ears when her mother informed her that David had arrived. She glared after her retreating figure before condescending to look at her husband. 'I told them not to send for you,' she whispered fiercely.

He stood and gazed down at her. In the white robe and paper hat she looked so vulnerable. 'I don't understand. Why did Neville call me if you don't want me here?'

'Because they're interfering busybodies, that's why! Look, since you're here, you may as well make yourself useful. They're going to do a caesarean section and foolishly think you might be interested. As my husband they need you to give your permission for the operation. It's all run-of-the-mill stuff. Nothing serious.'

Mind in a muddle, he continued to look at her blankly. Not serious? There must be some danger or they would not need his permission. Fear gripped his heart. What if she died?

598

Wanting to persuade him, she managed to sound appealing. 'I'm sorry. I know you're very busy at work and not really interested in my welfare but since you're here, you will sign, won't you? Please let me get this all over with. I want to hold my baby in my arms.'

She had been plucking feverishly at the bedclothes. Taking her hand gently between his, he said softly, 'Liz, you know I'll do anything you ask, but shouldn't Danny be in on this? Won't he be angry you didn't let him know?'

She closed her eyes and he was dismayed to see tears escape and run down her cheeks. 'If anyone else mentions Danny McGowan's name, I'll scream the place down.'

'I don't under...'

'And don't say that again! I'm beginning to think I'm surrounded by a bunch of imbeciles. I'm going to tell you something, David Atkinson, so you had better prepare yourself for a shock. Whether you like it or not, this baby is *yours*. Like it or lump it, you're the father! What do you think of that?'

'Mine? *Mine?*'

She nodded sheepishly. 'I promise you won't have to get involved with it. I know you never wanted a child and if things had been different, you need never have known. But will you please sign this form and let's get it over with?'

Still he gaped at her in speechless bewilderment.

'David, you will sign, won't you? Please?' she wheedled.

His grip on her hand tightened and he bent

lower. 'Are you telling me the truth? Am I really the father?'

'Let's not go over all that again. I haven't the time. Of course I'm telling the truth,' she whispered. 'I've never lied to you in all the time I've had the pleasure of knowing you.'

'Why did you say Danny was the father?'

'If you recall correctly, I didn't. Everyone else, including you, thought he was. I was just so fed up to the teeth of trying to explain myself to everyone, I decided, to hell with them. Let them believe what they like.'

'But why me, Liz? I'd the right to know.'

'Do you remember the day I asked you to meet me for lunch?' He nodded and she continued, 'I was going to tell you then. Instead you informed me that Irene said I was expecting Danny's child. You believed *her!* You were so bitter, you didn't even give me a chance to explain. After that, everything just spiralled out of control.'

'And what makes you think I don't want a child?' His bewilderment was obvious.

'Don't you?'

'Of course I do. I can't imagine anything more wonderful than to be a father. I just didn't think I was capable of it. That's why I was so easily led into believing Danny was the father.'

She eyed him apprehensively. 'David, if there is any doubt in your mind at all, speak now. There will never be a blood test carried out to prove otherwise! I won't hear tell of that. It's all a matter of trust. Without that we have nothing.'

His smile was tremulous. He was having difficulty taking it all in, but he believed her. 'I believe you, Liz. I really do.' He bent down and brushed his lips across hers, and whispered in her ear, 'I love you.' A doctor and nurse entered the room and he turned to face them. 'Where's this form you want me to sign?'

'Come with me, please.' The nurse led the way from the room and the doctor attended to a smiling Liz.

Giving Neville and Kath the thumbs up, David passed them in a daze. A large grin spread across his face as he followed the nurse down the corridor. *He*, David Atkinson, was going to become a father. Signing the form with a flourish, he handed it back.

'Would you like to be present at the birth, Mr Atkinson?' she asked.

Bursting with pride and happiness, he could only nod.

His grin was infectious and she returned it. 'Follow me, then. We'll have to prepare you too.'

Twenty minutes later, he was shown his son. Tears ran down his cheeks. Although straight from the womb, David could see he was either completely bald or very fair. He gazed over at Liz's still form. The doctors were still working on her. 'Is my wife all right?' he asked anxiously.

'She's going to be just fine. Everything went like clockwork.'

He returned to the waiting room still in a daze to break the good news. The instant they saw him, Kath and Neville sprang to their feet, moving anxiously towards him.

'It's a boy. Seven and a half pounds,' he informed them.

'Thanks be to God!' Kath sent the prayer heavenward. 'And Liz?'

'She's fine.'

'Mind you, that girl has a lot of explaining to do when she comes round. Come and sit down, son. You look as if you'd just had the baby.'

He grinned at them. 'I can't believe it. I'm the happiest man in the world! I'll never forget this day until the day I die.'

Neville was shaking his hand enthusiastically. 'Congratulations, son. Maybe now we can put the past behind us and look forward to being one big happy family. If you'll excuse us for a few minutes, Kath and I will just pop up and have a look at our grandson.'

Mary Larkin would like to hear from her readers. You are very welcome to visit her website at

www.marylarkin.co.uk

where she would be delighted to hear from you.

The publishers hope that this book has given you enjoyable reading. Large Print Books are especially designed to be as easy to see and hold as possible. If you wish a complete list of our books please ask at your local library or write directly to:

Magna Large Print Books
Magna House, Long Preston,
Skipton, North Yorkshire.
BD23 4ND

This Large Print Book for the partially sighted, who cannot read normal print, is published under the auspices of

THE ULVERSCROFT FOUNDATION